LETHAL LEGACY:
Thrill Of The Hunt

A Novel By

Sir Patrick Bijou

DESCRIPTION

***

Detective Andrew Martin had been in the homicide division of the Baltimore police force for twelve of his seventeen years in law enforcement. For the most part he loved his job except for the kind of cases that he was currently working on.

There was a string of unsolved murders the last count was ten that was driving him nuts. The problem was that the deaths had several things in common, they were all young healthy males, all of them had been drained of blood, and each of them had had a set of puncture marks that looked as if they were made by large bore needles that were surrounded by bright red lipstick.

Through some basic profiling it was determined that the killer was indeed female although it was rare for a serial killer to be female, she was between the ages of twenty-five to thirty-five, Caucasian and that she would have a well above average intelligence.

WHO IS THIS VAMPIRE KILLER?

The Question seems unsolvable but things changed when Agent Amelia comes in to help.

But What Happens After?

ABOUT THE AUTHOR

***

Sir Patrick is an eclectic writer, lives in the United Kingdom and was born in 1958 in Georgetown and raised in London, England.

His diverse writing prowess has been influenced by many experiences.

He pursued several courses of study at several universities, and declared two majors during his schooling which included the areas of Business and Economics and finally obtained his doctorate in Economics and International banking.

In all these scholastic studies though, the true treasures he took away are not the certificates (though those are very important), but instead the experiences he had, the people he met, the foods he ate and even the places he stayed.

"In truth, I am a citizen of the world and this greatly influences my writing.

So, if you are already a fan of mine, I appreciate you. If you are not yet one, then what are you waiting for? Read a book and then read some more. I create characters that resonate with you and infuse life into all I write".

Finding my Books

Sir Patrick has written over 15 published fictional and non-fictional books across several genres, I have realized the need to make it easier for my readers to find my books.

TABLE OF CONTENTS

CHAPTER 1

***

Detective Andrew Martin had been in the homicide division of the Baltimore police force for twelve of his seventeen years in law enforcement. For the most part he loved his job except for the kind of cases that he was currently working on.

There was a string of unsolved murders the last count was ten that was driving him nuts. The problem was that the deaths had several things in common, they were all young healthy males, all of them had been drained of blood, and each of them had had a set of puncture marks that looked as if they were made by large bore needles that were surrounded by bright red lipstick.

The similarities didn't end there, all of the victims were between the ages of eighteen and twenty-eight and all of the deaths occurred around four AM after apparently having sex. There was also no evidence that any of them struggled and there was no evidence of a robbery. The first victim had about 500.00 in cash on him; even his credit cards were still in his wallet as were the cash and credit cards of each subsequent victim.

As it stood the murders were occurring every four to five nights and the bodies were always found in plain view of passersby in the inner-city although each of them had rented a hotel room the night before their death. This struck Andrew as odd because three of the men lived alone and wouldn't have needed to rent a hotel room.

There had been no witnesses to the murders or the body dumps and in the cases of the males who had been out with friends no one could recall when or with whom the male had left the club. In one case, the club video equipment had actually been working and caught the victim leaving the club. The odd thing was that it appeared as though he had his arm around someone but the image of the person was missing.

The frustrating thing was what Andrew considered to be the lack of evidence; there were a few long black hairs, the lipstick left on the skin which the lab guys said was custom made and the vaginal secretions of a female. The lab also said that there was some type of anticoagulant around puncture marks.

"We don't know what in the hell it is." Bill said, "I can tell you that it's even more potent than heparin but not only that, you know that we have samples of vaginal secretions and hair."

"Yeah and?"

"We can't get any DNA from any of it. I won't lie to you." Bill said, "In all of my years on the job I've never seen anything like it."

"Can you give me anything to go on?" Andrew asked.

"Well, your perp is female and your victims didn't struggle or fight her which begs the question how in the hell did was she able to subdue them enough to get those puncture marks in their necks and what did she do with the blood?"

Andrew left the lab with more questions than he walked in with. The last victim, Akili Adoyo a Johns Hopkins's University student was in the United States on a student visa was from Kenya. According to his professors and his roommate, he was a serious young man whose focus was on his studies.

"Akili on a date?" his roommate asked shocked, "Are we talking about the same guy? All he did was go to work, class, came home and then stayed in his room and studied."

They got the same reaction from other students and the professors who knew the unfortunate young man; it simply wasn't like him to be out on a date when he had a paper due amongst other things. It just didn't make sense. What Andrew did know was that he had to catch a break within the next four days or another man was going to die.

Through some basic profiling it was determined that the killer was indeed female although it was rare for a serial killer to be female, she was between the ages of twenty-five to thirty-five, Caucasian and that she would have a well above average intelligence. Andrew was finding himself very grateful that he took the classes that the department offered on profiling, it was proving to be worth the Saturdays spent in a classroom.

The list of questions about the perp were continuing to grow, added to the ones that he already had were these, how was the perp able to kill the men without them struggling? From what the coroner said there was no indication that the men resisted having their heads moved to the position needed to get to their jugular vein, in fact, he said it was almost as though they offered themselves to her.

Andrew's cell phone chirping interrupted his thoughts.

"Andrew? Bill here, can you come back to the lab?"

On his way to the lab Andrew wondered how long it would be before the press heard about the murders, he was actually surprised that they hadn't already and thanked God for big and small favors alike. He could only imagine the headlines. They would be screaming about the fact that the murders were kept from the public and that they had the right to know so on and so forth. Added to the mix would be the accusations of the department being inadequate and or not caring.

Andrew had requested FBI involvement when the body count reached three but had been refused. Now that it was ten, they couldn't get the Feds here fast enough. "Better late than never." Andrew grumbled under his breath as he pulled in front of the lab.

"Hey Bill what you got for me?" Andrew asked as he walked into the lab.

Bill looked up from what he was doing and grinned; he loved the challenge of the hard cases and had helped solve some of the hardest ones in Andrews's career as a homicide detective.

"You sure brought us a doozy!" he replied, "the anticoagulant that was used on the victims was a highly concentrated version of the one used by the vampire bat when it feeds."

"Vampire bat?" Andrew asked and began to laugh, "What the fuck are you saying? That I have some kind of giant bat running around killing people?"

Bill chuckled and then turned serious, "No, but I did talk to someone over at the zoo and what he said was that when the vampire bat bites, it's only a small opening and they lap the blood up with their tongues. It would appear that whoever killed your guys is using a pump of some kind to take the blood from the bodies.

Here's another thing, mixed in with the anticoagulant in the dried saliva was a paralytic/anesthetic solution, which would explain why there was no struggle. We're still trying to figure out exactly what it is but I can tell you this much, whatever it was... it worked almost instantly."

Andrew listened carefully as Bill talked, mulling the information over for a few minutes when Bill was done talking.

"Why do you say that she used a pump?" he asked.

"That's the only explanation that makes sense." Bill replied. "All of the victims were drained almost dry, what other answer could there be? I also talked to a few colleagues and they agree that's the only way that she could have done it but that begs another question."

"I'm listening." Andrew replied.

"Did she have her victims already picked out or is it random? And... did or does she have an accomplice? Just think about it, how could she have done all of that alone? I know that there are some relatively small pumps but still, it takes planning."

Andrew's head began to hurt. It was bad enough that they had one that they couldn't catch but two?

"What else?" Andrew asked.

"Nothing, isn't what I've told you enough?" Bill asked. "I'll call you with any updates."

Andrew thanked Bill and left the lab feeling overwhelmed, he didn't know anymore than he did at the beginning and more questions had been added to his rapidly growing list. Time was running out, someone else was going to die and there wasn't a damned thing that he could do about it.

An hour later Andrew was back at his desk going over everything that he knew when the captain, Ted Conroy interrupted him.

"You're getting extra help on this and before you say it I'm well aware that you've been asking." The captain said holding his hand up when he saw that Andrew was about to say something. "I'm assigning Lisa, Paul and Drew to help you and we've contacted the FBI."

"It's about fucking time!" Andrew growled.

The captain ignored the comment and continued, "We've set up one of the conference rooms and copies of the file are being made as we speak. The Feds are sending Special Agent Amelia Hensley who will act as a liaison between us and the bureau."

As glad as he was for the extra help David was furious that it had taken ten deaths to get it.

"Anything else?" he asked watching his tone.

"Yes, you report directly to me, I want daily updates more if it's warranted. I almost forgot," the captain added," Shirley and Cindy will act as your extra pairs of hands. They had to take a prisoner to the courthouse and should be back in a couple of hours, Bill Wilson is the lab guy assigned to this and Jane Wiseman will be in charge of any press releases so run everything through her before talking to the press."

"Got it." Andrew said already planning how to best use the assets that he had finally been given.

"Andrew, I can't stress enough how important it is that we catch this suspect as quickly as possible...."

Andrew lost it.

"Why the fucking hurry now?" he asked, "I've been asking for support ever since the third death and the fucking budget was thrown in my face!" He was yelling and he didn't care. "And now you can't stress the importance of catching the suspect quickly? So what in the hell happened? Did the press find out or is your job on the line?"

His brain screamed for him to stop talking but he couldn't, the too many sleepless nights and exhaustion had finally caught up with him.

"My office, now!" Captain Conroy said and then walked away.

Andrew had no choice but to follow the order, had more than overstepped his bounds and hoped that he wasn't going to be suspended for insubordination.

"Shut the door." The captain said as he sat on the edge of his desk.

Andrew shut the door, turned to face the captain and waited for the dress down.

"Sit down."

Andrew was going to refuse but thought better of it.

"I know that you've been working your ass off on this case with little to no help and I'm sorry for that but that doesn't excuse insubordination." the captain said.

"I know and I'm sorry." Andre replied. "It's just that this could have been stopped a few bodies ago and no one was listening."

"That's not true." The captain replied. "I've been fighting for additional help ever since your first request, why they decided to give in is anyone's guess. "As to your outburst out there, I'm going to attribute it to exhaustion and lack of sleep, do it again and you'll be put on suspension without pay. We're done here."

"Captain? What about overtime?"

"Approved and I want every single hour of it justified."

Andrew nodded his understanding, left the office and went to the conference room to find that Special Agent Hensley had arrived and was already organizing the files.

"Hello." Andrew said interrupting her work, "I'm Detective Andrew Martin."

"Hello." Amelia replied extending her hand, "I'm Special Agent Amelia Hensley." she replied.

Andrew shook her hand liking that it was a firm, confident handshake.

"Where do we start?" Andrew asked.

"From the beginning." Amelia replied, "Please don't take this wrong but you were working on this alone and something may have been missed. With several pairs of new eyes maybe we'll find something that we can use to help us.

Andrew was far from offended, she was right and if it helped to stop the crazy bitch from killing again she could have as many people that she wanted look at the files. By the time the rest of the team got there, the files had been organized into neat stacks, a stack for each person and a timeline was already drawn up on the white board.

Introductions were made and the battle plan laid out,

"Each of you will read through the files." Amelia said, "Mark anything that jumps out at you no matter how unimportant it seems, sometimes it's the little things that break a case."

The team worked well past end of shift trying to glean every bit of information from the files that they could. After one was finished with a file, he or she exchanged it for another with someone else until all of the files had been looked at. After taking a short break, they all looked at the white board to fill in the blanks.

Andrew was getting impatient; a couple of more days and someone was going to die unless they got a major break.

On March fourteenth, Frank Barnes a sixth generation Baltimore cop had just finished his shift. For the most part he enjoyed his job except for days like today. There had been two domestic disputes with the second one being a nightmare. The husband had beaten the wife up pretty badly but when the police tried to intervene, the wife attacked the officers. They hadn't realized that there was a fifteen-year-old boy in the house or that there was a gun. They found out when the boy pulled the gun on them while they were trying to subdue the woman. It was a very tense few minutes until Frank had managed to talk the boy into giving up the weapon. Frank breathed a sigh of relief that neither he nor his partner had to shoot the boy. Although he usually stayed away from the bars because he preferred to drink alone, Frank decided to stop at the 'Driftwood bar and Grille.

The 'Driftwood bar and Grille' was a nice little place that was a favorite because it was cop friendly and served one of the best burgers around. Frank walked in, looked around and took a seat up at the bar ordering a draft as he sat.

He took a casual look around the rapidly filling bar and noticed that he was being watched by a gorgeous raven haired woman. He gave her a quick once over taking note of her figure that included large breasts and long sensuous legs. When she made eye contact, she smiled and gave Frank a slight nod of her head before turning away.

Frank's attention was pulled away from the woman by loud cheers when an older couple walked into the bar. When he turned around to face forward, the raven haired woman was sitting next on the stool next to him.

"Diamond," she said as she offered him her hand as her full lips curled up into a seductive smile.

"Frank, it's a pleasure to meet you." he said taking her hand and returning the smile.

He couldn't believe that this was happening. While he wasn't a bad looking man with dark wavy hair and dark eyes he wasn't the type that women like this one was attracted to. As they made small talk while they sipped on their drinks, Frank took in her scent. It reminded him of a freshly cut field after a rain shower on a warm spring day.

He felt himself becoming enamored with her and was powerless to stop. He hung on to every word that she spoke becoming drunk with the sound of her soft but melodic voice. When she suggested that they leave and go somewhere more private, Frank quickly agreed. He paid his tab while the woman called the 'Harbor

Inn' where she had decided to spend the evening with her friend for the evening.

Ten minutes later they were in the room where they quickly undressed. When Frank reached for her, Diamond stepped back; she wanted to see what he looked like without his clothes. She licked her lips as she started at the top of his head and slowly moved her eyes down his body.

"I have chosen an exceptionally fine donor this evening." she said as she continued her appraisal, "I shall enjoy feasting on you."

Frank wondered what she meant but didn't have time to ask as Diamond was pushing him back on the bed as she kissed his chest as she stroked his rapidly stiffening member. Frank cried out as Diamond gently stroked him while dragging her nails lightly across the skin of his cock. Her slow, leisurely strokes were driving Frank nuts but she wouldn't allow him to do anything to hurry her along.

"Trust me." she whispered in his ear, "this is going to be the best fuck of your life, a real heart stopper."

Diamond nipped at his earlobe and then slowly kissed and nipped at his skin until she was at his right nipple. She swirled her warm wet tongue around the nipple several times before finally taking it into her mouth gently biting on and tugging on it with her teeth.

Frank moaned and cried out as the sensations in his nipples traveled down to his cock. He moaned in frustration when her mouth left the left nipple and moaned in pleasure when he felt his right nipple being taken into her mouth and given the same treatment but biting to the point of pain.

Frank was out of his mind with lust, no other woman had ever driven him to such heights of pleasure and all she had done was suck his nipples and stroke him. His heart felt as if it was going to jump out of his chest as she began to make her way southward taking the time play with his belly button with her tongue. Diamond continued her trek southward, kissing his pelvic bone and then giving it a lick before blowing over the moist spot.

"Shit!" Frank exclaimed when he felt the head of his cock enter her hot, moist mouth.

Diamond smiled to herself as she began to slide her reddened lips down the length of the cock of her latest victim. Each time she took Frank's cock into her mouth she took more of him in until she had all of him deep in her throat. Every so often she would let his cock fall from her mouth so that she could lick the length of it like she was eating an ice cream cone. When she reached the sensitive spot where the head of his cock met the shaft she would give quick but firm licks until Frank began to beg her to end it.

"Soon lover." she murmured as she took the head of his cock back into her mouth.

He had to stop her, it was too much. Frank grabbed Diamond's arms and pulled her up to him for a kiss.

"What's the matter?" she asked teasingly, "is my warm mouth too much for the big strong man?"

Both of them laughed as Diamond positioned herself over his throbbing cock and eased down on it so slowly that Frank wanted to grab her by the hips and slam her down on him. Diamond began to rock back and forth and then moved up and down at that same maddening unhurried pace. Whenever he tried to alter her movements, Diamond would pin Frank down so tightly against the mattress that he couldn't move. In his lust he didn't seem to notice the strength that she had.

Frank felt his balls tighten signaling that his release was imminent. Diamond also sensing that his time was near, bent down kissed and then licked Frank's neck releasing the chemicals that would render him helpless. She looked down at Frank whose eyes widened in surprise and horror when he saw the fangs in her mouth.

Frank tried to scream as Diamond's face moved closer to his as she still rode him, her orgasm just beginning. She bit deep into his neck releasing the anticoagulant that would allow the blood to continue to flow freely until there was very little left.

Diamond gulped down the blood as fast as it came out while wondering why this donor's blood seemed to be sweeter than any of the others.

Frank's body was discovered early the next morning in an alley just off of Lexington Street. The first responding officers quickly blocked the area off, started interviewing the man who found the body and placed a call to Detective Andrew Martin.

Amelia and Andrew were having breakfast to discuss a few thoughts that Andrew was having about the case when the call came. Ten minutes later they were at the scene and so was a large crowd of people.

"Let's get someone to talk to the crowd," Amelia suggested, "sometimes the killer likes to watch and we need to take note of anyone who seems too anxious to help in any way."

After assigning officers to interview the crowd Amelia and Andrew went over to the body which had already been identified.

"Oh god!" Andrew said softly as he recognized the victim.

"You knew him?" Amelia asked.

"Yeah I knew him." Andrew replied, "I was his training officer before I got moved to homicide. He was a good cop with a good future in the department."

The murders were now in a whole new light; one of their own was now a victim.

"This is exactly like the others." Medical Examiner Walter Lassidar said as he examined the body, "down to the lipstick. Who in the hell is doing this?" he murmured under his breath.

"Here's a hotel receipt." The ME said after he emptied Frank's pockets.

"That's just two blocks from here." Andrew said as he motioned for Drew and Lisa to come over. He watched the crowd as Paul moved around taking pictures and sneaking in a few of the crowd. Somehow, he knew that whoever she was, she wasn't in the crowd but they needed to be thorough.

"Get over to the hotel and let's hope that housekeeping hasn't gotten to it yet" Andrew said, "a forensics team will be there in a few minutes, keep me posted."

A few minutes later Lisa was interviewing the manager of the hotel.

"Yes he was here." he said as he looked through the guest log from the night before, "checked in at eight-nineteen."

"Was there a woman with him?"

"Yes but don't ask me what she looked like because I can't tell you..... Why do I remember him but not her?" he asked.

"Good question." Lisa replied, "Are your security cameras working?" "Yes... I suppose you want the footage?"

"I would at least like to see it." Lisa replied.

While she waited for the manager to get the tape she checked on Drew.

"Anything?" she asked.

"No and housekeeping swears that they haven't been in here, you?"

"The manager is getting the security tapes as we speak." she replied, "keep your fingers crossed that something shows up."

Lisa watched the tape in disbelief, Frank was on the tape and his arm was positioned as though it was around someone but there was no one there.

"I have to take this." she told the manager who only shrugged not really seeming all that concerned that one of his guest who happened to be a cop was murdered.

"Didn't happen here did it?" he asked when Lisa asked about his reaction.

"No but..."

"Then I'm not going to obsess over it."

The team met back at the conference room to compare notes. Andrew had an appointment with the captain for later in the morning to give updates on the case; he hoped that they had something to tell him.

As with the other cases there was very little physical evidence that was of use. There was the single strand of black hair and body fluids from the couple having sex.

"Everything is exactly the same!" Bill exclaimed exasperated.

"Cindy, you talked to the man who called it in, what did he have to say?" Andrew asked.

"Not much, he's a city sanitation worker and was heading to work when he spotted the body. At first he thought that it was a bum but changed his mind when he saw how well dressed the vi.... Frank was. Then he thought that it was a mugging victim and called as soon as he realized that he was dead, he says that he didn't touch the body."

"He didn't see anyone around?" Andrew asked.

"He says he didn't." Cindy replied.

"Drew, what do you have?" Amelia asked.

Just as Drew was about to begin his report there was a tap at the door. A young patrolman nervously opened the door and stuck his head inside.

"Excuse me but could I please speak to Detective Martin?"

"I'm Detective Martin." Andrew said, "What do you need?"

"I'm Officer Hank Johnson, is it true that you think a woman killed Frank?"

Andrew gave the young officer a wary look before replying.

"You know that I can't divulge that information."

"I know... sorry. It's just that Frank was a friend of mine and..."

"Officer do you have something to tell us?" Andrew asked his tone curt.

"Oh, yes sir." The officer replied nervously. "Maybe it's nothing and I hope that I'm not wasting your time..."

"Hank," Amelia said softly, "tell us what you saw and heard."

"I saw Frank last night at the Driftwood; he came in alone but left around seven-forty five with a hot number on his arm."

Andrew sat up straighter, "Can you describe her?

"Sure! She was around five feet seven inches tall, one -hundred twenty pounds give or take a few, black hair that fell to about mid back and blue eyes. She was wearing a white blouse with a black miniskirt and stiletto heels."

"I want you to meet with a composite artist!" Andrew said excitedly. They had just gotten their first big break, now if they could only catch the bitch.

Andrew gave everyone assignments to do while he and Amelia met with the captain. Reenergized, everyone set out about their tasks. Bill set Hank up with a composite artist who would then make copies of the drawing to pass out to everyone and Drew and Shirley went back to canvas the area around the bar and hotel to talk to people that they may have missed.

After the meeting with the captain Amelia and Andrew went to the morgue so that they could sit in on Frank's autopsy. Each of them was hoping that the autopsy would give them more clues as to solving the mysteries of the case. Unfortunately the medical examiner could offer no new information with the exception of one thing.

"I doubt that a pump was used." he said. "If that were the case the veins and arteries would have been collapsed."

"Then how?" Andrew asked.

"Vampire?" the ME quipped, "I don't know but if you find out tell me."

As they drove back to the office Andrew decided to pick Amelia's brains.

"What are your impressions?" he asked.

Amelia took a moment to formulate her answer.

"This has got to be one of the most perplexing cases that I've ever worked on." she replied, "The unsub is very highly organized, intelligent and resourceful and to date her only mistake was being spotted by the officer which if you think about it was very careless on her part. These are the questions that are going through my head,

You heard the description of her, she's beautiful! So why doesn't the hotel manager remember her? How is she able to convince her victims to comply enough so that she can drug them and if she isn't using a pump to drain the bodies how is she doing it and what is she doing with the blood? There hasn't been a trace of blood spotted in any of the hotel rooms- how is she managing that?"

"And," Andrew added, "Where is she getting the anticoagulant? My understanding is that it's a hundred times more effective than heparin and the blood would be useless because of it."

"Maybe she's like Elizabeth Bathory- the so called Blood countess." Amelia said.

"Who?" Andrew asked.

"Elizabeth Bathory was a Hungarian Countess during the late sixteenth to early seventeenth centuries who is reported to have killed somewhere around 700 young women for their blood. The story is that she bathed in it because she thought that it would keep her looking young."

"Nice! What happened to her?"

She was tried and then walled up in a tower with only a slot big enough to slide her food and water through. She was never released and spent the last four years of her life there." Amelia replied.

"So that's your official profile?" Andrew asked laughing.

"No." Amelia replied with a smile, "just imparting some interesting history but here's something else that's bothering me, how did she get the body out of the room without attracting any attention?"

"And how do you not show up on camera?" Andrew added. "How do we proceed from here?"

"I would suggest that we keep the photo of her out of the press for now but we give one to every cop in the area, we also need to pick out the most likely places that she'll try to pick up her next victim. Maybe we'll get lucky and grab her before anyone else dies." Amelia replied as a feeling of dread settled in the pit of her stomach.

The rest of the ride passed in silence as Amelia tried to think if they had missed anything and Andrew was formulating a plan on how to best utilize his resources to catch this woman before she killed again. He wondered if the captain would give him at least one more person to help with some of the leg work.

Everyone was back at the station sitting in the conference room looking exhausted. They all needed to sleep; their brains were no longer functioning.

"Go home." Andrew said when he walked in, "Be back here by 8AM and bring an overnight bag, we have a lot to do before the next night that she kills."

Andrew was the first to arrive; his hope was that the captain would be there early so that he could get the meeting with the captain over with. Much to Andrew's surprise he received the extra help that he had requested.

"I'm giving you Jason Standish for your core group; he'll be a fresh pair of eyes and may have some insight that could make a difference. Also starting tonight we're adding extra patrols to the night shift just in case she changes her time table."

In the end the captain agreed that the sketch of the woman and all information should be kept away from the press for now.

"We don't want her getting a heads up and moving to another area." he said.

The day was spent going over clues and evidence and forming a plan. In the late afternoon several of them went to the bars and hotels that they thought the woman was likely to go to talk to the night staff. After several heated moments of conversation, Andrew decided to take a calculated risk and to leave a picture of the woman at each of the places of business. If the woman showed up she was not to be confronted but the police were to be called immediately.

By March seventeenth all of the surveillance was in place and after a long night in which four muggings and one attempted rape had been stopped it was clear that the guest of honor wasn't going to show. Andrew met with the Captain that morning already knowing that he was going to be taking some heat for the amount of overtime his task force was generating. He spent a good hour begging for one more night but it wasn't the captain that he needed to convince. Finally after a long and arduous talk with the mayor he was granted his one more night.

March 18

The night started out as the others had.

Quiet.

Andrew was starting to become concerned that he and the captain had stuck their necks out for nothing.

"Andrew," Amelia said seeing his anxiety, "this was a good call."

"Where in the hell is she?" Andrew asked not really expecting an answer.

It was quiet for the rest of the task force until about nine pm. Lisa who was partnered with Drew asked him to stop at 'O'Shay's Pub' so that she could use the bathroom. After parking they went inside where Lisa headed to the restrooms while Drew ordered a couple of sandwiches and diet cokes for them and settled in to wait for both the order and Lisa.

As soon as Lisa walked into the restroom, she saw the woman that they were looking for standing at the sink. Without saying anything, Lisa stepped into the first empty stall and pulled out her service weapon, a Glock twenty-two forty caliber pistol. Next, she pulled out her cell phone and called Drew.

"She's here in the restroom, hurry before anyone else comes in."

Lisa stepped out of the stall, aimed her gun and called out in a loud, clear voice, "Baltimore City Police! Place your hands on the wall and do not move!"

Diamond turned to face Lisa and sneered, "You've just made a mistake love." and began to approach her.

Lisa couldn't believe that the woman was still coming at her even though there was a gun pointed at her.

"Stop or I will shoot!" Lisa called out as she wondered where in the hell Drew was.

Diamond smiled and threw herself at Lisa who discharged two rounds into Diamond's chest. Lisa watched as the blood flowed from the woman's chest amazed that the woman was still coming for her, hadn't even slowed her down.

Diamond snarled as she felt the bullets slam into her. They weren't fatal but they would cause her considerable blood loss. She reached out, grabbed Lisa by her neck and twisted effectively snapping Lisa's neck as if it were no more than a twig.

She dropped Lisa's body and then heard Drew on the other side of the door. She launched herself at the door almost taking it off of its hinges and surprising Drew. Without looking back Diamond disappeared into the crowded pub and out onto the street. Blood continued to flow from her wound causing her to become weaker by the minute, she had to feed and soon. She cursed as she thought about the fine specimen that she had picked out for her meal that evening. If the clumsy woman sitting next to her hadn't spilled her drink on her she would be enjoying her dinner.

Drew had just gotten off of the phone with Lisa and was by the door when he heard the shots. Before he could open the door, it blew open and driving him backwards and slammed him into the wall knocking the wind out of him. He staggered to his feet and ran into the bathroom. The second he saw Lisa he knew that she was dead, there was no way that she could be alive with her neck and head at the unnatural angle in which it lay.

Panicked and grief stricken he called for help.

"Officer needs assistance O'Shay's pub on Baltimore Street! Shots fired! Officer down! Need backup and medical assistance!"

Andrew's heart stopped when he heard Drew's voice. He started the car and flew up Orleans Street and had just made the right-hand turn onto Central Avenue when Amelia spotted Diamond.

"There she is!" Amelia said pointing at Diamond who was running toward a school building.

Andrew sped into the school parking lot and parked his eyes on Diamond who stopped, looked at them with her face already changed into its true form, her eyes were nothing more than black orbs with no discernible pupil and her mouth hung open revealing her fangs. She seemed to be taunting them as she grinned and then jumped through a window twenty feet away.

Amelia and Andrew looked each other in disbelief.

"What in the fuck was that?" Andrew whispered, "Did she have fangs? And what was with that face?" he added.

"I... I don't know." Amelia replied in a shaky voice.

"Are you alright?" Andrew asked.

"I'm fine." Amelia replied after a minute. "Now let go get this bitch!"

Andrew went to the trunk of the car, got out a shotgun and handed it to Amelia.

"There are extra shells in the glove box and grab the flashlight too." he said as he checked his own weapon.

Amelia got the shells and flashlight before chambering the first shell and turning on the tact-light that was mounted on the shot gun.

Andrew had already called in giving all of the pertinent information. The thought to wait crossed his mind but he didn't want to take the chance that the subject would get away. He turned the volume of his radio all the way down and began to make his way to the window where they had seen the woman go in.

They cautiously peeked into the classroom hoping to spot the woman but she was already gone. Andrew used his jacket to cover the broken glass on the window pane, climbed in and then helped Amelia in.

Diamond knew that she was being followed, saw the car approaching and decided to let the cops see her as she truly was. Her goal was to lure them into the building so that she could feed from them so that she could speed her healing. Because she wouldn't be having an orgasm the paralytic/anesthetic component of her saliva would be ineffective but even so, they were no match for her, even together. She looked around for a place to lay in wait for them.

Andrew and Amelia slowly moved toward the door that led to the hallway and opened it. Andrew went first looking both ways and listening before proceeding.

"Cover the hall while I check out the room across the hall." Andrew whispered.

"Be careful!" Amelia whispered back as her eyes swept up and down the length of the hall.

Andrew ran across the hall as quickly as he could trying to make himself as small of a target as possible and opened the door. Finding the room empty, he went back to Amelia and they repeated the process until they reached the end of the hall which opened into a large common area. To the right was the office and the main entrance, the entrance to the cafeteria lay to the left. Next to the cafeteria was the gymnasium and directly across from it was another long hallway.

They cleared the cafeteria and office areas without seeing any sign of the woman. Andrew was beginning to wonder if the woman had somehow given them the slip but deep down, he knew that she was still in the building. He could almost feel her; he could almost feel her evilness and knew that Amelia was feeling it too.

They moved to the Gymnasium next. This was the room that was going to be the hardest to clear because of its size and many blind spots. Andrew leaned over to Amelia to give her instructions.

"Stay with me and keep your eyes and ears open. I'll watch our backs and you watch the front."

Amelia gave him a nervous nod and they slowly entered the gym. They were no more than ten feet in when a noise above them caught their attention. He saw the woman dropping down towards them and pushed Amelia out of the way. Amelia wasn't ready for the hard shove lost her balance and slid twenty feet across the slick gymnasium floor before coming to a stop.

Andrew had just enough time to raise his arm before the woman slammed into him knocking him to the floor as he grabbed his arm. Before he knew what was happening the woman had his wrist in her mouth, had bitten down and was greedily drinking from him. Managing to keep a hold of his weapon, Andrew fired off four rounds before the woman yanked it out of his hands and tossed it away.

Amelia struggled to her feet, ran over to the woman, and wrapped her arms around her neck from behind and pulled her back from Andrew. The woman snapped her head back making contact with Amelia's nose crushing it and dazing her. Diamond reached behind her, grabbed Amelia, and flipped her so that she was flat on her back.

Diamond looked at Amelia and smiled, "I don't usually drink from women as their blood isn't as sweet as a male's but for you, I will make an exception." Without pause Diamond grabbed Amelia by the hair and exposed her neck. She licked her lips and bit deep into Amelia's jugular vein and began to feast.

Distracted by feeding from Amelia, Diamond didn't notice Andrew now weakened by blood loss retrieve the shotgun. She didn't notice until she felt the weapon pressed tightly against her right side. She released Amelia to turn to Andrew and screamed in pain when she felt the shot slam into her side.

"Go to hell bitch!" Andrew murmured as he pulled the trigger again. He watched with satisfaction as what was her face was nothing more than a red mass. He dropped the gun, took out his radio and made a frantic cry for help.

"Two officers down! Need assistance now!" he screamed as he removed what was left of his shirt and tried to staunch the flow of blood that was coming from Amelia's neck. He passed out a few minutes later not realizing that he hadn't given their location in the school.

Four minutes later the first police unit arrived followed by medical support.

The medical examiner was at a loss as to how to explain why a woman who had just died and was still warm looked like a one-hundred-year-old mummified corpse.

Andrew died en route to the hospital. Nothing that the paramedics did slowed the blood as it flowed from his body. An IV was started in each arm and fluids were pushed as fast as possible but they couldn't even begin to keep up with the loss of blood. He was dead before they could drive less than three miles to the hospital.

Amelia was alive but unconscious arriving to the hospital in grave condition. The lead trauma doctor, Dr. Walter Dressler ordered two cut lines to be started in addition to the two IV's already in place.

"I want two units of 'O' negative right now!" he shouted, "I also want a CBC, CMP and a PT/PTT stat! Give 40 mg of Protamine Sulfate pushed and then 60 mg per hour! Come on! Where's that blood?"

Dr. Dressler was frantic, he could see that nothing they did was stopping the flow of blood from Amelia's neck, he had a nurse at Amelia's head applying pressure to the wound but to no avail.

"Call down to the blood bank and tell them to have fifteen units ready and to send what they have now!" He called out and then to another nurse, "fifty mg of Vitamin K IV push now! And get the hematologist up here... I think its Sanger."

Dr. Dressler had just stepped out of the trauma bay to talk to Sanger when Amelia crashed. He and his team put up a valiant fight but nothing they did worked. After twenty minutes, he called her death. When he got the lab results, he was shocked to see that according to the PT/PTT Amelia's blood had lost the ability to clot. Out of curiosity, he ran another PT/PTT even though Amelia was dead. He was amazed that the results hadn't changed even with the Vitamin K, Protamine Sulfate, and the blood that she had received. He requested and received permission to take blood and tissue samples from both her and Andrew's bodies before they were taken to the morgue.

Their autopsies would be performed first thing the next morning.

CHAPTER 2

****

Amelia opened her eyes and wondered what in the hell was going on. The last thing that she remembered was being in the car with Andrew when the "officer needs assistance" call came through. After that, she couldn't remember. "Where was Andrew?" she wondered as she tried to move. It was then that she realized that she was naked and lying on a cold hard bed of some type and covered from the face down with a sheet. She moved her arms and hit the sides of a wall and then the ceiling.

She yanked the sheet off her face and tried to take stock of her surroundings. Even though it was pitch black, she found that she had no problems with her vision and what she saw horrified her. She was in a stainless-steel box of some kind. She panicked and began kicking and hitting at the metal walls around her. One of her biggest fears was of being trapped in a small place.

Finally, the door opened and the bed was pulled out of the small space. She looked up to see Andrew looking down at her with a smile on his face.

"Come on, I'll help you up." he said.

He held out his hand, helped her into a sitting position, and kept a hand on her back to steady her, as she felt inexplicably weak. When the room stopped spinning, she looked at Andrew once again realizing how handsome he was but without the clothes, she had to admit that he was the best-looking man that she had ever seen.

"I was disorientated and weak too." he said, "but it should pass quickly. In case you're wondering, we're vampires and I'm still trying to wrap my head around it and what that means for us. I now understand how that woman managed not to be seen. It seems that we can control people to some degree with our minds, that's how I got the guy who released me to leave and not to come back."

Amelia looked at Andrew as if he had two heads.

"What the hell? What kind of game are you playing here? There are no such things as vampires and where are my clothes?" she asked looking around. "You'd better hope that I don't file sexual harassment charges against you!"

Andrew laughed, "I'm not playing games but we do have a few obstacles to overcome, the first and most obvious being clothes. The second thing is food, I don't know about you but I'm starving and I know that we're going to need blood in order to survive. It took me about an hour to remember what happened and it's around two am now. We need to find a place to go before sunrise so what do you say? Shall we get the hell out of here and find some food and clothes?"

Seeing Andrew's face change and his fangs extend jarred her memory a little. She recalled seeing the strange woman outside of the school and she looked as Andrew did now. She began to piece things together as she remembered the fight with the woman and being bitten on the he necks.

"T...t... this I... I f...f...f...r...r... real?" she stammered.

"Would you believe your toe tag?" Andrew asked.

Amelia's went wide in shock as she looked down at her feet. Somehow, that little tag made everything seem real. How could something so little have such a profound affect in her? Her thoughts went to her mother, she had just lost her husband, Amelia's father eight months ago. She would be devastated to think that her daughter was dead and what about her baby sister?

"How long have you been up?" Amelia asked.

"A few hours." Andrew replied, "It took a while for the memories to return plus I seem to know a lot of things like how to charm someone and how to incapacitate my victims and this..."

Andrew concentrated and after a few minutes began to fade away.

"How did you do that?" Amelia asked shocked.

He reappeared behind her and replied, "It's easy. Close your eyes and concentrate on being invisible."

Amelia closed her eyes and tried for several minutes managing to make herself translucent but not invisible. She finally became frustrated and gave up, "I can't seem to do that." she said.

Andrew however was impressed with what she could do.

"How did you do that?" he asked.

"Do what?" Amelia asked confused.

"You became translucent like a ghost; it was so cool!" Andrew replied.

"I pictured myself as a pane of glass, how do you do the invisibility thing?" she asked.

Andrew imagined himself as a pane of glass and became translucent before responding.

"I imagined myself as not being able to be seen like that guy in the movie 'The League of Extraordinary Gentlemen'."

Amelia closed her eyes and envisioned being like the invisible man. After a few seconds, she vanished.

"I did it!" she squealed excitedly and hugged Andrew.

As soon as she hugged him, he vanished.

"Now we know how she got the bodies out of the hotel unseen." Andrew said, "But as fun as this is, we need to get going, there's a clothing store down the street; let's head there."

Andrew took Amelia's hand and they both became invisible. They walked out of the morgue and headed toward the clothing store. Even in their weakened condition, they found it easy to force open the doors of "J. Brown's Fine Clothiers' an upscale clothing store.

They were both surprised at their strength when the door came off its hinges with what they thought was a gentle tug. They both laughed at their faux pas as Andrew set the door aside and then valiantly bowed as he gestured for Amelia to lead the way.

Amelia playfully fanned herself with her hand giggling as she proclaimed, "My you are such a gentleman my handsome knight."

Andrew chuckled, "We'd better hurry, I think that it would be wise to be out of here before the police arrived."

"How are we going to pay for this stuff?" Amelia asked.

"I seem to have left my wallet in my pants!" Andrew playfully remarked as he patted himself down. Seeing

Amelia's reaction, he became more serious, "we'll send him a money order once we have access to money unless you happen to have some hidden somewhere on your person?"

Amelia wasn't happy; she had never stolen anything in her life unless the fries she would steal from her sister counted. Andrew was right she realized but then she had an idea.

"How about we get my mother to pay the bill and we could pay her back?"

Andrew knew that she wasn't going to like his answer but he plowed ahead.

"Amelia, we can't contact our families. As far as they know, we're dead and it needs to stay that way at least for now."

"Why?" she asked angrily not seeing the issue.

Andrew looked away. He didn't like it anymore than she did. He didn't get to see his son Jake very often as it was and now, he would never see him again.

"If we go to our families several things could happen with the first thing being we could and probably would kill them." he paused to let this sink in before continuing, "and secondly, what do you think the government would do if they found us alive? May I suggest that we get some clothes and get out of here? The police will be here soon."

Amelia nodded and began to assemble an outfit consisting of a pair of black slacks, a white peasant top, a pair of comfortable shoes with a low heel and a leather jacket. A purse that matched her outfit completed her outfit. She looked over at Andrew to see how he had fared.

She gave a whistle of approval at the pair of tan khakis, black pullover shirt, and a leather jacket and pair of black loafers that completed the outfit.

"Looking good!" she said appreciatively, "how do I look?"

"You look as sexy as hell." Andrew replied as his eyes took in her appearance.

Just then, two police cruisers pulled up out front of the store. The two of them instantly vanished. Andrew wondered how Amelia was going to be able to see him and began to reappear.

"What are you doing?" she asked, "They'll see you!"

The two officers startled turned to see where the voice had come from. The store appeared to be empty as they looked around.

"Walt, did you hear that?"

"Yes, I heard it," Walt replied in a deep Jamaican accent, "but where did it come from?" he asked his partner.

"It sounded like it came from right here." Walt's partner replied.

While the officers continued to search, Amelia walked over to Andrew. Once she was standing in front of him, she leaned into him and whispered, "I'm sorry but I thought that you were visible to them. How did you make yourself visible to me but not to them?" she asked.

Andrew shrugged, "I just wanted you to see me, let's get out of here."

Amelia grabbed Andrew's hand and gestured for him to take the lead. Hand in hand, the two of them walked out into the night. Andrew was trying to find a place to shelter them from the sun, from everything that he knew and heard about vampires, the sun was dangerous to them and would burn them until they were nothing but ash. He couldn't imagine dying that way; he imagined it to be the most painful way to die.

"I know that you're trying to take care of us and I hate to add any more to your burden but I'm starving." Amelia said, "Do you think we could get something to eat? I would love a burger."

He was hungry too but knew that the only thing that would satisfy the hunger was human blood. He wondered why Amelia didn't realize this. He now had to come to grips with the fact that they would have to hunt and kill humans in order to survive. He was a realist and knew that it was either that or they starved to death. He made the decision to avoid people with families and children but he would do whatever it took to keep the two of them alive.

He wondered why he was so concerned about her; he really didn't know her that well but with her deep brown eyes and skin the color of rich chocolate, she was beautiful. A few minutes later, he had figured out the food and shelter issue, they would go to the hospital, steal some blood from the blood bank, and then go to his house. His ex-wife wouldn't arrive for a few days and it would give him and Amelia some time to plan their next move.

Andrew took a few minutes to reflect on his relationship with his ex wife. They had been high school sweethearts and became engaged their senior year. They married the year after he graduated from the academy. The only thing that he ever wanted to be was a cop but Shannon was miserable and worried constantly. The worry only increased when she found out that she was pregnant.

Their problems came to a head on the night that Andrew had been injured in a car accident while on patrol. A kid ran a red light and rammed into his patrol car. While Andrew only suffered a mild concussion and a dislocated shoulder, in Shannon's mind he almost died. As he recovered, she hovered over him, by the night he was supposed to return to work, she was a nervous wreck. After three weeks, she couldn't take anymore and moved out taking their son Jake with her.

They tried counseling and reconciliation several times but it never lasted for long. Every attempted reconciliation destroyed not only them but also Jake a little more each time so they decided to permanently part ways. By the time the divorce was finalized, Jake was four years old.

Eight years ago, Shannon met and married her current husband Tony and Andrew found that he liked the man. He was genuinely happy for Shannon and Tony was good to Jake not attempting to replace him as his father. Three years after Tony and Shannon married; Tony got a good job offer from a west coast company. Instead of just moving, Shannon and Tony talked with Andrew before he accepted the job. They wanted him to understand that they would make sure that he would get to spend time with Jake.

They stayed in contact via skype and this summer Andrew was planning to go out west for three weeks to spend time with Jake. Tony was going to charter a boat so that all of them could spend the day fishing. It hurt Andrew that it wasn't going to happen but took comfort in the fact that Shannon and Jake had Tony to help them through his death.

He dragged himself from his thoughts as he quietly said his goodbyes to his ex wife and son. He finally turned to Amelia and explained the food situation to her.

"I have an idea on how to get us through the next day or so." he said. "I know that you're hungry but it isn't human food that we need, it won't quell our hunger." he paused before continuing, "we need blood and it has to be human which gives us two choices, we either feed from a human or we steal the blood from a blood bank. Afterwards we can go to my place to figure out our next move, my ex and my kid won't arrive for a day or two and by then we should be gone."

Revulsion was on Amelia's face as she thought about drinking blood, "Are you fucking kidding me?" she asked.

Andrew laughed before replying, "No dear, I most certainly am not kidding. We're vampires, which means that we need blood in order to survive, now which is it? Blood bank or person?"

Amelia's shoulders slumped and she began to cry, "This isn't fair! I don't want to be a vampire and how can you act as if this is nothing? We're fiends who have to kill others so that we can live! Just let me die, I don't want to have to kill in order top live!"

"Do you eat meat?" Andrew asked as he hugged her.

"Yes but that's different." Amelia replied sniffling, "meat comes from animals and how can we feed from people when we're human?" she asked.

Andrew sighed as he held her, offering comfort, and making sure that she was still invisible.

"I'm not sure of what we are but we have to eat or we die and I refuse to let either of us die." Andrew said. "We'll get the blood from the blood bank, go to my house and then we'll sort this out.

Amelia held on to him until she was back under control.

"Okay, lead on." she said, "but this would be easier if we had a car. By the way, how is it that you seem to have the answers but I don't?"

Andrew shrugged, "maybe it's because I'm more accepting of the situation than you are. I'm not sure if that's the reason but we need to take advantage of any opportunity that we have, we have less than two hours before sunup. Come on; let's see if we can catch a cab, maybe I can make him forget us like I did the guy at the morgue."

Andrew looked around and saw a Wells Fargo Bank with an ATM machine in front of it. He was wishing that he could withdrawal some cash from it when suddenly the machine started spitting out cash. They rushed over and began picking up the money as fast as they could and by the time the machine stopped, they had a little over six-thousand dollars in cash.

"That was weird but lucky." Andrew said cheerfully as he stuffed the money in his pockets.

Amelia's elation quickly died as she looked at the money in her hands.

"As nice as this is, we have to return the money, it isn't ours and I don't want to be a thief."

Andrew blew out an exasperated breath. He wondered why she didn't understand that they had to forget their old values and do what they whatever they needed to do in order to survive. They had to have money in order to live and getting a job was out of the question for both of them.

He briefly thought about leaving her to her own devices but found that he couldn't bear the idea of leaving her.

"Amelia, listen to me." he said gently as he hugged her again. "We need the money and as soon as we are able, we'll pay everyone that we took from back."

After releasing her from the hug, Andrew picked Amelia up, slung her over his shoulder, and took off. Time was definitely against them. As he ran, he wondered about how he was going to convince Amelia that she was going to have to adapt. He didn't want to lose her and she was becoming important to him in a way that he had as of yet been unable to put into words.

What he did know was that it was imperative that she accept and adapt to what they were. The problem was figuring out a way to get her to that point. He was moving at a breakneck speed through the city streets, the building little more than a blur as he instinctively avoided all obstacles.

When he came out of his reverie, he they were standing in front if St. Agnes' Hospital. To his amazement, it had taken him less than twenty minutes to get from the inner harbor to the hospital, something that only someone who was driving could accomplish.

Amelia had been enjoying the comfort of Andrew holding her when suddenly she was tossed over his shoulder and he was running at a good speed and increasing it until everything they passed was a blur. He seemed to have no concept of how fast he was going and it scared the living shit out of her.

"Andrew!" she screamed, "Slow down, you're scaring me!"

Andrew seemed not to hear her as he kept up the breakneck pace just barely missing cars and buildings. She finally closed her eyes, held on, and screamed until she felt him slow down and come to a stop. She slowly opened her eyes and read the sign above the doors, "welcome to St. Agnes' Hospital"

Andrew gently set Amelia on her feet and held her until she steadied before whispering to her.

"We have to stay invisible and keep quiet." he said, "We'll take the blood and get out of here as quickly as possible."

Amelia nodded her understanding and gestured for Andrew to take the lead.

Andrew took Amelia's hand and led her to the hospital's blood bank where there was only one person visible. Andrew compelled the woman who was sitting behind a desk to go into the bathroom and not to return until he said that it was safe for her to do so. The woman stood up and walked to the bathroom without giving it any thought as to what she was doing.

Once she was out of sight, Andrew went to the doors of the blood bank, yanked the door open and walked in with Amelia on his heels. He grabbed one of the coolers used to transport the blood and began to fill it. His intention was to take twenty units, which he thought would be enough for a day or so.

As soon as Amelia walked in, the alluring scent of the blood hit her like a ton of bricks and she couldn't resist the pull. Her eyes turned red and her mouth watered as she grabbed two units of the delicious smelling liquid and ripped them open with her teeth. The blood poured into her mouth and all over her even as she grabbed two more units repeating the process of ripping them open and letting it run into her open mouth not caring that her clothes were becoming soaked with it. She was trying to drown herself in what she thought of as ambrosia that she couldn't get enough of, wanting more.

Andrew stopped loading the cooler and looked at her, "What in the fuck are you doing?" he whispered.

Amelia, who now had two units of blood in each hand, was lost in her lust. She opened her eyes, looked at Andrew and began ripping off her clothes even as she began to advance on him. She was not going to be denied. Andrew watched her advance shocked by the unadulterated lust in her eyes, surprised when she ripped his clothes off and tackled him to the cold floor. He tried to hold her off but because he hadn't fed, he was no match for her strength and speed. Amelia grabbed Andrew's turgid cock, slammed herself down on it, and began to bounce up and down on it.

She grabbed another bag, ripped it open and forced it to Andrew's mouth. As soon as the first drop touched his tongue, Andrew was lost in the in the new sensation of pleasure and lust. He grabbed two bags, ripped them open and poured them down his throat eagerly swallowing the cold, thick liquid. His admonishments that they had to remain invisible and silent were forgotten as he ripped open yet another bag of blood and drained it dry while Amelia continued riding him.

Finally, Andrew took control and rolled so that Amelia was beneath him. His cock made long, hard strokes in and out of Amelia's pussy making her beg him to go faster and harder requests with which he complied. Amelia in her lust grabbed two units of "AB" negative blood and squeezed them until they burst spraying blood all over the room.

As the two of them fucked each other senseless, they continued to gorge themselves on blood. Andrew tore open a unit of blood, dumped it all over Amelia's chest, and then began to lick it off paying particular attention to her firm, pert breasts. His ministrations to her breasts and the pounding in and out of her pussy soon had Amelia racing toward the mother of climaxes and when it hit, she came screaming Andrew's name. A moment later, Andrew grunted his explosive release into her.

Sated sexually and full they stood up and looked around the room taking note of the damage they had caused in their lust. The ceiling, walls and floor were covered with blood as were they. Andrew looked around for their clothes only to find that they were little more than blood-soaked rags.

Amelia sensed the woman still in the bathroom and asked, "What are we going to do about the woman in the bathroom?"

Without missing a beat, Andrew replied, "Dessert?"

Amelia sighed, "Andrew my love, while I now understand and accept that we must feed from humans I would prefer not to have too do it from innocents. She'll probably lose her job over this and she has two kids."

Andrew nodded in agreement, he really didn't want to make the woman's children orphans and he knew how he could save her job.

"Trust me." he told Amelia, "she won't lose her job."

He walked over to a wall, dipped his finger in some blood and wrote, "The blood of the innocent shall feed the dark lord of all eternity"

He then compelled the woman to come out of the bathroom, "what's your name hun?" he asked.

"Yvonne." the woman cautiously replied, "Are you going to kill me?"

Andrew gave the woman a gentle reassuring smile, "No my dear, we have no intentions of killing you."

He looked into her eyes and forced himself into her mind.

"You will remember that three large men forced their way into the room, one of them grabbed you and the next thing you remember is waking up covered in blood."

Before the woman could say anything, Andrew delivered a lightening fast right cross and knocked the woman out cold. He hated the fact that he hit her but it was important that her story was believable. He moved the unconscious woman to the wall where he wrote the message in blood and propped her against the wall. He grabbed a couple of units of blood, ripped them open and drenched her with it.

Amelia and Andrew then left the room taking off their shoes as they left so that they wouldn't leave bloody footprints to give them away. Andrew glanced outside and noticed that the sun was already beginning to rise; their little tryst had taken more time than he had planned and they now needed to find a place to hide for the day.

Andrew led them to a decontamination room that had been installed after nine-eleven. They quickly showered and scrounged around until they found some scrubs to wear before they found a supply closet to spend the day in until evening. Now that she had fed, Amelia was having no problems reaching out with her mind and dissuading people from investigating why the showers were wet.

They took turns keeping watch but thankfully, no one came to the closet that day. Andrew did a quick calculation of how much blood they had and figured that if they didn't waste it they had enough for two to three days. As soon as the sunset, the two of them left the closet invisible to everyone and headed out. On the way out Andrew snagged a newspaper and read the headlines.

"Two bodies disappear from the hospital morgue"

He folded the paper under his arm figuring that he could read it later when they arrived at his house. To his dismay, he saw a car parked in the driveway and his son sitting on the porch with Tony. He could tell even from where he stood that his son was crying and that Tony was doing his level best to comfort him.

Andrew stood frozen in place as he watched Shannon come out of the house, wrap her arms around Jake and talk to him. He could see the tears as they stained her pretty freckled face and wished that he could do something to take away their pain but he knew that they needed to grieve in peace.

"Goodbye my love," he said silently, "I hope that you find the happiness that you never had with me. Son, please be strong and grow up to be a better man than I was. Watch over and love your mother. Tony, do me a favor and take good care of them for me, love them and give them both what I never could."

Andrew turned to leave when Amelia wrapped her arms around him hugging him tight, "They'll be fine and you're right, we can never see our families again."

Andrew nodded and the two of them headed back toward the inner city as they tried to decide what they should do next aside from the fact that they needed clothing. They found a quick mart, which reminded Andrew that they needed ice for the blood. The problem was that he couldn't go in unless he was invisible; he was too well known here.

"I'm dying for a cup of coffee." he said to Amelia, "and we need ice for the blood so you're going to have to be the one to do it."

"Not a problem." Amelia replied with a smile as she walked into the store.

Andrew became invisible and followed her in watching as she prepared two cups of coffee hers with eight sugars and a quarter of a cup of creamer and Andrew's black. She stopped in the candy aisle and grabbed a payday for herself and a snicker bar for Andrew and as an afterthought a bag of beef jerky. The last item was a bag of ice that she found her way to the register.

While she was paying for their purchases, Andrew decided to have a little fun. He stood behind her, slipped his hands between her legs, and began to rub her center without warning her making her jump. Without thinking, she turned, looked behind her and glared at him before turning back around to see the man behind the counter looking at her as if she was crazy. She gave the man a sweet smile and shrugged as she counted her change and picked up the bag containing their purchases. As soon as she was out of sight, she turned toward Andrew, gave him her sternest stare before speaking to him.

"If you ever do that to me again, you'll be singing soprano for a month."

Andrew chuckled and then replied, "I'm sorry love but it was funny watching you squirm and admit it, it was as erotic as all hell having me feel you up while the clerk was watching."

Amelia laughed but issued a warning, "Just remember that the next time you go invisible." she said, "I'll be giving you the hand job from hell."

"I have no problem with that." Andrew said smiling wickedly, "as long as you don't mind me throwing you over the counter and fucking the shit out of you while they watch."

Amelia's eyes widened in shock and then she shuddered in anticipation, "You wouldn't dare!"

Andrew fought to keep a straight face, "Wouldn't I?" he asked.

Unable to keep a straight face, Andrew started laughing with Amelia joining in. Andrew packed the cooler with ice and counted the bags they had as he placed them in the cooler, they had eight bags and they couldn't afford to waste any if it.

They found a secluded spot where they could sit and talk. Neither of them could remember the last time that they had such good coffee and the candy bars were just heavenly.

"Is it me or does this stuff really taste better?" Amelia asked.

Andrew smiled as he relished the taste of the candy bar, "I have to admit that this is the best candy bar that I've ever had." Andrew replied but then changed the subject. "We have to make some fast decisions about our immediate future."

Amelia sighed, "We have to get out of this area." she said, "You're too well known around here and if we go to the DC or northern Virginia area, we'll have the same issue with me."

"So, what are you thinking?" Andrew asked.

"How about the Midwest or maybe the southwest?" she asked. "As far as money goes, we have somewhere around six thousand cash on us and I'm sure that we'll get more as we need it. Food wise, we'll have to make withdrawals from the blood bank and feed off scum when we can't. Agreed?"

"Agreed." Andrew said hugging her close, "One more thing though, no more talk about wanting to die. We either live or die together."

Amelia smiled and hugged Andrew back, "Agreed, forever, we stay together forever."

Andrew and Amelia walked toward the closest "Wally World" to go shopping. They bought clothes, pay as you go cell phones that they decided to activate one at a time, personal care items such as soap, toothpaste, and toothbrushes and for Amelia Tampons since she had no idea of whether she would need them or not.

They also bought a laptop, coffee, sugar, creamer, and snacks as well as a set of luggage, which included a makeup bag for Amelia. The last thing they grabbed was a couple of reusable credit cards. Andrew smiled at the as he asked her to put five hundred on each card and activated one of the phones while he waited.

In their zeal, neither of them thought about how they were going to get their purchases to wherever they were going. Andrew used the newly activated phone and called for a cab. While they waited, they packed their purchases into the new luggage leaving out clothes that they would change into when they found a secluded spot. By the time the cab arrived, they were comfortably dressed in tee shirts and Jeans.

Once the cab arrived, Andrew gave the driver an address that was located in the Lansdowne area. Amelia gave Andrew a confused look when the cab finally stopped in front of a large gated home. Andrew paid the driver and retrieved their luggage while Amelia erased the cab driver's memory of ever seeing them.

As soon as the cab was gone, they became invisible and Andrew began to explain who lived in the house.

"This place belongs to John Vincent; he happens to be the local drug supplier for over half of the gangs in Baltimore City and the surrounding counties."

"Nice." Amelia commented dryly.

"He is also responsible for at least six murders one of who was one of my confidential informants. He was a good guy but just trapped in the whole drug thing and was looking for a way out. The deal was that if he helped me then I would get him into a rehab program. Somehow, Vincent found out and my informant was murdered. What galls me is that I was never able to get anything to stick on the cocksucker when I was alive. How would you feel about inviting him to dine with us tonight?" Andrew asked.

"He sounds like such a charming gentleman that I have to say yes." Amelia replied smiling, "Does anyone else live with him?"

"His kid brothers." Andrew replied, "but watch him, that bastard is nuts. We had him on rape and murder charges a couple of years back but then the witnesses disappeared."

The two of them crept up to the porch and tried to enter but were blocked. It was then that Andrew realized what it was and groaned, "We have to be invited in."

"No problem." Amelia replied as she became visible, "Stay as you are." she said as she pulled the tee shirt up so that her stomach showed as an afterthought, she slipped off her bra and handed it to Andrew. She tied a knot so that it stayed up and then unbuttoned the button at the top of her jeans before sliding the zipper a quarter of the way down to show just a hint of her panties.

"Ready?" she whispered as she knocked on the door.

A few minutes passed before someone came to the door.

"Hi!" Amelia said cheerfully, "My car seems to have broken down and I seem to have misplaced my cell phone, can I use your phone?"

Paul Vincent couldn't believe what he was seeing as he looked Amelia up and down. She was gorgeous and although he knew that John would go ballistic, he invited her in. He had already decided that he wanted her. He smiled at her, stepped back, and invited her in.

Amelia stepped in, locked eyes with Paul and spoke, "Invite Andrew in too."

Right in cue, Andrew became visible and moved to Amelia's side.

"Welcome Andrew, please come in." Paul said politely.

Amelia's gaze went up the stairs, there was a woman here and she was frightened.

"Who's upstairs?" she asked, "Answer me." she added compelling Paul to tell her the truth,

"Just some bitch we gave a ride to and now she's going to pay for it."

Even before Paul could finish his statement, Andrew was flying up the stairs. He zeroed in on his target and burst through the door taking it off its hinges. He yanked John from off a girl who looked like she couldn't be more than fifteen or sixteen years old and pinned him against the wall.

Andrew didn't realize that when John looked at him that he wasn't seeing a human but the vampire part of him. His faced looked like that of a corpse, it was dried and drawn back, and his eyes were black and lifeless resembling the eyes of a shark. His fangs were visible against his thin, drawn back lips giving him an even more hideous appearance. The nails of his fingers had grown into long claws which were now poised at John's throat but hadn't punctured the skin. The woman on the bed looked at the horror that was Andrew, screamed and then fainted.

"Hello John," Andrew said with a cruel smile, "remember me?"

John studied Andrew's face for a long moment before recognition dawned. "Y... you're d..d... dead! I.... I saw it in...t... the p....papers!"

Andrew dropped the man to the floor and watched him cower. "That's what the papers say." Andrew agreed, "but here's my question, what were you doing to that poor girl?"

"She's just some street trash that I was going to party with tonight." John replied defensively. "You got a warrant Officer Martin?"

Andrew laughed before responding, "Warrant? I don't need one. I'm dead remember?" He looked back at the girl on the bed and then back at John, "she doesn't look like street trash to me, she looks like someone's little girl." by then Amelia had come up to the room and had taken in the scene.

"Please excuse my manners." Andrew said as he covered the naked girl with a blanket and then untied her, "This is my significant other Amelia, Amelia this is John Vincent." Amelia didn't reply but gave John a cold glare.

"Get some clothes on." Andrew said to John, "and we'll discuss why we're here, by the way, where'd you get the girl?"

"I picked the bitch up on Yale Avenue; she looked lonely so I decided to keep her company." John replied as she slipped into a pair of sweats and edged over to his dresser under the guise of getting a shirt. He reached into the drawer and was going to reach for the Glock 17 that he kept there when he heard a sweet voice coming from behind him.

"I really don't think that you want to reach for that gun as it would do nothing but upset my lover and believe me when I say you don't want to do that."

As Amelia spoke, her fangs dropped her voice remained sweet but her demeanor had become threatening. John moved his hand away from the gun, turned to look at her and realized that he was more afraid of her than he was of Andrew.

She turned to the doorway where Paul stood watching what was happening in the room. Amelia pointed to a spot on the floor and spoke to him.

"Paul come in here and kneel on that spot and don't move."

Paul walked to the designated spot, knelt down as he stared straight ahead and waited for the next command while John remained where he was.

"You really don't think that I didn't know about the gun did you?" Andrew asked Amelia good-naturedly.

Amelia looked at the still unconscious girl and compelled her to remain asleep before answering, "No love. I was actually worried that he would piss you off before we got the chance to invite him to dinner."

"Now Amelia, what would make you think that I would ever consider denying you a rare treat such as him?" Andrew replied teasing her.

John didn't know what they were talking about but he didn't like it. He was wishing that he had taken his chances with the gun. He looked over at Amelia, plastered a smile on his face and said, "I would love to join such a lovely lady for dinner, are we going out or eating in?"

Amelia smiled seductively, "I do believe that we'll be enjoying a quiet evening in." she said to Andrew, "won't we?"

"Yes," Andrew confirmed, "Once we see to the young lady and take out the trash... John, where are her clothes?"

John then knew that he wasn't going to make it through the night. He also knew that there was nothing that he could do to stop whatever it was that was going to happen and hoped that it wouldn't be too painful. He knew from reading the papers about the string of murders that these two cops had been working on when they died. His contact at central kept him up to date as well. He had started romancing Denise so that he could pump her for information. She had been the one who had given him the information on the witnesses in the rape/murder case that Paul had gotten off on a couple of years ago.

He had last seen her the night before and after fucking her she told him all about how Andrew and the FBI bitch had died and now here they were in his fucking bedroom. He ignored answering Andrew's question already knowing that Andrew would be pissed when he found out what he had done. The girl's clothes, now shreds were in the trashcan by the bed.

After he tied her to the bed, he cut her clothes off one piece at a time just so he could terrorize her even more than she already was. He also knew that the girl wasn't street trash but he wasn't about to tell Andrew that not that it would have made any difference.

"John, her clothes, where are they?" Andrew asked again.

"In the trash, I cut them up." John replied.

Amelia pointed at the spot next to Paul, locked eyes with John and commanded him to kneel next to him.

"Don't move unless I tell you to." she added.

John tried to resist but found himself walking to the spot next to Paul and kneeling down beside him.

Satisfied, Amelia turned to Andrew. "Sweetheart I'm hungry, how do you want to do this? One each or do we share one and save the other for tomorrow?"

Andrew gave it some thought. "One each would be great but I have some questions for Johnny boy such as the location of their safe including the combination, their bank and offshore account numbers and things like that."

"You heard him, talk." Amelia commanded.

Amelia stayed with the men and the sleeping girl while Andrew went to confirm the information. He found the safe easily and found fifty-thousand in cash, all of John's financial information including passwords and account numbers, a folder that listed all of his contacts and several CD's.

Andrew returned to the bedroom carrying all of the items from the safe and the cooler. He took two units of blood from the cooler and handed one to Amelia. In seconds, it was gone and she found herself feeling incredibly horny.

She looked at Andrew and walked toward him, "we have to settle things fast or they're going to get a show they won't soon forget."

Andrew saw the unbridled lust in her eyes and felt the blood rushing to his groin. "Amelia," he pleaded, "don't look at me like that or I won't be able to resist you."

Amelia gave him a seductive smile, licked her lips, and began pulling her tee shirt up stopping to massage her breasts and tweaking her nipples to hard points. "We could let her sleep and have Mike and Ike wait here while we have a little fun." she said.

Andrew smiled and pulled her into him, "Or we could take care of business first and have fun all day long, imagine what we could do with ice cream and whipped cream."

Amelia swirled her tongue around his ear while massaging his rapidly stiffening member, "Are you sure that you can wait?"

Andrew groaned as he struggled not to take her right there. His concern was that if they started, they would go into a frenzy like they did at the blood bank and that they would accidentally hurt the girl on the bed. The brothers he could have cared less about but he knew that Amelia wouldn't want the girl hurt.

"We need to take care of the girl first." he said "and we'll have more fun alone. Let's take care of business and I promise that you'll have the best day of your afterlife."

Amelia stroked Andrew with a firmer grip and rubbed a bare breast against him as she nibbled the side of his neck. Andrew closed his eyes as he fought for some semblance of control, "Love, if we lose control like we did last night we could hurt the girl. We need to care for her and then we can have John for dinner."

Amelia took a deep breath, then another and then a third one before she regained control over her lust. As much as she needed and wanted Andrew, she knew that he was right. "Alright, you win but you damned well better make it up to me."

Andrew reached out, tweaked the nipple of the exposed breast, and began to massage it slowly. "I want you more than I want or need air." he whispered, "but let's get the girl home, deal with those two and we'll spend the rest of the day in bed." He pulled her into a searing kiss and then released her.

Amelia straightened up her clothes while Andrew walked over to the brothers who had as instructed remained rooted to their spots on the floor. "Sweetheart, would you tell Mike and Ike to follow me? I want to get them out of here so that we can wake sleeping beauty over there."

"Alright you two stand up and follow Andrew." Amelia said, "And do whatever he says."

The two men stood and followed Andrew out of the room and down to the basement. "Nice." Andrew commented as he took in the large basement. The front of it was a combination game room/ multimedia area but it was the area in the back that he wanted.

In the back of the basement, he found a utility room that had an exposed pipe that ran along the ceiling. He made them raise their arms above their heads. The pipe was high enough that John and Paul had to stand on their tiptoes so that Andrew could tie them to the pipe.

Taking some old rags that he found on the floor, Andrew gagged both men as he issued a warning.

"If you behave yourselves, I might come back and release you tonight, if not, I might not come back for a day or two so do yourselves a favor and don't make a sound."

Amelia had retrieved their luggage and pulled out one of the summer dresses that she had just bought. Her Jeans and tee shirts would be too big for the girl but the dress while big would work. She went to the bed, sat down and gently released the sleep compulsion.

"Wake up, it's alright now."

The girl opened her eyes, looked around at the unfamiliar surroundings and seeing Amelia scooted back on the bed. Panicked, she curled into a tight little ball and began to beg as tears streamed down her face."

"Please don't hurt me! I don't want to die!"

Amelia tried to assure the very frightened young woman.

"We're not going to hurt you, I promise. The men that took you will never bother you again, Andrew and I have seen to that. What's your name?"

"Catherine Phillips." she replied, "who are you and what are you going to do to me?"

"First of all." Amelia replied, "You're going to put some clothes on and then you and I are going to have a serious talk about how to keep yourself safe. How old are you?" Amelia asked.

"Eighteen last week." Catherine replied as she slipped on the dress that Amelia handed to her.

"And just what is an eighteen-year-old girl doing walking the streets alone at night?" Amelia asked. "Did you not want to see your nineteenth birthday? The men that kidnapped you were going to rape you, pump you full of drugs and turn you loose. You would have ended up fucking anyone one just to get the money for your next fix! Is that what you want?"

Amelia knew that she was scaring the girl but that was her intent.

Catherine began to shake as tears ran down her face, "I was just walking home from a school dance! I never thought that I would be dragged into a car!" she sobbed. "He cut off my clothes and told me what he was going to do to me and I couldn't get away! He was ready to start when that.... Whatever that was crashed through the door and pulled him off me... oh god! You are going to kill me, aren't you?"

Amelia hugged the sobbing girl, "no dear, we aren't going to kill you." she said as she rocked the girl until she calmed down. "Just promise me that you won't go anywhere alone especially after dark unless it's with a group."

Catherine nodded her head as she promised. "I'll make sure that I'm with someone.... My parents! They have to be worried! They're going to kill me once they find out I'm okay."

Amelia smiled as she remembered what happened the one time she came home late, she was grounded for a month and had her mother had given her one hell of a lecture.

"Don't worry." she assured the girl, "I'll help you square things with your parents."

Andrew who had been waiting outside of the room for the girl to calm knocked on the wall, "is it safe to come in?"

Amelia noticed that Catherine had tensed at the sound of Andrew's voice. "That's Andrew, he won't hurt you."

After a brief hesitation, Catherine gave Andrew permission to come in. She braced herself to face the monster that she had seen earlier and was shocked to see a man who looked as if he could have been a model in one of her playgirl magazines. She took in his six feet inch height, tanned skin and was captivated by the way his muscles rippled when he moved. She could feel the moistness gather between her legs and wished that she had on a pair of panties to absorb the rapidly pooling liquid between her legs.

She looked at Andrew with lust-filled eyes as her imagination began to run wild with all that she would like to do to and with him.

Amelia noticed the reaction and fought not to yank Catherine's lust filled eyes from her head. Instead, she locked eyes with Catherine and spoke.

"You will forget about me and Andrew. You will only recall that you were kidnapped and almost raped by two men but you didn't see their faces. You will remember that a nice couple who scared your attackers off and helped you get home rescued you. The dress you are wearing was given to you by the woman of the couple who saved you, if asked; they didn't give you their names. The last thing is this; you will stop looking at my man with those lust filled eyes of yours. Do you understand?"

Catherine looked at Amelia and replied, "Do you really think that I could forget what my savior looked like? He's gorgeous! And do you seriously think that I could forget the face of the man that tried to rape me? What in the hell are you trying to pull?"

Amelia looked at Andrew in shock. Andrew looked into Catherine's eyes and tried to compel her as well, "You will do as she said, do you understand?"

Catherine looked at him and giggled, "What are you trying to do?"

Andrew and Amelia looked at each other and wondered what they should do. Amelia turned to Catherine and compelled her back to sleep.

"What are we going to do?" Amelia asked when Catherine was asleep. "She seems to be resistant to some of our compulsions."

Andrew was silent for several minutes, "As I see it, we have two choices; we either kill her or take her with us.... Really? We have only one choice."

He gave Catherine a sad look as he approached her. With tears in his eyes...

Andrew sadly looked at Catherine as he approached her. He looked from her and then to Amelia with tears in his eyes.

"I can't kill her even if it means our destruction... what are we going to do?" he asked.

Amelia sighed. She hated the feeling of uncertainty that flooded through her. She didn't want to kill Catherine but she was damned if she was going to share Andrew with her. The question that hung in her mind was how could they let her go? If they let her go and she told someone, it could mean their destruction if not something worse.

CHAPTER 3

***

Amelia went to Andrew, wrapped her arms around him and pulled him into an embrace relishing in the warmth and safety his arms provided. They weren't' safe and she knew it but she needed the illusion of safety that being held by him provided.

"We'll work it out." Andrew whispered, "We have to keep her with us until we can figure out a way to make her forget us."

"What kind of life is that?" Amelia asked. "What happens if we do take her with us and she escapes during the day when we can't follow her? She could go to the officials and we'd be trapped."

"Are you saying that we should kill her?" Andrew asked.

"No," Amelia replied shaking her head. "I don't want to hurt her but I don't want to lose what we have. I don't understand how you can mean so much to me after just a couple of days but at any rate, we have to talk to her and explain everything to her. We'll make our decision when we see her reaction."

Amelia sighed, "All I wanted to do was send her home, have a good meal and then enjoy a day of making passionate love with you." she added.

"It's still early." Andrew replied, "You may still get your wish. Tell you what, I'll put the rest of the bags of blood in the fridge and make us some food while you wake up sleeping beauty. The brothers are secured downstairs so she'll be safe.

Amelia waited until Andrew left the room before waking Amelia but not before reminding herself that she shouldn't remove the poor human's eyes for looking at her man. She released the compulsion and gently shook Catherine while calling her name.

Catherine opened her eyes, looked around and asked for Andrew.

Amelia's eyes became black orbs as the skin of her face became pale and drawn. Her fangs descended, her gums drawing back making them seem even larger.

"He's mine!" Amelia hissed, "And if you don't stop looking at him with lust in your eyes, I'll rip them out of your head and feast on them!"

Catherine's eyes widened in terror as she let out a blood-curdling scream as Amelia approached her. Amelia was now in full predator mode trying to protect her rights to her mate and the girl's fear wasn't helping. She violently grabbed Catherine's head, yanked it to the side and bit down her fangs piercing the jugular vein.

Amelia began draining the girl of her fear-laced blood thinking that it tasted sweeter than honey.

Andrew heard the scream, raced up the stairs and ran into the room. He saw Amelia in full vampire mode, her mouth latched onto the side of Catherine's neck. He raced across the room and yanked Amelia off Catherine as he screamed at her.

"Amelia! What in the fuck are you doing?"

Amelia struggled against Andrew as she hissed, "she was trying to steal you away from me! I won't allow anyone to come between us! She must die!"

Andrew turned Amelia around so that she was facing him and whispered to her, "she is a child, it's you that I want but you have to calm down so that we can help her before she dies."

Amelia regained control of herself and realized what she had done.

"My god Andrew!" she exclaimed, "help me! We have to save her! What came over me?" Amelia asked panicked.

Andrew went over to Catherine's side and tried to stop the blood flow knowing that if he didn't, she would die. Nothing he did stopped the blood from flowing from her neck. He looked over at Amelia and shook his head, "she'll be dead in a moment, and I guess our troubles are over."

"I didn't mean to attack her," Amelia said crying softly, "what came over me?"

Andrew wrapped his arms around Amelia as the girl took her last breath. He wished that he knew what to say to console Amelia.

"Maybe it's for the best." he said, "she won't have to travel with us and we won't have to worry about her betraying us."

Amelia was now beside herself with feelings of guilt, "What are we going to do with her body?" she asked, "She deserves a proper burial"

"We'll make sure that she gets one." Andrew replied. "We'll feed from the two downstairs, leave and then anonymously call it in."

"So we leave tomorrow night then." Amelia said softly. "Andrew, I am so sorry, maybe you'd be better off without me. You're better suited to the vampire life; I'll end up getting you killed."

"Did you forget our promise to each other?" Andrew asked firmly. "We promised to live or die together so which will it be? Get this through that thick head of yours! You are mine and no one or anything is going to separate us do you fucking understand me? I have been infatuated with you from the first time I saw you and after everything that we've been through you have no right to separate us."

Amelia threw her arms around Andrew's neck and kissed him. "I love you."

"I love you too." Andrew replied as he returned the hug

They went into another bedroom and quickly undressed. Andrew took a long slow perusal of the naked woman before him. He thought her more beautiful than any woman that he had ever seen and that included the mother of his son. He savored every inch of her flawless chocolate colored skin. Her scent was maddening. Her scent reminded him of the clean smell of a mountain rain and now that scent combined with the scent of her arousal, he thought that he could lose himself in her forever. It was as if the scent of her life's essence was a magnet drawing him in.

Amelia still aroused from her feeding wanted Andrew so badly that it hurt. His scent reminded her of new leather and musk. She was driven to a distraction by the scent of his life's essence that flowed beneath the surface of his skin. She had to taste it. She needed it more than she needed air.

Unable to wait any longer, Amelia dropped to her knees and took his member into her mouth. She rapidly bobbed her head up and down going deeper with each pass. She buried her nose in his pubic hair and worked her throat muscles trying to milk his cock. Andrew was fighting to control himself when he pulled Amelia up to her feet.

"I want to cum inside of you but not like that."

He picked her up, carried her to the bed and gently lay her down on it. He kissed her sliding his tongue into her mouth taking the time to explore her mouth with his tongue. He worked his left hand down to the junction between her legs and began rubbing her clit with his thumb varying the speed and pressure. He worked one and then two fingers into her hot wet pussy sawing them in and out while wiggling them around making sure that he reached every sensitive spot.

Andrew continued the ministrations with his fingers as he broke the kiss and began to nibble his way across his jaw then down to her neck. His fangs descended and he raked them across the skin of her neck causing her to shiver with anticipation. She wanted him to taste her essence as badly as he had wanted to taste hers it was a burning need that couldn't be ignored. When he reached her collarbone, Andrew retracted his fangs. He kissed, licked and nibbled his way across her collarbone; he could feel her building to her first orgasm.

He worked his way to her right breast and starting at the base and in a spiraling movement began to nip and lick his way up to her nipple. Once he reached the nipple, he gently took it into his mouth and began to tug on it as he flicked the tip of his tongue across the top of it. His left hand massaged her left breast gently pulling and pinching the nipple. His right hand tugged sharply on Amelia's clit making her sending her over the edge and screaming through the orgasm.

Inspired, Andrew didn't let up as he slid a third finger into her tight pussy. Amelia was out of her mind with lust and tried to rush him. She wanted him inside of her but when she tried to hurry him, he slowed down. He switched to her other breast but this time he used the tip of his tongue to spiral from the base of the breast to the nipple. Amelia tried to push her tit further into Andrew's mouth but he wouldn't allow it.

"I am the one who will decide how fast we go." he said as he held her in place. "If you insist on fighting me, I'll take great pleasure in tying you to the bed and teasing you for the next three days."

Amelia squealed, whether it was from lust or shock Andrew didn't know. He went back to teasing her nipple with the tip of his tongue and he could tell that her second orgasm was coming. He backed off but kept her right on the razor's edge of orgasm. She tried everything that she could to get Andrew to send her over the edge but he artfully dodged all of her attempts reducing her to begging.

"Andrew stop fucking teasing me!" she exclaimed, "and make me cum damn it!"

Andrew chuckled but continued to keep her on edge. Amelia tried to help herself go over the edge but Andrew wouldn't let her restraining her hands until she got the message.

"You are going to be sorry if you don't fucking make me cum right now!" Amelia demanded.

Andrew continued to ignore and slowly made his way down her stomach licking and then blowing across the moist skin making her shiver. He was taking great pleasure in driving her insane with lust never altering his pace no matter how much she demanded or begged him. She was getting to the point where she felt as if she was going to explode if Andrew didn't allow her to have her release. She couldn't even think clearly enough to use compulsion on him.

He swirled his tongue around her belly button as he worked her clit with his thumb just enough to keep her on edge but not enough to send her over the edge.

"Please Andrew," she begged, "Show me some mercy and let me cum."

Andrew rubbed his cheek across her patch of coarse dark hair reveling in the scent of her arousal as he slowly strummed her clit. Amelia was now begging in earnest offering him anything he wanted if only he would let her cum. He looked up at her and smiled as he got between her legs and slowly licked around the edges of her nether lips before going to the center and lapping at her. He stuck his tongue into her hole working it in and out like a small dick before licking his way to her clit. He began to nibble and suck on it as the bed became soaked with her juices.

He slid one and then two fingers into her pussy massaging her g-spot. Amelia began to shudder as the orgasm ripped through her body. All she could do was whimper as her breath raced in and out of her lungs. Her whole body trembled as she experienced the most intense orgasm of her life.

Andrew didn't let up, he kept sucking and nibbling at her as she rode wave after wave of pleasure that ripped through her body like a tidal wave. As soon as she began to come down from her orgasm, Andrew picked up his pace on her clit and the inside of her pussy. With a finger from his free hand, he began probing at her anal ring gently sliding it past the tight ring of muscle. The new sensation sent Amelia into another earth-shattering orgasm. She shuddered violently as wave after wave of rippled through her body. She was panting as if she had just finished running the New York City marathon in record time.

She couldn't wait any longer; she had to have him inside of her. She grabbed Andrew by his head and pulled him up to her.

"I need you now." she said as soon as she could look into his eyes. She gave him a searing kiss forcing her tongue into his mouth. Andrew repositioned himself, took his rock-hard cock in his hand and slowly slid it up and down her slit.

"What is it that you want love?" He teased.

Amelia wrapped her legs around Andrew's waist; her eyes now black orbs. "I want you now!"

Andrew inserted the head of his dick into her soaked pussy and held it there, "You don't intimidate me," he smirked, "I told you that this was at my pace not yours."

"Andrew please!" Amelia begged, "You're driving me insane!"

He began to work his way into her a little at a time then pull back until just the head of his cock was in her. He would pause for a couple of moments then slide in a little further only to pull back again. It took him a full five minutes to work his all of his cock in her. By this time, Amelia was beside herself with lust and desire, nothing she did could make Andrew speed up his slow, deliberate pace.

Amelia reached up, pulled Andrew down to her and bit into his shoulder. Andrew howled in pleasure and began to move at a frantic pace. His control gone, he let his fangs descend and bit into her shoulder as she had bitten into his. They each had only taken a couple of sips from each other but it was enough to send them into the most intense orgasm that either of them had ever experienced.

They released each other and lay in post orgasmic bliss. When they calmed, they realized that they needed to feed or else they would go into a frenzy. They headed to the basement where the brothers were still secured to the pipes. Andrew went to Paul, grabbed him as he turned his head to expose his neck and viciously bit down. He drank until the man was drained dry, released the lifeless body and left it hanging there.

While Andrew was feeding on Paul, Amelia calmly walked over to John and released the compulsion. She wanted him to be fully aware of what was going to happen to him. She wanted him to feel the same fear that Catherine felt when he had her tied to the bed and was going to rape her.

John watched as Andrew drained his brother and began to beg.

"Please! I'll do anything you want! Just don't kill me!"

"You have got to be kidding." Amelia said, "you expect mercy when you have none yourself? You're a pathetic piece of shit and I'm about to do the world a favor by getting rid of you."

She reached up, grabbed the rope that led to the pipe and snapped it. John tried to shove her out of the way but she didn't move other than to kick the side of his kneecap forcing it to dislocate to the side. John howled in pain as he fell, his leg no longer able to support him.

Amelia grabbed him by the hair, yanked his head to the side and bit down puncturing his jugular vein. She gulped it down not wanting to waste a single drop as she relished the sweet taste of it. When he was drained dry, she unceremoniously dropped the body to the floor.

She looked at Andrew and realized that she could feel everything that he felt for her. She felt his love and need for her just as he felt hers for him. She found it to be a very surreal experience. Amelia wanted and needed to be held by him and knew that he wanted the same as they came to grips with this new ability. She rushed over to Andrew and hugged him, holding on to him for dear life.

"I could stay like this forever." she heard him say.

Amelia smiled before replying, "So could I my love."

"You could what?" Andrew asked confused as to what she was talking about.

"Stay like this forever." she replied laughing, "You just said it and I'm agreeing with you."

"Amelia, I didn't say anything," Andrew said, 'I thought it but .... Are you telling me that you can read my mind?" he asked.

"If I did, it wasn't intentional," Amelia replied. "But it sounded as if you had spoken out loud and I'm not trying to spy on your personal thoughts."

Andrew heard what she said but also heard, "God why does he have to look so sexy?"

"You're very sexy yourself." Andrew said, "And I don't think that you were reading my mind on purpose, it just surprised me is all."

Amelia looked at Andrew and was confused for a moment until she understood what was happening.

"Andrew, we're not reading each other's minds; somehow we're projecting out thoughts to each other." She concentrated on what she wanted to say and then asked, "Did you hear me?"

Andrew shook his head, "sorry love but it didn't seem to work this time."

Amelia shrugged, "too bad, I was offering you something special but now you'll never know what it was."

Andrew's eyes lit up, "I can only imagine what you were thinking of."

He snapped the rope that was holding Paul's body up and let them fall to the floor.

"What do you think we should do with the bodies?" he asked.

"I don't know." Amelia replied, "How long are we going to be staying here?"

"I figured on a few days so that we could come up with a plan and maybe get a better handle on our abilities." Andrew said, "and I was hoping to get to know you a little better but I think that we should leave here as soon as possible." he added.

Amelia smiled at the "get to know you better" comment and asked a question, "why did we become vampires and not die like the others? And what if Catherine is in the process of becoming a vampire? If it weren't for you, I would be in big trouble. Think about how she's going to be when she wakes up and remembers that I attacked her."

Andrew frowned at the possibility that John and Paul could be vampires. He thought about what he knew about vampires from the books he read and the movies. The only thing that was consistent in all of them was that they died if they went into the sunlight and death was permanent if either they were decapitated or their bodies burned. He wondered how one was turned into a vampire although he did not intend to turn someone; it was something that they needed to know to prevent accidental turnings.

"I don't know why or how we turned but it's a good question." Andrew replied. "I also have to wonder what the difference between us and that woman's other victims are. And for the sake of argument, let's say that we started the process of creating three new vampires, what do we do? Do we allow it to happen or try to prevent it?"

"I don't think that we should let the brothers become vampires." Amelia replied, "But how do we stop it?"

"We cut off their heads." Andrew replied.

"Are you sure?" Amelia asked.

"No but according to the myths they can be killed in two ways and one of them is decapitating them and of the two methods, that is the more practical one." Andrew replied.

"Why is that the more practical choice? And what about the girl?" Amelia asked, "Are we going to cut her head off too?"

"The other option is burning the bodies, it would take too long and as for the girl, she was an innocent, we'll try to help her but we can't let the brothers return as vampires." Andrew replied. "I wonder if we can find any reliable information on the web?"

"Shall we try Google or Wikipedia?" Amelia asked laughing.

"Actually," Andrew replied, "I was thinking of trying both. We need to make some quick decisions; we have less than an hour before sunrise. We have to decide what we're going to do and where we're going to go from here. I don't know how much information is out there but we'll have to take what we can get."

"I'm sorry love, you're right and besides, it really can't hurt anything." Amelia said softly.

"There's nothing to be sorry for." Andrew said as he wrapped his arms around Amelia, "and it does sound like some kind of joke but I'm trying to keep us alive."

Andrew released her from the hug and went to the garage to see if there was anything that he could use to decapitate the brothers. He was impressed with the selection of cars that he saw in the garage-taking note of the Beemer and a viper but the Hummer H-3 Alpha was the vehicle that would best fit their needs. He took a few minutes to look it over and realized that it had everything that they would need including a small refrigerator. After looking over the Hummer, he looked for an axe and found a machete.

He went back into the house, pulled John's body out into the garage, and removed his head and hands before placing them in a trash bag. He repeated the process with Paul noting how little blood there was. Afterwards, he wrapped the bodies in comforters and with Amelia's help put the bodies in the back of the hummer.

Andrew knew that time was getting short but he didn't want the corpses in the house, it was bad enough that the girl was still there.

"I'll be back in a little while." he told Amelia, "I'm going to get rid of the bodies."

He knew that he had to be quick. Sunrise was rapidly approaching. He was about to pull out and head to the state park when he spotted a garbage truck about to empty a dumpster. He quickly got out of the hummer, ran over to the truck, and tapped on the driver's door. When the driver opened the door, Andrew quickly compelled him and instructed him to stay where he was.

He put the bodies in the dumpster and then erased the driver's memory of him. That done, he went to a twenty-four-hour grocery store and bought four bottle of drain cleaner with which he would use to dispose of the heads and hands of the brothers.

By the time he returned to the house, dawn was just touching the sky. He had just pulled in when he saw a trash truck headed their way. He had Amelia run the bags containing the body parts to the truck, throw them in and then compel the men to compact the trash and then to forget about seeing her.

While she was taking care of the remaining body parts, Andrew moved Catherine's body from upstairs to the downstairs sofa. He grabbed the file that he had taken from, the gun that had been in the dresser drawer, John's laptop, carried them down to the game room, and set himself up at the bar. Amelia came down a few minutes later with a tray containing two large omelets, a butler of coffee and utensils.

As they ate, the laptop was booting up, when it was ready, he googled vampires and was amazed at the number of hits that he received. He narrowed his search by typing in "real vampires" which knocked the number of results from fourteen million to about a million and a half. Not knowing where to start, he began picking random sites but a many of them were sites that retold the old myths about vampires. He was about to give up when he noticed that there were instructions on the lower right-hand corner of the screen, "if you can see this, click here."

"What the hell?" Andrew muttered as he clicked onto the link. The laptop went through a series of redirects until it came to a site. "Amelia, come see this." Andrew said.

They couldn't believe their luck as they read together, "welcome to the blood exchange, the first and only site for people who have been afflicted with vampirism. If you wish to continue, you must first call...."

The site kicked them off after about a minute. Andrew, using one of the prepaid phones dialed the number. The phone rang four times before someone answered. Instinctively Andrew knew that the voice that answered the phone belonged to a vampire.

"Hello," Andrew replied, "I hope that you can help us."

"Hello parvulus, where is your creator?" the voice asked.

"If you mean the bitch who turned us, in hell I hope." Andrew replied.

There was surprise in the man's voice as he responded, "Who is there with you? How did your creator die and do you know her name? I am assuming that it was a female since you used the term bitch."

"My name is Andrew and not parvulus and the name of the lady with me is Amelia. Diamond was the name of the woman who turned us and as to how she died; I blew her head off with a shotgun."

"Ahh Detective Martin! So Special Agent Hensley is still with you, this is good. We had a feeling that you two had been turned. The man paused a moment before continuing." Now the incident at St. Agnes makes sense. Nice cover up, the humans are looking for some kind of fringe cult but I must ask you to be more careful. How much blood do you have and when did you last feed?" he asked.

"We fed last night." Andrew replied, "And we have some important questions for you like how do we prevent from turning humans into vampires when we feed on them? How often do we have to feed and do we have to kill the human that we feed from?"

"First of all, "the voice said, "If you feed from a human, they will die. Whether they will turn or not depends on when you stopped feeding. If you stop feeding before the heart stops, they will come back as vampire. Therefore, when you feed from a human, make sure that you drink until the heart stops unless you are planning to turn them.

Andrew drew in a harsh breath, "Shit! I thought we turned her."

"Who are you talking about?" the vampire asked alarmed.

"When we got here the man that owned the place was in the process of raping a girl that he and his brother had kidnapped." Andrew explained, "When we freed her she started flirting with me which made Amelia so angry that she attacked her. She only bit her once and latched on for less than a minute but we couldn't save her."

"Have you and Amelia exchanged blood yet?" the vampire asked.

"Yes, just before we fed from the owners of the house." Andrew replied, smiling at Amelia's blush.

"Congratulations are in order then!" The vampire exclaimed sounding genuinely pleased. "The two that you fed from, did you feed until the heart stopped?"

"Mating?" Andrew asked. "And yes, their hearts were no longer beating not that it would have made any difference."

"What happened was when the two of you exchanged blood while having sex; you formed a bond that can never be broken. You will always be able to find each other no matter where you are or how far apart you are. You will also be able to feel the emotions of the other as if they were your own as well as project thoughts to each other. The down side to all of this is that it will be virtually impossible to remain sane after losing one's mate. More times than not, the remaining mate has to be put down." The vampire explained and then he asked about the bodies of the dead men.

"I decapitated them and cut off their hands." Andrew replied, "I was lucky enough to find a dumpster that was about to be emptied and tossed the bodies in there, they're probably in a landfill by now. The head and hands were tossed into a garbage truck and the driver was compelled to run the compactor."

"I am impressed." The vampire said. "Normally parvulus leave a trail of bodies behind them. How much blood do you have?" he asked.

"Six units and why do you keep calling me parvulus?" Andrew asked.

"Parvulus is Latin for infant or child. It is what we call newly turned vampires because in essence that is what you are in that you have to learn your abilities and how to manage them. As far as your blood supply is concerned, you don't have enough. The girl will require twelve to fifteen units when she wakes up. After that, you can choose your options. You can drink three to four units per day and not eat human food or you can eat human food and drink three to four units at least twice a week.

You should also keep ten units of plasma on hand for emergencies. It doesn't replace blood but it will hold off the blood lust for a day or so if you don't have blood, which by the way needs to be refrigerated. The plasma will keep for a year."

Andrew tried to think of where he could get that much blood and came up with one option, the hospital although getting a human would almost be easier.

"Alright," Andrew replied, "I'll go hit a couple of hospitals."

"No, that is too risky." The vampire said, "There is a place not far from you that acts as a blood supplier for vampires. I must warn you that it isn't cheap but the blood is always fresh and available. The blood cost two thousand a unit and the plasma is twenty-five hundred a unit."

"Where is this place?" Andrew asked.

"Do you know where Industrial Park on Lansdowne Road is?"

"I know the place." Andrew replied.

"Bio Medtronic is in building number sixteen. Go to the receptionist and ask for Susan Dorchester, she will be expecting you."

"Thanks," Andrew said, "I'll head out as soon as the sun goes down."

"Why are you waiting?" the vampire asked, "You need to have the blood ready by the time she wakes up which could be any time after sunset."

"I have no desire to be burned to death!" Andrew replied his voiced filled with sarcasm.

The vampire roared with laughter, "My friend, you have much to learn! While it is true that you will get sunburn faster than humans will you will not burst into flame. In order for that to happen, you would have tied down and left in the sun. It could take hours before death comes. The only thing that you will experience is a decrease in strength that will return to you at night.

Let me think of some of the more popular myths that I can dispel, we can't turn into bats or mist, we can't teleport, and we can go on holy ground, holy relics such as crosses and holy water have no effect on us. Garlic does nothing except to give us bad breath- I happen to love Italian food. A wooden stake while painful is not always fatal; in order for death to occur, the whole heart would have to be destroyed. The surest way to kill one of us is by decapitation; guns will hurt but are rarely fatal unless the brain or the heart is destroyed.

When you decide to leave Baltimore, come to Philadelphia. There is a night club called Sanguinem on Water Street and ask for me."

"And you are?" Andrew asked.

"I do apologize." The vampire said. "My name is Charles Black. I am the lead enforcer for the east coast. I can help you with the learning of your abilities and will show you how to locate blood suppliers as well as places where you can dispose of bodies. If you are in further need of assistance, please don't hesitate to call me. Here is a number that you may want to take down; it's the number to a body disposal service. They charge between five and fifteen thousand depending on the mess but it takes the responsibility away from you."

Charles gave Andrew the number and continued.

"You and Amelia are ultimately responsible for the clean-up of your own messes whether it be bodies or turnings. I will help you this one-time with the female that was accidentally turned and as I said, I am even willing to teach you what you need to know in order to survive but there are rules. These are rules that all of us follow and if these rules aren't followed you will be hunted down, imprisoned or killed."

Andrew didn't care for the implied threat but he could see the need for the rules.

"I understand and thank you for the help that you've given us already; we'll see you within a week."

After hanging up, Andrew went into the office and looked at the financial records of the brothers. He saw that they had several local bank accounts and even though he had the numbers, he didn't have the identification needed to cash a check and there was no way for him to access the offshore accounts. He backed up all of the information on the desktop to the laptop and disconnected the computer.

He looked at the clock noting that it wasn't quite nine am. He had spent more time than he had wanted to in getting ready to go buy the blood. He quickly dressed and grabbed the keys to the BMW parked in the garage and the Glock.

"I shouldn't be more than a couple of hours." he told Amelia, "Do you want me to bring anything back with me?"

"I'm going with you." Amelia replied. "The girl won't wake up until sometime tonight so I don't need to watch her and besides, I saw you pick up that gun. There's no way that you're going to leave me behind."

"I'm only taking the gun as a precaution." Andrew said. "And I know that Catherine isn't supposed to wake up until this evening but what if someone stops by and finds her?"

"Then we'll put her in the back of the truck and take it." she replied. "If not that then we hide her someplace but either way, I'm going with you."

Andrew was going to lose this battle and he knew it.

"Fine, let's find a good place to hide her." he said.

In the end, they decided on the attic. Andrew went up first and had Amelia hand him Catherine's body, which he laid on an old blanket that he found. After making sure that she at least looked comfortable, he climbed down and closed the door to the attic.

Amelia was waiting for him with a request, "Could we take the hummer? I love riding in it."

Andrew grabbed the keys to the hummer and led Amelia to the driver's side, kissed her and handed her the keys.

"What you really wanted was to drive it." Andrew said with a playful smirk on his face.

Amelia's eyes glowed with delight as she started the Hummer and then pulled out of the garage. Andrew hit the button to close the garage and gave her directions to Bio Medtronic. It occurred to him that they had nothing to keep the blood cold in so they made an unscheduled stop at "Wally World."

Amelia handled the truck as if she was a pro and had no problem maneuvering the large vehicle through traffic. Once at the store Amelia said that she had some things that she had forgotten to get the last time that they had been shopping.

"Alright." Andrew said, "as much as I would love to tell you to buy whatever you want, we have to watch the money until I can transfer more money into a local bank."

Amelia didn't argue as she grabbed a couple sets of undergarments, a pair of jeans and a tee shirt that looked to be about Catherine's size. She bypassed the other items that she wanted opting to wait until their finances were in order.

While Amelia shopped, Andrew grabbed a cooler that could be plugged into the cigarette lighter of the hummer. He also picked up a small apartment sized refrigerator as the hummer also had a power inverter as well as two house outlets located in the rear of the vehicle. The last thing he picked up was a couple of tarps for just in case they needed them.

He met Amelia at the cash register and used one of John's ATM cards to pay for their purchases. On the way out, Amelia handed him the keys.

"You drive, I want to look around."

Andrew helped Amelia into the hummer, put their purchases in and got in.

"How far away are we from our destination?" she asked.

"I don't know, twenty minutes give or take and depending on traffic." Andrew replied.

"Then I guess I'd better hurry." Amelia replied.

Before Andrew could ask her what she meant, his pants were unzipped and Amelia was pulling his rapidly hardening cock out. She bent down, wrapped her lips around his member and began to bob her head up and down each time taking more of him deeper into her mouth and throat. When she heard him moaning, she picked up the pace. After taking the full length of him in several times, she swirled her tongue around the head of his dick. Her ministrations were making it difficult for Andrew to concentrate on his driving.

She bathed the entire length of his swollen cock with her tongue before taking it back into her mouth. She kept going until she had every inch of him in her mouth and down her throat milking him for her reward. She stayed bottomed out on him for a few minutes and then began to bob her head up and down again. Once again, she took in his entire length using her throat muscles to massage him while a hand rubbed and tugged on his balls.

She only came up long enough to take a quick breath before returning to the task of milking him. Finally, it had become too much and Andrew exploded in her mouth as she greedily sucked down every drop and tried to get more. She had failed to notice that they had arrived at their destination and had been sitting there for a few minutes. She smiled at Andrew before straightening herself up. Andrew gave her a quick kiss before getting out of the truck and helping her out.

They entered a building that looked old and worn on the outside but was new and modern on the inside. The waiting area almost looked like the waiting room of a doctor's office with the magazines and the water cooler. There was only one person waiting and both Andrew and Amelia knew that she was vampire.

Andrew approached the receptionist and knew that she too was vampire. He gave her a polite smile and stated his business.

"We're here to see Susan Dorchester."

"Who may tell her is here to see her?" the receptionist asked.

"Andrew Martin and Amelia Hensley."

"She will be with you shortly, please have a seat after you remove that gun from the premises." The receptionist said returning the smile.

"Sorry." Andrew said sheepishly, "Old habits die hard."

"I understand that you used to be a cop." The receptionist said, "But let me give you a piece of advice, that gun will do little more than to piss a vampire off. If you're going to carry may I suggest a Forty-four Magnum or a Desert Eagle?"

"Thanks for the advice but I didn't think that it would kill a vampire, I thought that it might slow one down enough to give me an advantage." Andrew replied.

The receptionist chuckled, "you are very perceptive for a parvulus and congratulations on your mating."

"Thank you!" Amelia and Andrew replied in unison.

Andrew went out to the hummer and placed the weapon under the seat hoping that he wasn't making a mistake. He rejoined Amelia in the waiting room and noticed that much to Amelia's annoyance; the other vampire was making eyes at him.

He wasn't really paying attention to her until she got up and made a point of making sure that her cleavage showed as she bent over to pick up a magazine. Andrew glanced at her more for the fact that she was invading his personal space more than anything else. The female vampire flashed Andrew a predatory grin.

"Excuse me sweetheart."

That was Amelia's undoing. Before anyone could stop her, she launched herself at the woman grabbing her by the neck and lifting her off the ground.

"If you so much as look at my mate again, I will rip your fucking head off! Whore!" Amelia snarled.

"You bitch!" the woman snarled back as her eyes blackened and her fangs descended. "You dare attack me?"

The woman grabbed Amelia's arm, yanked it from her throat and twisted it to the side breaking it. Andrew seeing his mate in trouble roared and attacked. He threw himself at the woman grabbing her by the throat as he reached her. He hit her with so much force that the woman lost her grip on Amelia. Without thinking, Andrew snapped the woman's head to the side, viciously bit down and tore her jugular vein and carotid artery from her neck.

The receptionist couldn't believe how fast Andrew had moved. She didn't even have the chance to call for security. She watched fascinated as Andrew jumped to the defense of his mate and the offending female's blood sprayed around the room. She couldn't tear her eyes away as Andrew finally twisted the female's head until it separated from his body.

Andrew's primordial roar of victory had every member of the security team pouring into the reception area. Andrew now joined by Amelia turned to face their new attackers. Amelia's arm was broken and would need time to heal but otherwise she was unhurt.

Andrew placed himself between Amelia and the six new vampires that had entered the room. He knew that he didn't have much chance of surviving but he would defend his mate with the last ounce with his strength.

The new vampires formed a line between them, the receptionist, and the door to the back areas of the office. They held their defensive positions although they made no moves to advance or attack. Each of the new vampires had a sword and had a hand on the hilt.

After what seemed like an eternity, the tension was broken by the soft tinkle of laughter. Andrew glanced over to see who had laughed and saw a raven-haired Middle Eastern woman. The power that radiated from the woman was palpable as she surveyed the scene and then spoke to the security guards in a language that neither Amelia nor Andrew understood.

The guards stepped back clearing a path for the woman as she looked at the corpse on the floor. "Candace," she chuckled, "that look suits you and you have been warned about starting trouble at my place. You should thank the parvenus; he saved you from a lot of pain."

She then turned her attention to Andrew and Amelia taking notice of how Andrew was protecting Amelia.

"You have little to fear from me." she said with a chuckle, "but I will be adding five-thousand to your bill for the clean-up and you owe Ms. Vegas for her ruined outfit."

"My clothes being ruined was a very small price to pay for the show I just saw." Gloria replied laughing, "Not only is he nice eye candy......"

"While I agree with the eye-candy part," Susan said interrupting Gloria, "I would hate to have to find a new receptionist. His mate is still looking a bit anxious so I think that you should wait to finish that sentence. Mr. Martin, Ms. Hensley, if you would follow me? There was one person ahead of you but she seems to have changed her mind."

Andrew was shocked. He had expected to die. This woman wasn't in the least bit concerned about the woman that he had just killed. He hadn't intended to kill her but the sound of Amelia's arm breaking made him lose control. He looked down at Amelia to check on her.

"Sweetheart, are you alright?" he asked.

"I'm fine." Amelia replied her voice strong as she cradled her arm. Her eyes were pain filled but she showed no fear as she followed Susan to wherever she was taking them.

Susan heard the pain in Amelia's voice, stopped and looked her over. She could clearly see where the arm was broken. "We'll need to set that so that it will heal correctly." she said, "I could do that for you if you like."

"Thank you, Ms. Dorchester," Amelia replied shocked by the amount of compassion that she heard in the woman's voice. "I'm sorry for all of the trouble that I caused."

"It's no trouble." Susan replied with a chuckle, "there were no humans present but the next time please have your sexy mate take it outside." She added.

"I'll try." Amelia replied with a laugh, "but you know how hard -headed men can be."

Susan laughed as she led them to a locker room, "there's a shower in there and there's a couple of pairs of overalls in the closet but let's set your arm before it heals and we have to re-break it. Trust me, the second time is much more painful." she said.

She had Amelia sit on a bench and spoke to Andrew, "I need you to hold her in place while I do this."

Andrew sat next to Amelia and wrapped his arms tightly around her leaving the broken arm free. Susan grabbed the first aid kit and a broom breaking the broom into eighteen-inch pieces. She took Amelia's arm and set the bone with practiced ease. Amelia screamed in pain as Andrew whispered in her ear how much he loved her and that they would always be together. Amelia's fangs extended and she bit him.

The arm now splinted, Amelia released her bite and retracted her fangs. Andrew with his arms still around Amelia was dazed and trying to regain control of himself, her bite had acted as a powerful aphrodisiac.

Amelia now back in control thanked Susan and checked on Andrew.

"Andrew? Are you alright?"

"It's no problem." Susan replied, "I'll add it to your bill and please, call me Susan."

"Thank you, Susan." Andrew replied, "and please call me Andrew and this is Amelia and we'll be more than happy to pay for any damages." to Amelia he replied, "I'm fine."

"Good." Susan said. "I'm going to my office so you two can get cleaned up. I'll send someone for you in fifteen minutes and Amelia, be careful with that arm. It should be healed enough to remove the splint in about two to three hours."

Susan went to her office to change clothes. After she was changed, she placed a call, the phone rang twice before it was answered.

"Hello, Charles? It's Susan... Yes, they are here now, there was a slight altercation. No, they suffered no major injuries but Candace Carmichael is dead. She flirted with Andrew and Amelia responded... No, Andrew killed her when Candace broke Amelia's arm... dear, he's almost as fast as you are. Yes, I agree, they will be perfect. How would you like me to proceed? All right, I can help them get set up but what about the woman they turned? You're sure that it won't interfere with your plans? I see. You're hoping that she will be an asset to them and if she isn't? I agree. She will have to die... Yes, and I will see you next month, I am looking forward to the fun.... Bye lover toy!"

After she hung up, Susan pushed the button for the intercom.

"Gloria my love it you would, please cancel all of my appointments for today and close up the office until the repairs are completed. Also, call Ronald and tell him that we have to reschedule because of equipment issues and make sure that he has enough product to carry him until next week. What do you say about going to lunch for a private meeting? It's been far too long, what do you think?"

Susan smiled at Gloria's enthusiastic response, "Yes Ms. Dorchester! I agree that it has been far too long. I look forward to eating you.... Err with you."

Susan heard Gloria's chuckle as she released the button not fooled by her supposed slip of the tongue. In some ways, Susan envied Amelia for finding her mate so soon. Susan had been turned during the reign of Tiberius Julius Caesar Augustus when she was a house slave to one of the Tribuni of the Praetorian Guard. She was freed when Charles found her in 26 A.D.

Since then, the two of them had traveled the world together and there was very little that they had not done together. They had remained very close and although they hadn't felt the need to mate with each other, there was very little that they wouldn't do for each other.

Gloria had been turned during the Civil war by none other than Susan. She was about to be executed for helping slaves escape via the 'Underground Railroad'. Unfortunately, during the raid on their farm, her parents had been killed. Susan who had been there at the time begged Gloria to lay low but Gloria, set on avenging her parents refused to listen and killed eight of the twenty men responsible for the deaths of her parents.

Susan watched over Gloria and even helped her. Gloria, fully aware of what Susan was even gave her a couple of the men still alive to serve as dinner.

One night, Gloria went up against the leader of the men who killed her parents and killed him. The trouble came when the three men that had been with him came to his aid. Gloria managed to kill all three of them but during the exchange of gunfire, she was mortally wounded. Susan gave her the option of being turned or dying. Gloria chose to be turned. The two of them had been friends and occasional lovers ever since.

Andrew couldn't believe how hard Amelia's bite made him. He led her to the shower and helped her undress before undressing himself. After adjusting the temperature of the water, he moved her under the stream careful to keep her injured arm out of the water. Using the liquid soap available, he began to wash her starting with her hair and working his way down to her generous, perfectly shaped breasts paying special attention to her nipples.

His slow, deliberate massage was beginning to drive Amelia up the wall as his hands massaged in slow, lazy circles on her stomach working their way to her nether lips. His fingers spread her open and began to rub her bud with gradually increasing pressure.

Amelia was trembling with anticipation as Andrew began kissing his way down toward her waiting center. He didn't even pause at her breasts opting to go through the valley between them. He paused at her belly button, swirled his tongue in and around it before continuing his southward journey.

When he reached the apex of her legs, he traced the outline of her nether lips with the tip of his tongue before slipping it in between them. He licked back to front and when he reached her nub, he would flick his tongue like a snake sending little electrical jolts through her body.

Amelia was panting with excitement and began to beg, "Baby please fucking suck my clit!" She tried to get him to latch on but Andrew ignored her efforts and her pleas and continued the torture of her clit. Unable to withstand any more, Amelia's eyes changed from brown to black, "If you don't fuck me now, you will be sorry!"

Andrew ignored her and if anything, lightened his touch. Amelia screamed in frustration and with all of her strength shoved Andrew onto his back pinning him down as she impaled herself on him. She began riding him like a woman possessed as she bent down, bit into Andrew's shoulder causing him to explode inside of her. As soon as he began too cum, it triggered her orgasm; she shuddered with pleasure as it ripped through her body.

Just as she was coming down from her orgasm, she released her bite. Andrew bit into her shoulder causing her to shatter yet again. Her whole body convulsed as she screamed her release. Afterwards, Andrew held her as she came down from her pleasure high.

"You bastard, you did that on purpose." she said.

Andrew chuckled before replying, "guilty as charged but I think we'd better hurry, our escort will be here any minute if our hostess is prompt."

Susan chuckled when she heard Amelia scream her release. She picked up the phone and said, "Our guests should be ready for their escort in about ten minutes."

The male voice on the other end of the line was doing his best to contain his laughter as he replied, "Yes ma'am but I think that the lady will need a little more than ten minutes to get her legs back under her."

"Ok, give them twenty minutes then." Susan replied, "And for god's sake make sure you knock before you enter." she added.

Andrew and Amelia quickly finished their shower, dressed in the coveralls in the closet and threw the clothes that they had been wearing into the trash. Andrew cleaned their shoes as best he could use the wet clothes from their shower. They had just finished dressing when there was a tap on the door.

"Are you ready to go?" A voice called in.

"We sure are." Andrew replied.

"If you will follow me." The security officer said as he stepped back from the door and waited.

They followed the security officer until they reached a double set of wooden doors. The officer knocked and waited for a response. Susan invited them in and led them to a conference table.

"Please, sit and make yourselves comfortable." she said with a smile, "wine?"

Gloria brought in a tray containing glasses of wine. When she was gone, Susan turned back to them.

"How many units of blood would you like to purchase?" she asked.

"Twenty units." Andrew replied.

"That's a lot of blood, are you going on an all blood diet?' Susan asked. She already knew the answer but wanted to assess their honesty.

"No." Andrew replied, "We're going to eat food too but we have another who is going to become one of us tonight and we want to be sure that we have enough."

"What do you mean?" Susan asked, "What did you do with the body?"

"The place where we are staying was owned by a couple of low-life drug-dealing brothers. My plan was to make the world a better place and stay there for a while. When we got there, they had an eighteen-year-old girl tied up in one of the bedrooms intending to rape her. We rescued her but when Amelia tried to erase her memories and failed and then the girl came on to me, Amelia judged her a threat and bit her.

We hid the girl's body in the attic while we came here to get blood. We have six units back at the house and according to the information that Mr. Black gave us, she'll need between twelve and fifteen units of blood to satisfy her."

Susan smiled inwardly as she held her poker face, "very well thought out." she commented. "I'm sure that Charles also told you to buy some plasma for emergencies, how many units do you want?"

"Just the blood for now." Andrew replied, "I assume that cash is the preferred method of payment?"

Suddenly Susan understood that they didn't have much money and probably no identification. Under normal circumstances, the vampire that sired them would have taken care of getting them set up for life in the human world. That preparation would have included teaching them how to use and control their powers but their sire was Diamond. Even if she were alive, she wouldn't have done anything to help them.

"Andrew, I have an associate that can help you. He can get identification for the three of you assuming that you are right about the girl. He can also transfer any assets like the hummer and any financial assets as well into your name. If you like, Gloria and I can come out to where you're staying and help you with the girl. As you know, a newborn vampire can go into a blood frenzy. We know how to control it and we might be able to prevent it. I'll check to see if Mr. Allen is able to come too."

The offer of help surprised Andrew but before he could answer, Amelia spoke up.

"Thank you so much! We'll need all of the help that we can get. How about we do steaks on the grill... is six alright?" she asked.

"Sounds good to me but let me call Mark, he's the friend that I was talking about. She came back a few minutes later. "He's coming but he wants you have any and all financial records ready besides records of the brother's holdings, that way he'll be able to tell what he can and can't switch over to you."

"We can do that." Andrew replied and then grimaced when he received the total for the blood and damages to the reception area. Forty-eight thousand dollars.

On the way back to the house, they stopped at the store and picked up six large New York strip steaks, a dozen large baking potatoes, mushrooms, and fresh asparagus as well as a couple bottles of good wine.

When they got back to the house, they noticed a green Ford Focus with FOP (Fraternal Order of Police) tags on it parked in front of the house.

"It seems we have company." Andrew commented as he hit the button to open the garage door.

"I wonder why a car with FOP tags is here." Amelia said. "Let me go first and see what's going on."

"I'll be invisible and follow you." Andrew replied.

Amelia went into the house with Andrew following close behind. She could smell the scent of 'White Diamond' perfume and knew that the person wearing it was upstairs.

"John? Paul? Is that you? I just got back from the store!" Amelia called out.

Denise came out of the bedroom dressed in a sheer robe. "Who in the hell are you?" she demanded.

Andrew recognized her as Denise Samuels. She worked at central and now he understood how John was always ahead of the police, Denise was his contact. Andrew was beyond angry; he wanted to know why she had betrayed the force. Her betrayal had cost some good people their lives.

Amelia sensed Andrew's rage.

"Andrew! No!"

Denise looked at Amelia as if she had gone nuts, "Who are...."

Andrew threw himself at Denise grabbed the front of her robe and slammed her into the door knocking the wind out of her.

"How could you betray the badge like that?" he demanded as he shook her. "Your betrayal cost brother officers and civilian their lives! Why did you do it? Give me one good reason!" he demanded.

Denise was frightened out of her mind, Andrew, who was supposed to be dead had just appeared out of thin air and attacked her. His face had the look of death and he had fangs. When she looked into his cold uncaring eyes, she saw her death and knew that it wouldn't be a pleasant one. She couldn't remember ever being so afraid of anything in her life. She thought about her son and realized that she would never see him again.

"Andrew please!" she begged. "Think about my son Johnnie, I'm all that he has!"

Her begging had no effect on him, "What about Drew's twin daughters? They were just two weeks old when Paul killed him. Did you pass on the information that blew his cover?"

When Denise refused to meet his eyes and looked down, he had his answer. He was seriously considering ripping her throat out and feeding from her but he needed information. He wanted to find out if she knew of other corrupt cops. He looked at Amelia.

"Love, could you find out what she knows? Oh, and get her to write it all down." he added.

Amelia looked into Denise's eyes and compelled her to tell everything that she knew.

While Amelia was dealing with Denise, Andrew unloaded the car, put the groceries, and blood away. After looking into the well-stocked refrigerator, he realized that all that they had really needed for dinner was the steaks. After the groceries and blood were put away, he went to the attic to get a still unconscious Catherine and took her to one of the guest bedrooms.

He rejoined Amelia who was just finishing her interrogation of Denise.

"It's so much easier this way, this skill would be handy at the bureau." she said when Andrew came in.

"What fun would it be if all we had to do was to compel the criminals to tell us the truth?" Andrew asked laughing.

Less than twenty minutes later, they had a full confession of not only everything that she had done but also the names of everyone she knew had been involved.

"There's a disc in the safe." she told them. "It contains the complete list of John and Paul's contacts here and overseas. Everything is on there, please don't kill me!" She begged. "Don't make my son an orphan, my mother is too ill to raise him, he'll wind up in foster care."

Amelia ignored her, led her into a bedroom and compelled her into a deep sleep. That done, Amelia and Andrew changed into more comfortable clothing and began to prepare for their dinner guests. As they prepared the meal, Amelia thought about Denise and her child. She wasn't sure about making the child an orphan and she felt Denise's concern for her child.

Andrew sensed Amelia's unease about killing Denise but in his mind, the boy would be better off without her. Even if she went to prison, what would that do to him? Andrew sighed, "She deserves to die for what she did." he said.

"What capital offense has she committed?" Amelia asked. "From what I heard, what she did was protect the father of her child. Does she deserve to go to prison? Yes. Does she deserve to die? No and I really don't want to turn a child into an orphan, do you? Please Andrew, I'll do anything but that, please don't make me be a part of that."

CHAPTER 4

***

Andrew let out a harsh breath of frustration. What in the hell was he going to do? If he allowed Denise to live, she would end up in prison and the child in foster care. If he killed her, Amelia would be upset and angry with him and the child would be orphaned. But damn it! What the hell? A smile settled over his face as a plan began to form, if he couldn't kill her, he would use her to bring down all of the other corrupt bastards in the state.

He looked at the clock and realized that although he had been up for thirty hours, he felt fine. He took sometime to look at the discs. One disc contained all of the financial information and the other two would be of interests to federal prosecutors. He was sure that in the right hands the discs would cripple the drug empires of several cartels for years to come. He figured this way Denise had a chance at survival and if she died, it wouldn't be at his hands.

Satisfied with his plan, he told Amelia about it.

"Thank you!" she said hugging him thankful that the child wouldn't become an orphan by their hands. While Amelia continued dinner preparations, Andrew continued going through the disc and then made a salad and mousse for dessert.

Dinner was just about ready by the time their guests arrived. Susan made the introductions and Andrew remembered meeting Mark Allen once before. Mark had represented a person that Andrew had busted on a minor possession charge. The perp was the son of a council member and Mark had gotten him into rehab instead of serving jail time.

While they ate, Andrew told the group about the disc.

"While I agree that it would be a shame for her to get away with what she did," Mark said, "but if you turn her in or have her turn states evidence, you'll lose access to the house and a large portion of the assets. I'll think of something but I can tell you that killing her isn't a good idea, you should know better than anyone that cops take the disappearance or death of their own very hard."

Mark had just made an argument that Andrew couldn't refute. If Denise went missing, there would be an all -out search for her and more than likely, the feds would get involved.

"What does the vampire law say about killing a cop?" Andrew asked.

"Killing a cop isn't going to make you lose your head but it is frowned upon." Mark replied. "And since you are parvulus you may get a visit but going on a rampage like your sire did will definitely get you killed. I'm giving you generalities but what actually will happen depends on the lead enforcer for the area."

Amelia listened to the information and thought about it.

"Is there a way for her to be punished and not have her son be made a ward of the state?" she asked. "I just hate to see any child go into foster care."

"Is the child here?" Susan asked, "And if he isn't, then who is caring for him?"

Amelia grimaced. In all of the excitement, she hadn't thought about the whereabouts of the child.

"Let me go get her." she said. "We can find out where her son is and then figure out what we're going to do about them."

As soon as mark saw Denise, he tensed, his eyes going to black orbs. Susan and Gloria both recognized the reaction and Susan placed Denise's mind into a catatonic state. Susan stepped in front of Mark and snapped at him.

"Snap out of it! We need to talk and we also need to explain what just happened to the parvulus."

Mark blinked rapidly trying to clear his mind. Seeing his mate had hit him like a ton of bricks that he wasn't expecting. He knew that Andrew wanted Denise's blood and wondered if Andrew would want to fight him over it but he couldn't allow any harm to come to her.

"Denise is my mate." Mark said, "And I can no more allow any harm to come to her than you could Amelia."

Andrew couldn't believe the turn of events. He couldn't understand or believe that Mark would choose her of all people.

"Why in the hell would you choose her as your mate?" he asked angrily.

Mark's eyes changed into black, lifeless orbs as he angrily retorted, "I didn't choose her but she is mine! You cannot touch her and if you do, I will kill you."

Feeling threatened, Andrew dropped his fangs and allowed his primal side to come forth. He felt his senses sharpen especially his sight and smell. He smelled the sweet scent of fear roll of Mark, it was slight and he felt everyone else in the room go on the alert.

Susan knew that by showing fear Mark had made a potentially fatal mistake. Even though he was a much older vampire and had full command of his powers, he was no match for Andrew. Susan moved into a position where she would be able to protect mark if she had to. When this was over, she was either going to kick Mark's ass or kill him, she didn't know which. Challenging a parvulus and then showing fear? What in the fuck had he been thinking?

After he issued the challenge, Mark realized that Andrew was a superior predator and although he tried to control his fear, it seeped through. He saw the tenseness in Andrew's body and knew that he was getting ready to attack. How he would survive it if he did, he didn't know but he would go down defending his mate. He saw Amelia approach Andrew and reined in his primal side hoping that Amelia could talk her mate down.

Amelia seeing that Andrew was losing control stepped in between him and Mark. She could feel and smell the fear coming from mark and could tell that Andrew was relishing it but she could also sense his sensible side struggling for control.

"Andrew my love," she said softly, "he isn't threatening us. He was just protecting his mate as you protect me. Please look at me."

Slowly Andrew's gaze went to Amelia. She easily pushed into his mind and began to calm the feral side of him. After a few tense minutes Andrew felt his feral side relax and the logical part of him begin to take over. He wrapped his arms around Amelia and hugged her as the last of his aggressive feelings subsided.

"Impressive." Susan said. "I fully expected you to attack Mark especially with the scent of fear emanating from him. You did well in controlling your base form. Amelia, that was an impressive show of your ability to reach and calm your mate."

Neither Andrew of Amelia replied. Each of them was working through their emotions and trying to organize their thoughts. After several minutes, Andrew spoke. "I apologize for my outburst."

Amelia stayed close at his side while everyone took their seats. Susan took over the discussion.

"Mark, no one said that you couldn't claim your mate and Andrew never threatened her, he only said what the rest of us were thinking. Andrew, I know that you are new to this life but mates aren't choosing. it has something to do with genetics. Mates are always complimentary to each other and balance each other out, in other words, you keep each other on an even keel.

I believe that the reason that you and Amelia are adjusting so well is because you are mates. Andrew, what are you going to do now that you know that Denise is Mark's mate?"

Andrew took several seconds to respond, "Am I going to kill her? No, you have my word that I won't harm her but what about her son?"

Mark shrugged, "he will be raised as my own, what else can I do?"

"I'm not sure." Andrew replied, "But it sounds like a match made in hell, a lawyer and a corrupt cop. Who or whatever decides who the mated pairs are has one hell of a sense of humor."

Everyone had a quick laugh before Susan brought up the next topic. The disc.

"While it sounds nice to turn the disc over to the authorities, the reality of it is that the most that will happen is the arrest of a few of the low to medium level organization members and then it will be back to business as usual. I vote that we hold on to the disc, it could be invaluable in keeping the humans out of our hair.

Andrew and Amelia looked at each other trying to gage each other's thoughts. After a minute or two, they nodded at each other.

"Mark, if I turn the disc over to you for safe keeping it will be protected under attorney/ client privilege and I'm sure that you and Susan will each want a copy so that you can protect your interests, am I correct?"

"I'm not talking about just protecting my interests." Susan said, "I'm talking about using them to protect our species. Even now, there are members of a government organization who are aware of our existence and have been trying to capture one of us alive. They plan to study us and to use us as weapons. Can you even begin to imagine what would happen if someone had an entire army of vampires at their disposal? She asked.

Andrew could imagine the government dissecting them to see how they worked and looking for ways to make them even stronger. And because they were technically dead, they would have no rights. Andrew wondered if there were other things that went bump in the night.

"I have a question." Andrew said. "Are there such things as witches and werewolves?"

Susan chuckled before replying, "I was wondering when that question would come up. As far as I know, witches don't exist. I have been in existence for almost two-thousand years and have never seen a real witch or warlock. Weres do exist and not just as wolves but in many other species. Contrary to the legends, they are not the mindless bloodthirsty creatures that they are made out to be. They are able to shift from human to animal form, which is the main difference between them. They can live among humans with no problems and no, I do not know of any that are living in the area. The last one that I knew personally died almost two-hundred years ago, and they are not immortal."

Amelia listened to the conversation and agreed wholeheartedly that they needed to protect themselves from the government but she was more concerned about their abilities.

"How do we learn to control our abilities?" she asked. "Hell, how do we even find out what they are? When we first mated, we were able to speak to each other telepathically but haven't been able to do it since."

"It takes time and practice." Susan replied. "Normally your sire would help with that. A sire can sense their parvenus and that helps him or her guide their creation in discovering and mastering their powers. Unfortunately, you have no living sire. As for the talking to each other, it's easy once you know the trick. You must stop thinking about projecting thought and just think about what you want to say to him. Discovering the rest of your powers will be through trial and error although Charles may be of some help to you there."

While the women cleaned up, Andrew and Mark started going through the financial records, vehicle titles and property deeds. They noticed that the brothers had over ninety percent of their assets in off shore banks which would make Mark's job easier. He could start funneling the money into new shell companies and dummy corporations. He would also set Andrew and Amelia up with a long-term financial portfolio that would withstand even the most meticulous of federal investigations. He would also get them all of the identifications that they could possibly need not only for now but also for the next lifetime.

For the time being, the identification for Catherine would show her as being their daughter and she would have a trust fund valued at around twenty million dollars.

"It's going to take me about a week to set all of this up." Mark said. "Catherine will be able to take out about two-thousand a month to live on and that can easily be changed. She'll also have a stock portfolio valued at around forty-five million but she won't be able to access that until she is married. Sound good so far?" he asked.

He waited for Andrew's answer before continuing.

"As for you and Amelia, you'll have fifty million available to you by next week. I have to get the accounts set up, get the identification to you and transfer money into the accounts as well as transfer all of the vehicles and properties into your name. And so you won't have to worry about anything, I'll have a management company take care of the properties.

Even though I'm starting the process now, it will take about ten years before the entire process is completed and your net worth? It will be somewhere in the neighborhood of three to four hundred million. If you like I can manage your assets at the standard rate."

He made sure that Andrew understood the plan and that his cut would be approximately four million dollars.

After the kitchen was cleaned up, the women got everything ready for Catherine's waking. Susan tied her to the bed and had a cup and straw ready to go.

"Once we start feeding her the blood, she'll take it willingly." Susan explained. "We'll keep feeding her until she's full which should take about twelve to fifteen units and the men cannot come in, she'll want to have sex with them. When she's calmed down, we can start explaining things to her."

The women sat by the bed and started the vigil.

Catherine's eyes popped open around two am. She looked around the room trying to remember where she was and what had happened to her.

"You are restrained so that you do not harm yourself." Susan said to her softly. "I am going to give you something to drink that will make you feel better but you mustn't fight me."

Susan tried to push into Catherine's mind and met a wall of resistance.

Catherine was scared but the scent in the room was heavenly. Her reaction was the same one that she had whenever her mother made a fresh peach pie; she was salivating and her stomach was rumbling. As soon as the straw was placed at her lips, Catherine began to drink from it. Whatever it was that was in the cup, she had to have it.

She drank that cup and six more after it before she was calm enough to be untied and remembered where she was. She looked around the room, saw Amelia and started to back away.

"It's alright." Susan said as she wrapped her arms around the girl. "She will not harm you again. She was protecting her mate and she now understands that you are no threat to him or her."

"I just want to go home." Catherine whimpered. "My parents have to be worried sick and I promise not to say anything about what happened here."

"I'm sorry." Amelia said in a low voice, "That can never happen. It's too dangerous for you and for them."

"Why can't I go home?" Catherine asked as tears ran down her cheek. "Oh my god! You're going to kill me, aren't you?"

All of the women felt and sensed Catherine's fear as Amelia tried to reassure her.

"No dear, "she said with a sad smile, "we aren't going to kill you again."

Catherine's eyes widened, "What do you mean by again? You're fucking nuts!"

"Catherine," Susan said softly, "I am sorry to have to tell you this but what Amelia said is the truth. When she bit you, she released venom that stopped your blood from clotting... you died. She didn't drain you until your heart stopped and that is why you have returned as a vampire."

"All of you are fucking nuts!" Catherine said as she laughed hysterically.

"Do you realize that you just drank human blood?" Susan asked the laughing girl.

Catherine stopped laughing and looked at Susan as if she had grown a few more heads and then slowly looked into the cup. Her eyes widened in shock and the tears began again.

Several hours later, Catherine had calmed down enough to have her new life explained to her. By the end of the conversation she finally accepted the fact that she couldn't go home and she agreed that for the time being, she would stay with Andrew and Amelia.

Susan and Gloria left just before six am with profuse thanks from Andrew and Amelia.

"You're welcome and you owe us a favor which I assure you we will collect." Susan said as they walked out.

Mark asked Andrew if he or Amelia cared if he used one of the spare bedrooms to turn Denise.

"No problem." Andrew replied. "We'll even pick up some blood for you since we're going out." he added.

Andrew took Amelia and Catherine too the 'White Marsh Mall' where the women seemingly went into every store and dropped well over two-thousand dollars in clothes, jewelry, and accessories. Andrew rolled his eyes with his only purchase being a prepaid credit card on which he placed five-hundred dollars on for Catherine.

Before leaving the mall, Catherine changed into a pair of jeans and a shirt that actually fit her, the clothes that Amelia bough for her at Wal-Mart had been a bit too tight. Andrew waited until they were in the vehicle before giving her the credit card.

"This is for emergencies only." he told her. "Once the finances are in place, we'll get others that will have enough money on them to buy a couple of units of blood and plus leave a little extra for travel."

The last stop that they made before going home was at Bio Medtronic to pick up some blood for Mark. Mark had called ahead and the blood was ready for them. While they were waiting, Amelia had the feeling that they were being watched and that whoever it was; they wanted them dead.

"We're going to be attacked." Catherine said once they were back in the car. "He's going to strike before we get home."

"Are you sure?" Andrew asked.

Catherine's eyes had a slight glow to them as she replied. "Yes, he is preparing to attack us now. He wants all of us dead but especially you Andrew."

Andrew reached under the seat, retrieved the glock and handed it to Amelia who out of habit checked the clip to make sure that it was full. She reinserted the clip and chambered the first round as she spoke.

"I sensed that we were being watched and that whoever it was had strong feelings toward us. I can also tell you that he's a vampire and a lot older than us and I mean a lot older."

"First of all," Andrew said, "don't panic and if he does attack, I'll hold him off while you two run back to Susan's and tell her what happened. And I'll rejoin you as soon as I can."

"Fuck no!" Amelia exclaimed, "I'm not leaving you! Remember what you said? You said that we either live together or we die together."

'I'm not leaving either." Catherine said. "I'm not running away and besides we stand a better chance if we stay together. I may not like how things went down but you're all I've got."

Catherine's primal side began to come forth and unlike Amelia and Andrew, her eyes did not change to black but had an eerie glow about them.

"He's going to attack us when we get by the park." she said, "he has the road blocked; I can see it now."

"I would rather fight him in a place of our choosing." Andrew said as he made a U-turn. "Catherine, have you ever used a gun?"

"No but I'm a quick study." she replied.

"Good, Amelia call Susan and let me talk to her." Andrew said. "And Catherine, once this is over, we're definitely going to the shooting range." he added.

Amelia dialed Susan's private number and after two rings, Susan picked up.

"Susan, it's Amelia, Andrew needs to talk to you."

Andrew took the phone and started talking.

"It seems that we have a problem." he said. "A vampire is trying to ambush us. Catherine sensed the attack and warned us. Would you happen to have any idea of who we're dealing with and where a good place to resolve this would be?'

Susan didn't even have to think about who was responsible.

"The vampire is Victor Stone; it was his mate that you killed yesterday. Andrew, you have to be very careful, he has always been on the edge of sanity but without his mate, he is dangerously insane. If you can get back here, I'll be able to help."

"No but thanks, we'll take care of it." Andrew replied. "Where can we go that there will be no humans?"

"Andrew, listen to me." Susan said. "He is dangerous and has full control of his powers. Amongst other things, he is telekinetic and knows how to use it as a weapon."

"Susan you've been a great friend but we can't allow you to fight our battles for us. We'll take care of it. I just want an area where we can fight and not involve innocents." Andrew said.

"Damn its Andrew! He's going to have help! Let me and Gloria help you to at least even the odds, hell, I'll even bring my security force!"

"Susan, thank you but no. I can't let you get involved in this but if you will take care of Catherine, I would appreciate it. I doubt that he would have any interest in her."

Catherine shook her head vehemently. "Fuck no! I'm going with you two, we're doing this together."

"Catherine, please go with Susan and Gloria where you'll be safe." Amelia said.

"No way." Catherine replied. "You made me and now you're stuck with me so how do we beat this asshole? And we need to hurry. My shows are on tonight. It's bad enough that this bastard is going to make me miss GH today."

Time was getting short and it was obvious that neither Amelia nor Catherine was going to listen to him so Andrew turned his attention back to his call with Susan.

"Can you call him or give me his number?" Andrew asked.

"I can call him." Susan replied. "What do you want me to tell him?"

"Tell him to meet us on Gwynn's Falls Trail in Carroll Park right before it crosses the river in two hours.

"Hold on." Susan replied.

She buzzed Gloria to come to her office and while waiting called Victor.

"You couldn't leave well enough, alone could you?" she asked. "I told you that they were under Charles' protection and yet here you are. You are aware that if anything happens to them your entire line will be wiped out?"

"What do you want Susan? I'm busy." Charles replied.

"First I want to deliver a message. Andrew says to tell you that he will be at Gwynn's Falls Trails in Carroll Park right before it crosses the river in two hours. The second thing is to inform you that you or anyone even remotely associated with you is no longer welcome to the use of any of my services and that includes your sire whom I am planning to call as soon as we are finished talking. The third thing is this, if any of those three are harmed, I will personally put out a contract that will include your sire's line, which if I am not mistaken includes your sister. Her I will hunt down myself and take great pleasure in torturing and once I tire of her, she will be encased in concrete and then buried."

There was a long silence before Victor spoke.

"I am within my rights to avenge my mate."

"Did I also mention that they are under my protection as well? And even if they weren't, I would do it in support of Charles. Now, are you going to this meeting?' Susan asked.

"I don't believe that you will carry out your threats." Victor replied. "And even if you did, Charles will still kill me."

"Not just you but your entire line and you know that I don't make empty threats. Do you understand what being encased in cement means for your sister?" Susan asked.

"It will mean a slow painful death for her." Victor replied. "Let's talk about a trade, the lives of the two women in exchange for hers."

"There is no trade." Susan replied. "Either you stop or I will see to it that everyone even remotely associated with you dies. I will ask you again, are you still going to this meeting?"

"He has to die for what he did to my mate." Victor said. "There is nothing that you can do that will prevent his death,"

"You are going to lose this fight." Susan said her tone cool and confident.

Victor laughed. "I hardly think that three parvulus are a match for me and the men that I have with me."

"You stupid ass!" Susan hissed. "Don't you realize that you will be dealing with more than those three?" What fucking part of they are under my protection don't you understand?"

"We have been friends for centuries." Victor said softly, "I have no wish to fight with you."

"Then release your claim and swear to me that you will never go after them directly or indirectly." Susan shot back.

"I cannot make that promise." Victor replied. "He has to die, please do not make me kill you.'

Gloria who had been silent up until this point spoke up.

"Victor darling you never told me that you had a sense of humor. You can't even take me so how in the hell do you expect to take Amelia?" she asked. "And as far as that slut that you call a mate is concerned, she got what she deserved for trying to take another woman's mate. See you soon love.'

"You whore!" Victor screamed, "You will be dead by tonight!"

Gloria laughed, "Why wait? I'm here at the office. I know why you don't have the guts to face me you gutless cocksucker! You are only avenging your wife for one reason only, they are parvulus and you think that you can win and by the way, the only whore I know was Candace."

Victor raged. He wanted Gloria's blood almost as much as he wanted Andrew's.

"I will see you tonight." he said coldly. "And I will make you beg me to kill you. Not even your precious Susan will be able to save you this time."

Gloria and Susan heard the sound of glass breaking before the line went dead.

Gloria laughed, "I'd venture to say that he probably wants me more than Andrew right now."

Susan nodded her agreement. "I want every available man ready to go in twenty minutes." she said as she pressed the line that she had Andrew waiting on.

"He'll be there but please let us help you."

"No, you've already done more than enough." Andrew replied.

"Alright." Susan sighed, "But I hope that you know what you're doing."

"Me too." Andrew said as he headed for the park.

He wanted to get there before Victor and his men. All three of them made themselves invisible and headed for the meeting place. Neither Catherine nor Amelia could sense anyone there. Andrew had them wait at the bridge and asked Catherine about their chances of survival.

"I don't know but I don't get the sense that we're going to die either."

Victor and about twenty of his men appeared about twenty minutes later. He was nervously looking around when he stopped about twenty feet away from where Andrew, Amelia and Catherine stood.

"There's no sense in staying invisible." Victor said. "I can smell you even downwind."

Andrew motioned for the women to remain invisible while he made himself visible.

"So you're Victor." he said. "Do you think that you have enough men with you?"

Victor started to reply when Andrew launched his attack aiming for Victor's throat. Victor realized too late that the attack was coming but was able to turn slightly. Andrew bit and ripped into Victor's jugular. While it was a devastating attack, it wasn't the incapacitating one that he had hoped for but Andrew had Victor in a compromising position. Andrew reached up, popped out one of Victor's eyeballs, and crushed it between his fingers. Victor, surprised by the speed of Andrew's attack cried out in anger and pain.

One of Victor's men was about to hit Andrew in the back when Catherine became visible, locked eyes with the vampire and watched as blood gushed from his ears, eyes, and nose. He screamed once and then fell to the ground twitching.

Amelia looked at three of Victor's men, pushed into their minds and ordered them to attack the vampires standing closest to them causing even more confusion. One of the men managed to get a hold of Amelia and tried to break her concentration. Catherine attacked him from behind biting into his neck severing every major vein and artery there. While not fatal, it did incapacitate him. The problem was that the women had attracted the attention of the other vampires who were beginning to close in on them.

A couple of vampires had managed to pull Andrew off Victor. He continued to fight but knew that he was in trouble. As he watched, the damage to Victor's neck was already healing. Catherine saw this and began to concentrate on the head of one of the vampires. She imagined that it was a melon that she was crushing between her hands. The next thing she knew, the vampire was clutching his head as he screamed in pain collapsing to the ground. Suddenly, he went silent and his body began to decay. The problem was that Catherine was now exhausted and she wouldn't be able to do it again.

Eight vampires now surrounded Amelia and Catherine. Amelia forced herself into the minds of two of them and used them to shield her and Catherine but they were quickly disposed of and Amelia was too weak to do it again.

Andrew had gone into a totally defensive battle. Victor and two other vampires were attacking him and the only thing that was keeping them off him was his speed. He finally got an opening on one of the vampires and disemboweled him using his fingernails. He heard the report of the Glock, knew that the women were in trouble, and tried to get to them but Victor and three others effectively blocked him.

Victor thought that it was a shame that he had to kill them; they could have proved useful. The parvulus had managed to take out some of his best men. Out of twenty, only nine were able to stand. He was thankful that he brought as many with him as he did or that he hadn't come alone. If he had, Andrew's initial attack would have worked and he would be with his beloved Candace.

Andrew moved to his left hoping to draw an attack from the vampire that he sensed to be the weakest. The vampire thinking that he had an opening launched his attack. Andrew spun away from the flying tackle and brought his nails down into the back of the vampire severing his spine taking him out of the fight. Andrew was exhausted. He knew that he wouldn't be keep going for much longer.

Victor sensed that victory was at hand. The women were surrounded and Andrew was tiring and slowing down.

"If you stop fighting and accept your fate, I will spare the women." Victor said gloating.

Before Andrew could answer, Amelia shouted, "hey asshole! What makes you think that I'm going to let you live?"

Victor couldn't believe Amelia's insolence.

"You may have just signed your death warrant bitch; your death will be slow and painful."

Suddenly, Victor felt a crushing pain in his head. Blood ran from his nose as he dropped to one knee, his head in his hands. Catherine's eyes were glowing brightly but were dimming. She couldn't stave the fatigue off long enough to finish Victor off. Finally, she gave in to the exhaustion and went down to one knee panting hard.

Andrew took advantage of the distraction to launch another attack and charged the vampire standing between him and the women. On one level, he knew that it was a mistake not to go after Victor but he needed to protect his mate and her creation. He hit the vampire from behind, savagely jammed his fingers into the back of his neck and severed his brain stem from the spinal cord. While it wasn't a killing blow, the vampire was definitely out of the fight.

As Andrew started his attack, Amelia used the last of her strength to push into the mind of the vampire that had gone to help Victor and ordered him to attack him.

Using a fingernail, the vampire slashed Victor across the chest tearing deeply into the muscles. It was the last offensive move that he would make. Victor, recovered from the effects of Catherine's mental attack made short work of the vampire, tearing off his head with no effort.

The odds were turning in their favor but they were all exhausted. Andrew hadn't gotten away without being injured. He had several gashes that were bleeding and one eye was swollen completely shut. Amelia's arm while not broken was sore as well as her wrist from when the vampire had tried to disarm her. She also had a couple of deep gashes. Of the three of them, only Catherine was virtually untouched. She only had a gash on her right arm from when she ripped the side of a vampire's neck out.

The next problem was that some of the vampires while injured were healing enough to rejoin the fight. Andrew realized that they should have killed them instead of incapacitating them. It was a lesson that he hoped that they would live to remember.

Victor felt better now that he had six other vampires in addition to himself. It had been a painful battle. His eye would take weeks to heal and he intended to make Andrew pay for the insult to him by crushing both of his eyes before killing him. He wanted to spare the women and have them work for him. Catherine in particular.

"You fought well." he said to Andrew. "I will only extend this offer to you once, if you surrender yourself, I will let the women live and your death will be quick."

"Fuck you dick head!" Catherine responded her voice dripping with venom.

Victor was about to respond when he heard laughter ringing through the air. It was soft female voice that he knew well and made him cringe when he heard it.

"Victor darling, I thought that you and I had a date. I thought that you were going to teach me how to be a whore like your wife." Gloria said.

"Victor!" Susan called out, "did you tell your men that these three are under the protection of Charles Black?"

His men were shocked. Every one of them knew that their lives had just ended and those with mates knew that the lives of their mates were over as well. They all looked at Victor as they raised their hands in surrender.

Susan continued speaking, "I will forget the face of anyone that I saw here if you leave here now and you may take the dead with you. Victor, you aren't included in that offer." she added.

Victor's men scattered like roaches when the kitchen light was turned on. Victor knew that he was dead but was hoping to find a way to save the lives of his line and that of his sires. When he started this fight, he knew that it was a gamble but he figured that he would kill Andrew, Amelia and Catherine with no problem and then remove the bodies leaving no evidence. However, they had been much stronger than he had imagined.

"Susan, would you grant me two favors for old times sake?" he asked.

Susan looked at him for several seconds before responding, "What are the favors?"

"Leave my sire and the rest of my line out of this and tell me who sired these three." Victor replied.

Susan thought for a moment. Victor had always been a bit of a flake but at one time he had been a friend but that was before he mated Candace.

"I warned you about what would happen if you touched them, I told you that you would lose. Charles will be the one deciding your fate and has ordered that you be taken to him. Because we were friends at one time, I will grant you the lives of your sire and of your sister. I cannot however; answer for your line, that decision is for Charles to make.

As to who sired them, you really should take more of an interest in reading the human papers. If you had, then you would know whom you were going up against. Amelia and Andrew are Diamond's parvulus; Andrew is first, Amelia second. Catherine is Amelia's first."

Victor now understood why they were so powerful. Until Amelia and Andrew, Diamond had never sired another vampire in her long life. While she wasn't the oldest of vampires, going almost a thousand years without siring was rare to say the least. He had heard the rumors about her getting out of hand and that she was going to be put down. He saw Gloria approach and spoke to her.

"Well whore, it looks as though you've gotten a reprieve, at least until I get back."

"I doubt that you'll be getting back." Gloria said with a smile. "Do you really think that Charles is going to let this slight go?" she asked.

"Then I guess killing you is free." Victor said as his eyes became black orbs and the skin of his face became drawn and leathery. His fangs dropped as he readied himself to attack.

Susan's eyes went black and she used her mind to stun him.

"Enough." she said, "If you cannot control yourself, then I will do it for you."

Victor's shoulders slumped. He knew that Susan wouldn't let him die in battle. He wondered if he could attack Andrew and at least avenge the death of his wife. Victor watched as they fed and knew that they would recover from their injuries quickly but he believed that he could get Andrew with a surprise attack. He forced himself to relax and bided his time. Once the guards surrounding the group began to relax, Victor began to move slowly toward Andrew trying not to draw attention to himself.

He was almost three feet away and about to launch his attack when Amelia and Susan looked at him at the same time.

"Andrew! Look out!" Susan shouted.

Amelia's eyes darkened and began to glow. Everyone could feel the power that emanated from her as she glared at Victor. As he dropped to the ground, Amelia grabbed her head and howled in pain.

Andrew heard Susan's shout of warning, turned to look for the threat and felt the power spike that came from Amelia. He glanced at her and couldn't believe what he was seeing. Her eyes were not the normal brown but black including the whites and glowing. He watched as Victor's eyes widened in surprise as he collapsed to the ground. Amelia's howl of pain came seconds later and before she hit the ground, Andrew had her in his arms. She recovered quickly but was still shaky. After a minute or so, she could stand and the pain from the power spike was almost gone.

Everyone looked at Victor who was lying on the ground. His eyes were wide open and staring blankly into space. His breathing was slow but steady and there were no signs of cognitive thought. Susan tried to read his thoughts but there was nothing there. It was completely blank.

"Amelia, what did you do to him and why?" Susan asked.

"He was going to attack Andrew!" she replied angrily. "I erased his mind and no, I don't know how I did it." she replied. "He'll be like that for the rest of his life and I hope that he has a long life."

"It's true." Catherine said, "I sensed him about to attack Andrew, he was going to kill him."

Susan sighed, "Charles wanted him alive to use as an example."

"Well," Gloria snickered, "he is alive and physically unharmed."

Susan glared at her and Gloria grinned at her unrepentantly, "come on Susan, you know that Charles will understand and this may work out better for his purposes... how in the fuck can you destroy someone's mind like that?"

Susan debated on how much to tell Gloria. The problem with Gloria was that she tended to talk too much especially in bed and she rarely slept alone. If word got out about Amelia and Catherine's powers, the danger to them would only increase. Susan made the decision to keep Gloria close to home for the time being.

"Yes Gloria, I have seen this before." she replied.

She wasn't lying. She had seen that particular power a few times before in her life but she had never seen it manifest in a parvulus so young. She was more than a little curious about Catherine's powers, that she was clairvoyant was obvious but to what degree was still to be determined. Her other ability while interesting, was secondary.

As of yet, Andrew hadn't shown much in the way of power except for his incredible speed and strength. Susan was sure that he had more mental powers than being able to make money spit out of an ATM machine. She had to wonder if he wasn't hiding his powers as an ace in the hole. In theory, Andrew should have been the most powerful of the three but that would depend on what his powers turned out to be. Given the trick with the ATM, Susan was certain that he was to some degree, telekinetic.

Susan shielded her thoughts from the three of them; she wanted no misunderstandings because of an errant thought. She could already see that Gloria was planning some great escapade for them and if her past capers were any indication; it would be highly profitable for all of them.

Gloria, while not an evil person was always looking for the next big score. It was a trait that Susan liked but at times, like now, it could be distracting. But overall, it kept life interesting and it would be a few years before Gloria brought them in on any of her schemes.

"Andrew, "she called, "make sure that all of you feed." she said.

She suggested that they each drink four to five units explaining that it would increase the rate of their healing as well as help them regain their strength. After they fed, she pulled Andrew aside and warned him to be extra vigilant.

"There may be others who will come looking for revenge. I will also keep an ear out and call you if I hear anything."

"What does Charles want with us?" Andrew asked abruptly changing the subject.

"That isn't for me to say." Susan replied with a smile, "But I would carefully consider any offer that he makes." she added.

"Is he trustworthy?" Andrew asked.

"I trust him with my life." Susan replied, "It is something that I have had to do many times in the past. He was and is an honorable man that has never betrayed a friend, has always kept his word and says exactly what he means."

Gloria stood behind Susan nodding her head in agreement. Amelia listened, but was reading Gloria who read like an open book. She was forming some kind of plan that involved the three of them. It didn't feel malicious and she seemed almost amused by it. Susan, on the other hand, was trying very hard to conceal something. What it was, Amelia couldn't tell but whatever it was, it was causing her great concern. Amelia could sense that while Susan was interested in all of them but her main interest seemed to be Catherine. She was also interested in Andrew but not in a romantic sort of way. It was more the kind of interest that a scientist would have toward an experiment. Amelia was glad when Susan finally told them that they could leave.

Amelia kept what she knew to herself by imagining that the access to her mind was behind a vault door that was tightly sealed. Amelia kept her eyes on Susan the entire time and had actually considered declining the offer of a ride home and would have if Catherine who was the only one of them physically able to drive knew how to.

Catherine sensed the added tension coming from her sire and it worried her. She moved so that she was standing closer to Amelia and Andrew even though she sensed no immediate threat. She tried to get a handle on everyone's intentions but when she got to Susan, she couldn't sense anything. She was sure that this was why Amelia was nervous and it made her nervous too. She looked over at Andrew wondering if he was aware of what was happening and noticed that he was his usual calm, pleasant self.

Andrew had in fact noticed Amelia's concern regarding Susan but wasn't sure of why. He was aware that in their current condition that they couldn't offer much resistance if there should be an attack. In the end, it really wouldn't have mattered. He felt Susan's power at the office and if she chose to attack, she would have very little problem with the three of them. He did wonder what it was that had set Amelia off but because her mind was blocked, he couldn't read her. Surreptitiously, he moved until he was between the women and the rest of the group and watched every move anyone made. He would be more than happy to leave as soon as it was possible.

Gloria had been around Susan long enough to know that she had blocked off her mind. She knew that it would happen at some point since Amelia was a mind reader and that Susan wouldn't take the chance of her finding something out. The intent was to prevent Amelia from finding out something that could be used against her and Charles or that she would misunderstand something now that emotions were running high.

The problem was that it was having the opposite effect. Gloria's gifts were subtle by nature and she could see the auras of others. She knew that Amelia could sense Susan's interest in Catherine and Andrew and she had raised the alarm of them as well. Now all three of them were on edge and it wouldn't take much to ignite the powder keg. Gloria also noticed that Andrew had moved so that he was between the women and everyone else. Although he gave the appearance of being at ease, he was far from it.

Susan also noticed the change in the parvulus but wrote it off as fatigue not thinking that Amelia was strong enough to know that she was purposely being blocked. As she felt the tension rise and noticed Andrew's position, she decided that it was for the best that she get them home as soon as possible before the day spiraled out of control any more than it had.

She breathed a sigh of relief when they were on their way home; the tension was slowly diminishing. All evidence of the fight had been carefully erased although there were no bodies. There was however, plenty of blood and Victor to contend with. She wondered if it wouldn't be more merciful to put him down but then decided that the decision wasn't for her to make. She would take him to Charles and let him decide. Once again, she was glad that she wasn't the one who had to make those calls.

Susan looked up to see Gloria approaching her and could tell from her body language that she was displeased about something. She met her partway so that she could find out what had her so upset. When they met, Gloria grabbed Susan's arm and led her away from the group.

"What in the fuck do you think you're doing?" Susan asked angrily.

Gloria waited until they were out of hearing range of the others before replying.

"You fucked up." she said.

"I fucked up? How?" Susan asked.

"You blocked off your mind and you weren't very subtle in your interests in the three of them, especially Andrew." Gloria replied. "Amelia picked up on it."

"There is no way that she could have picked up on that." Susan protested, "She's much too young to have her power developed to that degree."

Gloria sighed, "Susan, have you forgotten my abilities? As soon as Amelia sensed your interest in Catherine, her defenses went up and so did Catherine's. I also know that she tried to probe you and judging by her reaction, she knew that you were blocking her. To be honest, I'm surprised that she didn't confront you right then and there. You had to have noticed that the defenses of the other two went up in response to Amelia's alarm. All I'm saying is that you had better stop underestimating them if you don't want to be the subject of an attack by them."

Susan blushed. She knew and trusted Gloria and if she was this adamant, then it was the truth.

"What do you think that I should do?" she asked.

Gloria thought a moment before responding.

"Tell them the truth. Tell them that you are a bitch and that you hate being around people who can read your mind and that you were trying to figure out the best way of getting all five of us into bed... oh wait... that was me." she said laughing.

The two friends laughed before Gloria continued, "Seriously, I would advise against lying, they would know it. I would suggest letting them be for a few days so they can calm down and regroup before you approach them with anything else."

Amelia, Andrew, and Catherine looked forward to going back to their house. Andrew wanted to know what had the other two so on edge. He could still feel their anxiety although it had decreased some in the hummer. They were almost home when the driver spoke.

"Miss, I know that you are worried about the mistress closing her mind off to you. I just wanted to tell you not to worry; it's just her way of handling tense situations, a defense mechanism if you will. I can also tell you that she has no romantic interest in your mate and that she likes all three of you. This is the first time in the three centuries that I have been with her that I've seen her go to the defense of someone else's parvulus. She wouldn't involve us if it wasn't for Mr. Black."

Amelia sensed no deception in the vampire who was serving as their driver and decided to probe him for more information.

"Do you know what the interest in my mate was about?" she asked.

Andrea thought for a moment and couldn't answer the question.

"I'm sorry ma'am I haven't a clue except for maybe its just curiosity. You and Catherine have shown remarkable control over your powers and from what I have been led to understand, Andrew has shown incredible speed and strength. Correct me if I am mistaken, but Andrew was the first to be turned and should be the more powerful of the three of you."

Amelia found herself liking Andrea, he seemed honest and he wasn't trying to be deceitful.

"Thank you ... umm sir."

Andrea frowned slightly. "Please accept my apologies for my lack of manners. I am Andrea Susan's head of security. It is a pleasure to meet you."

Pleasantries were exchanged as he pulled into the driveway of the house and parked the hummer in the garage.

"I wonder if I can talk my mate into letting me buy one of these." he mused.

"My mate is the one who loves it." Andrew said laughing.

"Damn!" Andrea exclaimed, "How in the hell did you get so lucky?" he asked as he looked to see if his ride had arrived. He stepped aside so that the hummer could be unloaded. Andrew took the cooler out of the hummer and headed toward the house. Amelia invited Andrea in to wait for his ride.

"What in the hell happened to you?" Mark asked when he saw them.

"Victor wanted revenge." Andrea replied, "and if you think that they look bad, you should see the ones that attacked them." he added.

"What do you mean?" Mark asked.

"The other side has nine dead, two that will be permanently disfigured and one that may be crippled as well, his spine was severed. Victor no longer has a mind; he is a vegetable." Andrea replied.

"Has no mind?" Mark asked flabbergasted, "who could do something like that?"

"Amelia." Andrea replied, "All she did was look at him and he collapsed staring blankly into space."

Andrea had just poured a cup of coffee when he heard his ride blow his horn.

"I'll take care of it." Catherine said as she stood and went to the door.

Andrea sat down to drink his coffee. Greg, Andrea's ride came in a few minutes later following Catherine.

"There's coffee if you want some." Catherine said pointing to the coffee pot and mugs.

Greg and Andrea left after drinking a cup of coffee stating that they had things to do. Amelia started dinner while Catherine set the table and Andrew poured blood into four large glasses for them to sip on while they waited for meal of spaghetti, meatballs, and salad.

As they ate, Mark explained what he had done so far.

"I've gotten everything arranged to get new identification which includes social security cards, birth certificates and drivers licenses for all of you." he said. "Each of you also has a line of credit and for you Andrew and Amelia, I have a marriage certificate. Your last name is now Barnes and Catherine are your daughter. I've already transferred the vehicles into your name and you have accounts at several local banks but it will be a few days before money will be transferred into them.

I've also set up accounts in a couple of internet banks that are run by vampires and I've started transferring stocks into your name. Your portfolios look good and I've supplemented them with a few long-term investments. The last thing we have to do other than signing the contract for you to buy the house is to set up a line of credit with Susan so you can get blood whenever you need it until the funds become available."

"Thank you." Andrew said meaning it.

"You're welcome." Mark replied happy that he was able to help.

The next two weeks were spent teaching Catherine how to drive and how to care for and use firearms. It turned out that the brothers had quite an extensive collection of guns and other weapons. Hand to hand combat was added to Catherine's teaching and they were amazed at how quickly she learned. By the end of the first week Catherine could drive the hummer and shoot well enough to hit center mass. Her hand-to-hand combat skills were improving as well. They spent a few hours of each day working on their skills. Andrew's powers had begun to manifest and he was definitely telekinetic as well as having the gift of psychometry. That particular gift they found out about when he handled one of the guns that the brothers had and he had been able to see Paul shoot his confidential informant to death with it.

Amelia was able to fine-tune her clairvoyant ability to the point that she could go just a little beyond surface thoughts and probe into distant or forgotten memories. However, she still had quite a bit of work to do in that area. Her mind control abilities were progressing as well. She could maintain active control over her victims, which still drained her, but she was getting stronger.

Catherine's precognitive ability continued to be hit or miss but she was fine-tuning it by practicing on animals. At first, she would just kill them but with practice, she was now able to control the amount of damage that she did to them. She could make them uncomfortable and progress too crushing their brains.

After a couple of days, they headed to Biomedtronic to replenish their blood and plasma supply. They also talked with Charles informing him that they had to get their affairs in order before they left.

"I understand." he replied. "But when you get here, I have a proposition for you. I will only discuss it in person and of course you are under no obligation to accept." he assured them.

The third week after they had begun their training, they were out and decided to stop in to see Gloria and Susan. After a few minutes of friendly chatting, Susan invited them to a club that was run by and for vampires. They eagerly accepted looking forward to a chance to relax and have a little fun. They agreed to meet at the club which was located on Key Highway.

"Don't be fooled by the building." Susan warned, "It looks abandoned but it isn't and your vehicle will be safe."

She also informed them that Mark and Denise would be there and that Denise was taking to her new life better than anyone could have predicted. Her son Johnny had no problems with Mark. He had fully accepted him as a father figure.

When Friday finally arrived, they had mutually agreed to take Saturday off as well as they planned to be out late. They arrived at the club a few minutes early and waited by the hummer for the others to show up. As they waited, they noticed a young vampire being held by two older and bigger vampires while a third one was working him over.

"If we don't stop them, they're going to kill him." Catherine said as her eyes turned white and began to glow.

Andrew calmly approached the group with Amelia and Catherine flanking him.

"I think that you've had enough fun, let him go." he called out when he was close enough.

The vampire administering the beating turned toward Andrew, his eyes black orbs. When he spoke, it was with a thick Russian accent.

"I would suggest stay out of this parvulus. This one interrupted my meal."

"I could leave." Andrew replied locking eyes with the vampire, "but then I'd always wonder."

"Wonder what parvenus?" The Russian asked.

"Whether that young man is exceptionally strong or if you're that weak and cowardly that it takes three of you to fight him." Andrew replied.

The anger that rolled off the middle vampire was palpable as he spoke.

"I will give you one more chance to leave. If you choose to stay, I will kill you and enjoy the bitc..."

Andrew had his hands around the vampire's throat before he could finish his sentence. Andrew lifted him off the ground by his throat crushing it. The other two vampires released the young man, went to the aid of their friend stopping when Amelia with her eyes glowing pushed into their minds, and ordered them not to move.

Andrew still holding on to the vampire unleashed several powerful blows to his face relishing the feeling of destroying the vampire's face one crushing blow at a time. His primal side was now in full control.

Catherine rushed over to the young vampire and could tell that he was very badly hurt. She picked him up and carried him over to the hummer. She eased him into the seat and got two bags of blood from the small refrigerator, ripped holes into it and fed it to him.

In the meantime, security from the club rushed out and tried to pull Andrew off the vampire. When one of them aimed a Taser at Andrew, Catherine used just enough of her ability to stun the security officer.

"The next one to raise a weapon to my sire's mate will die." she said loudly.

Finally, Andrew managed to gain some semblance of control of himself and released the vampire.

"Bet you won't ever call my mate a bitch again!" he said angrily.

"Sir," one of the security guards said, "I need you and your mate to go wait with her parvulus."

Andrew wrapped an arm around Amelia and led her to the hummer.

"Is he alright?" he asked Catherine when they reached it.

Catherine nodded the affirmative and continued to feed the young vampire blood watching as he healed.

"What happened that they were kicking your ass like that?" Andrew asked.

The vampire blushed.

"My name is Scott Mitchell. I saw that guy over there trying to rape a woman and when I tried to help his two friends grabbed me. Fortunately, the woman was able to get away."

Andrew turned to look at the vampire still lying on the ground and wished that he had killed him. Amelia pushed into his mind and sent soothing thoughts to him. They watched as the vampire was being fed blood and saw that he was rapidly healing. The other two vampires that were with him were still standing and waiting for orders from Amelia.

Susan and Gloria pulled up, noticed the throng of people, and finally noticed Andrew standing by the hummer with Amelia by his side.

"Now what?" Susan muttered as she parked the car. Gloria was openly laughing as they got out of the car and walked toward them.

One of the security officers stopped her and told her that she would have to wait a few minutes before she talks to Andrew. She nodded in understanding and scanned the area. When she saw who was lying on the ground, she knew that she was in for a headache. Gregori Demidov, the vampire lying on the ground was the first to the lead to all of Russia.

After Demidov was healed enough to talk, he spoke to who Andrew assumed to be the head of security for the club. Andrew had a bad feeling and he moved to the back of the hummer, retrieved a couple of pistols that he passed to the women. Catherine had a three eighty caliber and Amelia a nine mm Glock 17 that they hid in their purses in the hopes that they wouldn't be needed.

Susan saw Andrew getting the pistols and made a quick phone call to Charles to apprise him of the situation.

"Stay out of it if at all possible." he told her, "and whatever you do, do not let the parvulus go with Gregori."

"I understand." Susan replied, "I'll do my best."

She was relieved when Mark showed up a few minutes later if for no other reason that it evened up the odds a little.

After what seemed to be an eternity, the head of security walked over to Andrew.

"Mr. Demidov has decided not to press charges against you and the women but he demands that the other one be turned over to him."

"I don't think so." Andrew replied. "He stays with us and I already know that Demidov is too much of a coward to try and take him away from me. The fucking bastard was trying to rape a woman when Scott came up on them. I demand that he be arrested and taken into custody pending a formal investigation and it you're too afraid to do it, then I will."

"Sir," the head of security said patiently, "do you know who that is?"

"Some piece of shit rapist!" Andrew retorted.

"He's the first of the lead enforcer for Russia."

"Good for him," Andrew replied, "but the last I heard, Charles Black was the lead enforcer here and I demand that you turn Demidov over to him to face charges for rape and attempted murder.

While Andrew and the head of security were arguing, one of the security people tried to grab Scott. Catherine saw what was happening and used just enough of her ability to give the security office pain. He went to his knees while holding on to his head as blood ran from his nose.

"The next one of you that tries to take him will die." Catherine announced.

Amelia tired of the game ordered Gregori's two goons to take Gregori into custody. They immediately grabbed him and began to drag him over to Andrew and Amelia. The security watched not knowing how to react since it was Demidov's own men who were dragging him to the parvulus. A couple of the security officers blocked the vampires' progress and after a brief altercation, the two goons lay on the ground incapacitated.

The head of security issued a warning to Andrew.

"If you don't stop right now and surrender yourselves and Scott, I will order my men to use lethal force."

"Then you'll have a bunch of dead men." Andrew replied coldly. "And you and that bastard will be the first to die." he added.

Andrew refused to give ground. His eyes scanned the group in front of him wondering which of them would be the first to die. Another security person made the mistake of making a sudden move but before the movement was complete, there was the loud report of a gun being fired. The man clutched his stomach in the area where Catherine's bullet had entered.

The head of security had to use every bit of influence he had in order to keep his men under control. He knew that the human police would come to investigate the report of a gunshot, which would be a very bad thing. He blinked rapidly as he recognized who was standing in front of him. If the rumors were true, they were under the protection of Charles Black. God, he hated days like this. If he didn't turn the young vampire over, Demidov would have his ass. If he tried to take Scott by force, he would be up against three vampires who were under the protection of one of the oldest and most powerful vampires in the world. As he looked around wondering what to do, he spotted Susan who was Charles Black's right hand ...umm woman.

He ordered his men to stay away from the small group and approached Susan.

"Ms. Dorchester, it's a pleasure to see you." he said when he reached her. "Would you mind talking with the parvulus? Maybe you could get them to get them to see reason."

"Why would I get involved?" Susan asked.

"I was under the impression that they are of interest to Mr. Black... am I mistaken?"

"You are not mistaken; tell Demidov that he can't have them." Susan replied.

"It's not them that he wants." The security officer replied, "It's the young one that he wants. The other three are protecting him and are insisting that Mr. Demidov be arrested for rape and attempted murder."

Susan looked over at them and noticed how protective Catherine was acting toward the vampire in question. She also realized that the vampire was very young, not more than a week old. Where in the hell was his sire? She wondered. She then realized that Catherine was acting like his mate. "Fuck!" she said harshly.

"What?" the security officer asked.

Susan sighed before replying, "If I'm right, you're not going to get that boy away from them."

Susan glanced at Gloria, waved her over and explained the situation to her. Gloria said that she understood and that she would do nothing to inflame an already volatile situation.

As Susan and Gloria approached the hummer, they could see how on edge Catherine was and realized that she was definitely protecting her mate. Susan hated this part of her job. Since Charles hadn't extended his protection to the young vampire, there wasn't much that she could do for him. Her job was to protect

Andrew, Amelia, and Catherine from others and that included protecting them from themselves.

"Andrew," she explained patiently, "You may have to let the boy be taken into custody. He attacked Demidov and endangered all of us by allowing the woman to escape."

Andrew's eyes and voice hardened as he replied, "That cowardly bastard was raping a woman and Scott tried to help. If Demidov wants him all he has to do is get past us but we both know that he doesn't have the balls to try."

"I'll kill anyone who tries to take him away from me." Catherine said calmly although the skin of her face was drawn back and her fangs were descended. Her eyes were white and glowing like spotlights. The power that radiated from her had Susan's hair standing on end. She turned to look at Susan. "Tell that cocksucker that all he has to do is get past me if he has the balls or to go home until he grows a set. Tell him to choose now."

Before Susan could explain that she would be the one to hold him in order to defuse the situation, Amelia spoke.

"It ends now."

"NO!" Susan screamed.

But it was too late. Amelia's eyes were glowing as she turned her gaze to Demidov. She stared at him for one brief moment watching as his eyes widened and he dropped to the ground. His eyes were fixed and dilated; he was still breathing but it as well as his heartbeat was slow.

Amelia's eyes went back to their normal color and she was a little shaky but she recovered quickly.

"No one comes after my family and lives."

Susan's eyes widened in disbelief. This was going to be a fucking nightmare and there was going to be hell to pay. She knew that she needed to call Charles right away and it was a call that she wasn't looking forward to making. The phone rang one time before Charles answered it. She quickly explained what happened and waited for the fall out. Instead he laughed.

"It's about time somebody put that piece of shit down."

"Charles, he's the first of Vladimir Demidov, the lead enforcer for all of Russia, won't he be upset?"

Charles chuckled, "he will do what is required of him. He'll make a formal complaint demanding that the ones who perpetrated the crime be turned over to him. I'll refuse, he'll pay me a personal visit in order to plead his case and we'll get as drunk as vampires can get and exchange stories.

The part that you're going to hate is this." Charles said. "Since you are the closest thing that I have to a mate, you will have to be here and entertain his mate Misha plus act as hostess at all of the formal dinners."

"But Demidov was his first." Susan repeated.

"Susan, the only reason that Demidov was Vladimir's first was because Innokenti and Lenka died. Don't you remember attending their remembrance ceremony?"

Susan thought for a few seconds. She recalled meeting Gregori at the funeral. He was still a parvulus but he had made her skin crawl as he looked at her as if she was a piece of meat. She had been trapped into dancing with him at the welcome dinner and he had been way to free with his hands. She had been relieved when Charles cut in much to Gregori's displeasure. During the dinner, Gregori had invited her out but she had politely refused deciding that it would be bad taste to have to kill him while at the funeral for his sire number one.

"So are you telling me that I should get the credit increased on the credit card you gave me?" she teased feeling much relieved.

"Enjoy your night out." Charles replied chuckling, "and try to keep them from killing or maiming anyone else. I'll see you in a couple of weeks."

"Now you are asking for the impossible." she replied laughing. "I'll see you in a couple of weeks."

She disconnected the call and was walking over to her friends when she recognized Vlad. He was standing in front of Andrew and saying something. As she approached, she heard Vlad say in his thick Russian accent.

"The four of you will surrender yourselves immediately or I will take you by force."

Instead of responding, Andrew delivered a lightening uppercut to Vlad's jaw. Everyone heard the sound of his jaw breaking and watched as the larger vampire went down.

"I bet you'll think twice before you threaten my family again." Andrew said. "I would suggest that you not get up." he added.

Six large vampires stepped forward and made a half-circle around Andrew, Amelia, Gloria, Scott and Catherine. Vlad sat up, looked at Andrew and asked, "What are you going to do now parvulus?"

"First," Andrew said, 'I would suggest that you let Ms. Vegas get clear. Then if you insist on pushing this, I guess we'll be sending you to hell."

"I have my orders." Gloria said. 'I'm here to help protect you so you have to count me in."

"I don't want you or Susan involved in this." Andrew replied. "But I do appreciate the offer."

"My orders came from Charles." Gloria replied, "And there's no way that I'm going to piss him off."

"Fine, if you're not going to listen to reason, then stand behind me." Andrew replied.

"I can do that." Gloria replied. "I hope that Amelia won't mind if I enjoy the view." she added with a chuckle.

Amelia laughed and allowed her feral side to come forth. The only difference was that instead of her eyes going to black lifeless orbs, they glowed even brighter than Catherine's did. She looked to the right and then to the left and saw that the others had gone over to their feral side as well.

Andrew took another step forward and then spoke.

"This is your last chance to leave here alive. Decide now."

Police sirens could be heard approaching from the distance. Vlad and his men stepped back.

"Another time." Vlad growled, "Humans cannot be involved in this."

"Why another time/" Andrew asked. "So you can try to ambush us? I don't think so. Either surrender yourselves now or get ready to defend yourselves. You have ten seconds."

"Andrew!" Gloria said urgently, "You can't be seen by the cops, they know you."

"We'll finish this after the cops leave." Vlad hissed and started to walk away.

Susan finally spoke.

"As interesting as it was to see the Barnes' in action, it's over. The four of them are under the personal protection of Charles Black. One thing though, if I were you, I'd thank Charles for saving your life."

Vlad gave her a disbelieving stare before replying.

"You have a lot of faith in these parvulus."

Susan smirked.

"First, you forgot about my first Gloria but these are the ones who took out Victor and most of his men."

Susan turned to Andrew and Amelia.

"Please become invisible, we don't need any more headaches."

CHAPTER 5

***

The police showed up a couple of minutes later and asked about the gunfire. When everyone insisted that it had come from somewhere else, they left. Susan led the group to a private room in the club and gave them a chance to order their drinks and settle down. When they were all situated, she turned her attention to Scott.

"How long ago were you turned and who and where is your sire?"

Scott sighed and looked into his drink,

"My sire is Flora and I don't know where she is. She stayed with me for four days after she turned me and then we traveled her from Mississippi. The first night that we got here, she took me to a club on Monroe Street and then went to the hotel. When I woke up, she was gone but left me a note saying that it was fun but that I was a waste of her time. She left me three-hundred dollars and four units of blood in the freezer. That was four days ago."

"Do you know her last name?" Susan asked.

"No ma'am I don't." Scott replied, "But I'm pretty sure that it started with a T. she was wearing a necklace with the initials FT on it. Is there anyway that I can get blood without killing anyone?" he asked.

"I have a company that sells blood but it's expensive." Susan replied. "The only thing that I can do is to see if I can find someone who is willing to take you in and who will be willing to teach you all that you need to know in order to survive. The only thing is this, if someone takes you in you will have to become their servant and since you aren't of their line, you would be subservient to those who are."

"He can stay with us." Catherine said, "We'll help him."

Andrew shrugged. "I have no objections especially since he was brave enough to face that asshole Demidov and as long as he realizes that we will be traveling."

Amelia noticed Catherine's less than subtle interest in Scott. "As long as Scott has no objections, he's more than welcome to come with us and we can all learn together." Amelia said.

Scott was surprised at how easily they accepted him, a stranger, into their company and wondered what they wanted in exchange especially after what Susan told him. He decided that the best thing to do was to be honest.

"I appreciate the offer but before I accept, I want to know what it is you want in return. Don't get me wrong, I'm more than willing to work and to carry my share of the load but I refuse to be a slave or anyone's whipping boy."

Andrew smiled at Scott's straightforwardness.

"We're not offering you a job." Andrew said. "We're offering you a place to live and to do what the rest of us are doing... learning to survive as vampires. We haven't been vampires much longer than you have and we're still trying to figure out how to fit in."

Gloria and Susan laughed at the last comment.

"You might try going for more than a week without picking a fight with someone." Gloria suggested. "It isn't bad enough that you picked a fight but it had to be with either the head of a family or their first." she added

"I didn't start that fight." Andrew replied. "What was I supposed to do? Let them kill him?"

The look on their faces told Andrew all that he needed to know. That was exactly what they thought he should have done. Scott was both shocked and angry.

"Are you saying that you would have let that slimy bastard rape that woman? You would have let him get away?"

"Scott, "Susan said sympathetically, "you have to understand that its part of out physiology. We become aroused when we feed so rape isn't a crime in our society. It is a byproduct of who we are."

Andrew was incensed as he replied, "All I can say is this, if I see someone raping, I'm going to tear their heads off."

Amelia was appalled, her expression showed shock and disgust.

"You have to be kidding me! What the fuck kind of bullshit is this?" she asked as she looked at Susan. "With places like yours, there should be no need to hunt humans."

"I understand how you feel and how you see it as revolting." Gloria said, "But you have to understand that when we go to our base level, we operate purely in instinct. Amelia that's why you attacked Catherine and why you Andrew, killed that female vampire. Blood laced with fear has a much sweeter taste and when a person is raped, the level of fear rises. Part of our instinct is to make our victims fear us.

When we orgasm, we release a toxin in our saliva that paralyzes out victim. When we bite, we release venom that is an anticoagulant. We can survive on bagged blood but the blood from a frightened victim is so much better. The difference between the two would be like having hamburger versus prime rib for dinner. I know that this is hard but you have to turn a blind eye to certain things."

"Another thing," Susan added, "Charles can only cover you for so much and if you don't stop, you're going to become a detriment to him. Victor was necessary but it wasn't necessary to fry Demidov's brain. Vlad, the last vampire that you tried to pick a fight with is a member of the Ubertas Venator. They act as bounty hunters for the various enforcers. He is one of the best and the only reason that you got him was because he underestimated your speed. The only reason that I said what I did was to deter him from hunting you.

Amelia, I would suggest that you watch the use of your powers. It will draw unwanted attention and there are those who will be able to resists you... look at what happened with Catherine. I want the four of you to settle down and I'm going to have Gloria tutor you on the things that you need to know. She will contact you with a time that is convenient for her and unless you want to find out how much of a bitch, I can be... I would suggest that you listen to her."

Susan had stopped suppressing her power. The whole room seemed to be filled with electricity. The hair of the seven occupants at the table stood up on end as if they had touched a Van De Graff Generator. As quickly as she had released her power, she reined it back in. A few minutes later, things had gone back to normal

People who had been staring at their table went back to their drinks and conversations.

"I didn't do that to threaten you." Susan said, "But you have to realize that ours is a dangerous world. Most newly turned vampires don't survive past fifty years even with the help of their sire. At the rate that you're going, you'll be dead in three months. Andrew and Amelia, I know that because of your previous line of work that the rape thing is a hard pill too swallow but it is a part of our world. You're going to have to find a way to deal with it. If you can't let me know and I'll tell Charles that you're a lost cause. I'm sorry to be so harsh but you've caused much too much trouble in such a short period of time."

Andrew took a moment to gather his thoughts before replying.

"I know that we've been a major headache to you and for that I apologize. We only intervened because there were three of them beating him to death. Catherine saw it as well."

"It wasn't so much that you intervened to help Scott, even Gregori took that in stride." Susan said, "It was all the shouting about rape and that Amelia fried Demidov's brain. I would have kept Scott safe by using my authority to take him into my custody but Amelia didn't give me the chance. The attack on Vlad was beyond stupid and Gloria can tell you that he isn't one to trifle with. I hope that he decides to drop it.

Andrew blew out a frustrated breath. Who would have thought that this would have been so complicated? He wondered.

"I would appreciate any help that Gloria can give us and working around her schedule is no problem." Andrew said. "And... I promise that we'll try to stay out of trouble." he added.

"By the way," Amelia said, "I don't fry their minds, I just erased them."

Gloria had never seen a power like Amelia's and was curious about it.

"Could you undo it?" she asked.

"I don't think so." Amelia replied. "I think that I can implant memories but undo the erasure? I'm pretty sure that I can't."

"Are you saying that they can be re-taught?" Susan asked.

Amelia's confusion was evident as she replied, "I think so but I don't know how. I don't know very much about the power."

"Amelia," Susan said, "It is part of the gift of power. You always know what your powers do, not what they appear to do. I find the information that you just shared intriguing and I'll ask Charles to look into it.

Scott sat quietly trying to remain inconspicuous as possible. He had no abilities that he knew of. He had seen Flora go invisible but he hadn't been able to do it. She explained to him that all vampires had the gift of compulsion and invisibility and laughed at him when he failed. When he tried to live feed, the thought of killing a human kept him from biting. It was then that Flora declared him a mongrel with no hopes of surviving.

He hoped that they continued to ignore him. His fear was that if they discovered that he was a substandard vampire, that they would want no parts of him. He had been so deep in thought that he didn't realize that Catherine was talking to him until she nudged him.

"Sorry, I was lost in thought for a minute." he said sheepishly.

"I was wondering if you would dance with me." Catherine said.

Scott was enamored with her. He loved how her shoulder length blonde hair framed her face and how her jade green eyes sparkled with mischief. Her full lips had a slight smile on them as she waited for him to answer her. Catherine was about five inches shorter than his five feet-eleven-inch frame and he thought her to be the prettiest woman that he had ever seen. The next thing that he noticed was her scent. It reminded him of lying in a field of wild honeysuckle.

As they got to the dance floor, the DJ began to play 'My Heart Will Go On'. As they danced Scott began to relax and enjoyed the feeling of having Catherine in his arms.

As soon as the young couple was out of earshot, Denise spoke.

"Something is bothering him, he's ashamed of himself. Something has shattered his confidence and he's going to need careful guidance to rebuild his self-esteem."

"It was his sire." Amelia said while nodding her agreement. "She called him a mongrel and a waste of her time because of his reluctance to live feed. To make matters worse, he hasn't discovered his abilities so he feels substandard."

"You are doing well with your abilities." Susan said to Amelia with a smile. "I'm also glad that you're taking him in. From what I can read, he's a good kid but a bad candidate for vampirism. I also doubt that he will ever be able to bring himself to live feed. You do realize what he is to Catherine don't you?"

"He's her mate." Amelia replied.

The song ended with an announcement by the DJ.

"The next hour is for all of you lovers so grab your mate or significant other and get out on the floor. I will be spinning some of the best slow-dance hits ever. I will start and end this segment with 'Endless Love'.

Mark and Denise excused themselves and made their way to the dance floor. Amelia ordered another round of drinks for everyone still at the table and enjoyed listening to the first couple of selections. When the DJ started playing 'When You Say Nothing At All', Amelia led Andrew to the dance floor and kept him there for the remainder of the hour.

Everyone, Susan, and Gloria included was having a good time until a drunk human tried to cut in on Scott. Even though both Scott and Catherine told him no, the human became insistent and then belligerent. He threw a punch and was restrained by Scott and Susan who to their credit did nothing to harm the man. The vampire who he came with, a rather attractive South-American woman thanked them for not killing him and dragged him out of the club.

It was well after two when the group left the club. Scott was silent during the ride back to the house. He had enjoyed his evening with Catherine and didn't understand why he felt so drawn to her.

The next afternoon Gloria called to arrange a time to meet with them for the tutoring sessions. Mark called an hour after she did ask what they wanted to do about Scott as far as identification and finances.

"I'll call you back." Andrew said.

Andrew went to Scott who was mowing the lawn.

"We need to talk about what you want to do." Andrew said.

"What do you mean?" Scott asked confused.

"What are your plans for the future?" Andrew asked. "I know that you're concerned about not being able to use your abilities but don't worry about that, we can help you. We can also teach you how to defend yourself better."

"Why would you help a substandard vampire like me?" Scott asked visibly confused.

"Who in the hell gave you the idea that you were substandard?" Andrew asked. "You certainly don't lack for guts! You went up against three vampires who were much bigger and older than you are in defense of a woman that you didn't know. For that alone you've earned our respect. Scott, you do know that Catherine cares about you don't you?"

"I know," Scott said looking away, "but she's too good for me."

"Probably." Andrew replied laughing, "But that's not going to stop her. But you still haven't told me why you think that you're substandard."

Scott blushed but began to answer the question.

"Flora was the first woman that I had ever been with. She told me that I was lacking but that she thought that she could teach me how to please a woman. After she turned me, she called me a mongrel and told me that more than likely; I would be dead in a few weeks since I couldn't use my gifts. When I couldn't bring myself to kill so that I could feed, she called me a pussy and told me that I either needed to man up or she would leave me to die."

"First," Andrew said, "let me give you a little bit of wisdom about sex. No one does it right their first time. It's a learning experience and what works on one woman may not work on another. Secondly, if Susan is right about you being Catherine's mate, she'll kill you before she lets you leave. About the mongrel thing, it isn't true and I'm positive that I can teach you how to become invisible. Susan told me that it could take as long as a year for all of your abilities to manifest. But Scott, even if you never develop a power, you're welcome here or wherever we may be. We rarely live feed and when we do it's on those who are scum."

Scott couldn't believe how nice they were being to him. They took him in and were willing to keep him around even if he was a mongrel.

"Thank you." he said softly. "You've all been so nice to me and I don't know if I'll ever be able to repay you."

Andrew shook his head as he replied.

"There's no repayment. You are now one of our strange little group. The only real rule that we have is that we take care of us first. I'll have Mark set you up with new identification and access to money. The next thing is that we need to go shopping and get you clothes that fit. While I'm making the call, why don't you finish cutting the grass and I'll send Catherine out with something to drink. By the way, do you have a preference on last names?"

"Not really." Scott replied, "Just so it isn't anything hideous."

"So I guess latrine is out?" Andrew asked laughing.

"Yes," Scott replied laughing, "I would prefer something else but I guess that would be better than shithouse."

Andrew walked away still laughing to make the call to Mark. He dialed the now familiar number and Denise answered the phone.

"Allen and Associates, how may I direct your call?"

"Denise, its Andrew, is Mark available?"

"Hey Andrew!" she replied. "Mark's on the other line, can you hold?"

"Sure, how's the house hunting going?" he asked.

"Do we really want to go there?" Denise asked with a sigh.

Andrew smiled as an idea hit him.

"Denise, why don't you and Mark swing by later? I have something that I want to run past you."

"Depends on what you have in mind." Denise replied teasingly.

"I guess you'll have to use your imagination." Andrew replied in a husky voice.

At this point, Mark cut in his voice angry but Andrew could tell that he was trying not to laugh.

"That's enough! Stop propositioning my mate!" he growled and then started to laugh. "What do you need?"

"Damn!" Denise said just before hanging up, "just when it was getting interesting. Would seven be ok for tonight?"

"That's perfect." Andrew replied. "Bring Johnny too; he can play in the playroom while we talk business. Mark, I was just getting back to you about Scott. He isn't picky about a last name as long as it isn't something hideous. He'll need a full set of identification including driver's license and credit cards. As far as money, give him the same limits as Catherine."

"Got it." Mark replied as he made notes. "I'll bring his identification and banking information with me tonight. The credit cards will take a day or two but I'll put ten-thousand dollars in his account for now. I think I'll give him the last name of Hawkins, how does that sound?"

"Sounds good." Andrew replied, "We'll see you later."

Andrew waited until Scott had finished cutting the grass before asking everyone to come into the kitchen.

"I was talking to Denise about the search for a house and I came up with something that I want to run by all of you. According to her, the search isn't going well and I thought that maybe we could let them have this place as long as we could store a few things here. Thoughts?" he asked.

Amelia was the first to speak.

"Mark has helped us so much and we won't be coming back this way any time soon, so yes. This place would be perfect for them especially with a kid."

"Catherine?" Andrew asked.

"I think that it's a great idea. I agree with Amelia, he has helped us and the house would just sit empty. What do you think Scott?"

"Why are you asking me?" Scott asked surprised. "Give him the house if you want to, it's yours not mine."

"Scott," Amelia said, "when you came home with us you became a part of this family. That means that you have a say in whatever decisions are being made. Now what do you think?"

Scott hesitated before speaking, "well, if he's helped you as much as you say he has and you all seem to be friends, then why not?"

"It seems as if we are all in agreement so on to the next piece of business." Andrew said. "Scott, I'm going to teach you how to become invisible. Close your eyes and imagine that you are a piece of glass."

"What do you mean?" Scott asked confused.

"Listen to him." Amelia advised. "It helped me when I couldn't become invisible."

"You had trouble going invisible?" he asked shocked.

"I sure did." Amelia replied. "And just think, I woke up naked in a morgue!" she added laughing.

"I would like to see him like that." Catherine said with a faraway look in her eyes.

Scott turned beet red making everyone laugh.

"Alright," Andrew said, "let's get serious. Scott, clear your mind, imagine that you are a pane of glass, relax and just let it happen."

Scott closed his eyes, relaxed and slowly he began to become transparent taking on the same ghostlike appearance that Amelia had the first time she tried.

"Are you sure he isn't related to you?" Andrew asked Amelia laughing.

"It's the way that you teach it." Amelia replied laughing.

Andrew shook with laughter as he replied, "I know but it's the neatest effect, too bad it isn't Halloween, we could have a blast answering the door."

Scott opened his eyes with a disappointed expression on his face.

"See, I told you that I couldn't do it."

"I did the exact same thing." Amelia told him in an effort to comfort him. "And it's what the ass wanted you to do- he thinks it neat."

"Now," Andrew said bringing everyone back to the task at hand, "All you have to do is imagine you're like the invisible man in "The League of Extraordinary Gentlemen"

A moment later, Scott was invisible.

"Thank you, thank you." he said over the cheers. "I can't believe that I really did it!"

"Good job." Andrew complimented. "Now I want you to let only Catherine see you. You do that by just thinking about her being the only one that you're visible to."

The first several times he was visible to everyone and Andrew would gently coach him until he was able to show himself to anyone he picked at will. It was a major step for him. He could now accept the fact that he wasn't a mongrel as his sire had told him he was. The lesson had worn him out and he wanted to lie down.

He went to his room, lay down and was just dosing off when he felt a hand massaging his cock through his pants. He watched shocked, as his zipper lowered itself. A warm hand reached in, freed his cock, and began to pump up and down his shaft. The touch was light but it was driving him crazy.

"Catherine, you have to stop or I may not be able to."

He couldn't figure out how she was staying invisible to him but he could feel her hand on his cock. He moaned when he felt her lips wrap around his stiffened member. Her mouth was warm and felt like heaven as she moved up and down, her tongue swiping at the sensitive underside when she approached the head.

"Please, let me see you." Scott said between gasps of breath.

Catherine complied. When she appeared, she was naked. She pulled her mouth from the head of his cock with a popping sound but kept stroking him with her hands.

"Understand this." she said as she stroked him, "you are mine. I am claiming you and there is nothing anyone or anything can do to stop me."

She had a feral look on her face and she looked at her claim daring her to stop her.

Scott grabbed her, pulled her on top of him and then rolled so that Catherine was beneath him.

"Mine! And I will have you MY way!" he exclaimed.

He gave her a fierce kiss letting his tongue slip into her willing mouth. Their tongues dueled. Scott's kiss was long and forceful calling to Catherine in a way that no one ever had. She wanted to taste his blood but more than that, she wanted him to taste her.

Scott broke the kiss and began to nibble his way to her collarbone while he slid one hand down her belly and then between her legs. He began to massage her clit, his feral nature more than making up for his lack of experience. He pulled back and looked at her breast with admiration making Catherine blush. He bent down over a breast and dragged the tips of his fangs across them. No skin was broken but it was a promise of things to come. Catherine squirmed with anticipation as she felt warm liquid pool between her legs.

He began probing her with his finger and stopped when he reached her maidenhead. His eyes glowed with the anticipation of knowing that he would be the first and only one to touch her. He sucked on her nipples alternating from one to the other before making his way down her stomach not stopping until he reached her target.

He started by taking long slow laps of the length of her nether lips making her jump every time he did. Scott gently opened her lips, slid his tongue deep inside of her pushing in until he felt her barrier with the tip of his tongue. He gently probed at it taking care not to break it before going back to her clit. He sucked on it gently gradually increasing the strength and speed until

Catherine began to cum. He quickly moved into position and gently slid in, breaking her hymen. As he broke her hymen, Catherine bit into his shoulder and began to drink from him.

Catherine's drinking from him overrode Scott's control. He bit into her shoulder drinking from her as he spilled his seed deep within her womb. They released their bites at the same time as Scott rolled over to his side holding Catherine tight against his side.

"I love you." he whispered.

"I love you too." Catherine replied.

They lay in each other's arms until a knock on the door disturbed them.

"Hurry up and get decent! You need to feed soon!"

Reluctantly, Scott grabbed his pants and pulled them on. In her haste to mate with him, Catherine hadn't thought about needing clothes afterwards so she put on his shirt thankful that it was long enough to cover her. She opened the door and took the tray containing two large glasses and a pitcher of blood from Amelia.

"Let me be the first to congratulate you on your mating." Amelia said with a smile. "You have about forty-five minutes before our company arrives so you might want to get cleaned up.

They drank the blood quickly and then got ready for their guests.

They were making small talk when Catherine and Scott joined them.

"Where's Johnny?" Amelia was asking.

"He wanted to stay over at a friend's house." Denise replied. "Since there's no school and you wanted to talk business, we allowed it."

Andrew called 'Nick's' and ordered pizza and then sat down.

Mark handed Scott his new identification.

"Stop by the office tomorrow and I'll have new identification for Catherine ready and we'll set up the trust fund so that they both have access to it." he said. "And while you're there, Scott and Catherine can sign the marriage license. If I had known earlier that we were going to see you tonight, I could have had all of this done."

"If I were clairvoyant, I would have told you." Andrew replied laughing. "They've only been mated for about an hour."

"Ok, then what's up or did you just want to flirt with my mate in person?" Mark asked teasingly.

"Damn! You caught me!" Andrew joked back. "Seriously, we know that you've been looking for a place and we were wondering if you would like this one."

Denise was shocked.

"We would love a place like this but there's no way that we could afford it." she said.

"We'll tell our lawyer to draw up the papers transferring the house to you." Andrew said. "The only thing is we'll need to store a few things here." he added.

Mark was speechless. When the shock wore off, he spoke.

"As much as we appreciate the offer, there is no way that we can accept it."

"First of all," Andrew said, "it's from all of us. Secondly, we're still your clients and you said that you would handle our legal matters. So, stop arguing and draw up the papers."

A knock on the door interrupted any further conversation. Scott went to answer the door and called back.

"Mommy or daddy-in-law! Do either of you have any cash? The bill is twenty-three fifty-three."

Andrew handed him forty dollars.

"Tell him to keep the change."

Denise was still in shock.

"I can't believe that you're giving us this house... Thank you!"

Once Mark recovered from his shock, he thanked them as well.

"If you ever need anything, just let me know."

As they ate, Mark explained the financial planning that he had done.

"I've arranged for a management company to take care of the real-estate which includes as you know the condos in Ocean City, Florida and L.A. The same company will handle the strip malls and warehouses. Of course, I had the company checked out and they are highly regarded."

He explained that he was going to set up a corporation and would put them on the board of directors so that they would draw a paycheck.

"You'll be paying taxes so it will keep the feds off your back. I've created a fictitious past for you as well." he said. "Everything including the documentation of your births and medical history will be available if by some chance someone starts nosing around."

He kept their academic records average or just slightly above and included participation in groups such as the '4H' club.

"These little additions are the difference between a good false identification and a great one." he said.

He wanted to take additional picture of them so that he would have fresh ones to use on any new identification.

"Becoming vampires did alter your physical appearance slightly making you more appealing." Mark explained. "If you were fat before being turned, you would remain fat. Unfortunately, becoming a vampire doesn't turn on into six -feet tall dark hero with washboard abs or if you're a woman, it doesn't make you some sexy goddess that belongs on the cover of 'Playboy'."

He went on to explain that the blocking of cameras and surveillance was an automatic defense mechanism that was controlled by their subconscious minds.

"It's a modified use of your ability to become invisible. All you have to do in order for the camera to see you is to turn off the defense mechanism. You may need to allow your picture to be taken from time to time for things such as flying commercially."

He had them practice until he was sure that they were able to do it without any trouble.

"Why don't we go to the pub to celebrate Catherine and Scott's mating?" Mark suggested when they were through practicing. "I know of a place that is run by an older vampire and his mate."

A few minutes later, all of them were piled into the hummer with Catherine sitting in Scott's lap for the ride to the pub.

They had been sitting in the pub for about an hour enjoying themselves when a female vampire came in accompanied by a man wearing a UMBC tee shirt came in. She was five three with generous curves and smooth toffee colored skin. Her face was framed by long brown/auburn hair that was braided and brought out the highlights of her deep brown eyes. Scott tensed as soon as he saw her.

Catherine noticed, put a hand on his arm and asked who the female vampire was although she had her suspicions.

"That's Flora my sire." he replied as he kept his eyes on Flora.

Scott felt the tension level of the group rise but it was mostly from Catherine.

"I know that she has no hold over me but it's the guy that she's with that I'm concerned about." Scott said. "She'll do to him what she did to me."

Flora, sensing that she was being watched slowly looked around the club until her eyes rested on the table with six vampires sitting around it. She noticed Scott and saw the changes in him. There was no indication of the shy, weak boy that he had been when she turned him. What she saw was a young vampire who was confident in himself. Next, she noticed the two other male vampires. One was all right to look at and she could tell by the way that he was dressed that he was a professional of some kind and not much older than she was. The other male was a knockout and exuded power. She no longer found the human male that she had come in with interesting. Using compulsion, she made him leave. She wanted any and all of the males sitting at the table.

As she approached the table, she could tell that all of the males, Scott included were mated. She glanced at Catherine who was glaring at her and mentally dismissed her.

"Scott darling." she said in a sweet, honey-drenched voice, "I've been so worried about you, are you alright?"

Scott looked at her with disdain.

"You dare to come over and try this bullshit after what you did to me?" he asked incredulously. "You called me a substandard vampire and a mongrel and then you left me to die!"

"It wasn't like that." she crooned, "You needed a little push and I didn't leave you alone. I paid someone to watch you and he didn't do his job. I've been searching for you ever since."

Catherine could see that Flora was lying and fought to maintain control.

"You looked really concerned when you walked in here with that human male." she said. "And from what I've been told, a sire can always find their creation if they want to. Care to try again?"

Flora knew that she had been caught in a lie and hated that a parvenus had called her on it. She pasted a false smile on her face and forced herself to remain calm.

"You have no idea of what you're talking about." she replied.

"Flora, we know that you're lying." Catherine said with a smile. "But it makes little difference. Scott said that you called him a lousy lover. Well, I guess it takes a real woman to make him perform and god did he perform on me. Just think about what you lost bitch."

"I'm going to rip your fucking...."

That was all that Flora got out. Scott's temper exploded and he grabbed Flora by the throat.

"If you ever threaten my mate again, I will kill you. You're nothing but a used up two-bit whore who used me for your own pleasure and then threw me away. You call me a mongrel and a waste of your time but guess who the waste is bitch? You and if I were you, I'd leave and make sure that we never crossed paths again."

Scott released Flora letting her fall to the floor. Flora quickly recovered not believing that Scott had spoken to her as he had. She realized that she had underestimated him and wasn't about to let him get away with it.

"You are my parvenus." she said. "That means that until I decide that you are able to survive on your own you belong to me. So, either get over here and do as you are told or I'll contact the lead enforcer representative for the area and have her put a termination order on you."

Mark laughed. "Would you like me to call Susan for you? I know that she was very interested in meeting you last night after all the trouble that he created."

"Who is this Susan?" Flora demanded. "And what kind of trouble could he have caused? It wasn't as if he was in blood lust."

"No." Mark replied. "He just picked a fight that caused great harm to the number one of the lead enforcers of Russia. Susan Dorchester is Charles Black's number one and his right-hand woman. You have a lot to answer for and I believe that she has already procured the services of the Ubertas Venator to track you down."

"Are you going to stop me from leaving?" Flora asked suddenly worried.

"It isn't my job to stop you." Mark said with a shrug. "But I am required to report your location. If I were you? I'd get the hell out of dodge and live on bagged blood for a while."

Flora cursed. She hated bagged blood but knew that the male was right. It would be too easy to track her if she kept feeding from humans. She would have to be careful. She knew that the Ubertas Venator went to a larger contract and they paid well for information on their quarry. She knew that she was fucked and that all she could hope to do was to delay the inevitable. She turned invisible and vanished from the club.

Mark turned back to his friends unable to contain his laugher. He took note of the confused looks on their faces, ordered another round of drinks and began to explain.

"Legally she did nothing wrong and while it is true that Susan wanted to speak to her, it was only to tell her to stop making parvulus. The Ubertas Venator wouldn't accept a contract on a petty criminal like her. I think that she'll be running and looking over her shoulder for at least the next decade or so."

Everyone at the table laughed. The celebration continued until the pub closed. They all agreed to meet at Mark's office at two pm to do paperwork and to work out the details for the house. When they got home, the two couples went to their respective rooms and settled in for the night.

Amelia and Andrew undressed and got into bed and began to kiss and caress each other while deepening the kiss. They took their time to allow the passion to build and to enjoy the closeness of being in each other's arms.

Andrew massaged Amelia's breast as she nibbled at his eat and neck while tweaking his ripples with her fingers. Gently, Andrew lifted her chin so that he could look into her eyes.

"I love you." he said softly.

"I love you too." Amelia replied.

Andrew slowly moved his hand down her body and toward her center. When he reached it, he began to massage her clit as he slid a finger inside of her and began a slow in and out motion. He lowered his head to her breast, caught a nipple in his lips, and began to tug on it sending shivers throughout her body.

Amelia nibbled on Andrew's neck then softly whispered, "I need you now."

Andrew lined himself up with her entrance and slowly slid into her. They made love at a leisurely pace letting the climax slowly build. Andrew was the first of them to go over the edge with Amelia following a few seconds later. They fell asleep in each other's arms and awoke the same way later that morning.

As soon as Scott and Catherine reached their room, Scott picked Catherine up, threw her on the bed and quickly stripped her of her clothes. He began to kiss and nibble on her body while Catherine began ripping his clothes off. Their hands frantically roamed each other's bodies as they kissed. Catherine reached down between them, took his rigid cock in her hand, and began to pump him. She moaned when Scott worked a finger into her soaked pussy.

Scott moved so that he was on top of her and impaled her with his rigid cock. He set a quick pace sawing in and out of her body. He moved a hand down, found her clit and began to massage and tug on it never slowing down his pace. Catherine felt the orgasm begin to overtake her, pulled Scott down to her and bit into his shoulder.

As soon as her fangs pierced his shoulder, he howled out his orgasm and bit into Catherine's shoulder sending her over the edge for the second time. Afterwards, they lay in each other's arms feeling the afterglow of their lovemaking. As they lay there, Catherine got a strange feeling in her nether region. It was a fleeting sensation and not one that she could easily describe. Scott felt her uneasiness and gave her a questioning look.

"Are you ok?" he asked.

"I'm fine." Catherine replied with a smile, "I just had a weird feeling in my vagina."

"Was I too rough?" Scott asked his voice filled with concern.

"No, I'm fine and you didn't hurt me. Whatever it was is gone." she replied.

Andrew and Amelia woke up around nine, showered and quickly dressed. They went to the kitchen and started a breakfast of eggs, toast, and coffee. Catherine joined them a short time later.

"Are you alright?" Amelia asked. "You look pale."

"I'm just a little tired." Catherine replied. "I guess Scott took a little too much blood last night."

Andrew sat a large glass of blood in front of her.

"Drink up and if you sip from each other make sure that you get some blood right afterwards." he said

"Yes Papa." Catherine replied with a smile.

"You two need to be more careful." Amelia said sternly. "And if you don't start looking better soon, I'm taking you to see Gloria or Susan."

Catherine sighed but agreed.

Amelia softened her tone.

"I know how you feel." she said. "I'm newly mated too but I'm worried about you and I don't want anything to happen to you."

Catherine gave Amelia a quick hug and then turned on the television. On the screen were her parents pleading for information about her whereabouts and for her safe return home. Suddenly, she felt guilty. She was having a good time, found her mate and her parents were going out of their minds with worry. Scott walked up behind her and wrapped his arms around her.

"I have to let them know that I'm alright or this will kill them." she whispered.

"Catherine," Andrew said in a voice filled with compassion. "It's going to be easier for them in the long run if you don't contact them. What will it do to them if you keep going in and out of their lives? And how will you explain where you've been all of this time? You sure as hell can't tell them the truth."

"So, what am I supposed to do?" Catherine asked. "Let them wonder and worry about me for the rest of their lives?"

"Why don't we see what Susan suggests?" Amelia asked. "We can stop in and talk to her on our way to Mark's office.

There was a knock on the door and Scott answered it.

"Good morning officer, can I help you?"

"Good morning." the officer replied. "I'm Officer Franklin and we're looking for this girl, have you seen her?" he asked as he handed Scott a picture of Catherine.

Scott looked at the picture making sure that enough time had passed before he replied.

"No sir I haven't. My wife and I are the only ones here; the in-laws had to go out this morning. Oh, please excuse my manners, would you like to come in?"

The officer stepped in and looked around before saying anything.

"You see Mr....."

"Hawkins, Scott Hawkins."

"You see Mr. Hawkins; we have a report about someone who looks like this girl being seen around this house." the officer said.

Scott looked at the picture again and smiled, "I can see why, my wife resembles her." he said.

"I see." the officer said. "Is it possible to speak with your wife? Maybe she's seen her."

Scott hesitated.

"Give me a minute, she's still in bed."

The officer sensed Scott's reluctance and went on alert.

"If you wouldn't mind, I'd appreciate it." He said looking around again.

"Scott? Who's was that?" Catherine called down the stairs.

"The police." he called back. "He wants to talk to you for a minute."

"The police? Ok I'll be right down.' Catherine called back.

"I'm sorry." Scot said relaxing. "I just hate waking her up." he lowered his voice and then said, "She can be a real terror in the morning."

The officer relaxed and chuckled. "I understand," the Officer, said, "my wife isn't a morning person either."

"Can I get you something to drink?" Scott asked.

"Sure, a cup of coffee if you have it." the officer replied. "Are you new to the area?"

"Yes, I guess my accent gave it away." Scott replied. My in-laws got this property when they were here on business and decided to stay."

The officer followed Scott into the kitchen and came face to face with Amelia. She locked eyes with the officer and spoke.

"All that you will remember is that you met a nice southern gentleman. While our daughter does resemble the Catherine that you are looking for, it is clearly not her. You had a cup of coffee while you chatted with us, we answered your questions and you left here satisfied that the one you seek is not here. Now drink your coffee and have a nice day."

The officer drank the coffee, thanked them, and followed Scott to the front door.

"I'm sorry that we couldn't be of help." Scott said.

The officer thanked Scott for their cooperation and the coffee. After he was in his car, he called in and reported that the woman at the house wasn't the one that they were looking for. He checked his next report certain that if they found the girl, she would most likely be dead. He was thankful that he only had five years left before he could retire. He hated looking into the faces of grieving parents and saying "I'm sorry for your loss." He had hoped that this time he wouldn't have to do it. He sighed and continued on his way.

Everyone breathed a sigh of relief when the officer was gone. Catherine now realized that no matter how much she wanted to, she couldn't contact her parents.

It would be dangerous not only for them but for her and the others as well.

"Maybe we'd better leave before anyone else noses around," she said.

They started packing what they would need for the trip. Andrew packed a pistol and a shotgun for each of them leaving the rest for Mark to do with what he wished. The vehicles were another matter. Amelia suggested that they give the 2011 BMW Z-4 to Susan and that they give Gloria the Viper. The rest of the vehicles with the exception of the Hummer would go to Mark and Denise.

Catherine took stock of the blood supply and noticed that they were down to twelve units.

"How many units of blood should I order and what about plasma?" she asked. "We have twelve units in the fridge and I think that there's two in the hummer."

"Order twenty-four units of blood and twenty units of plasma." Andrew said. "And when you talk to Susan, ask her if she had an hour to spare when we get there this afternoon. We have some things to go over with her."

After the Hummer was loaded, they headed to Mark's office. They knew that they would be early but they didn't want to take the chance that someone else would show up at the house.

"You're early." Denise said when they walked into the office.

Andrew shrugged. "We're going to be leaving sooner than planned." he said. "The police showed up this morning looking for Catherine. Someone reported seeing her around the house."

"I'm going to miss all of you." Denise said frowning. "We'll have to find a way to get together from time to time."

"Don't worry." Amelia said hugging her. "We will."

"You're early." Mark said when he walked in. "I was about to take the wife out to lunch. Care to join us?"

"Please come." Denise said her voice tight, "it will give us a little more time together before you go."

"Go?" Mark asked surprised. "What happened?"

Andrew told Mark about the visit from the police.

"So we think that we'd better get moving before someone else sees her and it turns ugly."

"Have you told Susan yet?" Mark asked.

"We're going to see her next." Andrew replied.

"We can wait for lunch if you're in a hurry." Mark offered.

"No, lunch sounds good." Andrew said.

Mark called the restaurant that he frequently used for meetings and reserved a side room. After the meal, Andrew told Mark what they wanted to do with the vehicles.

"Everything else is yours to do with whatever you please." he said.

"I have everything ready to go at the office." Mark said in response. "All I need are signatures."

The business part of the meal over, the talk turned to more personal and social matters. Denise beamed as she told them that Johnny had gotten straight "A's" on his report card.

Soon it was time to leave though none of them wanted to. As they were leaving, a man walked up to Catherine.

"I know who you are." he said. "You're the one on television."

"I'm sorry." Catherine said with a smile. "But you have me confused with someone else."

"No I don't!" the man insisted. "I know it's you and I'm going to take you in for the reward."

Scott stepped between the man and Catherine.

"I would suggest that you back away from my wife before I rip your fucking throat out and feast on your blood!"

His eyes began to change into lifeless orbs. Amelia quickly pushed into his head forcing him to calm down. At the same time, Andrew stepped between Catherine and the man.

"Sir, please back away from my daughter unless you want the police called."

When the man didn't move, Catherine used her compulsion.

"Sir, I am not who you think I am. Apologize and leave."

The man blinked twice before doing as he was told.

"I apologize. I thought that you were someone else."

The man turned away red-faced that he had caused a scene. The manager of the restaurant made his way to them and apologized for the inconvenience. They assured him that all was well and that they enjoyed their meal and they would return. As a further show of goodwill, he took Catherine's meal off the bill.

The incident was further proof that they needed to get out of the areas as soon as possible. When they were out of the restaurant, Amelia gave Scott a warning about controlling himself in public.

"If you had changed, you would have endangered all of us."

"I know and I'm sorry." Scott said softly.

Once back at Mark's office, it took three hours to complete all of the necessary paperwork. After the last document was signed, they said their goodbyes to Mark and Denise and headed over to Biomedtronic to see Gloria and Susan.

Gloria greeted them when they arrived.

"Susan is in a meeting and will be another forty-five minutes. So what's new?" she asked.

"What are you doing this evening?" Andrew asked after a few minutes.

"Nothing really." Gloria replied, "A good book and a hot bath were all that I had planned. Why?"

"Do you think that I could convince you and Susan to take a ride with me? I'll even throw in dinner." Andrew said.

"You sure know how to tempt a woman." Gloria said batting her eyes. "Dinner with two handsome men? Who could turn down an offer like that?"

"Good." Andrew replied, "It will also be our goodbye dinner."

"What?" Gloria asked shocked. "Why is it a goodbye dinner? And you can't leave until I've taught you what you need to know to survive."

"I know." Andrew replied. "And I wish that we could stay for those lessons but we have to leave."

For the second time that day, he told Gloria about the visit from the police and then about the man at the restaurant.

"Where are you going?' she asked.

"We'll go see Charles first, after that? I don't know yet" Andrew replied.

"Why don't you talk to Susan about it?" Gloria suggested. "She might have some ideas."

"So I take it that you'll be joining us for dinner?" Andrew asked.

"I can't answer for Susan but I'm going." she replied.

While they waited for Susan's meeting to be over, Andrew called and made the dinner reservations including Susan in case she decided to go with them.

About an hour later, a very angry vampire emerged from Susan's office.

"This isn't over!" he shouted. "I'll take this to Charles!"

Immediately, Andrew and Scott stood in front of their mates but ready to defend Susan if need be. The vampire noticed and laughed.

"Look at the parvulus ready to come to your rescue! How pathetic!"

Susan glared at the vampire.

"Fredrick, take note that it is their mates that they are protecting and not me. I've had more than enough of your shit today and my decision stands. If you want to go to Charles, be my guest but I'll tell him the same thing that I just told you. This is my business and no one tells me how to run it. Now please remove yourself from my property before I call security and have you removed."

Fredrick took a step toward Susan and both Andrew and Scott took a step forward. He looked at them and laughed as he taunted them.

"Oh, look at the mice that roared! Really Susan, is this the best you can do?"

"You were asked to leave." Andrew said taking another step forward. "Please do so now."

"This is too precious." Fredrick said to Susan and ignoring Andrew. "You must tell me who sired this parvulus."

Amelia stood and moved to Andrew's side.

"Sir, you've been asked to leave and I suggest that you do so. No one wants any trouble." she said the warning obvious.

Susan had finally had enough.

"Ms. Vega please call security and have Mr. Marquise removed from my property."

Fredrick took yet another step toward Susan, stopped, grabbed his head, and dropped to his knees. Catherine's soft voice filled his head.

"You were asked to leave do it now or it will only get more painful."

Fredrick's eyes widened when he saw Catherine's glowing eyes. He couldn't believe that a parvulus could hurt him. It was impossible and he wanted her for his.

"Of course, my dear." He said in a silky voice. "I'm sorry that I upset you. Let me apologize over dinner."

He didn't care that she was mated and he didn't consider her mate a threat. If her mate attacked and he killed him, she would be a free female again.

Scott's eyes darkened until they were black orbs as his temper flared.

"My mate will not be having dinner with you tonight or any other night and if you speak to her again you will die."

Before anyone could respond, Susan's security burst into the room and formed a line between Fredrick and everyone else. Four very large vampires grabbed Fredrick while Catherine wrapped her arms around Scott to keep him from going after Fredrick.

Amelia looked at Fredrick and issued a warning.

"You'd better get the idea of coming after my number one out of your head or it will be the last thought that you have."

"What was he planning?" Susan asked.

"He was thinking about kidnapping Catherine and using her for his own benefit." Amelia replied. "Like we would let that happen." she added.

Susan turned to her head of security.

"Andrea, drain and then dispose of him."

"Yes ma'am!" Andrea replied.

"Wait!" Fredrick shouted. "You can't do this top me! This is neutral ground!"

"That's why he's taking you to the processing plant." Susan said with a chuckle.

They watched as security dragged Fredrick out of the building and stuffed him into a van.

"Thank you for coming to my rescue and for not ruining my new reception area." Susan said.

"You're welcome." Andrew replied. "How about coming to dinner with us? We have some things to discuss with you plus we have an order to pick up." he added.

Susan motioned for them to follow her back to her office. Once they were all inside, she closed the door.

"I was surprised to see the plasma order." she said as she sat down.

"I'm afraid that we have to leave." Andrew said. "There were two incidents today both within hours of each other. First, the police show up at our house and then a man at a restaurant recognized Catherine. It's only a matter of time before a person or a group of people spots her again and then we'll really be in trouble. Everyone is looking for her especially since her parents are offering a large reward."

"I understand but what are your plans?" Susan asked.

"We'll go see Charles first and then maybe head west." Andrew replied.

"I know that Charles wants to offer you some work," Susan said. "But even if you decline I'm sure that he'll help you settle down somewhere. I'm going to miss all of you."

While Andrew settled accounts with Susan, Scott loaded the Hummer with their purchases from Susan. Afterwards, they all piled into the Hummer and went to dinner. An effort was made to keep the conversation friendly and light. After dinner, Andrew told Susan and Gloria that he needed to go to the house before taking them back to the office.

He pulled into the driveway, parked and then handed each of them an envelope that contained the keys and the title to the cars that they had decided to give them. Gloria reacted like a kid who had just gotten her first car after graduation while Susan was much more reserved but no less grateful.

Gloria hugged and kissed each of them twice while Susan gave them a light hug and kiss on the cheek. After Susan and Gloria were gone, the four of them took one last look at the house and the surrounding area before getting into the Hummer. They headed toward Philly and a new life unsure of where their travels would eventually lead them.

Andrew decided to take the ninety five through the new tunnel. He would get off at Pulaski Highway and then take that into Philadelphia. It was a longer route but he was in no hurry. It would take about three to four hours before they reached their destination making their arrival time between midnight and one am.

Meatloaf's 'bat out of hell' played in the CD player, and everyone was singing although a bit off key. No one seemed to mind, they were just having a good time. When the song was over, Andrew made a suggestion.

"Let's find a motel when we get into Delaware."

Everyone agreed and then continued to sing with the music. When 'Objects in the Rear View Window' came on.

"if they had to keep listening to such ancient music. Can we stop for a Slurpee?" Catherine teasingly asked.

Andrew pulled into the first seven-eleven he saw, and they all went in. Amelia loaded up on snacks saying that no matter how much you ate, you still had to have snacks for a trip.

Andrew found a nice roadside motel just outside of Wilmington. He rented two rooms and asked the clerk for a nine am wake up call. After checking in, they each went to their respective rooms. Andrew and Amelia went to bed, and fell asleep in each other's arms.

Scott was trying to make love to Catherine, but she was just too tired.

"You shouldn't be this tired." Scott said concerned, "let me go get Andrew and Amelia."

"I'm fine." Catherine said. "It's been a stressful day, and there've been a lot of changes for me in a short period of time. And after last night, I think that I have the right to be tired. You wore me out."

Scott looked at her. He knew that something was wrong. Her color was off and she looked exhausted. He didn't care if she objected or not, he was going to get Andrew and Amelia. Catherine could feel the fear coming from Scott and knew that the fear wasn't for him, but for her.

As he dressed, Catherine argued with him.

"You're being foolish." She said. "I'll kick your ass if you go and wake them up."

"Then you can kick my ass." He replied as he continued to get dressed. "I'm going to get Amelia and if you don't like it, tough shit."

Scott left the room before she could say anything. Catherine knew that was worried, but so was she. She couldn't come up with a logical reason for why she was so tired. She thought that maybe it was because of her powers, but she hadn't been using them all that much or had she? The next thought was that something had gone wrong with the change. She lay in bed and tried to keep her imagination at bay.

Scott went to Andrew and Amelia's room and knocked on the door.

"Scott?" What's wrong? Andrew asked when he opened the door to the room.

"I think that there's something wrong with Catherine." Scott nervously replied. She's exhausted and her color is all wrong."

Andrew could smell Scott's fear, and knew that it was for Catherine.

"Go back and sit with her." Andrew said. "We'll be over in a minute.

Amelia was already getting dressed even before the door closed. Andrew quickly dressed and they rushed over to Scott and Catherine's room. They were shocked at Catherine's appearance.

"Did you drink from her again?" Andrew asked.

"No, I swear." Scott replied shaking his head.

Andrew went out to the hummer, and took four bags of blood from the fridge. He put them in a bag and hurried back to Catherine and Scott's room. When he returned, he sent Scott to his room to get his cell phone.

"I need to call Susan." Andrew said. "Maybe she can shed some light on what's happening."

Andrew took a unit of blood out of the bag and handed the bag to Amelia. He began feeding Catherine the blood, but it wasn't until the third unit that she began to look and feel better.

"Why do I need so much blood?" she asked.

"I don't know." Amelia replied." We're going to call Susan and see if she can help us."

Andrew dialed Susan's number speaking as soon as he heard her pick up.

"Susan, we have a problem with Catherine."

"Andrew?" Susan asked. "Sorry, you woke me up. What's the problem with Catherine?"

He could hear Gloria in the background asking what the problem was, and waited until he had Susan's full attention. He described what Catherine looked like and her symptoms.

"Yesterday she woke up pale and tired." He said. "We weren't too concerned because she and Scott shared blood. We thought that they had gotten overzealous so we gave her some blood and warned them to be more careful. Tonight, she looked really bad, and it took three units of just to get her color back."

"Where are you?" Susan asked.

"We're at a motel by Wilmington." Andrew replied wishing that he had kept driving to Philly. "We weren't in any hurry so we decided to stop, and get a fresh start in the morning. We planned to arrive early so that we could find a decent place to stay before we called Charles."

"Alright," Susan said with a sigh. "Don't drive like a maniac to get here. If I'm right, Catherine will be fine. Just give her a large cup filled with blood to sip on while you travel. If Charles isn't there, see Emma. She is Charles' business manager, and her mate is his personal assistant.

"What do you think is wrong with her?" Andrew asked worriedly.

"Nothing is wrong with her." Susan replied. "Just get her to the club. Someone will be there to check her out and help her. I don't want to say anything more until

I'm sure. Gloria and I will be there by the end of the week."

"Alright, we'll see you then." Andrew replied. He felt a little better but was still concerned.

"Scott, go to the hummer and grab one of the large cups and wash it out. After that, help Catherine get dressed and pack up your things. We'll be back after we pack up our things."

Andrew went back to their room, packed up their few belongings, packed the hummer and checked them out of the hotel. He settled the bill explaining that they had gotten an emergency call and that they had to get on the road.

Twenty minutes later, they were on their way to Philly. The drive took almost three hours because of construction that had closed all but one lane on the ninety-five.

The club looked as if it was closed when they drove up. They were about to leave when Catherine saw a sign instructing anyone having business with the club after hours to go to the rear door. Andrew quickly parked the hummer and reached under the seat for the Glock.

"Baby leave it." Amelia said. "We aren't here for trouble."

"Old habits die hard." Andrew replied with a smile as he got out of the hummer.

Andrew helped Amelia out of the hummer while Scott helped Catherine who for the moment seemed to be in perfect health. They walked to the back of the building, and were surprised to find a parking lot full of vehicles. There casually dressed vampires standing by the back door that smiled at and then greeted them. Andrew could tell that they were all packing and judging by their appearance was a professional security team. The smallest of them stood six feet three inches tall and was built like a middle linebacker.

"Where is your car?" he asked.

"It's parked out in the front." Andrew replied. "We're here to see Mr. Black, is he here?"

I'm sorry." The vampire replied, "But he's gone for the evening. Is there something that I can help you with? I am Mitchel Orion, Mr. Black's head of security."

"I'm Andrew Barnes." Andrew said extending his hand. "Is Emma here?"

He noticed that at the mention of Emma's name, the vampires began to fan out and took defensive postures.

"What is your business with Ms. Black?" Mitchel asked.

"We aren't here to cause trouble." Andrew replied keeping his tone neutral. "Susan Dorchester sent us and told us to ask for Emma if Mr. Black wasn't here."

After the briefest of seconds, everyone began to relax.

"Ah... Officer Martin." Mitchel said with a smile. "Ms. Dorchester told me that you were coming. I apologize for what just happened; we didn't know who you were. If you'll give the keys of your vehicle to Kirk, he'll move it to the back of the building. In the meantime, we can get Ms. Catherine taken care of."

Andrew handed the keys of the hummer to Kirk, and followed Mitchel and the others into the club. They were led up a set of rear stairs to a private office. Mitchel knocked on the door, and waited for a response.

"Enter." A feminine voice said.

Mitchel opened the door, and showed them in.

"Catherine." Emma said, "Please sit. If mother is correct, you'll need to save your strength. Mitchel, could you please get Agatha? I think she's in one of the private rooms."

Scott helped Catherine to one of the couches as Mitchel left the office to find Agatha.

"Can I get any of you anything while we wait for Agatha?" Emma asked.

They all declined. They were too worried about Catherine. Emma watched as Scott hovered over Catherine. She could see that he was worried and could imagine his reaction once he knew the truth.

"Why don't you and Amelia go have a drink?" she said to Andrew. "Agatha needs to examine Catherine, and I don't think that she will be comfortable with you here. Scott can stay as long as he behaves himself and lets Agatha do her job."

"Who is Agatha?" Amelia asked.

"Agatha is a vigoratus, a medium uxor specifically." Emma replied.

Amelia's eyes widened in shock as her high school Latin came back to her.

"Why in the hell would she need a midwife?"

"There's only one reason why a woman would need a midwife." Emma replied chuckling.

The meaning of Amelia's question hit the rest of them like a ton of bricks. Scott's eyes widened. His lips twitched, and then broke into a big smile as he let out a loud whoop.

"Ho... I mean we just mated. There was no one else before him." Catherine sputtered in disbelief.

"Congratulations!" Andrew exclaimed clapping Scott on the back.

"It's different for vampires." Emma explained to Catherine. "When one of us becomes pregnant, we know it almost immediately. The gestation period is considerably shorter than that of a human. A human pregnancy lasts approximately two-hundred and eighty days whereas ours last about one -hundred and forty days.

During your pregnancy you will need six to eight units of blood per day, and once the baby is born, he or she will require blood as well as mother's milk. The best way is to breast feed the baby so that he gets both milk and blood at the same time. That means that your blood intake will be high for the first two years of the child's life.

Catherine paled as the implications of the pregnancy hit her.

"How long before the baby comes? What are we going to do? I don't know anything about babies! I'm only eighteen! I can't have a child yet!"

"I don't think we have a choice." Scott said laughing. "We'll figure it out together." He added.

"You'll have plenty of help." Emma assured her, "but the first order of business is to confirm that you are in fact, pregnant. After that you can begin to make plans as to where you will live. I understand that both the Baltimore and the Jackson, Mississippi areas are out, but there are plenty of other areas to choose from."

"We won't abandon you." Amelia assured Catherine, "You and Scott are family and you're my number one." She turned to Andrew and beamed. "We're going to be grandparents!"

"I know." Andrew replied smiling. "We're going to need a place to stay while we get them settled, are there any nice hotels around here?"

"There are several." Emma replied. "We also have some rooms here that are available for rent. They're up on the third floor."

"That would be great." Andrew replied. "I gather that this place never really closes?"

"No, it doesn't. They serve excellent food here, and you can buy special diet items. Would you like a couple of rooms?" Emma asked.

"You make it difficult to say anything but yes." Andrew replied. "Yes, we'll take a couple of rooms."

"Fine, but I hope that you aren't going to cause any trouble in my club." Emma said the warning in her voice clear.

"I promise that we won't cause any trouble." Andrew said holding his hands up in surrender.

Andrew could see that Emma was a force to be reckoned with. Under that soft demeanor was a core of iron. He had no doubt that she would enforce the peace in any way that she deemed necessary, including taking someone apart.

There was a single tap on the door before a large Native American male walked in without waiting for the invitation to enter. He spoke before he realized that there were other people in the office.

"Sweetheart, I was wondering if we were staying here or going home tonight."

When he realized that Emma had company, he apologized.

"I'm sorry; I didn't realize that you had visitors."

"It's alright." Emma replied with a smile. "They're friends of mothers. The ones that father invited to visit."

"Oh yes, the parvulus." The big man said, "But I thought that they weren't coming until tomorrow night."

"That was the plan, but they thought that something was wrong with Catherine and called mother. She told them to come tonight."

"Is everything alright with her?" He asked.

"She's fine." Emma replied. "She's pregnant and wasn't taking enough blood. "

Emma turned to address the group.

"This is my mate Neil Redcloud. Neil, this is Andrew and his mate Amelia. The young lady on the couch is Catherine and the nervous looking young man is her mate Scott."

Pleasantries were exchanged but Neil was still concerned.

"How much blood has she had today?" he asked.

"She's fine." Emma replied, "And we'll be staying here tonight."

There was another tap on the door and a woman walked in.

"Agatha! It's about time you got your ass up here." Emma said when the woman walked in. "Is your age catching up with you?"

An extended middle finger was the only reply Agatha gave. Andrew and Amelia excused themselves, and headed toward the bar for a drink. Emma and Neil followed them to give Agatha the privacy she needed to perform her examination.

Agatha started out by smiling at Catherine in an attempt to put her at ease. Next, she asked what seemed to be a strange question.

"Did you get any funny feelings in your vaginal area or in your lower abdominal area after making love?"

Catherine looked at her and nodded her head yes.

"Did you exchange blood while you were making love?" Agatha asked.

Catherine's face turned a bright red, but Scott was the one who answered.

"She mentioned that she had a weird feeling when we exchanged blood. How can you be so sure that she's pregnant? I mean this just happened last night."

Agatha did a quick but thorough examination. Unlike human doctors, the only thing that she needed to tell if the girl was pregnant was her nose. She could smell the subtle odors of the hormones that a woman gave of when she was pregnant.

"Most vampires can tell you the moment they conceive." Agatha explained. "I'm sure that you've been told the gestation period for vampires is approximately half that of humans. In one hundred and thirty-nine days, you will be parents.

CHAPTER 6

Catherine, you will need to drink at least six units of blood in addition to what you usually drink. In the old days, pregnancy was a very dangerous time for us. The female needed increased amount blood which invariable drew attention to the area without her having her abilities to protect herself it's much easier now that we have blood banks. I thought for sure that we were going to lose Susan, and we might have if not for Charles but that is their story to tell. The biggest indicator that you are going into labor is that the day or two before, your blood intake will dramatically increase.

If you are staying in the area, and would like to use me as a doctor, I would like to see you in my office on Monday. If you are leaving the area or don't want to use me, I would suggest that you find a doctor soon. Chances are that sometime in the next two or three weeks your powers will stop working. They won't return until after the birth of the baby. Here's my card. Call me tomorrow if you want to set up an appointment. I want to get back to that delicious man I was with before Mitchel told me you were here."

"How are we going to do this" Catherine asked Scott when they were alone.

"The same way every other parent on the planet does it...one day at a time." Scott said. "I'm sure that we'll make mistakes, but we'll learn and we'll be good parents. I like Agatha, how do you feel about her taking care of you and the baby?"

"I like her too." Catherine replied.

They held each other as they began to plan their future and began the dreaded task of picking a name for the baby. Catherine soon gave in to exhaustion and fell asleep with her head resting on Scott's shoulder.

Andrew and Amelia went to the bar area. After finding a table, Andrew went to the bar and ordered drinks. He returned to the table with a beer for himself and a glass of wine for Amelia. For several minutes they listened to the music; neither of them speaking.

Finally, Amelia spoke.

"Andrew, what are we going to do?"

"We're going to follow our plan." He replied. "If Scott and Catherine want to settle down here, we'll help them and then go about making a life for ourselves. The thing is I don't know what I want to do. The only thing that I ever wanted to be was a cop. I don't know if I can go back to that; but I'd like to try.

What about you? Have you thought about what you would like to do?"

"I wanted to be a psychologist and was in the process of deciding what kind when a recruiter from the bureau showed up and gave a talk. I was fascinated. I ended up signing up and ended up working with VICAP. My first assignment was helping to provide background info on the Seaside Strangler case. I like everyone else worked on the aftermath of nine-eleven.

I was assigned to the team that profiled several suspected terrorists. I also headed up the team that helped to prevent the attack on Pearl Harbor that was scheduled for December 7, 2006. That never made the news because we took the terrorist out before they reached the U.S. I had just returned to VICAP when I pulled your case and I'm glad that I did.'

Andrew was surprised, proud and amazed at Amelia's accomplishments.

"What was it like to work those kinds of cases?" he asked.

Amelia closed her eyes to think about her answer.

"I was under a lot of pressure especially with the nine-eleven case." She replied. "Don't get me wrong, it felt good that our profile helped in breaking the network that enabled those bastards to attack us. There's still a lot of information that hasn't been released to the public and may never be. But the pressure was horrendous."

"What degrees do you have?" Andrew asked.

"I have a doctorate in psychology and a JD degree." Amelia replied. "When I was I college, I had no life; I think I had a total of three dates. I went into the academy right after graduation. I was happy and my parents were so proud. My dad carried a picture of my graduation from the academy in his wallet and was even buried with it."

Amelia stopped talking and looked away. Tears stung her eyes as she thought about her father. She still missed him. She regretted that she hadn't spent more time with him, but she had been busy building a career and thought that she had more time.

Andrew wrapped his arms around her ad gave her time to work through her grief.

Amelia returned the hug and asked Andrew about himself.

"There isn't much to tell." He replied shrugging his shoulders. "As you know, I was married and I have a kid. She remarried and lives on the west coast with my son. I was on the force for seventeen years with three of those years being on patrol. I did two years with vice and twelve with homicide. I actually started with cold cases; I was actually good at it.

I was in the group of officers that went to New York City after nine-eleven and spent two months at ground zero. Three years ago, I was sent to Quantico for three weeks of training on how to properly use a criminal investigative analysis tool. By the way, I like the simpler term profile.

Diamond was my fourth task force that I was a part of and the second that I led. The first one was the Victor Robles case. He raped sixteen women and murdered seven of them. The youngest victim was seventeen, the oldest fifty-three. All of them were brunettes under five-five and overweight. It took six weeks and a lucky break to catch him.

He was in the process of raping another woman when her boyfriend stopped by for a surprise visit. Robles jumped off the balcony when the boyfriend chased him and in the process; twisted his knee. That was the first time that I worked Lisa. Anyway, we contacted all of the emergency rooms and clinics and asked them to report if any males in his age bracket came in with a knee injury.

Three hours after the alert went out, we got a call from Harbor Hospital. They had a man who said that he had accidentally fallen from his balcony. We busted him and he's sitting on death row. It's too bad that she's gone. She was a good cop and a good friend. Enough about the past." Andrew said. "What would you like to do in the future?"

"Go to Egypt and see the sphinx and pyramids up close." Amelia replied without hesitation.

"I would like to go to Europe." Andrew replied. "And I've always wanted to go on one of those photo safaris in Africa."

"Excuse me." A vampire from the next table said. "I couldn't help but overhear your conversation. How nice it is to be in love and to make plans for the future. If you don't mind a little advice from an old vampire, stay out of the Middle East until you are a little older. The head enforcer there is a real bitch and would insist that you are there to cause trouble. She would make your life a living hell. She's been the lead enforcer of that area for close to.... Umm let me think... Charles gave it up in twelve-fifty so that's... umm. What year is this anyway?" he asked.

"Twenty-twelve." Andrew replied trying to contain his chuckle.

"So that makes it seven hundred and fifty years." The vampire mused. "Please excuse my manners, I am Amsu."

"I'm Andrew and the lovely woman with me is my mate Amelia." Andrew said offering his hand.

"I am pleased to meet you." Amsu said as he rose from his seat and kissed Amelia's hand. "Young man, you are very lucky to have such a rare flower as your mate."

Amsu studied them for a moment. It was obvious to Andrew that he recognized them.

"You are the two new vampires that Charles has been anxious for me to meet." He said. "You are the ones that were created by Diamond. You managed to kill a rabid ancient vampire while you were still human. I am honored to meet you."

Emma approached Andrew and Amelia's table. As soon as Amsu saw her he stood, picked her up and hugged her.

"Emma! It's so good to see you!" He said excitedly.

"Amsu! When did you get here?" Emma asked as she returned the hug.

"I've been here for about an hour.' He replied. "I haven't seen your father yet. I last spoke to him on Tuesday when he told me about the whole Diamond fiasco and Andrew and Amelia. I'm still a bit upset that he didn't tell me how pretty Amelia was. He knew that I was heading this way; we have some details to discuss about Diamond's assets. Plus, I think that he wanted he wanted me here when Vladimir calls."

"Have you met Andrew and Amelia yet?" she asked.

"I just had the pleasure." Amsu replied. "They were talking about going to Egypt to do some sightseeing. We were just starting a good conversation when you came in. Where is that scalp happy husband of yours?" Amsu asked teasing her.

"He never took any scalps." Emma replied chuckling, "wrong tribe."

"I know." Amsu replied." I just love getting you riled up."

"Are you going to need a room?" Emma asked.

"If you have one available. If not; then I'll take your father's room."

"I have a room available." Emma replied as she rolled her eyes. She turned to Amelia and Andrew. "Your room is ready. Agatha is finished with Catherine. Her confirmed due date is September."

"Amelia, isn't Catherine your number one?" Amsu asked confused.

"Yes, she is and she's pregnant." Amelia replied her voice filled with excitement.

Amsu shook his head in disbelief.

"You young kids move way to fast." He said. "Emma, how long have your parents been doing the same dance? Everyone knows that they're mates; but those two are still courting each other."

Emma chuckled as she replied. "They say that they are going to mate on January first, twenty-thirteen. They also said that they would stay in bed all day December twenty-first just in case."

Amsu roared with laughter.

"Oh, come on!" he said. "They're staying in bed all day just to fuck. It has nothing to do with the end of the world."

"Thanks for an image that I definitely didn't want in my mind." Emma said cringing. "Come on Amsu no kid wants to imagine their parents fucking like that." She added.

"Then I'll switch to a subject that you're more comfortable with." Amsu replied. "When are you and the scalp hunter going to have kids?"

"Subtlety isn't one of your gifts." Emma replied laughing. "Let me guess, you want to spoil the child like you tried to spoil me." Emma's eyes lit up with laughter as she looked at Andrew and Amelia. "Poor Catherine! You two are going to spoil that child rotten and god help her if it's a boy."

"I can understand that Amsu feels a link to you because he sired your father; but why would he be concerned about my number one's child?" Amelia asked.

"Diamond was sired by Amsu about three hundred years after he sired father." Emma replied.

Amelia's eyes widened as Andrew stepped between her and the rest of the group.

"I am not looking for retribution." Amsu said when Andrew moved. "If anything, I'm thankful that you put her out of her misery. She lost her humanity and became a cruel and vicious predator murdering without remorse. Her only joy in life was to cause others the pain that she was feeling.

Please don't misunderstand my next question, but how did you defeat her? She was one of our best ubertas venators. She had centuries of training and practice of hunting rogue vampires. She should have been able to use compulsion on both of you and feed from you at will, so how did you do it?"

"Let Amelia go see Catherine and I'll be more than happy to tell you everything that I remember." Andrew replied.

After sending Amelia off with a quick kiss, Andrew began his story.

"I was a Baltimore City detective and was handed this case..."

Two hours later, the story was finished. He admitted that given the fact that he and Amelia were human; he couldn't fathom how they even stood a chance against Diamond.

Amsu closed his eyes in silent prayer for his second oldest parvulus. He had spent over two-hundred centuries teaching her how to master her abilities and training her to hunt rogues. Not that he would ever admit it, but in many ways; he was more proud of her than Charles.

Diamond had been a street urchin who had tried to steal his purse when he was in Rome. He almost turned her over to his guard, but something about her eyes captivated him; and he turned her. Theirs was never a romantic relationship as he considered her a daughter. He would carry the regret of preventing her from going rogue for the rest of his days. His hope was that he would be able to find some measure of peace on the other side.

Amsu pulled himself together before he spoke.

"She wanted to toy with you." He said sadly. "She didn't consider you a worthy opponent and she paid for her conceit with her life. I hope that she is at peace and you my young friend uses her story as a lesson."

"What's your story?" Andrew asked.

"As I said, I first saw Didiana or Diamond as you call her in Rome. I grabbed her hand as she tried to steal my purse." Amsu said. His voice was almost hypnotic as he spoke. "I was about to call the guards when I saw her eyes. Even though they held fear, there was a strength and fire about them. I compelled her to follow me and turned her that night. Over the next two centuries, I made sure that she received the finest education available and that she knew how to defend herself with a blade and her hands. To everyone who knew us, she was my daughter; there was never a romantic relationship between us.

When she wasn't on a hunt, she would spend time with me and we would travel the world seeing the sights. Eventually she found someone that she wanted as a mate, but he was human. He refused to change until after he completed his service to his country. You see, he was in the Marines. He lost his life in Vietnam in nineteen-seventy-two.

After that Diamond withdrew. For almost twenty years after his death, she went on mission after mission hunting for rogues. My biggest regret is that I didn't intervene sooner than I did. I thought that it was her way of working through the pain and coming to terms with her loss. At the turn of the century I received word that she had stopped taking missions and that she had fallen off the radar. I had friends looking for her, but I would only get reports of occasional sightings until a year ago. She was seen in former eastern bloc countries openly killing and leaving a trail of bodies behind her.

I asked the ubertas venators to find her ad bring her to me so that I could save her; but she disappeared again. She reappeared in Canada, was there for a few weeks and then moved on to America. By this time, her behavior was much worse. She was openly taunting the human law enforcement.

You have no idea of what it took to keep the human law enforcement community from finding out that she wasn't just some local psychopath. I still held hope that we would find her and bring her back. That hope was dashed two weeks before she arrived in Baltimore. A group of ubertas venators caught up with her and gave her my message. In response, she killed all but one of them. She only left him alive so that he could deliver a message.

Amsu stopped for a moment and then continued.

"She told him to tell me and everyone else that she would kill anyone who tried to bring her in. That was when I knew that we had lost her soul and that she had to be put down. You know the rest of the story. Diamond was like a daughter to me so you will have to have to forgive me if I choose to remember her as the good person I loved and not the monster she became."

"I'm sorry." Andrew said quietly. "But we had no choice. She killed two cops and left behind forensic mysteries that aren't going to go away. For one, the coroner still has Diamond's corpse. Second, the anticoagulant was identified as a highly concentrated form of saliva found in vampire bats."

Amsu grimaced.

"I wasn't aware that the humans found out about the venom. That is of great concern to me. Diamond's corpse should be of little value to them as it will decay quickly."

"I hope so." Andrew replied. "But if I know Doc Lassider, he would have wasted no time in performing the autopsy. Not only that, the FBI would have the files because a federal officer died during the case."

Amsu blew out a frustrated breath.

"This is most distressing." Amsu said. "If he managed to autopsy her before she decayed he would confirm that she wasn't human. I assume that they would have preserved tissue and fluid samples?"

Andrew nodded.

"If he sent copies to the FBI they could run tests not normally run and they have tests not available to regular law enforcement. If they find out that her DNA isn't human; they won't stop until they figure out what it is.

Amsu swallowed hard. "This is not good." He said. "Charles will need to look into this immediately. How long does it take to take to get the results back from DNA testing?"

"That depends on the test." Andrew replied. "It also depends on which lab he used and how backed up they are. If he wanted a rush, and he more than likely did because this was a high priority case; it would be two weeks to a month before the results were back. He probably used the FBI lab which means that the feds will have the results first."

Amsu pulled out his cell phone and began speaking as soon as the person on the other end picked up.

"Charles? Amsu here... we may have a problem with the Diamond situation... yes... the humans analyzed the saliva and may have gotten a viable tissue sample from Diamond."

There was a moment of silence as he listened to Charles' response.

"You were aware and someone is already handling it? I apologize; I should have known that you had the situation under control... I was just talking to Andrew. Yes they're here...that was the plan but they thought Catherine was ill...No she just has the one --hundred and forty day flu...Yes she is pregnant... she didn't know that she wasn't taking in enough blood... Charles slow down. Agatha has already seen her and Emma is making sure that she is being taking care of... yes, hold on; I'll ask him."

Amsu covered the mouthpiece of the phone and spoke to Andrew.

"Charles would like to know if you and your mate will be available around ten this morning."

Andrew looked at his watch. It was just after six am.

"Amelia." He called telepathically, 'Charles would like to meet with us at ten this morning. Is that okay?"

"That's fine." Amelia replied. "I'm going to the room to take a shower. Try not to be too much longer. You need to clean up and we need to get some breakfast."

Amsu could see that Andrew was communicating with someone telepathically. Sure that it was Amelia, he waited.

"Ten is fine." Andrew said. "I'm going to go to the room, get cleaned up and take Amelia out for breakfast. We'll see you at the meeting and it was a pleasure meeting you."

Andrew held out his hand to Amsu.

"The pleasure is al mine." Amsu said shaking Andrew's hand. "I look forward to getting to know the two of you better."

Amsu turned his attention back to the phone.

"Charles... yes ten is fine... I'll let Emma know... I'll see you at ten.

Andrew found Emma behind the bar taking stock. She stopped long enough to tell him how to get to his room and hand him the electronic key needed to access the elevator. Out of habit, she informed him that the key would be deactivated once they were gone. She bid him a good night commenting that if she didn't get a few hours rest; she would be a total bitch.

Andrew thanked her and went to the room. It was a large room that had a furnished sitting area with a large flat screen TV. There was also a small kitchen area complete with a fridge that was stocked with blood. There were two doors that led off the main door. To the left was a small furnished office and to the right, was the bedroom. The bedroom was large enough that it had a king-sized bed and two armoires plus a walk in closet. Their luggage was lying on the bed along with a note.

Dear Sir,

This is to inform you that all of your firearms have been placed in our vault for safekeeping. We hope that you understand that we do not allow firearms in the club or in the guest rooms.

If you have any additional items that you would like to place in the vault, please call security. If there are any questions regarding out policies, please contact management. To do this; please use the house phone and ask for the office.

Also take note of the second page. It will inform you of the wide variety of services that we offer our guest. We hope that you enjoy your stay and thank you for choosing us.

The management.

P.s: We took the liberty of plugging the refrigerator in your vehicle into a power source in order to preserve the battery.

Andrew read the note and then began to unpack while Amelia finished her shower. Once she was finished, Andrew grabbed a quick shower. They quickly dressed and went to breakfast.

After ordering coffee, eggs, and bacon with orange juice for Amelia and tomato juice for him, Andrew told Amelia about his talk with Amsu and what he learned about Diamond. After they ate, they still had an hour before the meeting. They decided to take a walk around the neighborhood to kill some time.

As they were leaving, they ran into Amsu who was on his way to breakfast.

"Good morning!" he greeted with a smile. "Have you had breakfast yet?"

"Good morning." Amelia replied. "We've just finished. We were just going for a walk before the meeting."

"Then don't let me delay you." Amsu said as he shook Andrew's hand. "I shall see you at the meeting."

Andrew led Amelia out into the morning light. It was a bright, but slightly chilly early spring morning. The city was just beginning to come to life. They joined hands and began to walk up Water Street with no real destination in mind.

Neither of them spokes as they slowly walked enjoying the quiet companionship of their early morning walk.

"We're being followed." Amelia said telepathically after a few minutes into their walk. "I can feel them but I don't know where they are yet."

"Are you sure that there's more than one?" Andrew asked.

"I just started feeling them and yes there's more than one; but I don't know how many."

Andrew couldn't feel them but trusted Amelia's instincts.

"Can you tell if they are Vampire?" He asked,

Amelia closed her eyes for a moment trying to focus on their followers. After a moment, she had a clear picture of their pursuers and their intentions.

"There are four maybe five of them. They are waiting by the alley for us. They plan to rob us and are armed with knives. The leader has a katana."

Andrew readied himself as he telepathically spoke to Amelia.

"I want you to get behind me just as we reach them and watch our backs. I'm willing to bet that they have someone shadowing us. I'll try to keep them on me while you get control of the guy with the sword. If you can; have him attack the others."

"I'll do my best." Amelia replied.

Just as they reached the Alley, five vampires appeared before them. The vampire in the middle had a katana and two others had wicked looking daggers. Two other vampires blocked the way to the street. One had a butcher knife and the other had a kukri.

"My my, what do we have here?" The vampire holding the katana said. "A pair of parvulus out for a romantic walk. How nice. I hope that you have your wallet with you. You have to pay for the privilege to walk our streets. If no wallet, maybe your sire is willing to cover for you."

"I have no money." Andrew replied. "And our sire is dead. Unless you want to join her, I would suggest you leave."

"Well then," The leader sneered. "I guess we'll just have to take it out of her ass rig..."

Before the leader could finish his statement, Andrew had his head in his hands. Before the others saw him move, he threw the leaders head at the vampire to the left of him. Andrew grabbed the one to his right by the throat and threw him to the ground. The vampire to the left of Andrew had recovered and stabbed Andrew in the side of his neck. The blade went in about an inch but managed to nick the jugular vein.

Andrew felt the sharp pain and then the felt the hot blood as it pulsed from the wound. He looked at the vampire that stabbed him with glowing eyes. Seconds later, the vampire burst into flame. He screamed in pain as the flames quickly engulfed him. The vampire fell to his knees, screamed one last time, and was claimed by the flames. The Vampire that Andrew still had a hold of began to beg for his life.

Amelia was surprised by Andrew's sudden attack. She quickly forced her mind into the minds of the two vampires that were blocking their way to the street and took control of their minds. She sensed another vampire coming up from behind them and ordered the two that she had control of to subdue him. She had just turned to face the new threat when she felt Andrew's pain. She turned in time to see the vampire that had stabbed Andrew burst into flames. She heard the last vampire that Andrew had engaged pleading for Andrew not to kill him.

"Andrew love, he's giving up."

The vampire that the others were holding indicated that he was going to surrender. It was then that Amelia realized that he had a broken jaw. She has one of the vampires that were under her control take care of Andrew's prisoner. The blood had stopped flowing from Andrew's neck but he was weak from the loss of blood.

Amelia had just taken out her cellphone to call for help when four dark paneled vans pulled up. Emma and her mate Neal got out of one and Amsu followed by a vampire who stood six feet, seven inches tall with long black hair and gray eyes got out of a second one. It was clear that he was of Middle Eastern descent. Amelia had to admit that he made a very pretty package.

"Susan did say that you two attract trouble." He said with an amused smile.

"How did you know we were in trouble?" Amelia asked.

"How else?" Emma replied. "Catherine told us. She knew that you were going to be attacked, but she was unfamiliar with the city. We misunderstood her description and thought that you had gone the other direction on Water Street.

The vampires that came with Emma quickly disposed of the smoldering corpse and cleaned up the scene. Two vampires helped Andrew to a van, checked him over, and handed him a bottle of blood.

The vampire that arrived with Amsu approached Amelia.

"Ms. Hensley, I am Charles Black. Could you please tell me what happened here?"

Even though it was worded as a request, Amelia knew that it was anything but. Getting into her facing the review board mode, she stood straight and began her report.

"First, please call me Amelia. Andrew and I decided to go for a walk after breakfast..."

Charles was surprised by the clear and detailed report that Amelia gave, but was confused about how the vampire had been set ablaze.

"Please do not take this wrong, but are you sure that it was Andrew and not you that set the vampire on fire?"

"I'm positive." Amelia replied. "I felt him do it. I really can't explain it except to say that I felt the power as it welled up in his mind. I also heard him say the words burn in hell. The next thing I know, the vampire is on fire. I've never seen Andrew project like that and I'm not sure of how long it will take us to master this."

"Please call me Charles." He said. "I'm hoping that we will be able to develop a friendship such as the one that you have with Susan. Are you saying that the two of you have been helping each other learn control of your powers? That is remarkable normal vampires who have no sire have to learn how to control their abilities on their own."

"Andrew and I have been working on developing our powers together." Amelia explained. "I haven't been as much help to him as he's been to me, but he anchors me and keeps me focused. When the need arises, he lends me his strength. I know that this is going to sound strange, but just his being there helps me."

"I understand." Charles replied. "But you will both need to be very careful with this ability. Pyrokinesis is one of our least understood abilities. I would also suggest that you limit the number of people that you tell about this. It seems that you have some form of sixth sense that is nowhere as developed as Catherine's, but it's there."

"Is there some place where we could go where Andrew can safely learn to control his gift?" Amelia asked.

"If you're asking if there is a school or a training facility, the answer is no. You must understand that until recently, vampires had a house to which they were loyal to. The enemies of the house became your enemies; it was the same with alliances. For the most part, it is still that way in Europe and in Mexico except Mexico they are called cartels but this isn't the place to discuss such things."

After she and Charles were finished talking, Amelia went to check on Andrew. He was still weak from the blood loss and from using the Pyrokinesis. He was still trying to figure out how he had done it and if he could do it again.

Amelia wrapped her arms around him and hugged him. Andrew knew that she thought that she had lost him and could feel her anger boiling under the calm façade that she as showing. He wasn't looking forward to having that anger turned loose on him.

Once she saw that Andrew was all right, Amelia took his face in her hands.

"You ass! What in the fuck was that? I thought we had a plan and you let him goad you into attacking him! If you had stuck to the plan, I would have had him and the two flanking him under my control. You wouldn't have been hurt and we may not have had to kill any of them."

"I know." Andrew said sheepishly, "But when he threatened you, I attacked."

Amelia's eyes narrowed as she spoke in a deceptively calm voice. "Andrew Martin, if you ever pull a hair brained stunt like that again; I'll kick your ass. You tell me a plan and then with no fucking warning you change it and almost got yourself killed. Then, you try to justify it by saying that your mate was threatened. You asshole! You could have gotten us both killed! What would have happened if I did what you originally planned and grabbed the guy with the sword to help us? I would have been wasting energy taking control of a dead vampire. We would have been outnumbered and in trouble because of your caveman tactics. You know as well as I do that, he used his words t throw you off and it worked"

Andrew let out a harsh breath.

"I did the same thing that you did twice and I never berated you for it! In fact, neither of those vampires was going to attack me. They flirted with me and you lashed out. It is well within my rights to protect my mate from those who threaten her."

Amelia's eyes began to glow. The vampires who were caring for Andrew began to back away.

"How dare you throw that up in my face!" She said angrily. "I don't know why I attacked Catherine, but that other bitch was trying to steal you from me and you looked at her!"

"The only reason that I was looking at her was because she was invading my personal space." Andrew replied his voice just as angry as Amelia's did. "I was going to tell her that I wasn't interested when you went all psycho on her ass and almost got yourself killed! I will reiterate what I said earlier; I have the right to protect my mate."

"You may have the right to defend me," Amelia said, "But you don't have the right to get yourself killed while doing it. If you had just stuck to the original plan, not only would you have defended me; you wouldn't have gotten stabbed."

At this point, Charles intervened.

"Perhaps this is best discussed in private after you've both had a chance to cool off."

They looked at each other and nodded in agreement. They rode back in the same van as Charles and Amsu. The only conversation that took place was when Charles formally introduced himself to Andrew.

Andrew felt badly about the way he had jumped Amelia and had to admit that she was right; he should have stuck to the pan.

"Amelia, I'm sorry. You were right; I should have stuck to the plan. I never should have brought up the past. Forgive me." He said telepathically.

Amelia snuggled closer not caring that he was covered in blood.

"I'm sorry too. I was so scared that I had lost you when you were stabbed. According to Charles, we have a lot of work ahead of us. He also said that Pyrokinesis is one of their least understood gifts. He told me that we should be careful about who we reveal our powers to."

Once they arrived back at the club, the vans that they were riding in pulled into a building next to the club. After they unloaded Emma lead, Andrew, and Amelia to a rear set of stairs that took them to the third floor.

"Get cleaned up and join us in the office where we met last night." Emma said.

"Give us fifteen minutes." Andrew replied. "Thank you for your help this morning."

Emma shook her head.

"I'll never doubt mother again. I'm just glad that you're alright."

They took a quick shower and got ready for the meeting.

"How are you going to learn to control this ability?" Amelia asked.

"I'm not sure." Andrew replied. "I guess we'll have to find an area where there is nothing to burn. I'll just keep practicing until I have it under control. I'm not sure that I like using that power, it drained me; I feel worn out."

Amelia nodded as she finished getting dressed. She chose a summer dress with floral print on it and a pair of flat shoes.

"It'll get better once you have it under control." She said. "I was worn out when I first started using my abilities. Now I can use it several times and I don't get near as drained as I used to."

Andrew buttoned his shirt and slipped on his loafers.

"But if I make a mistake, I could burn a whole neighborhood down." He replied.

"I'm sure that you'll get it under control." Amelia said hugging him. "We'll just have to be careful until you do."

She stepped back while Andrew grabbed his wallet and room key. They held hands as they walked to their meeting with Charles.

When they got to the office, Charles was not there.

"Please have a seat." Emma said. "Father had to take a conference call. He shouldn't be too long."

As they were taking their seats, Andrew saw a newspaper and asked if he could borrow it. After getting permission, he read the headlines:

"Three men decapitated in downtown nightclub"

"Amelia." Andrew said telepathically, "You may want to read this with me."

"Three men were beheaded at the Club Nuveen last night. However, there were security cameras on scene a source close to the investigation said there is no clear images of the suspect. No one from inside of the club could recall anything about the suspect. However, a man who was the club reported seeing a Hispanic male running from the club. He was described between twenty and twenty -five with shoulder length black or grey hair his height was reported somewhere between five foot-eight to five foot --ten. weight was said to be between one- hundred and thirty to one- hundred and forty pounds. He was wearing a light grey business suit with a light pink shirt. If anyone can offer any information as to the identity of this unknown person please contact your local police department"

The victims are Carlos Martinez, Juan, and Raul Hierra. All three me are reported to have ties to the Martinez drug cartel. Carlos Martinez was the grandson of Santiago Martinez, the reputed head of the cartel. The Hierra brothers both have long police records and Raul was wanted for questioning in connection with a triple homicide in Pensacola, Florida..."

The story continued with giving more background information.

"The attacker sounds like a vampire." Andrew said quietly. "I wonder what in the hell is going on?"

"I agree." Amelia said. "Do you think that the cartel is being run by vampires?"

Amelia went to mind speak

"If they are, does that mean that Charles Black is nothing more than a two-bit drug king pin?"

Andrew grimaced at the thought.

"I guess we can ask him about it." Andrew said before switching to telepathy. "I sure as hell hope not, but we need to be prepared. Do you know where Scott and Catherine are?"

Amelia closed her eyes for a moment and smiled.

"They're at the mall looking at baby things. They're safe for the moment. How do you want to play this?"

"Loosely." Andrew replied. "If things go wrong in there, I'll try to keep Charles occupied long enough for you to either take control of or wipe Amsu out. If you can't do anything with him, then we'll switch targets. The problem is I don't know how long I'll be able to stand against them; I'm still weak from the fight this morning."

Emma watched them and could tell that they had gone on alert although she didn't know why. She saw that they were having a private conversation and that something in the paper made them nervous. She entertained the idea of reading their thoughts, but if she were caught; they would never trust her again.

"Is everything alright?" She asked. "You seem tense; did you see something in the paper?"

Andrew was in the process of deciding if Emma was a threat when Amelia spoke to him telepathically.

"She is genuinely worried about us. She is wondering what it is that has us concerned."

Andrew gave Amelia a nod and spoke to Emma.

"We were just reading about the murders at Club Nuveen. We were wondering if vampires were involved."

Emma gave them a confused look as she got a copy of the paper and read the story. As they watched, her demeanor changed.

"Son of a bitch! I'm not going to let them get away with this! Philly is neutral territory and Rodrigues knows this. Now the emergency conference call makes sense. Damn it! I should be in on it."

"Would you mind explaining what's going on?" Andrew asked.

"Fuck it!" Emma swore. "I'll bring you up to speed and if father doesn't like it; tough fucking shit. There's some of this that you may be aware of, but I'll go through it anyway just in case you aren't up to date. Right now, there are six cartels running drugs through North America. Normally we wouldn't care, but the lead enforcer for Mexico has decided to supplement his income with drug money. He's already taken over the Rios cartel and was either destroying or taking over the other cartels. The problem is that he's turning humans to act as guards and enforcers for his drug empire.

The Martinez cartel is run by a vampire who has been running it since the twenties. Outside of his immediate family and a few of his guards, it was always a human operation. That is until Rodrigues set his sights on him. Santiago sent his grandson Carlos to see father about intervening to stop Rodrigues from using his position of enforcer to cover up his illegal activities. According to what I've been told, in the last month he's turned twenty of his men into vampires. I need a big favor from you. Name your price, but I want the assassin alive and able to answer questions."

"We'll need access to our weapons and the crime scene." Andrew said. "Any information on the suspect pool would also be helpful."

"I can have your truck out back in ten minutes with your weapons inside. There will also be a disc with all of the pertinent information. Hand me your cell phone and I'll program my number in for you. Also need to know what you are going to charge me so that I can have it ready." Emma said.

"We'll take a good steak dinner plus any expenses we incur." Andrew said. "We'll be sure to save the receipts."

"Are you sure?" Emma asked shocked. "Isn't there anything else that you want?"

"Yes." Andrew said after thinking for a minute. "A copy of the crime scene reports from last night and you have to explain to your father why we aren't here."

Emma gave him a mocking smile as she handed the cell phone back to him.

"Now you're asking for something hard. Neil's number is in there as well as mine. Keep me posted."

Amelia and Andrew went to their room to change into more appropriate attire. They packed a change of clothes just in case they needed them. As they got ready to go, Andrew wondered what else other than Amelia's powers could be used to restrain a vampire.

As they were heading out, Andrew saw Mitchel and stopped to talk to him.

"What can be used to restrain a vampire?" he asked.

Mitchel handed him a pair of handcuffs.

"These are made from a special metal that inhibits a vampire's abilities and takes away their strength." He said.

"Can I buy a couple of sets?" Andrew asked as he handled the cuffs.

"Why do you need them?" Mitchel asked.

"We're thinking about doing some bounty hunting and may need a couple of sets." Andrew replied.

"I'll talk to Ms. Black about it." Mitchel replied. "If she approves it I can sell you four sets. Let me give her a call now."

Andrew nodded and loaded the duffel bag in the back of the truck. He pulled out the Glock and handed it to Amelia along with an extra clip. He placed the three-eighty under the driver's seat while Amelia placed the Glock under the passenger seat and the extra clip in the glove box.

A few minutes later, Mitchel came out and handed Andrew four sets of the restraints.

"Ms. Black charged them to your account." He said.

Andrew put the cuffs in the duffel bag, programmed the GPS system, and headed toward the crime scene. Amelia booted up the laptop, inserted the disc that Emma had given them and started going through the files.

She stopped to look at the information on Carlos. It was more or less, what she expected to find. He was the suspect in over a dozen murders and the witnesses either forgot or disappeared. Amelia also noted that Carlos had been born vampire and that his father had been killed when Rios firebombed one of their warehouses. His mother, in her grief had gone over the edge and had to be put down. The report also mentioned that his two guards were humans that had been turned twenty years before. Amelia relayed the information to Andrew as she read it.

As she read the files, she made notes on the victims. The next file she opened was on Rodrigues. He had become lead enforcer for Mexico in nineteen-ten. He had run it without incident until the nineteen seventies when he got greedy and took over a little-known cartel.

Initially it was weed and meth, but then he expanded adding crack, weapons, and women to his available merchandise. The latest report was that he was trying to take over the Mexican drug trade. It would get interesting if the rumors that he turned a Mexican Army General were true.

Andrew pulled up in front of the club but it was a beehive of activity. He drove to a side street and found a parking spot. He and Amelia became invisible and went into the club. They could see the forensics team still collecting evidence from the crime.

"I could use a distraction." He said telepathically.

Amelia smiled and went to the kitchen. A few moments later, Andrew heard her scream and then the sound of a door slamming. The four technicians and the officer who was acting as guard charged into the kitchen leaving the evidence that they collected unattended.

Andrew quickly gathered the evidence and the camera that was being used to take pictures of the crime scene. He went through the evidence and saw that outside of the blood spatters and the two ornate knives; most of it was useless. He was sure that the knives belonged to the victims.

When he picked up the knives, he saw the assassin. He was a six-foot Hispanic male with shoulder length brown hair and a vicious looking scar on his neck. It looked as if someone had tried to slit his throat. He had also used a wakizashi and not a katana as a weapon.

Still holding the knife, Andrew watched as the assassin killed one of the victims. One of the victims however had wounded the assassin before dying. That meant that the assassin had to feed and wouldn't have time to dispose of the body.

Amelia alerted him that the crew was returning. He grabbed as much of the evidence as he could and headed for the hummer. As he left, he told Amelia to meet him there. He heard the technicians cursing because they realized that the majority of their evidence was missing. He could see that their clothes were a mess and that they were bruised.

"What did you do to them?" He asked telepathically.

"I poured cooking oil on the floor and dumped the pots and pans on them." Amelia replied with a chuckle. "I figured when they heard me scream they would come rushing in. The oil did the rest. Honestly, it was like watching the Keystone Cops."

Andrew put the evidence in the rear of the truck and got in. Amelia joined him a minute later still chuckling. He handed her the SD card from the camera so that she could load the pictures onto the laptop. He heard the beep from his cellphone indicating that he had messages. When he looked, he saw that there were two from Emma.

Andrew hit speed dial and she picked up after two rings.

"Hi Emma... yes we've already been there. The techs aren't too happy though. Tell your dad that we're fine... yes... where is the local blood supplier? The assassin was injured in the fight and he's going to need blood... yes, he's Hispanic with shoulder length brown hair and a scar across his neck. It looks like someone tried to slit his throat... no I don't think that he'd risk coming there to buy blood... I would monitor the police bands to see if they get any calls about a body drained of blood... I want to check the local supplier and then we'll come by to give you the evidence we have. Yes, we'll talk to your father... just be ready in case the lab calls to check our credentials... we'll see you soon."

Forty minutes later, they were sitting in front of the lab. Andrew slid the three-eighty from under his seat and placed it in the back of his waistband. Amelia retrieved the Glock from under her seat and placed it in her purse. They walked in to see that it was set up much like the facility in Baltimore was.

A thin blonde with brown eyes was sitting behind the desk greeted them snidely.

"What do you want parvulus?"

"Is the manager available?" Andrew asked pleasantly.

"The manger doesn't have time for the likes of you." She replied impatiently. "If you're here to make a purchase, its thirty-five hundred a unit and you go through me. If you aren't here to make a purchase; leave or I'll call security."

Andrew quickly lost his pleasant attitude.

"I tried to be pleasant but you're being a stuck-up bitch. I work for Emma Black; I take it that you know who she is? Now, take me to the manager or I'll be making a call. A security force will be here within minutes and we'll tear this place apart. You won't be able to reopen for a week and you'll have to explain it to your boss."

The woman laughed dismissively.

"Do you know who owns this place? Obviously, you don't so I'll tell you. Her mother Susan Dorchester owns it. Do you really think that she'll close her mother's business?"

"That's good." Amelia said with a smile. "Why don't I give Susan a call?"

"The number is ready." Andrew said as he handed her the phone. "Just hit send."

"Alright, the fun is over." The woman behind the desk snorted. "If you don't leave right now; I'm calling security."

"Tell your boss that we'll be out front." Andrew said.

Amelia hit the send button as they walked toward the door.

"Hi Susan, its Amelia... sorry to bother you but the receptionist at your Philly location is refusing to let us see the manager... no we don't need blood. We're helping your daughter... we're out front, the receptionist threatened to call security... ok... thanks... we'll see you tomorrow."

"Is everything alright?" Andrew asked.

'It's fine." Amelia replied. "She thanked us for not pushing the issue and for calling her. She said to give her five minutes and it should be straightened out."

A few minutes later, fiftyish, balding vampire came out.

"Mr. and Mrs. Barnes? I'm Stephan Noah. I must apologize, I had no idea that my receptionist was interfering with your work. Please come into my office so that I may be of assistance to you."

Andrew plastered a smile on his face.

"Thank you. Your cooperation is appreciated.

When they walked past the receptionist, she wouldn't make eye contact.

"He's a lying sack of shit." Amelia said telepathically. "He knew what she was doing because he told her to do it. He's also charging extra for the blood and pocketing the difference. The receptionist is afraid of him."

"Alright, let's get the information that we need and then we'll handle the rest of it." Andrew replied.

Once they were in the office and sitting, Andrew began asking questions.

"Did you sell blood to an injured Hispanic male? He would have had a scar that ran across his neck and he would have been in late last night or early this morning. You might have also gotten a clean-up call from him."

"No, I didn't." Noah replied. "But I can check with the night manager."

"Ask if he sold to any Hispanic males. The gentleman that we're looking for may not have been working alone. While you do that, I'm going to talk to your receptionist in case she was the one who sold it to him or received any phone calls."

"I can do that for you." Noah said quickly.

"No thanks... I'll talk to her while you help my mate. Is there a reason why you don't want me to talk to her?" Amelia asked.

"Ummm Susan warned me about you." he replied after a moment. "I don't want to have to replace my receptionist.

Amelia knew that he was lying. As soon as they left, he was going to kill the receptionists and replace her.

"I promise not to harm her." Amelia said as she walked out of the office.

Noah tried to hide his nervousness. He knew that Amelia knew that he had lied. He stared at her as she walked out and was still staring when Andrew started tapping on the phone.

"If you don't mind, we're in a bit of a hurry. We're late for a meeting with Mr. Black."

"I'm sorry." Noah said sheepishly. "But your mate is a remarkable woman."

When Amelia reached the receptionist, she noticed a couple of humans waiting in the reception area. She ignored them and spoke to the receptionist.

"Did a Hispanic male with a scar across his neck come in for blood or any other services?"

The receptionist became nervous and looked around the room before replying.

"I'm sorry about earlier. Mr. Noah is trying to get rid of all but a few select clients. The man that you're looking for was in here yesterday morning. Mr. Noah took care of him."

Amelia sent the information to Andrew and then spoke to the receptionist.

"I want you to gather your things; you're leaving with us. Don't panic, we're doing this to save your life."

The receptionist gave Amelia a wary look and then nodded.

"I'm sorry, but no one fitting that description bought blood or ordered services last night or today. My receptionist may have helped him."

"What about the man that you took care of yesterday morning?" Andrew asked.

Noah paled and became nervous. He silently cursed his air headed receptionist and put a weak smile on his face.

"That was Mr. Santos. He's an old associate from Barbados. He just stopped in to say hello and he didn't purchase any blood."

"I guess that it's a coincidence that Mr. Santos had a scar across his throat?" Andrew asked. "You're coming with us to answer a few questions. I'm sure that Ms. Black would love to meet you."

"You can't do this!" Noah protested. "You have no right!"

Andrew however didn't agree. He grabbed Noah, slammed him across the desk, and handcuffed him.

"You should have cooperated." He said as he patted the man down. "You could have walked out of here with your dignity."

Andrew sat the man back in his chair and called Emma.

"Hi, I have a question for you... Is there someone who could run your mom's shop for a few days?... I have him in handcuffs. I'm sure that you're going to want to talk to him and if what Amelia says is true; you mom will want to talk to him too. I'll call her if you like... tell your father not to get his panties in a bunch, we'll be there soon. "I'll call her... Neil is coming over? Good... what do you know about the head of security for this place? Ok... we'll see you then."

"Amelia." Andrew called telepathically, "we're going to be getting a lot of company in about twenty minutes. Emma, Neil and a security detachment are on their way."

Andrew looked at Noah with a small grin on his face.

"Perhaps you would like to spare yourself some pain and tell me what you know before Ms. Black gets here." He said.

"He'll kill me if I say anything." Noah whimpered.

Andrew pulled the pistol from his waistband and put it against his knee.

"What do you think I'll do to you?" he asked. "When you blow a human knee cap apart, it's a onetime thing. I wonder how many times I can blow your kneecap out. Shall we find out?"

"No! For the love of god don't shoot! I'll tell you what you want to know!"

"I'm waiting." Andrew said.

There was a tremor in Noah's voice as he began speaking.

"I was contacted by a man who claimed to be a representative of Mr. Rodrigues the lead enforcer for Mexico. He wanted to use us to distribute drugs and women all over the city. I knew that Susan wouldn't have gone for it simply because it would have drawn the attention of the human authorities. However, the money was too good to pass up so I agreed to do it without Susan's knowledge. At first, it was just a couple of shipments a month, but now its three to five a week for drugs and at least two shipments a month of women. I was allowed to tap the women for blood and keep the money that we normally paid our donors.

I even started dating a woman in Black's office so I could monitor what was happening there. Between the innocent pillow talk and compulsion, I was kept informed. Two weeks ago, Becky told me that she overheard that Santiago Martinez had been in contact with Mr. Black. According to her, he wanted to talk to

Mr. Black about Rodrigues using his position to commit crimes, which included turning vampires who would be loyal to him.

I was afraid that he knew about me so I called my contact. They told me to find out where the Martinez party was staying and that he would send a man to handle it. He met me here yesterday and I gave him blood and the information about the room I had reserved for him. I put him up at the Holiday Inn express over by the airport. The room is his until tomorrow but his flight leaves at three-twenty am. His name is Antonio Munoz and he's staying in room one-ten."

"Do you have a number where he can be reached?" Andrew asked.

"I gave him a burn phone." Noah replied. "If you want the number, then we deal for it plus the location of the disc that has all of my contacts and shipping information on it."

"What do you want in exchange?" Andrew asked.

"Let me go before Ms. Black gets here."

"I could start with your knee and then move on to other areas." Andrew said as he moved the gun to Noah's groin. "Do you think that will grow back?"

Andrew watched as a bead of sweat formed across the vampire's forehead.

"Don't worry." Andrew said. "I don't have time for games. I'll let my mate handle you." Andrew said as he pushed the intercom button. "Amelia my love, could you come in here?"

A moment later, Amelia was in the office. Andrew wrapped an arm around her when she stood next to him.

"I'm sure you remember her." he said. "Your eyes were glued to her ass when she walked out of the door. Don't worry. I find myself doing the same thing; but for a much different reason. The reason that I called her back in is because she has the ability to read minds. I know that you're thinking that you can block her and under normal circumstances, you might be able to do that. However, if you try, I'll take great pleasure in seeing how many times I can blow your kneecap out before it won't grow back anymore. If you fight her, I'll ask my lovely mate to wipe every thought from your head. You'll be nothing but a dribbling fool."

Noah's shoulders slumped in defeat as he lowered his barriers so that Amelia could search his memories. He had heard about what she did to Gregori Demidov and didn't want to end up like that. He felt her presence as she examined his memories experiencing them as if she was him.

"You are one sick son of a bitch." She said when she was done. "You made your father watch as you drained your mother and sister."

Charles and Emma arrived a few minutes later.

"Why the hell is Stephen in handcuffs?" Charles demanded. "You'd better have a damned good reason for it!"

"Charles! You've got to help me!" Noah said. "They're crazy! They're accusing me of all kinds of shit. He threatened to shoot me and then have her destroy my mind!"

"I'm waiting for an explanation." Charles said looking at Amelia and then Andrew. "I've known Stephen for almost a century."

"He's the one who helped the assassin kill Carlos Martinez." Andrew replied. "We have the assassin's name, room number and the time his flight leaves. Your friend has been using the office to smuggle drugs and women and he's been skimming your profits."

Charles' eyes narrowed in anger. He knew that there had been some irregularities that Susan had planned to address; but she hadn't indicated that it was anything serious. He had believed that they were simple errors in communication.

"Stephen, you'd better start talking.' Charles said.

"Charles," Stephen said, "We've been friends for almost a century! Surely you don't believe that I would do anything to jeopardize that friendship... are you going to believe a couple of parvulus over me?"

"Do you have any proof?" Charles asked Andrew.

Amelia knew how to prove it; but didn't know where the knowledge came from. She walked over to Charles, placed her hands on his face, and locked her eyes onto his.

"These are his thoughts." She said.

Charles' eyes widened as Amelia shared Stephen's memories with him. He was enthralled with what was happening. There was no pain; just pressure and a weird sensation that he couldn't quite describe. It felt as if five people were trying to force their way through a doorway designed for two.

Amelia released her hold on him and stepped back. It had only been for a couple of minutes, but to Charles; it had felt much longer. He stood silent for a few minutes trying to process the information that Amelia had shared with him.

Everyone watched as Amelia placed her hands-on Charles' face. Her eyes began to glow as she murmured something about his memories. Charles' body had gone as stiff as a board and his eyes seemed captivated by her. It was almost as if she was a snake and he was the prey.

Emma was going to pull him away from Amelia, but Andrew stopped her. She began to shout for help but by the time, security came rushing in; Amelia had already released Charles.

Amelia began to slump to the floor but was caught by Andrew.

"Emma, your father is fine." She said. "He is processing the information that I gave him."

Andrew helped Amelia to a chair and let her sit for a moment. After a couple of minutes that seemed like hours, Charles started to blink rapidly and began to collapse. Andrew and a very angry looking security man helped him to a seat. Emma was immediately at her father's side.

"Dad? Are you all right? Talk to me."

Charles shook his head to clear the cobwebs.

"Sweetie, I'm fine; but that was one hell of an experience. Amelia do me a favor and warn me the next time."

He turned to look at Stephen.

"Your ass is mine." He said quietly. "Mitchel get that piece of shit out of here and contact team two; they have a pickup to do."

"Dad, what did she do to you?" Emma asked. "It scared the hell out of me."

"She did something that I had only heard about." Charles replied. "She shared the memories that she mined from Stephen with me. It was a unique experience."

"I'm sorry." Amelia said. "I wasn't even sure that it would work. I wanted to get the information to you quickly; I hope that I didn't hurt you."

"No, you didn't hurt me." Charles replied with a smile. "It was interesting to say the least. I gather that the two of you would like to be present when we capture the assassin?"

"Yes." Andrew replied speaking for the both of them. "If you like, we could go stake the place out. We'll call you if he starts to move."

"That would be great." Charles replied. "I don't want to lose this asshole. It will make removing Rodrigues much easier. Do you know where the hotel is?"

"We have the address and a GPS system so we're good." Andrew replied.

Andrew and Amelia got into the truck and drove to the hotel where the assassin was staying. Once there they found a spot where they could watch the main entrance and the only road in and out of the hotel parking lot.

"This isn't exactly an inconspicuous stake out vehicle." Amelia said as she looked around the hummer."

"Maybe not." Andrew replied with a chuckle, "But how many police agencies could afford an H-3?"

"True." Amelia conceded. "How do we know that he's in there?" she asked.

"I was thinking about going in to rent a room and compelling the clerk into giving me information and then erasing his memory." Andrew replied.

"Pull up front and act like you're on the phone." Amelia said. 'I'll go in and see what I can find out."

"Fine, but be careful that he doesn't spot you." Andrew said as he started the hummer. "We don't want to tip him off."

"I've done this a time or two before." Amelia replied. "And besides, my mental skills are much better than yours."

CHAPTER 7

***

Amelia walked into the hotel and was headed for the counter when she saw the vampire, they were looking for coming out of the business center. She sensed that he was tense but didn't think that he noticed her. She played it cool and decided to see about renting a room.

"Do you have any rooms available?" she asked when she got to the counter.

"Yes, we do." The clerk replied. "How many will be staying in the room?" he asked.

"There will be just two of us." Amelia replied. "We also prefer the bottom floor."

"How long will you be staying?" The clerk asked.

"Three nights." Amelia replied.

She handed the clerk a credit card and began filling out the registration paperwork.

"Will he ever get off the damned phone?" she asked as she looked toward the front door.

The man stifled a chuckle as he handed her a room key.

"Room one-twelve." He said. "It's through that door and it's the third room to the right. The ice and vending machines are across the hall from it."

"Thank you," she said with a polite smile.

She stormed out of the hotel and opened the door to the truck.

"For the love of Christ!" she exclaimed. "Will you get off of that damned phone? I've got a room and I'm hungry!"

"This is an important call." Andrew replied. 'What's the room number? I'll park the truck and be up as soon as I'm done with this phone call."

"He's here." Amelia said telepathically. "I just saw him come out of the business center."

"Good." Andrew replied. "I'll call Charles and let him know. You check to be sure that we can watch him from our room and let me know if we can't."

Amelia grabbed the duffle bag with their clothes in it. She checked the Glock to be sure that it had a full clip and that the first round was chambered and safe before putting it in the bag.

"I'm going to take a shower and try to lay down for a while." She said. "Try not to take too long."

Andrew nodded.

"I'll grab the other bag and the laptop." He said still holding the phone to his ear.

Amelia walked into the hotel and saw the assassin at the soda machine. She had the impression that he was going to attack her.

"Andrew, I need you; I think he spotted me." She said telepathically.

Antonio Munoz pulled a pistol with a silencer on it out of his pocket.

"Agent Hensley," He said with a thick accent, "let's keep this civil. I have no desire to hurt someone under the protection of Mr. Black. I know that you have already warned your mate. Tell him to come to my room where the three of us can talk. I must warn you that these are exploding bullet. They may not kill you, but they will incapacitate you making it easier to finish you. So please senorita; do not do anything stupid."

"He has a gun with exploding bullet." Amelia sent to Andrew. "He wants us to go to his room so we can talk."

"He's coming." Amelia said. "You know that you won't leave, here don't you?"

"We shall see." Antonio said with a smile. "Now move."

Amelia started to move toward his room and felt the cold steel of the silencer press against the back of her head.

"I am sorry that you have to die." Antonio muttered.

"Andrew, I'm sorry; I will always love you."

She heard the soft cough of the silenced gun firing and a burning sensation on her neck.

Andrew heard Amelia telepathically say that she was sorry and Good-bye. He burst through the front doors of the hotel ripping them off the frame as he rushed into the hall where Amelia was. When he saw the gun to the back of her head, everything seemed to go into slow motion. Andrew used his telekinesis to push the gun away from his mate just as he heard the weapon discharge. He watched in horror as he saw Amelia drop to the floor.

When the smell of Amelia's blood hit him, he saw red and gave himself over to his primal side. Andrew performed a flying tackle driving them both through the door of Antonio's room. The two of them crashed into the far wall as Andrew jammed claw like fingernails in to Antonio's lower back wrapped his fingers around the base of his spine snapping it off and ripped it out of his body and threw it to the floor. Antonio let lose an inhuman howl of pain. Antonio's lower half of his body was crippled and even with a vampire's regenerative abilities he knew it was most likely permanent. Andrew flipped him over and unleashed blow after blow in to his face and chest each blow smashed something else. Antonio was no longer moving.

Amelia was sure she was going to die permanently this time. Here only regret is what it would do to Andrew she prayed that he would find some way to overcome her death. She heard the soft cough of the silenced gun as it discharged and wondered if she would still be able to go to heaven. She felt a burning sensation as the bullet passed through the side of her neck and the world went fuzzy as she felt her legs give out. After a few moments, the world started to refocus and she realized the wound to the side of her neck was serious but far from fatal.

It took her a few minutes for her to heal enough for her to regain her senses. She opened her eyes, looked around, and saw Andrew was in the process of beating Antonio to death. As her eyes focused more, she could see blood splattered from floor to ceiling and. Amelia knew that the humans were watching and only hoped that Charles' people would get here soon. She quickly pushed into Andrew mind. "Love we need him alive, please stop." She pleaded through their bond.

Andrew didn't even so much as acknowledge her all she could sense through their bond was all consuming rage that blinded him to everything but he needs to kill. She began to worry when she could find no part of the man she knew through their bond. She rose to her feet but was unsteady as waves of Dizziness and nausea over took her. She closed her eyes until they passed then slowly approached Andrew calling to him through their bond. Amelia could sense the terrified humans and knew they didn't have long until the police showed up. Just as she got close enough to touch him, he quickly rose and spun on her. He had a wild look in his eyes and for a fleeting moment, Amelia thought he might attack her but he just stood there looking at her as if he was trying to recall who she was

"Love I need you," Amelia whispered, as she pulled Andrew into a fierce hug.

Amelia declaration had the desired effect it started his logical mind working again. He quickly wrapped his arms around her and let her scent wash over him. Slowly the closeness to his mate and her sending images of the two of them together was allowing him to reign in his feral side "My god, I thought I lost you forever. I have never felt so empty in my life." Andrew quietly confessed as tears started to flow down the side of his face.

Amelia said nothing just held on to him for dear life allowing him to regain control of himself. She would deal with the humans when it became necessary. At this moment, her only concern was for her mate and his state of mind. She could feel he was still on the razor edge of sanity and it wouldn't take much for his feral side to reassert itself and if that happened, she was, afraid she would lose him forever.

Charles had been on the phone with Andrew. He had just confirmed that their target was there and gave him the room number when he heard Andrew say he has her at gunpoint and then the phone fell. He and the strike team were within ten minutes of the hotel. He and his strike team flooded into the hotel and seized control they cordoned off the area and would control the scene. He had left a couple of his people to deal with the human authorities and press. He wondered how much damage control he would have to do an experienced vampire who had a mate threatened was bad enough but parvulus could go on a rampage and kill everyone in the hotel.

When he finally entered the hallway, where Amelia and Andrew were, to say he was shock would have been an understatement. He saw a large pool of blood that had Amelia's scent staining the carpet. He looked down the hallway and saw Amelia with her arms wrapped around Andrew his eyes were still black and lifeless. Charles had the rest of his people hold back and he cautiously approached the two of them. As he got a view into the room it looked like just about every surface had blood splattered on it. He stopped before getting too close to Amelia and Andrew; he didn't want to cause Andrew to attack him. He could see what was left of Antonio he had no distinguishing facial features and the only sign that he was still alive was the soft gurgling sound he mad as he tried to breathe.

"Perhaps you should take Andrew into one of the other rooms here so he can finish calming down. Then get cleaned up and I will bring you some blood to aid with your healing," Charles suggested. He was trying to see just how bad Antonio was hurt when he noticed a four-inch piece of his spine lying on the floor. He was shocked to see the amount of devastation Andrew had done to Antonio.

Amelia nodded and started to lead Andrew from the room. Charles made sure that everyone gave them a wide berth so as not to inflame and already volatile Andrew. As soon as the two of them were in the room Charles placed two of his people on the door with order to keep the two of them in there until he said it was all right to let them out. He wasn't worried about Amelia but knew if he tried to separate them right now Andrew would lose himself.

He had one of his men run out and get overalls for them and a couple of bottles of blood. He had Susan start package blood in soda style bottles one it made it easier to transport and secondly since the bottles were opaque it made it harder to see what was inside. Franklin gave Charles the items, he had requested. "Charles the human authorities have been dealt with. The guest and staff have had the memories altered.

What do you want us to do with their hummer? It is on the lot with keys in the ignition," Franklin reported. Then as an afterthought he added," Antonio is alive but just barely. He will most likely be a paraplegic. Andrew smashed his skull and crushed part of his brain. According to Heidi it will be a few days until we can tell the extent of the brain damage, however she feels it will be extensive."

"I love Hummers, but it is a lousy choice for undercover work because everyone notices them. Have Louise take it to Sanguinem and park it in the underground garage. Ask Heidi to keep me posted on Antonio's condition. I'm hoping to be able to use him as a witness against Rodrigues." Charles instructed he then headed to the room that Amelia was using. He softly knocked on the door and waited.

Andrew held on to Amelia who was still shaking and not believing she was alive. When he heard, the pistol shot and saw her fall he was sure she was gone. Andrew decided he didn't want to live anymore and just gave himself over to the feral beast that now lives within him. From that moment, until he heard Amelia's plea, he had no recollection of what he had done. Even now, he couldn't suppress his feral side and was not even sure if he should.

Amelia was weakened by her blood lose, but right now her only concern was Andrew. His eyes had still not changed back and he was acting like a caged tiger. He had refused to let her go, the only time he had spoken was when they were in the hall when he first found out she was still alive. He tensed and locked his eyes on the door when someone had knocked on it. Amelia could sense it was Charles on the other side of the door. "Love I am going to answer the door it is just Charles," Amelia said telepathically.

"The door is open," She called out after Andrew refused to let her go.

Charles slowly opened the door and stepped in. "I have some blood for you. How is he doing?" Charles said.

"I have never seen him like this. He refuses to let me go and his eyes have not changed back. Charles what is a matter with him? And more importantly how do I help him?" Amelia nervously pleaded.

The whole time they spoke Andrew's eyes followed Charles' every movement like a snake watching a mongoose. He was ready to strike at the slightest provocation. Charles knowing the danger of the state that he was in kept his movements slow and deliberate." By stop worrying and doing what you are doing. It will take some time for him to rein in his feral side. Just stay at his side and keep reassuring him you are alright." Charles responded reassuringly.

He laid the items down on the table and exited the room. He reminded the two men he had guarding the door no one in or out without his permission. He exited the hotel for some privacy as he dialed the familiar number on his cell. After the second ring, he heard Susan's voice greet him. "Hi, we may have a problem." He said.

Charles had already called apprising her of the situation caused by Stephan. The fucking idiot had to use her place to smuggle and store illegal drugs and human slaves. No one really care about the drug smuggling except that it could garner the attention of the human authorities and they could inadvertently cause them to find out the true purpose of Bio Medtronic. However, trafficking in human slaves was a different animal. It would cause the humans to investigate on a national and possible international level. That kind of attention was something every vampire feared. Susan knew she was going to have a lot to answer for and the other enforcers would demand her record be opened up to their investigation. She would need to prove she had no part in the smuggling of the humans. This fiasco was going to cost her dearly and she just hoped that when it was finished, she would be allowed to deal with Stephan in her own way.

The other nightmare was the assassination of the three vampires in the human nightclub the assassination itself was of little concern outside of the victims being under Charles personal protection. It was common knowledge that you dealt with those kinds of affairs outside the prying eyes of the human authorities and you never walk into a club full of humans and decapitate three other vampires. Thankfully, Amelia and Andrew had retrieved the evidence before the humans could process it and that it did not really concern her yet.

"What happened now?" Susan asked her voice a mixture of concern and frustration.

Charles brought Susan up to date. He expressed his concern that Andrew's eyes had not reverted to normal. Charles did add that he was encouraged that Andrew hadn't attacked him when he gave Amelia blood. Charles informed her that he had the two of them isolated in a room. The door is guarded by his security men." As much as I hate to say this, I may have to put him down for everyone's safety," Charles said solemnly.

"I hope it doesn't come to that, you will lose them both and possible make an enemy of Catherine. I will be there in about forty-five minutes please don't make any decision until I get there." Susan replied.

Amelia drank a bottle of blood while she wondered how to settle Andrew down. She was glad to feel her strength return and the Queasiness in her stomach settled. She led Andrew to the bathroom for a long shower. She stripped the clothes off both of them She washed the blood off him then herself. She made him stay under the stream while she slowly massaged his shoulders. Slowly his eyes started to revert to their normal color.

"Are you OK?" Andrew asked his tone full of concern.

"I am OK, but love I was ..." Amelia replied.

"I know, you were set up," Andrew interrupted

"He knew I use to be a FBI agent and that we were here for him; not just that I was but WE. I had my mind shielded." Amelia stated her voice full of concern.

Andrew hugged Amelia and kissed her forehead." Do you still have your weapon?" Andrew asked not releasing the embrace.

"No I left it in the duffel bag in the hall. Why?" Amelia replied.

Andrew released the embrace then handed her a set of the overalls. The two of them dressed quickly Andrew once again cleaning their shoes up. "This is getting to be a habit." He quipped.

Once he was finished and the two of them were dressed, he retrieved the three-eighty from the counter where Amelia had laid it and handed it her. She quickly checked to make sure the gun was loaded and safe, more out of habit then need. She then placed the weapon in her pocket.

Andrew handed Amelia the other bottle of blood and insisted that she drink it all. "Love we need to get to that business center and see if we can find out who tipped Antonio off. I hate to think this but it can only be Charles or one of his people, no one else knew who we were here."

Amelia hoped that Andrew was wrong and that it was someone else. She followed Andrew to the door hoping to get their answers. Andrew opened the door to leave. He was stopped by two large vampires blocking their way. "I am sorry, but I am ordered to detain you until Mr. Black releases you. I will summon him, please wait inside," The Larger vampire stated in a firm but calm voice.

Andrew didn't argue because he knew it was pointless. He stepped back into the room and closed the door. He quickly surveyed the room. "We need to get out of here. That window looks like our best option," He mentally said

"Damn I really thought we could trust Black. What are we going to do now? And how do we help Catherine and Scott?" Amelia replied with telepathy.

"I not sure yet, I think they are safe for the moment. Let's get out of here then we can decide." Andrew suggested mentally. He then opened the window and the two of them turned invisible as they slipped out into the night.

Andrew started to go to where he had parked the H-3 but saw it was gone. Andrew quickly picked Amelia up and speed away from the hotel at his top speed. He headed towards the heart of town. Once he was sure that they were a reasonable distance away, he placed Amelia back on her feet. They wondered around until they found a Target and used the ATM machine. The two of them were thankful that they still had Andrew's wallet and access to cash. The downside was it would be a relatively easy task to trace them if they kept using the card.

"Love while I get us some fresh clothes and a new cell phone you call Catherine. Warn her to get away and make sure they have their cells so we can contact them to arrange to meet up." Andrew said telepathically.

Andrew quickly picked out clothes for the two of them he included a medium size purse so Amelia could conceal the gun and a new burn phone. This time he even got them each a new pair of Reeboks. He grabbed some snack food and drinks then paid for their purchases with his card wanting to save their precious cash. As he was exited, he saw that Amelia was still on the phone so he went out and found a place to change while he waited for her.

Charles received word that Andrew was trying to leave their room From Hank and went to meet with them straight away." Hank, did Andrew give you any trouble about not letting him leave?" Charles inquired trying to gauge Andrew's mental state.

"He clearly wasn't happy but didn't say a word just went back in the room and closed the door," Hank replied earnestly.

"How was his state of mind? Did he seem feral in any way? Were his eyes normal?" Charles asked.

"He seemed normal to me. He didn't get combative or aggressive. I would have to say that he was most definitely in control of his primal side since he didn't attack. You know how the beast hates to be caged. His eyes were normal with no signs of any wildness," Hank responded honestly.

Charles let out a small sigh of relief as he knocked on the door and paused for a few minutes to wait for an answer. When no answer came, he opened the door. "Andrew! Amelia! It is me Charles," He called out. He sensed there was no one in the room and quickly opened the door the rest of the way and saw the window opened with the screen removed." Damn it! They have left," Charles exclaimed in surprise.

The two security men rushed into the room in disbelief." I am sorry Mr. Black. I didn't sense he was going to attempt to escape." Hank responded.

Charles sighed shaking his head." I should have expected this. Hank, start a search I want them located.

Do not make contact with them; just watch them discreetly. As soon as they are located, I want to be notified," Charles said bemused.

Susan and Gloria walked into the room just as Charles finished speaking." Is there a problem, lover?" Susan inquired as she raised her eyebrow.

"Amelia and Andrew left without saying goodbye," Charles responded shaking his head while pointing at the window.

Susan looked at Gloria and motioned with her eyes. Gloria nodded and left the room to go find the two of them. Susan knew that if anyone could find them it would be Gloria, one of her many talents was tracking people. "Charles! Why the fuck were they being held as prisoners?" Susan demanded a stern look on her face had most of the others in the room looking to leave.

Charles blew out a frustrated breath the last thing he needed now; was Susan upset with him. "Clear the room." Charles announced in a loud voice.

He watched to make sure everyone heeded his command. He took Susan in his arms." Amor, the only reason I had them detained was for everyone's safety. Andrew had given himself over to his primal side. He was having trouble reining it back in. I placed the two of them in this room to allow Amelia time to help Andrew without outside influences hampering her. I had to place security on them, for we both know what could have happened if he lost control. I guess I should have explained the security to Amelia but she was already stressed enough and I did not want to add to it." Charles explained hoping it would satisfy Susan.

"OK I can understand that and I am sure so will Amelia and Andrew once we explain it. What I can't understand is why they ran before giving you a chance to explain." Susan replied with a much softer demeanor.

"Most likely because they know they were set-up or at least suspect it strongly. The two of them probably are not sure whom to trust right now." Charles quietly whispered.

"Why do you think that? Who would dare try to betray you like that?" Susan asked shocked, barely able to maintain her composure.

Charles handed Susan a couple dozen sheets of printer paper. The papers contained complete dossier on Amelia and Andrew. The files not only contained pictures of the both of them but also their work histories and location all know living family members. The lasts sheet was orders for him to kill them both and a note about a ticket to Denver for him at the airport.

Susan didn't need to read the dossier; she had prepared it for Charles when he decided that they might be a useful addition to the organization. The family information was compiled in case they went rogue. Rogue vampires always seemed to seek out living family members and it never ends well for the living family members. Normally this information is held by the sire or coven leader however since the two of them had neither, Charles decided since he was going to help them, he would hold onto the information.

Susan thought over who would possibly have access to this information and the list was disturbing to say the least. Charles, Gloria, Emma, Neil, Andrea, and possibly Mitchel besides herself, the list was all family or people she considered as close as family. The very thought that one of these people had betrayed Charles and her was sickening and it tore at her heart.

While she was lost in her thoughts, her cell phone rang, forcing back to the here and now. "Hello, what did you find?" Susan asked expectantly.

"They went out the window and headed towards downtown. Andrew is carrying Amelia." Gloria responded.

"How do you know he is carrying her? And where the hell are you?" Susan inquired.

"I tracked them to a muddy field about a mile from the hotel. There was only one set of footprints and by the length of the stride he was moving," Gloria replied.

"Are you going to keep tracking them or are you coming back?" Susan asked.

"Unless you order me not to, I'm finding them. When I do what do you want me to do?" Gloria inquired.

"When you find them make contact and ask them to call me and be extra careful. I will join you as soon as I can slip out of here," Susan commanded.

"Susan what the hell is going on, Are you safe?" Gloria demanded. Worry crept into her voice.

Susan saw Charles talking to Mitch as the two of them headed towards her." OK Gloria, keep me up to date on your location and status. When you locate them, contact me immediately," Susan said changing the subject.

Susan quickly hung up her phone and shielded her mind against intrusion. She tried to give off a nonchalant air about her as she headed towards Charles. She stopped a step or so behind Charles while he finished talking with Mitch.

Charles knew the minute that Susan had shielded her mind. He wondered what had her so worried even though he gave no visible sign anything was wrong. When he was done with Mitch he immediately, lead Susan to a secluded spot. "What has you on such high alert?" Charles inquired.

"What makes you think I am on high alert, Charles?" Susan responded keeping her expression and tone carefully neutral.

"How about knowing you for nearly twenty centuries?" Charles countered, his body language clearly saying, "I'm not impressed."

"What did you think that I would do once you showed me those papers? Most of them were from the dossier that I sent to you by carrier. Between both of our organizations, I can only come up with a total of ten people that had access to them, two of which are standing right here. My god Charles one of the main suspects is our own daughter!" Susan responded. Her eyes showed just how much the obvious betrayal had hurt her. Susan quickly buried her feelings and resumed her calm facade.

"I know love that is why I want you personally to take charge of who betrayed us. You have my full authority to do what you must to find out and bring guilty person or persons to me. Then we will judge them together," Charles decreed then pulled Susan into a hug and kissed her on the top of her head as he whispered, "I love you."

Susan relaxed into Charles embrace and allowed the tension to be drawn from her body. She wrapped her arms around Charles' neck and pulled him into passionate kiss." God, how I have missed you," Susan softly whispered.

Susan then broke the embrace replacing her mask of indifference. "What about Andrew and Amelia?" She asked.

"I can't think of a better person to find them then Gloria, can you? " Charles replied.

"No, I can't. What do you want to do once we find them?" Susan asked.

"I would like to arrange a place I can talk to them. I am even willing to let them to name the place, as long as it is within reason." Charles answered honestly.

Susan pulled her cell out and started to dial Emma's number." I'm going to explain everything to Catherine. I hope that she will be willing to help us when they call her," Susan said.

Charles acknowledged her with a wave he was already on his cell answering a call he had ignored three times while talking with Susan. Susan told Catherine everything and explained the reason why they had to isolate the two of them. Susan promised her that all she wanted was a chance to explain everything. Catherine said she would ask them to call her if she heard from them but she stated clearly, that she wouldn't betray them.

Amelia headed to the two pay phones at the front of the store. One of the phones was occupied and the other was out of order. She waited while the man finished, thank fully he keep it short. Amelia dialed

Catherine's cell number and while it rang, she discretely kept looking around for threats. She was counting on the fact that they wouldn't try anything in a crowded store.

As soon as she heard the call connect, and before Catherine could speak." Please just listen. Andrew and I were set-up and I were almost killed. We were betrayed by Charles or someone in his organization. Is anyone associated with Charles in the room with you? Is Scott with you?"

"Umm yes and yes," Catherine responded quietly as she casually went to a more private spot to talk.

"Can the two of you slip away? If you can, procure transportation and leave. Make sure you have your cell phones with you and we will contact you." Amelia said.

"Amelia I am where I can talk now. There is no way for us to leave undetected but we aren't prisoners here we can come and go as we please. I have the keys to the Hummer. Where are you?" Catherine asked.

"Listen to me I want you and Scott to take the Hummer and go. Get somewhere safe and stay out of sight. Do not tell anyone where you are going. Once it is safe to do so, we will contact you." Amelia pleaded.

"Amelia, we are as safe as we can be. I talked to Susan and they're aware that you were set-up. Susan asked that you contact Gloria and no one else. Charles was not behind this and he wants a chance to explain everything to you. Please trust me and call Gloria before you do anything else," Catherine begged.

"I will talk to Andrew about it and we will call you in a day or two. We will be fine; you just make sure you take care of yourself and that baby," Amelia responded. She got the feeling someone was watching her. She turned around slowly and saw Gloria Standing there staring at her. She continued quietly, "I have to go and I hope you were right about Gloria. She is standing here looking at me. I will talk to you later. I hope."

"Hun, Gloria is standing out front of the store looking at me." Amelia sent mentally.

"I know I am working my way behind her as we speak. Please tell me you have that gun handy," Andrew responded the same way.

"I do and I am coming out. Are you in position?" Amelia telepathically said. She started walking slowly towards the door.

"Yup, I hope I don't ruin my new clothes," Andrew responded as before.

Amelia came out of the store and stepped about ten feet from Gloria. Gloria cautiously closed the distance all the while she kept glancing to where Andrew was trying to determine if he was going to attack. She could see that Andrew was relaxed but Amelia was nervous and tensed but surprisingly neither of them showed any fear. "All I want to do is talk to you and Andrew. Can the three of us go somewhere more private so we can talk," Gloria asked cautiously.

Andrew stepped back into the shadows became visible. He could tell by the way that Gloria kept looking at him that she knew he was there. He stepped beside Amelia and handed her the bag. "Let her get changed, then we will talk," Andrew responded.

The three of them walked around a corner of the building. Amelia turned invisible and quickly changed her clothes. Amelia returned to being visible and the three of them stood there a moment sizing each other up. Andrew and Amelia were trying to decide if they could trust Gloria. "There is a small cafe down the street where we can get a coffee and we can talk. Would the two of you do me a favor and allow me to call Susan. She is worried about the two of you and I want to let her know you are OK," Gloria requested

Amelia visibly relaxed she could sense no deceit from Gloria and the only other vampire she sensed was her mate. Andrew on the other hand was still on alert. Even though he could sense no other vampires besides the three of them he still wasn't convinced, that this wasn't a trap. "Andrew darling, I was hoping that you would trust me," Gloria said, a little hurt.

"I do trust you, if I didn't, I would have attacked you on sight. I am worried that Black may have had you followed. I am sure you are as expendable as we obviously are," Andrew dispassionately said, as he looked Gloria directly in the eyes.

"Andrew what happened? I know that the two of you were attacked but there is something else going on. Susan wanted me to contact her, without Charles knowing. She is never gone behind his back before. Please, I am asking you as a friend tell me what happened." Gloria beseeched.

Andrew did not say anything at first; he just started leading them away from the area. He finally found a secluded spot and stopped; he quickly looked around to make sure no one was around. He started describing the events of the day in detail. He explained that Emma had asked them to investigate the assassinations at a human club. He explained about Stephen's illegal activities and his involvement with Antonio. He also told her that Antonio had recognized Amelia and knew that she was a former FBI agent and that they were there for him.

He explained that the only people knew that they were there for Antonio was Blacks' own inner circle. Finally, he explained that Charles had locked them in a room and placed guard and the door. He also had moved their vehicle effectively trapping them there. "If he wasn't going to eliminate us, why would he lock us in that room and take away transportation?" Andrew demanded.

Gloria could not believe what she was hearing; one of Charles' closest associates had betrayed him. From what Andrew said, the most likely suspect was Emma his own daughter. She now understood why Susan was being so cautious. Gloria was now worried for Susan she could be in danger. "Andrew, will you please trust Susan enough to allow me to call her. She needs to know what is going on and I will get her to come alone," Gloria requested.

"I want some were more public than a small cafe," he responded after considering for a few minutes. He quickly surveyed his surroundings, showing McDonald's across from the mall. He then continued, "I hope you like McDonald's sweet tea. Call Susan and have her meet you here and please don't mention us. It isn't, I don't trust Susan; I'm just afraid someone might listen in and follow her," Andrew said.

Gloria didn't like lying to Susan but she knew that she would understand this instance. Gloria was one the few vampires that could lie to her sire. The fact that Gloria could tell a lie to anyone, and it not be detected was a blessing in her work. That ability coupled with her being able to track anyone or anything was the reason that Susan had never needed the services of the Ubertas Venator.

Gloria dialed Susan's number and waited for the call to connect. "Hello..." Gloria said.

"Did you find them? I heard you caught up with them at Target," Susan interrupted.

"No I lost them; as soon as they saw me Andrew grabbed Amelia and bolted. Damn he is fast! I manage to track them as far as Mac Dade mall then I lost their scent. Would you mind picking me up at the McDonald's across the street? And about how long will it take?" Gloria lied.

"How did you manage to lose their scent? If you are giving up, I can be there in about 20 minutes." Susan responded; her suspicions colored her voice.

"I am sorry, Susan. I think they must have hopped a bus since I lost their trail by a bus stop," Gloria stated. She quickly disconnected the call after that. The three of them walked over to McDonald's ordered sweet teas while they waited for Susan. Gloria had suggested that they sit near the exit in case something went wrong. Gloria volunteered to delay any pursuit to give Amelia and Andrew a chance to get away.

"Gloria, we wouldn't abandon you. If it became necessary, we would all fight together and if anyone was going to stay behind it would be me,' Andrew stated firmly.

"Andrew, I appreciate that, but I would never abandon either of you," Gloria replied. She carefully considered how to broach the next subject. After a few minutes of considering she continued, "I do not believe that Charles is the one who betrayed you two. I understand that he put guards on your door and I know you don't want to hear this, but if I were in his shoes, I would've done the same. Andrew from what I was told you had gone completely over to your feral side and we're having trouble regaining control. The reason he had placed the guards on the door was because in that state you were a danger to everyone around you except Amelia. Frankly, I'm surprised that you did not attack Charles and his men one sight," Gloria explained sincerely. She then took a sip of her iced tea before continuing, "By Charles isolating you the way that he did it gave you a chance to calm down and regain control of yourself. I am not sure why he had the Hummer moved without your permission. If it was me and he didn't have a good reason for it, I would ask Susan to kick his ass for me."

The three of them chuckled at Gloria's comment. The talk then turned to trying to figure out who had betrayed them. The list of suspects was short and it concerned Gloria greatly, specifically the main suspect Emma.

CHAPTER 8

***

Susan was confused as she hung up the phone from Gloria. It was so very much unlike Gloria to give up so easily, normally Susan would have to drag her in from a chase. "Charles, if you do not need me and Greagor pick up Gloria. I have a couple errands to run. I will meet recalled later," Susan said as she got a quick hug and kiss from Charles.

"Would you like me to ride with you?" Charles asked.

"I would love for you to join me but my car has two seats," Susan responded.

"I thought you brought your Prius?" Charles asked confused.

"No love, I brought my Z --4," Susan replied with a chuckle.

Charles followed Susan out to the car. He whistled as he admired it. "Sweet ride, when did you get it?" Charles inquired gleefully.

Susan knew how to get his hackles up. She decided it would be fun to tease him. "Umm, a few days ago, it was a gift from a friend," Susan responded nonchalantly.

"What friend?" Charles demanded. His words were icy cold as his eyes started to darkened.

"Well to be honest four friends Amelia, Catherine, Scott, and Andrew. They gave me the car as a thank you gift for all of the help I gave them. You should see the Viper that they gave Gloria." Susan teased while laughing.

Charles calm down and his eyes returned to normal. He smiled ruefully as he opened the car door for Susan. "You did that just to get me to react. Please be careful, and I love you. O' by the way, are you coming back to the club tonight?" Charles asked.

"Yes, I'm looking forward to spending time with you. Let me take care of these errands then I will be all yours for the rest of the evening," Susan replied.

"I am looking forward to this evening," Charles said lustfully. He smiled as he leaned into the car for a quick kiss before continuing, "I am heading back to the club, but I am leaving Hank and Belinda here in Andrew's room just in case they come back. I will also have them monitor the situation with the humans."

Charles closed the door and stepped back. Susan took off knowing something was not right about

Gloria's call. It concerned her greatly and she was going to find out what the fuck was going on.

Somewhere across town a cell phone rang and a second ring, it was answered. "We have found them; they are with Gloria. What do you want me to do?" the mysterious voice said.

"Kill the female it will cause the male to go berserk, then he will have to be put down. Try not to touch Gloria, I do not wish Susan upset," a cold hard voice replied.

"Understood, I shall call you once I am finished," the mysterious voice responded.

The man with a mysterious voice was parked in the lot across the street from McDonalds. He had the perfect snipers roost set up in the back of his van. In the rear door, he had a disguise panel that he could slide open and take the shot without having to open the doors. He figured he was about 400 meters away; he knew it would take just over a second for a bullet to strike its target. He looked through the scope and he saw Gloria setting with her back to him. This meant he had to shoot over her shoulder to hit his target, not an ideal shot but he had made it many times before.

He loaded the 800 grain exploding head round in to his specially converted to sharp's .50 -140 caliber rifle. He adjusted the windage and elevation settings and his four-powered Leopold scope. He patiently waited until

Gloria moved slightly to her right clearing his shot. Just after he squeezed the trigger, Gloria moved right into the path of the bullet.

The window exploded into a million shards and Gloria's body lurched from the impact of the bullet. Blood came pouring out of her wound. She also had blood coming from her nose and mouth. She had a large entrance wound just to the right of her left shoulder blade. Andrew immediately knocked Amelia to the floor as the store exploded into pandemonium, people running and screaming. Andrew carefully slid Gloria off the table and got her on to the floor. She was still alive but gravely wounded. Andrew grabbed Amelia purse and handed it to her. "Amelia give me the gun and call Susan now," Andrew demanded sharply.

Amelia handed Andrew the .380. She then found Gloria's phone and called Susan. "Susan it is Amelia. Gloria has been shot and she is hurt bad. We need help!" Amelia said as she assessed her wounds. She was pale but the blood loss had slowed down. She estimated by the amount of blood lying around she had lost over half of her volume. She kept pressure applied to the wound as she looked around the store noting that it was almost completely empty. Then she could here sirens and knew the police would be there any moment.

Susan was in shock she could not believe that Gloria was hurt. "Where the fuck are you?" she asked harshly.

"We're at the McDonalds across from the mall, waiting on you," Amelia replied.

"I will be there within 5 minutes," Susan said.

"Susan wait, we don't know where the shooter is and the police will be here any minute. Just tell me how to help Gloria, please," Amelia responded. She glanced down to check the condition of Gloria she may have died. She frantically continued, "Hold on a second, I need to check on Gloria."

Gloria was still alive just barely. Her skin had almost no color at all and her body was ice cold. She quickly got back to the phone. "What do we do about the human police?" Amelia desperately pleaded.

Andrew turned invisible and cautiously peeked out the window just in time to see Ford cargo van racing out of the lot of the mall. He slowly scanned the area seeing no threats "how is Gloria doing? And do you sense any other vampires around?" Andrew asked telepathically.

"Gloria is hurt bad, I do not think she will last much longer. I do not sense any other vampires out there. Not that this means much, but I do not sense any threats either; however, I didn't sense any before the shot was fired," Amelia responded mentally.

Andrew moved back to where Gloria was while Amelia was on the phone. He knew they had to get moving soon or they would have to explain things to the local police that didn't want to explain. He thought back to all those old vampire novels he read while on stakeouts. He was not sure this would work but he knew Gloria had to have some blood and she needed now. He used his fingernail to slice into his wrist and stuck it into Gloria's mouth letting his blood run down her throat. Gloria's eyes popped open and immediately turned black as her fangs extended. She viciously bit into Andrew's wrist and greedily gulped down his blood.

Amelia saw Andrew feeding Gloria his blood and her feral side came rushing forward." What do you think you are doing?" She hissed at him.

Andrew quickly wrapped his free arm around Amelia and pulled her to him. "I am trying to save our friends life, my love," Andrew said soothingly.

Amelia started to struggle against him. She wanted to kill the woman she now saw a competition. "Love you are the only woman I want." Andrew said in a soft voice as he started to kiss her. He deepened the kiss then continued, "I could not just watch our friend die. Would you have wanted me to?"

Amelia laid her head on his shoulder and soaked up his warmth. The feeling of closeness with her mate helped to calm her, quickly. Amelia kissed Andrew one last time before releasing him. Andrew chuckled and pointed at the phone lying on the floor.

Andrew was beginning to feel the effects of the blood lose." Gloria, you need to stop now!" Andrew commanded a bit harsher than he intended.

Gloria released the bite and looked up at Andrew in disbelief no vampire would do what he had just done. She was surprised that Amelia had not killed her for feeding from him. She had never heard of a vampire allowing another vampire feed from them. The only exception was if the vampire was directly related to them, such as mate or child. She tried to figure out why they had allowed her to feed from him, but Gloria's mind was too clouded to think straight because she was in a world of pain and the room was spinning. She could smell her blood on the floor and wondered what in the hell had happened. She closed her eyes to try to steady herself and quickly was unconscious again.

Susan thought about Amelia's question, she knew what the proper answer was but dreaded saying it. She swallowed back her tears I was just about to answer when she heard Amelia growl and the phone hit the floor. She repeatedly called for Amelia received no answer. She tried to imagine what was going on and hope that the human authorities had not arrived yet.

She had stopped her car at a mile before to McDonalds and she was waiting for Amelia and tells her what was going on. Susan's frustration grew and she said the hell with it. She put the car in gear and was just about ready to pull off when Amelia came back to the phone. Susan knew she had to say what to do before she changed her mind.

"Amelia listens to me. You have to finish Gloria off and get the hell out of there. She cannot be taken alive," Susan explained with tears rolling down her cheeks.

"That won't be necessary Andrew feed Gloria some of his blood. It should be enough to stabilize her so we can move her. I will call you back in a few minutes once we find somewhere safe," Amelia said then ended the call.

Andrew scooped up Gloria in his arms and both Amelia and he turned invisible. They went out through the broken window just as the police arrived. Andrew headed the three of them away from the mall looking for a secluded spot. They found a hiding spot behind a Wal-Mart's about quarter of a mile from the McDonalds. Amelia grabbed one of the pallets laying there and a piece of clean car board for Gloria to lie on. Amelia examined Gloria and noted even though her wounds had sealed she still was very pale and weak. She knew that if a fight came Gloria would not be able to help them. "Andrew, I'm going to feed Gloria so my blood will help her regain her strength. Please do not get riled up like I did," Amelia stated with a little humor in her voice.

"Just don't let her take too much. I'm feeling a little week from blood loss myself," Andrew responded chuckling.

"No worries love, I will only give her a little," Amelia replied. She then took her finger and sliced her wrist like Andrew did. As soon as she stuck her wrist in Gloria's mouth, Gloria's eyes popped open but maintained their normal color. She began to drink the blood and when the wound to Amelia's wrist closed, Gloria extended her fangs, gently bit down, and drank more. After a couple minutes, Gloria released her bite and retracted her fangs.

"Why did you two do that?" Gloria asked.

"What would you had us do stand there and watch you die?" Amelia retorted confused by her question.

Gloria laughed harshly. "Please do not think that I am not grateful. I have never heard of a vampire allowing another vampire to feed from them who wasn't their mate or child, no matter what the circumstances were. I do not know how I will be able to thank you for what you have done for me. Could you please tell me what happened?" Gloria responded.

"You were shot by someone. I am pretty sure, either Andrew or myself was the target. I called Susan so she is aware of what has happened. I told her we would call her back once we were safe but I have not done it yet. I am still trying to decide if we can trust her especially after what she said to do with you," Amelia reported.

"Let me guess; she told you to finish me off? Amelia, I know you don't want to hear this but she was right. If I had been discovered, I would have been turned into a guinea pig or worse. I know that Susan wouldn't have made that decision easily." Gloria explained.

"Well we took the decision out of her hands and yours. You are our friend and we don't abandon our friends," Amelia stated firmly.

Gloria closed her eyes and let Amelia's blood finish healing her. She was still in awe that they had saved her by feeding her their blood. Andrew blood had saved her life and started the healing process. Amelia's blood would finish healing her and allow some of her strength to return. After about 15 minutes, Gloria felt a lot better she was still a bit sore and felt weak least now she could stand. "Can I call Susan now?" Gloria asked.

"You may want to change into these overalls first. I know they're not the height of fashion but they're a lot better than walking around in bloody clothes. Then call Susan but we're going to have to move very soon. The cops are searching the area and are starting to get close. Any suggestions to where we can meet?" Andrew said.

Amelia helped Gloria to her feet. She turned invisible and changed quickly. "There is a small bar that serves a mean burger a couple mile from here. How about if we have her meet us there?" Gloria asked.

"That sounds like a good idea, I'm getting hungry anyway," Amelia said.

The Gloria and Andrew nodded in agreement with her. "OK, I will call Susan and make the arrangements," Gloria stated.

Susan was about to confirm what Amelia said, when Amelia hung up on her. Susan quickly called Charles. "Hello baby, what's up?" Charles said cheerfully.

"Charles, Amelia just called me someone just shot Gloria," Susan replied sorrowfully.

"Is she alright? Andrew and Amelia, are they okay? Wait; was this the McDonald's across from the mall?" Charles asked his voice full of concern.

"Amelia and Andrew were untouched, they are pissed but fine. Gloria was hit badly; I had to tell them that they should finish her," Amelia responded hoarsely her eyes flooded with tears.

"My god did they do it?" Charles asked not really wanting to hear the answer. If they had then it would destroy Susan's soul. If they didn't then Gloria could become a major threat to the vampire's way of life. He unconsciously held his breath waiting for the answer.

"No, they did not have to. Andrew feed her some of his blood," Amelia answered after recomposing herself.

"He...he did what? Amelia allowed this?" Charles shakily asked, not being able to hide his shock in his face or voice.

"Charles, I do not know why Amelia did not attack her and to be honest do not care. I am just glad that they saved her. The rest of the ramification they will have to work out between them," Susan replied.

"You are right babe; I just cannot figure out what possessed Andrew to do that doesn't he know the ramification and how did Amelia keep her feral side in check to allow Gloria to feed from Andrew. By all rights she should have attacked the instant, she saw Gloria start to drink. They are most remarkable individuals and I look forward to getting to know them better. I am coming to join you in one of the Escalades your car will be too small to carry everyone. Also, I am having a few of my response teams in the area to act as back- up," Charles said.

"Once they make contact with me, I will call you and let you know what the plan is," Amelia responded before hanging up. She looked at her watch and started to get concerned she had expected to hear from them long before this. She was just about to try them on Gloria's number when the phone rang. Once she saw it was Gloria's phone, she quickly answered it." Amelia thank god, I was getting concerned. Is everything all right?" Susan asked in a rush.

"I thought you would be happy to talk to me, but if you don't want to speak to me that's OK. I will get you Amelia," Gloria teased while giggling.

Susan could hardly speak she was so choked up. She was laughing and crying at the same time." I thought I lost you. How are you up and about so quickly, there is no way you should have recovered this fast unless you drained Andrew dry... I am sorry for rambling. By god, it is good to hear your voice. How are you? How are Amelia and Andrew?" Susan rambled excitedly.

"Susan calm down before you burst something. I am up because both Amelia and Andrew feed me blood. Can you believe what they did for me? The two of them are fine and want to talk to you. What do you think about meeting at that little bar over off Maryland Avenue? Unless you can think of someplace better," Gloria replied.

"Is it alright if we invite Charles? What do you think about that diner on Kedron Avenue right off of Mac Dade Boulevard?" Susan suggested.

"I forgot about that place and I will ask them about Charles give me a sec," Gloria replied. She then took the phone from her ear and asked," What about Charles? Also do you mind if we change where we go there is a Fifties themed diner right up the street?'

Andrew looked at Amelia and shrugged." Up to you love," Andrew said.

"The diner sounds great and Charles is invited but please only him," Amelia responded.

Andrew looked at the way the three of them were dressed all of them had blood on them. Gloria also had blood all over her skin." Gloria what size clothes do you wear?" Andrew asked.

Gloria told Andrew her sizes. He then handed Amelia the gun. "I will be right back," Andrew said.

Gloria went back to her call." Charles is welcome to but only him at the diner you suggested. Please make sure he has a few bottles of blood." Gloria stated.

Andrew returned about fifteen minutes later with a bag for Gloria it contained a nice pair of gray slacks, a white blouse and a pair of low heel shoes. He also had purchased a bottle of water less soap and couple washcloths. Andrew handed Amelia a bag that contained a nice navy-blue skirt and a navy blue blouse. He had already changed into a pair of tan khakis and black pull over shirt. "Gloria, I suggest you let Amelia try to get some of that blood off of your back." Andrew suggested.

"I was hoping you were going to be the one washing me up. O' well looks like us, girls will have to have all of the fun," Gloria chided with a wink of her eye.

Andrew turned his back to allow Gloria some privacy. Amelia quickly cleaned as much blood off Gloria's back as she possible could. Then the two ladies changed, quickly into their new clothes. The three of them headed towards the place they were supposed to meet Susan making sure that they stayed invisible. They tried to stay out of open areas where a sniper could get a clear shot at them being invisible was no guarantee. They all knew a vampire with the right powers could see them. Andrew stopped them he wanted to watch the area for a few minutes. He couldn t place his finger on it but something felt wrong. "Let's just watch from here for a few minutes. I have a bad feeling," Andrew said.

The sniper had seen Gloria move just after he squeezed the trigger. He watched as his round slammed into her back. He quickly chambered the next round and waited a few seconds he was hoping that one of the parvulus would pop their head up. After a few minutes, he realized that either they weren't going to pop their heads up or they had managed to slip out of another door and maybe even working their way to him now. He had heard what Andrew had done to Antonio. He jumped into the driver's seat, took off flying across the lot. He quickly fled heading away from the scene. He pressed the speed dial on his phone and waited for it to connect he heard." Report!"

He swallowed hard knowing that his news was not going to go over well. "Sir, Unfortunately Gloria was hit, I'm unsure if it was fatal. The parvulus still live. I had to leave the area before the human authorities responded," the man nervously reported.

"Let me get this straight not only did you fail to eliminate your target but you hit the person whom I distinctly told you to avoid hitting. I would suggest that you never allow us to cross paths again, do you understand me?" The voice warned his anger was palpable.

The assassin knew he was now a target the boss would put a large contract out on him to make an example of him. Weighing his options, he wonder what he should do make a run for it that would buy him at best a couple decades; most likely only a few weeks. If he surrendered to Black, most likely black would torture him and then kill him slowly and painfully. Then a plan hit him he would send the information about the trader anonymously to black it should tie up the boss long enough for him to get away and who knows if Black is as powerful as it is said he is maybe he will eliminate the boss.

The assassin arrived at the hotel he was staying stepped from the van before the valet could assist him from the van, he made the mistake of assuming the guy was just some working class vampire and ignored him. He had failed to notice the thin knife he had in his hand. He heard the valet call him and as he turned, he never saw or felt the blade as it sliced through his neck.

The slice was not meant to kill but to incapacitate him. He looked at the man who was about to end his long life and watched with detached interest as the man cut his head off. The valet then calmly got into his van and drove away.

As soon as Susan finished the call with Gloria, she hung up and immediately dialed Charles number. "Love, Amelia, and Andrew want to meet with us, but only the two of us. The meeting is set for about an hour at that fifties themed diner on Kedron Avenue. DO you happen to have blood with you?" Amelia Said.

"Yes love, I have ten units in the Truck with me. If you think, we need more I can arrange for one of the other units in the area to drop off more. Do you want to meet up and go together? If everything goes well, we can have one of them drive the Escalade back to your car and drop us off," Charles suggested.

"You just want to get behind the wheel of my new car," Susan countered with a chuckle.

"Damn you caught me. What do you say?" Charles asked as he was laughing.

"Who do you have with you?" Susan inquired.

"Neil is with me, why?" Charles replied.

"I will meet you at that old gas station by Maple Avenue. He can drive my car back to the club. Then after we're done with this you can drive me to your house tonight," Susan suggested.

"I love your way of thinking. We will meet you there in about fifteen minutes." Charles said with a smile.

Charles hung up the phone. "Neil, don't tell anyone about our meeting with Amelia and Andrew. I do mean anyone not even Emma. Do I make myself clear," Charles ordered?

Neil was surprised at first, then when he realized what Charles was implying, he became upset. "Surely you don't think that Emma would betray you?" Neil retorted anger evident in his voice.

"I Trust my daughter, but we do have a leak and right now the only people that know we're meeting with those two is Gloria and the three of us. I want to keep it that way! The fewer the people that know it the less likely it will be that someone will betray us," Charles replied harshly.

"OK Charles I should not have lost my temper and I do understand. What you have to understand is that I do not make it a habit of hiding things from my wife. You know that she will question me if I return without you," Neil said.

Charles thought about when Neil was saying have realized he was right. He also knew given Emma's talents Neil would never be able to lie to her, even if he was willing to. "Take the car to my house and wait there for me. I will call Emma and cover for you," Charles replied softening his tone.

Charles called Emma. "Baby girl, you can relax Gloria is fine. We are going to meet up with her and find out what the hell happened," Charles said.

"What about Amelia and Andrew?" Emma worriedly asked.

"We're not sure dear. As soon as Gloria was stable, they left her hidden and called your mother. We are both racing to get to her now, but Susan has talked to her, besides being pissed, and weakened from blood loss, she is fine. Once we get to her and make sure she's all right, we will call you. It shouldn't be more than a couple of hours," Charles replied in a reassuring tone.

"There you're covered," Charles said after he hung up the phone.

The two of them pulled onto the lot of the gas station and saw that Susan was waiting for them. She quickly got out of the car and walked to Neil. She handed him the keys. "Take it easy with my baby, please," Susan requested.

"I will take good care of her," Neil promised then gave her a quick kiss on the cheek.

Once Susan was in the truck with Charles, he headed towards the diner. "What you think about trying to switch the meeting to Patricia s bar and grill. I know Patty will let us use the back room where we can talk in private." Charles suggested.

Susan smiled she liked Patricia and knew she was one hell of a cook. The place was nice and since it catered to vampires, it was the perfect place to talk. It even had special menu items for vampires.

"Sounds like a great idea, if Amelia and Andrew are willing to go. The first thing is that we have to get blood into all three of them."

Susan and Charles arrived at the diner a few minutes later he figured they were about 10 minutes early. Even though the diner was not busy, they park in the back corner of the lot. Charles' eyes glowed for a moment. "We are being watched and I can sense the vampire," Charles said.

"Could it be Andrew and Amelia watching us?" Susan asked, forcing herself not to react.

Charles closed his eyes for a few moments, concentrating on the area. He could sense Gloria, Amelia, and Andrew were watching them. The one that his senses had alerted him to had a more malicious feel about them. Charles concentrated on the one that had alerted him. He could sense the vampire was somewhere on the lot across the street from them. "No love, the one that alerted me is somewhere on the lot across the street." Charles replied while still trying to zero in on the vampire.

While Susan called Gloria's cell, Charles called Neil. "Neil did you tell anyone about the meeting with Amelia and Andrew?" Charles asked.

"No, Charles I swear I did not call anyone. Why what is the matter?" Neil replied suddenly concerned.

"It seems we were followed here. Do not worry we will handle it," Charles said.

"Charles, what do you want me to do?" Neil asked.

Charles thought about it for a few moments, trying to decide the best course of action. "I want you to take Susan's car to the club. Then I want you to join Emma, Catherine, and Scott in the emergency shelter. I will contact Mitchel and have him move the rest down to the shelter. Be careful that there could directly to the shelter. Do not talk to anyone and call me once you are in locked down." Charles ordered his voice brokered no arguments.

Charles then called Mitchel's cell. "Mitch, its Charles I want Emma, Catherine, Scott, and yourself to immediately precede to the family shelter. Neil should be joining you shortly. Also, call Linda and have her prepared to be picked up to join you in the shelter. Have David pick her up. After Neil and Linda arrive, lock it down. I want no one else admitted except Susan or me. Tell Emma that I will call her shortly explain everything. Please give are my love," Charles directed.

"I will take care of it immediately sir. Are you and Susan safe?" Mitchel replied.

"We are fine for now. Just please take care of my family," Charles requested.

Gloria, Amelia, and Andrew watched Charles pull into the parking lot and go to the rear corner. He had made them wait a few minutes while he surveyed the area looking for threats. He was just about to say it was safe when Amelia stopped him." Andrew something isn't right I have a bad feeling and I can sense the stress level in the truck had ratcheted up in the last few minutes." Amelia warned.

Gloria wanted to go to the truck she knew that Charles would have bottles of blood she desperately needed. She heard Amelia's warning and tried to get a sense from her sire but Susan still had their link blocked off. She tried to use her senses but could not find anything.

Andrew slowly scanned the area and couldn't see any threats. He knew better than to just ignore Amelia, when she got a feeling. "Gloria, I know you're anxious to get to the blood and to see Susan, but until we figure out what triggered Amelia's senses we stay put. If Amelia says there is something wrong, we go with her instincts," Andrew explained.

Gloria considered what she knew and while she was anxious to see Susan and trust her implicitly, her gut instincts told her to listen to Amelia. "Amelia, can you sense anything more? Do you..." Gloria started to ask, when the cell phone rang. "Susan, what's happening? Amelia said she sensed something and that your stress," she said into the phone.

"We have someone watching us. We're pretty sure he is going to attempt to finish what they started earlier. Stay where you are for right now and give us a chance to get a couple things in place. When we're ready, we will call you and if this is the assassin head out of the area get somewhere safe. Once you are safe call us; we will arrange to meet with you all," Susan replied.

Gloria removed the phone from her ear. "Susan said that they were being watched, they think that is the assassin from this morning," Gloria said.

"Where is he at?" Andrew asked his eyes glowing with anticipation.

Gloria put the phone back to her ear. "You have any idea where the assassin is?" Gloria inquired.

"Charles is pretty sure he is on the lot across a street from us. Why do you want to know? Please do not do anything stupid," Susan pleaded.

Gloria relayed the information to Andrew. Andrew moved to a good vantage point and saw the black Ford van. It was parked in the middle of the lot across the street where Susan said it would be. He was sure it was the same van he saw racing away after the shooting. "I want his fucking ass! Amelia how would you like to go on the offensive?" Andrew said his eyes: dark with anger.

"Are we going to be able to feast on his blood?" Amelia responded with a bone-chilling smile, as her feral side came forward.

"In due time, you will have our revenge but first we need to have a pleasant chat with that person," Andrew said his eyes darkened even more.

"Are you two sure you know what you are doing? That vampire is a trained killer in full control of his powers," Gloria warned as worry colored her voice.

"Gloria! What the fuck is going on?" Susan shouted into the phone.

"Sorry, Andrew and Amelia are going after the assassin," Gloria replied.

"Stop them! All they will wind up doing is getting themselves kill," Susan demanded.

"Andrew, Susan has requested that you not try it," Gloria said.

"Tell Susan we will be fine. Gloria please wait here for us," Andrew responded rolling his eyes.

"There is no way in hell I'm going to stay here while the two of you run off and get yourselves killed!" Gloria retorted her eyes narrowing in anger.

"I need you to wait here! Amelia and I instinctively know each other's move and we cannot afford any mistakes. We'll be back soon," Andrew replied his voice icy at best.

Gloria growled her eyes almost went feral. "I am going god damn it! So shut the fuck up and lead on. The two of you aren't going anywhere without me so get use to the idea," Gloria demanded.

"Fine, then you will play over watch." Andrew growled in frustration. He handed Gloria the gun pointed at the phone, "Tell her good bye and turn it the fuck off."

"Andrew, who the fuck do you think you are talking to? I was hunting vampires before your grandfather was a sperm in his father's balls," Gloria retorted harshly. She then hung up the phone and turned it off.

Andrew just walked away; he did not have the time or the energy to waste arguing with Gloria. For her part, Gloria realized her mood was results of what they had done earlier to save her life she knew that the three of them had to have a long talk about the ramifications of them sharing blood with her. Andrew led the three of them a few blocks away from the diner then circled back to where the van was parked. The three of them carefully shielded their minds and made sure to approach the van from downwind.

Andrew picked a spot where Gloria could cover them in case things went sideways. Andrew moved cautiously towards the van staying invisible and trying to make himself as small of a target as possible. Amelia held back a bit giving Andrew plenty of room to react if necessary

"I can sense him love he is in the rear of the van," Amelia mental said to Andrew.

"Can you take control of his mind?" Andrew asked telepathically.

"I can if I can see his eyes," Amelia replied the same way.

"So that is your Achilles heel, huh?" Andrew sent with a fair amount of conceit.

Andrew heard Amelia chuckle in his head. He singled for her to move to a position where she could cover the side door. Andrew was hoping that if the vampire opened the side door Amelia would be able to see his eyes and take control of his mind. Andrew crept up to passenger side. He saw that the wing window was open and the keys were still hanging in the ignition. He used his telekinesis to remove the keys from the ignition and float them out the passenger wing window into his hands. He isn't going anywhere soon Andrew thought to himself.

Gloria realized something; the vampire inside of the van should have sensed Andrew by now. Even with them shielding themselves, even a newly changed parvenus should have sensed him by now. Gloria concentrated on Andrew and couldn't sense him he managed to hide his presence completely. Gloria had heard that Diamond had been able to do that but never had believed. It hit her that Amelia had the same ability.

Andrew moved to the side door of the van. "I am going to yank the door open and snatch the vampire out of the van. Please get control of his mind as quickly as you can. Let me know when you are ready," Andrew said telepathically.

Amelia cleared her mind and was just about to tell Andrew to go, when it hit her that the vampire inside should have known they were there. Andrew wait something is wrong!" Amelia screamed through their mental link.

Andrew ready himself for an attack trying to figure out where it was going to come from. he quickly surveyed the area and saw no threats. "What's a matter?" Andrew mentally asked.

"He should have sensed you by now even with you shielding yourself. I am sure he is laying a trap for us love," Amelia sent.

Andrew quickly backed away from the van to cover beside Amelia "Any suggestions on how we proceed from here?" Andrew asked using his mind.

"Can you use your telekinesis to open the door from cover?" Amelia suggested mentally.

"I should be able to and I like the idea of being out of the line of fire," Andrew responded telepathically.

He took a few minutes to prepare himself for the task "Here goes nothing," He warned Amelia through her link.

Amelia nodded her readiness. Andrew concentrated on the door of the van, and a moment later, the door was ripped wide open. He had opened it with such force the he had ripped the door out of its track. The assassin caught by surprise quickly drew his pistol and wildly fired striking a half of dozen cars in the process. Andrew waited until he ran out ammo in the clip then charged him while he was reloading. He snatched the assassin out of the van and delivered a lighting right cross to the other vampires' jaw. The assassin dropped his weapon and was dazed from Andrew blow. Andrew quickly slammed the vampire to the ground knocking the wind out of him. Amelia rushed forward to be able to look into the assassin's eyes and quickly took control of his mind.

Amelia ordered the Assassin to stop resisting his arrest. As soon as Andrew realized Amelia had control of the vampire, he looked into the rear of the van and when he saw that there was a spotter's scope but no rifle, he suddenly had a bad feeling. He quickly shoved Amelia into the back of the van. "Stay down!" Andrew ordered as he shoved the assassin the van with Amelia.

"Andrew what's the matter?" Amelia asked.

"He only has a spotter's scope which means there could be a sniper around here." Andrew said as he started scanning the area.

Gloria was confused by Andrew's reaction and started to walk towards the van. She knew they needed to get out of there soon the human police were already on their way. "Gloria get down! There may be another sniper in the area." Andrew shouted. He then glanced inside of the van at the man they had captured.

"Love, try to see if he knows where the sniper is? If there is one," Andrew asked telepathically.

Gloria quickly went to cover and slowly made her way towards Andrew and Amelia. She kept low and used the cars for cover. "Andrew, we need to get out of here the human police will be here soon." Gloria said.

Amelia managed to probe the assassin's surface thoughts while he was still dazed by Andrew's attack. "He is alone. He was ordered to follow Charles and report if he made contact with us. When he saw Charles rendezvous with Susan, he decided to follow them figuring they would lead him to us, "Amelia informed him through their link.

Charles was extremely angry at Amelia and Andrew's stupidity. Two parvenus going after a trained vampiric assassin was suicidal at best. He hoped the two of them survived so that he could strangle them himself. The two of them waited forever then they heard the gunshots and both his and Susan's hearts stopped. Susan called Gloria's cell and it immediately went to voice mail. "It went straight to voice mail god damn it. While you are strangling Amelia and Andrew, I am going to strangle Gloria damn her for following them," Susan exclaimed in anger, fueled by worry.

Charles threw the Escalade into gear and speed off the lot as Susan's phone rang. Susan answered it and listened for a couple seconds." Thank the Maker you all are OK," She exclaimed then listen to the rest of Gloria's report," OK! Take him to the building we own out by the airport. Charles and I will meet you there."

"What happened?' Charles demanded without realizing how harsh his words came out.

"Amelia and Andrew caught the vampire who was spying on us. He was to follow you hoping that you would lead him to them. I am having them go to the private sanctum we have out by the airport." Susan replied ignoring his harsh tone.

"Excellent idea it will provide us the privacy we need to get answer from him." Charles said his demeanor suddenly brightening up.

"It should considering only three people know of its existence Gloria, you, and me." Susan replied.

Charles and Susan arrived right behind the others. It was just finishing the elaborate security checks to enter a place. As soon as the large garage doors opened, she waved them in and then door behind them closed. They were effectively trapped in a Sally port. Gloria walked over to the wall and punched another code in causing the inner door to open giving them access to the rest of the garage. The garage area was large isolated; so that once you were in this area, you were effectively trapped. Amelia and Andrew were lead through a door into a long very narrow hallway. The hallway was only couple of inches wider than the width of Andrew shoulders. At the end of the hall was a heavy steel door with an electronic lock that had a 16-digit pass code. In the center of the door was a firing port, Andrew could see it would take only one man with an automatic to hold off an Army trying to get through the hallway.

The reception area was the first room you entered even though it looked benign. It was anything but, the way it was designed and the layout of the furnishings would make it very easily defended by a couple people. Even if a force did manage to take control of the reception area, they would be facing four strong steel doors of highly advanced, locking systems. From the looks of the doors and the walls, it would take a considerable number of high explosives to breach either of them. Susan took great joy in explaining about her creation. She also mentioned if they needed, could house over 200 people on this floor.

The six of them went down a hall to a storage room in the back of the room hidden behind a shelf was a pocket style steel door that covered an elevator. Charles and Susan rode down first since the elevator could only hold four people. It was purposely designed that way to prevent a large-scale force from being able to storm the lower floor. The basement was a lavish living area it had all the comforts of home plus room for full staff and dozens of security personnel. Gloria showed Andrew where the cells were for their prisoner. While they were gone, Charles went and retrieved bottles of blood for the three of them. While Charles was getting the blood, Mitchel called letting him know everyone that he requested was now in the shelter.

When Mitchel received the call from Charles, he quickly escorted Emma, Catherine, and Scott down to the secure shelter it was in the sub-basement of the club. He dispatched a team to pick up his mate Linda and bring her to the club. Mitchell had already called her and told her he was bringing her to the club for a few days. Linda offered no objections even though she didn't want to be sequestered, but had learned a long time ago that Mr. Black only gave this order when necessary.

Within an hour, everyone who needed to be was in the secure shelter. Mitchell had station guards at the door leading to the shelter and at the only elevator that came down to this floor. Once everything was secured, he called Mr. Black and let him know him that his orders had been carried out.

Charles had just handed out the bottles of blood, when his cell phone rang, he recognized Emma's phone number. "Hello baby girl," Charles greeted.

"Daddy, where are you? And what is going on?" Emma asked her voice full of concern.

"Sweetheart there's a lot going on which I cannot discuss over the phone. I am safe for now as is your mother, Gloria, Amelia, and Andrew. I will explain everything to you as soon as I can. Please for now just stay where you are and listen to Mitchell. I love you and will talk to you later," Charles responded.

"Okay daddy, I love you to. Talk to you later," Emma said before hanging up.

Charles let everyone know that their loved ones were safe. While Charles was handling security arrangements for the rest of the people, they loved. Susan made sure that Gloria, Amelia, and Andrew drank a couple bottles of blood. Gloria then went to her room to get a quick shower to wash the rest of the blood off her and change into something more comfortable.

Susan showed Amelia and Andrew to their room so they could get cleaned up and changed into something more comfortable. Susan then headed to the kitchen to make them all something to eat. A few minutes later Charles joined her to help. They decided on a simple meal of steak, asparagus, herb-roasted potatoes, and a salad. Everyone ate dinner in silence, each trying to process the day's events. After dinner, Charles, and Susan excuse themselves saying there will go check on the prisoner.

Andrew could sense Gloria's nervousness and knew she had been edgy all day. "Gloria, you're been edgy around us all day. We do something to upset you?" Andrew asked concerned for his friend.

" No! What you two did for me, was unbelievable. I was serious when I said it was unheard of for a vampire to allow anyone but there mate to feed off them. In the case of a female vampire, you have to add her offspring while the child is nursing from her. The only other case of when a vampire will exchange blood with vampires is when they would join a coven.

The difference then was it was an exchange between two vampires to establish the familial link. The link was used to identify members of the coven and to locate members in times of need. When one joined the coven, he or she would exchange blood with every member of the coven. The exchange was at the most a mouth full of blood and normally they would do it at the same time from the wrist. In addition, fangs were never used. When you two feed me your blood today you forge half of the link, I am offering both of you the chance to forge the other half of that link." Gloria carefully explained. She hoped that her friends would not wind up hating her, or regret saving her life.

"This some kind of joke Gloria? You are now linked to my Andrew?" Amelia angrily growled as her eyes started to darken with anger.

Andrew sensed his mate starting to lose control as her anger mounted quickly wrapped his arms around her and pulled her into the crook of his neck. He started soothingly rubbing her back. As Andrew scent started to wash over Amelia, she started to relax.

"Amelia it's not like you think, the link is more like what you have with Catherine. A few centuries ago, you would have had to live in a coven to survive. In most covens, you would have exchanged blood with 20 to 50 other vampires. The reason it was done was for mutual protection and it also gave a sense of family to keep the members of the coven loyal to each other than," Gloria continued with her explanation.

Andrew mulled over what Gloria was telling them, to him it didn't sound too bad. However, at the moment, he was more concerned with Amelia's reaction. "What are you thinking, my love?" Andrew asked her telepathically. He had noted that she was strangely muted.

"I am not sure what to think. I do not like the idea of sharing any part of you with anyone else. Not to mention I am not too thrilled with the idea that she will be able to located us anytime she wants. What if we do not want to be found?" Amelia replied mentally, after long couple of minutes.

Andrew had to admit he had not thought about it that way. He thought about how he would feel about it if it were male vampire. He admitted to himself that he would be less than thrilled even for Mark. The only thing that would help his mark was mated. Andrew did understand Amelia's apprehension about Gloria.

"I know you're not overly thrilled about this. Let me ask you this, if we had known would you have let her die? Worse yet, would you have been able to kill her yourself? I know we both think of Gloria as a friend but now I know you're also worried she may be competition. Please remember this I only want one woman in my bed and that woman is you, my love.

Amelia the decision is yours how we proceed from here. I am not doing this to be an ass and dump it in your lap, but your happiness comes first as does your peace of mind. I will fully support whatever decision you make." Andrew telepathically said reassuringly. At the same time, he asked, "Gloria if we decide to do this coven how does the link work? In addition, if we so desired or needed to could it be blocked?

"Any connection can be blocked even the one you have with Amelia if you so desire. If you would like I could teach you how to do it. No matter what if you are destroyed everyone linked with you will instantly know it and approximately where it happened," Gloria answered earnestly.

"If we had known I would like to think that we would've done the same thing maybe with one difference, me sharing the blood instead of you," Amelia responded with the link.

"Do you think it is any easier on me, having to share you with someone else? How do you think I feel about your link with Catherine?" Andrew mentally replied before asking his next question, "Are you linked with anyone else like this?"

Gloria looked down and her eyes got a faraway look as if she was recalling something. She closed her eyes fighting back the tears and forcing the memory back down. "Just once but he had to be put down. You know the person I am linked with is Susan and that is because she is my sire," Gloria replied visibly shaken.

Amelia could sense her great sorrow and now that her guard was down Amelia could sense loneliness and emptiness in Gloria soul. Amelia before she realized what she was doing she started probing to find the source of Gloria's pain. Amelia saw the day that Gloria lost her parents, when she was sixteen, and she never really had a chance to grieve for them. It was just before her nineteenth birthday when she became a vampire.

She was hunting her parent's killers when she meant Lenard. He was an older vampire that was full of compassion, once he saw how badly she was hurting, he offered her comfort for the next century the two of them were constant companions. He was the one that convinced her to let what happened to her parents go. He was like a kindly old grandfather who helped to train her and showed her the world. He made sure she was educated and knew how to defend herself with swords and her bare hands. He gave her a sense of self-worth she had not had since her parents died. In the late fifties, he told her he had to go away for a while to the old country for family business.

When he returned five years later, he was changed. He had lost himself somehow and for some reason went rogue. It was Gloria who had put him down that incident had scarred her soul and was even to this day very painful. Amelia hadn't meant to pry by once she saw the events play out she could not look away it was as if she was a dear in a caught in a set headlights. Gloria barely registered Amelia mind invading hers and thought that Amelia had only brushed her mind before Gloria had closed her mind off.

"Gloria, I am sorry; I did not mean to pry. I felt your pain it was drawn in," Amelia apologized, realizing what she had done.

"It's okay, mistakes happen," Gloria replied. Not knowing how far she had gotten into her mind

Amelia was relieved that Gloria wasn't mad but she felt terrible for her friend. She could not imagine having to kill someone who was like a grandparent to her. She had seen that Gloria had no choice, but Gloria's had closed off her mind before she could get to the memory of what happened. Amelia hadn't realized she had tears leaking from her eyes until she heard Andrew's concerned voice in her mind, "love, are you are right. You seemed awfully upset. "

Amelia wiped her eyes and noticed that Gloria was looking at her with a curious look on her face. "Sweetheart, I want to do the blood exchange with her and I also want to do it with Scott. I want you to do it also with the two of them and Catherine. That way we will be like a real family. After what I saw in Gloria's head, I realized that I want to do it. Can we please do this? " Amelia pleaded telepathically.

"As long as you are sure you can handle it. I do not want you to regret it and I see how you get when she flirts with me. I do not want this to cause any trouble between us. " Andrew responded mentally.

"I know why she flirts now; this is her way of dealing with her pain. I do not want to betray her by telling you what I saw in her mind. Now I understand her and respect her strength. I also know she would never try to come between mates." Amelia explained with her mind.

"Gloria, how do we do this?" Amelia asked.

"I just cut my wrist and you take a mouthful of my blood. You do not even need your fangs," Gloria said with a genuine smile.

Amelia nodded and Gloria's pierced her wrist with her nail. Amelia took about a mouthful of the blood and immediately felt the bond established itself. Amelia did agree it felt like the bond she had with Catherine.

Andrew followed suit and marveled at the bond. Having never sired anyone, he was unprepared for the sensation of feeling Gloria's presence in the back of his head. He could feel her happiness but he also felt underlying sadness from her. He realized that the bond was more empathic than telepathic. He could get impressions of her general mood and health. He could also sense that she was directly ahead and very close.

Gloria gave them time to get used to the new bond. "Now I want you to use your link to try to locate me," Gloria instructed.

Gloria turned invisible and moved quietly to a different part of room. Andrew was having trouble using the link to track her but Amelia was almost immediately in front of her. She had Andrew keep practicing and after about 20 minutes, he could track her easily. She next taught them how to shut down their bond not only with her but also with each other. Both of them felt it disconcerting, when they would block the bond between them. "I know it's disconcerting when you do it but there are times when you want to be able to block out even your mate. Without this skill, you could never plan a surprise for your mate. The two of you should keep practicing once you do a little better at it you will be able to use it as a filter. Amelia dear, it is a skill that you will need when you go shopping with me," Gloria explained. She could not help but chuckle at their reaction.

All three of them laughed at Gloria's comment and then they continue to work on different skills they would need to survive as a vampire. By the end of the evening Gloria had given them a good education in the nuances of using the bond, not only the one between the three of them but also Amelia's bond with Catherine, and finally the mating bond. The evening had been mentally tiring and not one of them had trouble falling asleep that night.

Even though it was after three AM before they got to bed, Charles woke them up a little before seven. He said that they had to get the information from their prisoner in order to protect their families. Andrew and

Amelia rose and quickly dressed. When the two of them walked into the room by where the prisoner was housed Susan pointed at a tray with coffee on it.

The guest had a rather uncomfortable night hanging inverted by his ankles with his two arms anchored to the floor. He had spent the night with a bright strobe link flashing in his face and music blared all night in the soundproof room. Throughout the night, Susan would attempt to breach his mental shield. The intention of doing all this was to prevent the vampire from resting at all and it had worked like a charm.

Charles explained that Amelia and Susan would take turns probing his mind. Unfortunately, Gloria, Andrew, or himself would be of little use, since this job was outside the scope of their abilities. Charles cautioned Amelia not to push their guest to hard or she could accidentally damage his mind and then they would lose whatever information he had.

Susan went first and she carefully tried to force her way into the prisoner's mind. The prisoner had managed to hold fast against her probing and even at times to push back. Susan quickly realizes that he was well trained and it would take a while to wear him down. Susan started putting constant pressure against his mental shield. After about a half-hour, she stepped back and allowed Amelia to take over.

Amelia applied just enough force to let him know she was there and then she nicely asked him to relent so she wouldn't have to hurt him. Amelia heard the guy laugh at her calling her weak and said this was going to be easy. Amelia softly requested that he please not fight her. The Assassin thought she was weak and relaxed his barrier just ever so slightly to give himself a break. Amelia told him if he lowered his defenses and allowed her to get the information she needed; she would get Charles to allow him to live. The guy refused one last time.

Amelia mentally sighed and then she locked eyes with the guy and her eyes started to glow and after about ten minutes of mentally dueling him, the assassin eyes went wide. She ordered him to lower his mental barrier and allow her to enter. The assassin tried to resist her but found he couldn't resist and he opened his mind to her. She rifled through his mind. He didn't know the name of the man he was working for; he had only talked to him on the phone. He knew that he was someone who had many resources and was very familiar with Charles organization. Amelia heard the voice of the man in the head of the vampire and thought she recognized it but couldn't place whose it was.

Amelia felt Susan tapping her on the shoulder telling her it was time to switch but she was not ready to back out when he felt Amelia being slightly distracted by Susan he tried again to reestablish his mental barrier and it took just about every ounce of reserve to maintain over control of Uwais she had gotten his name. She also learned that the sniper that had taken the shot earlier was now dead and that the sniper was ordered to kill Amelia in order that Andrew would have to be put down. Gloria was supposed to be left untouched. Amelia could no longer keep him under her control and he managed to push her out of his mind but everyone could see he was in pain and totally exhausted. Charles was concerned the Amelia may have pushed him to hard and decided to let him rest.

Andrew went to Amelia's side concerned about how pale and unsteady she was. He heard her softly whisper that she managed to get in before collapsing. Andrew scooped Amelia up in his arms before she fell to the floor and gently cradled her. Gloria rushed to their side; she was concerned Amelia may have hurt herself. Gloria quickly checked Amelia over. "She is just exhausted. Let her rest for a few minutes while you give her a bottle of blood," Gloria suggested feeling much relieved.

Andrew was relieved that Amelia was going to be all right. He held her in his arms while softly stroking her back waiting for her to wake. "Amelia says she got in just before she passed out," Andrew said.

Susan was surprised to say the least she thought it would take days to break him. She wondered how

Amelia managed to do it in minutes. Susan once again wondered just how strong Amelia would become from early signs she imagined she would be quite powerful and a welcome addition to the organization.

Charles was pleasantly surprised by the power and control that Amelia had shown. He had known that Diamond had been very pale for her mental abilities and he imagined that Amelia had inherited them from her. "Andrew, you have yourself one hell of a woman there." Charles exclaimed then quickly added, "Almost as good as mine."

"Almost, a nice recovery," Susan teased as she laughed at Charles.

Andrew laughed quietly as he held Amelia letting her head, rest against his chest while he slowly stroked the side of her face. Charles watch as Andrew held her filing the deep attachment, he had to her for possible future use attachment were a duel edged sword in their world the good thing was the helped to ground you and in the case of a mated pair they give you a reason to want to live. In Charles's memory, no mated pair had ever had one of the partners go rogue while the other was still living. The bad thing was that the person you are attached to could be used against you.

"Andrew be careful developing attachments. When you do develop them guard closely who knows about them. A mate is a powerful ally among other things they are also a potent weapon against you. At the very least, connection you make can be held over your head. That is why both Susan and I have always made sure that Emma was always well guarded." Charles warned.

Andrew nodded his understanding as he wondered what Amelia had learned. He was beginning to get concerned with the amount of time Amelia had been unconscious. He watched as Gloria returned with the bottle of blood and wet washrag. He was relieved when he felt Amelia starting to stir.

Gloria set the bottle of blood on the table. She then carefully laid the washcloth across Amelia's for head. "I imagine she could have a monster of a migraine when she awakes. Hopefully that will help her," Gloria said.

Susan tried to probe the assassin's mind one more time even while asleep he was able to keep his mental shield in place. She once again wondered just how powerful Amelia was. Charles was thinking along the same lines but for different reasons. Although he found himself liking the young couple, he knew that in a few years they could become a threat to his organization. He was considering, rather it would be more prudent to eliminate them now and save himself a possible future headache. He sat there trying to decide what the best course of action was. He knew that Susan was of the opinion that they would be a major asset to the organization. Finally, he decided that he would use them until they became a threat and then eliminate them.

Charles also wondered who ordered the hit on the two of them. He doubted that any of the other lead enforcers had had the time to learn about them and even if they had, they hadn't had the time to get enough information on them to gauge what potential risk they pose. He hated to concede this but the threat he was facing now was coming from within his organization and he knew that the list of suspects was short and painful to him they were all people he considered family. Charles thought about the list of suspects with only cold hard logic and came up with two possibilities outside of the people here. He eliminated Gloria and Susan simple because they didn't know of Carlos Martinez's visit. Emma and Mitchel were the only two others besides himself, which knew about Andrew and Amelia going to watch Antonio Munoz.

Emma was the only one besides him who had access to the files that Antonio Munoz had in his possession yes, Mitchell could have conceivably accessed the files, but he had Amelia and Andrew flat sheets that contained all of the information that Antonio would have needed. Charles was sick to his stomach to think that his baby girl was the one who betrayed them. He ran through everyone he could think of that who could have done it the only other person who had that kind of access was Neil and that was no better. Neil would be the last person he suspects once Neil was turned all he wanted was for him and Emma go someplace out of the limelight and live quiet comfortable lives.

As predicted Amelia, had awaken with a massive migraine. She sensed her mate holding her close to him and even though her head was killing her, she smiled. She slowly opened her eyes and looked into a very worried set of eyes belonging to her mate. "You scared the hell out of me," Andrew's whispered softly as he smiled while looking into her eyes.

Amelia grabbed her arms around him and pulled him down for a kiss. "I am sorry love but I think it was worth it. I got into his mind," Amelia said triumphantly.

As anxious, as Charles was to learn which he had found out he knew she needed some time to pull herself together. "Amelia that is great news why don't you drink some blood and go grab a quick shower. I am sure that either Susan or Gloria has something that will fit you. Meanwhile Andrew and I will make some food for all us, and we can go over what you have learned while we eat," Charles suggested.

Amelia was happy for a chance to get over her headache before having to report what she had learned. She opened the bottle of blood and drank it as she headed to the room that she and Andrew had used the night before. Susan was closer to Amelia size and found her a nice housedress to wear. Amelia was a little larger in the chest but had smaller hips then Susan.

While Amelia was getting herself, together Andrew and Charles made a quick brunch, of Scrabble eggs with sausage and home fries. Once everyone was seated and had food in front of them. Amelia began relaying what she had learned. "His name is Uwais and despite his appearance he is a highly trained assassin. He has never seen the man he works for but has talked to him. I heard the voice in his memory. I swear I have heard that voice but I cannot place whom it belongs to. The man who shot Gloria earlier is dead; he was made an example of for his failure. I was supposed to be his target so that Andrew would have to be put down," Amelia reported matter-of-factually.

"Excuse me did you say that you were supposed to be the target, so that Andrew would be put down?" Susan asked interrupting Amelia.

"Yes, why what difference does that make?" Amelia inquired.

"Amelia not all mates have that strong of a bond that the death of one mate instantly causes the need to put the other down. That means the person who ordered the hits would have to have knowledge of what happened at the hotel. Look at Victor he was nowhere near the point where he needed to be put down and may have been able to survive losing his mate," Susan explained not liking where this was leading her. Susan knew that this limited suspect pool down to Emma, Neil, or Mitchell with Emma being the most likely.

Amelia gather her thoughts before she continued, "Their orders to kill us was to prevent Andrew and I from investigating the hotel incident, or at least that is what he was led to believe." Amelia paused trying to concentrate on the voice she heard. "I know that voice but I just can't place it," Amelia said frustrated.

"Amelia you did better than my wildest expectations. I have one question; do you think you will be able to share your memories with one of us in hopes that we can recognize the voice? Like what you did to me at Bio Medtronic," Charles asked with a smile trying to relax her.

Amelia thought it over for a few minutes. "I will try to but the last time it took a lot out of me. Can I please try it with Susan? I think I may have an easier time since her abilities are like mine," Amelia requested.

"Whomever you think is best. As long as Susan has no objections," Charles replied looking at Susan.

"What am I being asked to do?" Susan asked bemused as she looked at the two of them.

"I can share my memories with you, so that you can hear the voice and maybe you will recognize it." Amelia explained.

"She did it to you, Charles? What was it like?" Susan asked looking impressed.

"It was a unique experience to say the least. There was some pressure but no pain and as I was unprepared for it; it was a shock. It was not an unpleasant experience I once she gets the power under control, I could see where it would be an invaluable tool for an investigator," Charles explained with a laugh.

"I am game if you are," Susan excitedly said, her eyes alight with curiosity

"Just relax and I will do the rest," Amelia explained.

Amelia placed her hands on the sides and Susan's face and locked eyes with her. After a couple moments, Amelia's eyes started to glow and Susan's eyes went wide. Susan felt Amelia starting to come into her mind and relaxed. She heard the voice that Amelia had pulled from Uwais' memories. Susan felt no pressure and while it was a little unnerving at first once she got used to it, she felt at ease with the feeling. Amelia started to pull her mind back and just for moment, Susan felt as if she lost something.

While Amelia was showing her memories, Andrew and Charles moved behind the respective woman to be ready to catch them if necessary. They watched as Amelia released her link was Susan both of the women staggered for second.

"I know whose voice that was. It is..." Both women said in unison.

"Who did you two, say it was?" Charles asked shakily hoping he had somehow misheard them.

"You heard what we said and I know it is a shock to you," Susan softly responded as she took Charles' hands in hers.

"I am going to rip his fucking head off," Andrew angrily exclaimed as his eyes turned to black orbs.

"Andrew we must be very careful here. I can't believe he would betray me. He had never shown any interest in power. Amelia, are you sure you didn't somehow make a mistake or somehow altered the memory to make it sound like his voice?" Charles quietly said.

"I would never bare false witness against someone," Amelia retorted sternly.

"That isn't what I meant. I have no doubt that you honestly believe that you are being as honest as you can. What I am asking is by you trying so hard to identify the person who voice you heard in his memory did you accidentally misidentify it, and then accidentally alter the memory in your mind to match his voice?" Charles explained.

Amelia pondered what Charles was asking and considered his wisdom carefully before speaking. She didn't understand how she knew the answer to his inquiry but she did. "I do not think I could do it even if

I tried. But even if I could why do Susan come up with the same name?" Amelia responded.

Charles listened to not only what she said but how she said what she said looking for any signs of deception. "Just for argument sake, let's say in your mind you thought it was Amsu then wouldn't your mind alter the memory so that the voice Susan heard was who you wanted it to be. I mean on a subconscious level, where you are not aware of it?" Charles inquired.

"No, I don't think I could alter the memory. The memory I shared with Susan is a direct copy of what I saw in his mind like a picture or a recording of it and I don't have the ability to alter it as far as I know. Can I swear to this beyond all doubt? No, but I can beyond a reasonable doubt. The only reason I say it that way is I don't know how I know what I know," Amelia replied. She went quiet for a minute as if considering what Charles wisdom then continued," If I was going to pick someone; Why would I pick Amsu? There are far better suspects like Emma or Neil."

"Amelia please don't think that I doubt your integrity, but I have to make sure of my facts before I proceed. If we make one misstep, it could result in a civil war that could very well destroy everything we have worked for as a species. For the record, I do believe that the information you are giving me is truthful and accurate. I hope you understand I am just trying to gauge the extent of your powers," Charles explained earnestly.

"I wish I knew the extent of my abilities but I have no idea, and as I have said before, I can't explain how I know what I know about my powers; I just know. So how do we proceed from here?" Amelia responded conceding that Charles had a right to be concerned about the validity of her information.

Everyone was staring at Charles waiting to hear the answer to that very question. Charles was not sure how to proceed, there was no way the other enforcers would take a parvulus word over Amsu. Charles knew he had to prove that Amsu's plans were a threat to the vampires as a species to get the other enforcers to act and even then, he would be hard pressed with the amount of support Amsu has among the older vampires and other species.

Susan knew what Charles was thinking and understood that no matter what they said none of other enforcer would believe Amelia since she was a parvulus. She cleared her throat to get Charles attention. "I have a suggestion; let me try to break through Uwais' mental barriers. That way I can validate what Amelia said is accurate." Susan suggested.

Charles nodded his agreement. Susan tried to penetrate but his mental shield held and the harder she pushed the stronger the shield became. Finally, she realized he was not going to give and stopped trying. She looked at Charles and shook her head. Susan wondered how Amelia managed to get a past his mental barrier. "How did you get past his mental shield so quickly without damaging his mind?" Susan asked.

"I made him think that I was weaker than I am and when he eased off I took control of his mind and ordered him to lower his mental barriers and then it was easy for me to access his mind. He did try to fight but it was far easier for me to fend his attempts to regain control off then to constantly fight for each individual memory." Amelia replied.

Susan redoubled her efforts but it seemed that Uwais only got stronger the more she tried to force her way through. She couldn't believe that Amelia had walked through Uwais defenses with relative ease when she had not been able to even make a small dent in his defenses." Damn it! I wasn't able to break through his mental shield. Sorry Charles," Susan said frustration evident in her voice.

"I will start the attempt and try to take control of him as I did before and force him to lower his defenses. While you try the direct route to his mind one of us should be able to pierce his mental barrier," Amelia suggested.

Susan nodded her approval. Amelia walked over and looked Uwais in the eyes and began to push into his mind he tried to fight her but she easily pushed in and seizes control of his mind. Uwais eyes went wide then he got a blank look in his eyes and stared straight ahead as Amelia ordered him to lower all of his mental barriers and allow Susan to probe his mind.

Susan had little trouble confirming that Amelia was correct. She even saw a few of the vampires who he worked with and knew that Amsu employed them. Susan pulled out his mind and the two of them walked out of the room that served as his cell.

"She is correct I not only recognized his voice but I saw Layla giving him instructions on this mission. He was to follow them and watch for a chance to not only destroy Amelia and Andrew but you also Charles." Susan sadly said.

Charles was visible shaken. If Layla was giving orders, it left no doubt. There was no way for Amelia to have implanted that memory into the assassin since she didn't even know Layla. The room now vibrated with his power; it was an order of magnitude above even Susan's. The air literally crackled and it felt like a lightning storm was about to appear within the room as arcs of energy danced around Charles. Both Amelia and Andrew could feel every hair on their bodies stand up.

Susan laid a soft hand on Charles' shoulder and just let her calming presence wash over him. After a few minutes, his breathing evened out as the storm in his eyes calmed. Finally, the electrical storm that was bouncing around the room calmed as well.

"This fight is between Amsu and myself. I would appreciate any support that you can give me. I don't want you all directly involved. It is too dangerous." Charles ordered in a tone that let it be known he would broker no argument.

"He tried to kill my mate and injured my friend. When I get my hands on him, I am going to rip his beating heart from his chest and ram it down his throat. I don't care who I have to go through to get it done." Andrew angrily retorted.

Andrew's control shattered and his powers came rushing forward like a freight train. His eyes turned to pure black orbs showing no life in them at all. Everything not nailed down or secured in the room began to float in the air and the temperature began to rise. Within a minute, it was almost ninety-five degrees in the room and climbing rapidly. Andrew pictured Uwais in his mind and his anger turned on him. Uwais felt incredible amount of pressure on the sides of his head. He let out a scream as blood began to pour from his nose and ears. The blood then started to run out of his mouth as his eye bulged from his head. He tried to scream in pain but could not get it out as his mouth was filled with blood. He felt his body getting hotter; from uncomfortable to burning hot. The last thing Uwais saw before his head popped like a balloon was flames erupting from his midsection.

Most of the brains and blood that exploded from his head when it popped caught fire and burned up before it could even reach the walls or the floor. The fire was so hot that it completely consumed the rest of the body. The only remains were a small pile of ashes and a few smears of blood from when his head popped. What was most miraculous to all of those that observed the event was that the sprinkler system never activated.

The temperature was steadily rising in the room it was now over one hundred and thirty degrees. Andrew stood their unaware of anything or anyone around him. He was lost in a war between his two halves and the feral side was winning for the moment, partially because the human half-wanted revenge as much as the baser half did.

Charles couldn't believe the amount of power that Andrew had shown; he was much too young to be able to wield the kind of power. He was concerned that Andrew could lose control of his powers or worse yet he could potentially challenge him and in a few decades be able to usurp him. He was originally worried about Amelia and her powers but now he realized that Andrew was a much larger of a threat and he would have to watch him very carefully.

Amelia wrapped her arms around Andrew's waist and looked into his eyes as she pushed into his mind and tried to calm him. She could sense he was almost to the same state he was in earlier and she worried this time he may not be able to come back.

" Love, you need to lower the temperature in the room. It is getting way too hot in here and we are roasting." Amelia whispered.

She was right; the temperature in the room was pushing one hundred and fifty degrees now. She grabbed the sides of his face and started sharing memories of them being together. Slowly she managed to break through his feral state and bring him back to a more centered state of mind. Everything gently settled back down to the ground, Andrew's eyes went back to his normal color of hazel, and the temperature in the room slowly began to drop back to normal. Andrew looked into Amelia's eyes and smiled slightly just before he collapsed. Amelia scooped his limp form up in her arms and gentle laid him down on the couch. Gloria quickly retrieved a wet cloth for Amelia to lie across the top of his forehead.

Susan felt Andrew's powers explode forth and watched in amazement as everything in the room not nailed down began to float into the air. She could feel the temperature rapidly rise. She heard Uwais scream she then watched as the blood began pouring from his nose and ears. Susan watched in both fascination and horror as the top of Uwais' head exploded just before he was consumed by flames. She had never seen anything like that in her long life and it called to her baser side; the raw power Andrew had just shown was like an aphrodisiac. The sudden arousal surprised Susan; it had been centuries since a parvulus had caused such a reaction in her. Susan realized that she would have to be careful around Andrew so she didn't upset his mate, whom she dearly liked. She realized why she felt such a kinship with Andrew and Amelia as they reminded her of Lenard and Gabriel. Susan fought with her sadness as she thought about the two of them.

Lenard had been with Charles off and on for over eight hundred years. Once Lenard had met Gabriel, the four of them had traveled the world and seen the sights. They had decided to spend the turning of the new century in Spain. Gabriel had only been mated with Lenard for little over five years but everyone could tell those two had that magical union and their two souls had become one. All it took was a glance to see how deeply they loved each other. When the bell tolled signaling that seventeen hundred had arrived, the streets erupted in a party and during the wild, dancing Gabriel had been separated from the three of them. Archibald, who had claimed Gabriel was his mate, was embarrassed when Gabriel mated with Lenard and took the opportunity to take his revenge and murdered Gabriel. He claimed that Lenard had stolen her from him. Lenard knew the second she died and started attacking everyone in sight while screaming for Gabriel. Charles had no choice but to put his friend down. The four of them had been so close they decided to form their own coven and it had scarred the two of them so deeply that they had never formed another coven with anyone.

It had only taken six hours for Susan to track Archibald down. Susan had taken great pleasure in beating and torturing him for hours causing as much pain as she possibly could. By the time Archibald was turned over to Charles, Susan had broken nearly every bone in his body.

Charles had taken great pleasure in announcing Archibald's fate. He personally removed Archibald's fangs and buried him alive in a steel coffin. Charles knew it would take months for him to starve and before he did, he would go mad. It may well be the cruelest punishment that could be inflicted on a vampire. It had been the first, and only, time Charles had ordered that punishment.

Susan pulled herself back to the present and wiped the tears from her eyes. She looked around the room and was surprised that everything was set back in place with no apparent damage to it. She watched as Amelia took care of Andrew unconscious form worrying over him. Susan looked at Charles and he smiled at her shaking his head. She could see the concern he was hiding behind his smile.

She knew that Andrew could become a threat but she doubted that he ever would she knew that by nature he is a protector hence his choice to be a cop. He was a natural leader but he wasn't a politician and she doubted that he ever would be. Amelia was the politically minded one of the two but she had no desire to be a leader. She would do it when her job called for it, but she was happiest when someone else was in charge and she could do her job. Susan was sure the two of them would be an asset to Charles and given the chance, they would most likely become close friends. Susan decided that she would do everything with in her power to help the two of them except to attack Charles, and she hoped that Charles wouldn't jump the gun and order them destroyed. If he did, Susan decided she would, for the first time in their long relationship, refuse to carry out his order. She would never forgive him if he did it, but she couldn't attack him.

CHAPTER 9

****

Charles could see that Susan was worrying over if he would order Andrew death because of his potential threat, and he knew that it was the prudent thing to do, but he would wait for the time being. Unbeknownst to him Amelia had picked up on his line of thought and was watching him while preparing to defend herself and, more importantly, her mate. She slammed her mind closed preventing anyone from gaining access and closing all bonds but Andrew's with her. Gloria immediately went on alert once she sensed what Amelia had done, wondering what had set her off.

Across town, Catherine felt Amelia slam close her link to her and immediately panicked. She thought that something had happened to Amelia. She begged to be taken to her sire but Emma explained that she had no idea where they were and that if they called her it may endanger their lives. Scott finally demanded that they contact them somehow; he was worried that the stress would hurt Catherine or the baby. Emma promised to try to get in touch with her parents and see if she could get some information.

Andrew slowly came back to consciousness. He couldn't recall what had happened and he had a pounding headache. When he looked into Amelia's eyes, he gave her a weak smile. He felt as if he had just run a marathon while having the flu.

"This should fix you right up." Gloria said as she handed him a bottle of blood. She sat a second bottle of blood on the table in front of Andrew encase he needed it.

"Andrew you need to regain your strength as quickly as possible. Charles thinks you may be a threat to him and is trying to decide if he should attack you. Please don't react to this we need to bide our time until we can even the odds love. Block your mind off to everyone but me," Amelia telepathically said.

Andrew sat there for a few moments trying to recall what had happened then he quickly drained the bottle of blood and closed off his mind to everyone but Amelia. As soon as he finished the bottle, his headache subsided and the memories of what he had done came flooding back in. Andrew looked over to the cell where Uwais had been housed and realized what he had done. He couldn't help but smile in satisfaction. "Why the hell does he think that?" Andrew asked mentally.

"He saw how strong you already are and he thinks in the very near future you could usurp him and take over his precious empire," Amelia responded through their mental link.

"Is he fucking nuts?! I do not want his fucking empire; I would kill someone. What an egotistical bastard." Andrew responded the same way.

Amelia started to chuckle then quickly covered it up with a cough. Damn it Andrew be careful, I don't want to tip him off. "Amelia admonished him through their link.

Andrew chuckled softly as he pulled Amelia into a hug. All of a sudden, his senses sharpened dramatically. He could sense everything around him not only in the room but also outside of the building. It was a surreal experience when someone walked past the front of the building and Andrew could tell that it was a vampire. His sense of smell also dramatically increased. Before, he could smell blood flowing beneath a person skin if he was close to them but now, he could smell Susan and Charles' blood from across the room and tell the difference between them. He also smelled the remnants of the coffee they had earlier and even the cleaning products that had been used in here. Andrew was a bit overwhelmed and staggered for a second.

He closed his eyes to bring the overwhelming sensations under control. He slowly managed to tune his senses down a bit. He was still hyper-sensitive to everything but at least now, it was at a level where he could function. He sensed Charles start to move and spun around on him suddenly. Andrew was clearly startled and took a defensive posture

Charles was about to get up to go get more coffee, unaware of Andrew's heightened senses, when Andrew spun on him. He knew that the two of them were on alert but decided that it was just from the events from this morning. He would have never believed that Amelia had not only been able to read his thoughts but also Susan's thoughts. Charles was surprised by Andrew's sudden movement.

"I sensed him starting to move. I felt his muscles tense and it surprised me. How did I do that?" Andrew asked clearly confused.

"I would say that you have tapped into more of your abilities Andrew and if what I suspect is true, it will be very hard for someone to sneak up on you. What else do you sense?" Susan calmly explained with a smile.

Andrew opened up his senses to see what all he could pick up. "I can sense everyone and everything around the building and I can tell if they are human, vampire or something else. It is almost like radar but I am not sure how far I can sense."

"May I ask why you and Amelia are blocking yourselves off?" Susan inquired.

Andrew considered lying but decided it was far better to confront Charles here and now. This way, they have somewhat of a chance to defend themselves. He locked eyes with Charles and prepared himself to attack if necessary." To protect ourselves; it would seem someone in this room thinks I may be a threat." Andrew responded in a measured tone.

Andrew was coiled tightly and was ready to strike at the slightest provocation, not that you could tell from appearance. He was watching Charles waiting to see what his reaction was. If Charles tried to attack, he would do whatever he had to do to protect Amelia.

"Why would you think that?" Susan asked.

"I do not think it. Amelia knows it, she warned me that Charles considers me a possible threat. What I would like to know is what is he going to do about it? Secondly, why does he think I am threat? I am not going to be going around looking over my shoulder." Andrew replied in the same easygoing demeanor as before.

What Charles found most disconcerting was Andrew's easy stance he looked as if he was discussing the weather, he showed no apprehension or fear. Charles could not believe that a parvulus could have such control over his emotions. He could feel the apprehension and even a bit of fear off everyone else but him, as if he had the ability to turn off every emotion. Amelia quickly rose and moved beside Andrew; her body language showed her tensed and ready to strike.

Charles felt Susan take a quick reading on him and he knew that not only did she know what he was thinking, but also that she wouldn't help him this time. He was now reconsidering his original assessment of the two of them. The two of them were proving that they very well could become a major threat to him in the near future. He was beginning to think that it might be in his best interest to strike now. He knew that Susan would set this fight out, but for the first time he was unsure if Gloria would get involved or not. If she did and he had to destroy her, it would hurt Susan deeply.

Charles knew if he struck now, he would have to do some fast-talking to prevent Catherine from seeking revenge. Of course, eliminating her would be the easiest of all. Just has he had that thought Amelia scowled at him. Charles now realized she was still able to read his mind even though he was blocking her. The only person who had ever been able to read him like that was Diamond. He tried to reinforce his mental barrier as he muttered, "Fuck!"

Gloria was torn she knew that if a fight broke out that Susan would side with Charles and attack Andrew and Amelia. Gloria had no desire to attack anyone in this room. She looked at Susan, her eyes pleading. Susan shook her head telling her not to get involved. Susan then looked at Charles, so he could see the displeasure in her eyes.

"Why are you doing this now Charles?" Susan demanded.

"I was just doing a threat assessment. I didn't think anyone would be probing my mind and to be honest I am not happy that she did it or even that she has the ability to do it. I have to protect the species." Charles lied hoping it would defuse the situation.

Amelia was incensed that he had the balls to try to lie. She mustered as much venom as she could as she accused, "Your only concern was your empire, and that in a few decades Andrew could be strong enough to take it from you. Well asshole I will tell you this; neither of us want anything from you, and if you try to go after Catherine, I will do everything in my powers to kill you. You leave her, Scott, and their baby alone. You have a problem with the two of us, then let's settle it here and now."

Susan went wide in shock as she looked at Amelia in disbelief. She had never seen anyone but her stand up to Charles like Amelia had just done. Susan was concerned that Charles would take offense or worse yet make him believe that they were truly a threat to him and strike. Susan subtly positioned herself to be able to intercede between the two of them.

The surprise in Charles' face was evident; no one had had the balls to stand up to him in this way in centuries, not even Susan. Not only was Amelia standing up to him but she was actually calling him out. The both of them were ready to face him. Knowing they didn't stand a chance in hell of winning was extremely impressive. What astonished him the most was how protective they were of each other; they were both ready to throw their lives away to give the other a chance to survive. He found himself growing in respect for the two of them by the minute

"Please forgive me. She is right I was trying to decide if the two of you were a threat. You two are impressive and could be a very real threat in the future. Usually I would have watched the two of you but with everything going on right now I am hyper-vigilant and very much on edge. I will give both of you my word of honor that at this moment I have no intention of striking against either one of you, and I hope that the two of you will forgive me for making you believe that I was intending to.

Susan has repeatedly told me that the two of you would be a good addition to our organization, and she doesn't feel that you two would ever be a threat to what we have built. I normally take her word, it is just with being betrayed as I was and not knowing the two of you, I was overly concerned. I ask that you understand my motives. I have to always be on guard against people who would try to conduct a coup against me and I guess this time I let the circumstances of the past few days' events cloud my better judgment. Amelia please believe me that while I may think about doing such things, I have never destroyed someone without just cause and in an instance like this before I would act against the two of you, I would have discussed it with not only Susan but Emma. I give you my word I have no intentions of acting against any of you." Charles explained earnestly with a hint of regret in his voice.

Susan placed herself between Amelia, Andrew, and Charles to try to defuse the tension before it spiraled out of control. "Why don't we all..."Susan started to say when her cell phone interrupted her.

"Hello Emma what is a matter? ... No, it was just a misunderstanding; tell Catherine that Amelia will call her in a couple minutes. Also, remind her worrying isn't good for the baby... Yes dear, we are all fine. Is everything OK there? ... No, I do not want him anywhere near you. I want you to get everyone to move now. Let me talk to Mitchel... Mitchel this is Susan I want you to take everyone including your mate and leave now. Make sure everyone is armed, and use the emergency exit. I want you on the road within fifteen minutes... You know which members we picked and under no circumstance is Amsu allowed in with Emma... once you are in route call me... thank you and please be careful." Susan said in a concerned voice.

Susan hung up the phone and saw five very concerned faces staring at her. All of the troubles between them were placed on the back burner. "What is the matter?" Charles asked.

"Emma said that Amsu has been demanding to see her, and that if he wasn't allowed to see her soon it would be dire consequences. Damn its Charles that bastard is threatening our family." Susan replied her eyes filling with rage.

Charles wrapped his arms around Susan, "Love, calm yourself down and we will get her here were she is safe. Then we will deal with Amsu and he shall pay dearly." Charles whispered while comforting Susan.

"Love I know we need to settle things with Charles, but please let's bide our time. Catherine and Scott are in trouble and we can't protect them on our own," Amelia pleaded using their link.

"I will let it go for now so we can all work together and protector our families. I warn you, no matter the outcome, if I even suspect for a second that he will try anything I will strike without hesitation or warning," Andrew replied mentally with a sigh.

"Thank you, my love, I just hope Susan is right about Charles being a man of his word. However, if things do go bad what do we do about Susan and Gloria? Susan is sure to defend Charles. I am pretty sure Gloria will not idle set by and allow Susan to be destroyed so we will also have those two to contend with." Amelia warned using telepathy.

"Let's just worry about protecting our family and pray that everything here was just a big misunderstanding escalated by frayed nerves and not knowing each other well enough. We will just be vigilant and watch each other's' backs." Andrew replied the same way, as he said while motioning towards the cell," I guess if Catherine, Emma and the others are coming here I better clean up my mess."

The tension in the room lowered immensely and Gloria breathed a sigh of relief. "I will go get some cleaning supplies and help you," She offered cheerfully.

Charles headed to the armory and started to pull out a side arm for each one of them. He reached up and grabbed two gold plated .454 Casull Taurus revolvers and the six speed loaders beside them. He then retrieved three .50 Action Express Desert Eagles and half of dozen magazines for them. He knew that all of the weapons here were supposed to be loaded with Teflon coated rounds, so called cop-killers because their bullet resistant vest could not stop these rounds. He laid the pistols carefully on the table before him. He made sure that all of the guns were properly cleaned and loaded then placed them in shoulder holsters.

Andrew made quick work of cleaning up what was left of Uwais. He then went to see if he could help Charles while keeping an eye on him. He couldn't fully trust him yet and didn't want to give him a chance to ambush Amelia or himself. Charles was just finishing when Andrew joined him. Andrew was impressed with the collection of firearms stored in this room; everything from modern semi- and fully automatics to Antique match locks. He took a quick look around and he seen a Schofield Cavalry revolver. "You have quite the collection here." Andrew said.

"Most of the older ones Susan, Gloria, or myself carried at one time. That Remington over there was one of the guns that Gloria used to avenge her parents." Charles explained with a smile. He indicated an old Remington Navy .36 caliber cap and ball pistol. Andrew looked around the room while Charles continued, "This collection is nothing compared to what I have at my home. Once we get out of this mess, I would love for you and Amelia to come over and see it"

Andrew was a still wary of him but thought it better to try to keep thing friendly for the time being. He figured Charles and he would settle things one way or the other once everyone was safe. He said, "I look forward to seeing that collection."

"Andrew, I know we got off to a bad start here but I really would like the chance to get to know you and your lovely mate. I was concerned for my organization and yes, you and she could be a real threat in the future to it. I am willing to gamble that Susan is correct and that you will be an asset to it. What I am asking is for a chance for us to become friends. What do you say?' Charles asked while offering his hand.

Andrew quickly assessed what Charles had said, looking for any deceit and not finding any. He accepted the offered hand letting go the remaining tension. "I would like to be able to call you friend." Andrew replied.

Charles handed Andrew one of the Desert Eagles." It is loaded with Teflon coated rounds so be mindful of what is behind your target." Charles warned.

While the others saw to their various tasks, Susan and Amelia started preparing rooms for the others that were coming. They had just finished the second room when Susan's cell rang. "Hello," Susan said into the phone.

"Mother, Amsu was waiting for us in the garage and won't let us leave; he said we will die if we try to go. Mother, it almost sounded as if he was threatening us. What do you want us to do?" Emma asked her concern evident in her voice. While they were talking, Susan could hear Amsu arguing with Mitchel.

"Let me talk to Amsu," Susan ordered.

"Susan, I sense that Emma is in grave danger." Amsu said without any greetings after he was handed the phone.

"Amsu, we were trying to move the children and their friends to a safe location when you interfered. Please let us get this done, then we will contact you in arrange a time and place to meet to discuss how best to alleviate the threat." Susan calmly stated biting back her anger.

"I am telling you if they try to leave here, they will die. If you are insistent on this foolish move then I insist that you allow me to accompany them." Amsu demanded angrily.

"No, you are not going with them. I will just put a larger escort around them. This is none of your concern Amsu, now remove yourself from the secured area and we will contact you once they are safe." Susan ordered her anger starting to leach into her tone.

"It is my concern; Emma is my grandchild. Please let me speak with Charles." Amsu retorted.

"Hold on a minute I will get him." Susan replied coldly.

Susan muted the phone and went to get Charles." You better talk to this asshole Charles or I am going after him and consequences be dammed." Susan angrily demanded.

"Talk to whom? My love," Charles asked clearly confused.

"Amsu. He has just threatened our daughter. I will kill that fucker and anything that gets in my way." Susan threatened. Charles could sense the anger rolling off her in waves. He knew that if her control slipped, she could very well destroy a large portion of the city.

"Love, calm down" Charles said. "Don't you remember what happened in 1871 when you went after Carl Misère? I don't think that the humans will blame Mrs. O'Leary's cow this time."

Charles took the phone and started to talk to Amsu. He was concerned that Susan would threaten Amsu and it would get out of hand. He knew under normal circumstances Susan would be able to maintain a level head but with Emma being threatened, she would very quickly loose her perspective and could very well make the situation much worse.

"You started the great Chicago fire?" Andrew asked his surprise evident.

"Yes." Susan replied flatly, as she walked over to the bar. She poured herself a glass of whiskey and drank it straight down. Andrew noted that her eyes were in beginning stages of change.

"Susan, we will do whatever we have to do to protect our family. I am including Emma and Neil in that statement. Amsu will pay, and it will cost him dearly; once we have our love ones safe." Andrew promised.

"Thank you, I cannot tell you how much that means to me." Susan replied as she gave Andrew a friendly hug.

"You and Gloria have been there for Amelia and me from the beginning and there is no way we would abandon you when you need us even if Catherine wasn't involved." Andrew said.

"Amsu, what are you doing?' Charles demanded without the normal preliminary small talk.

"I am trying to protect my Granddaughter. If you take her from here, she will die. Call it a premonition." Amsu said inject the correct amount of concern in his voice.

Charles realized that Amsu was indeed threatening Emma. He fought to maintain control of his baser self. After a brief struggle, he came up with a way to buy them some time and maybe throw Amsu off-kilter enough to give them a chance to rescue Emma and the others. "Perhaps it would be best if they stayed there. Let me talk to Mitchel then I will call you back. I need a favor from you." Charles responded, carefully keeping his anger in check. He waited until Amsu handed the phone to Mitchel then said, "I want all of you in the secure family room. Stay there and await further orders from me. Have Vernon's team put the club on lockdown."

"Consider it done. Any other orders?" Mitchel asked.

"Just be ready at a moment's notice and tell Amsu, I will call him back in about ten minutes," Charles replied. He then disconnected the call.

"Gloria call Andrea and tell him to get his team to BWI, then call Keith and tell him I want the jet at North Philly within three hours; I don't care how he gets it done. Also, tell him that Andrea will be joining him. Once he lands tell him to prepare the plane for a trip to Cancun. Susan call Ulysses tell him to prep my jet and prepare flight planes for both LAX and Miami International. Amelia would you please go back over everything you picked up from Uwais' mind and try to find out what Amsu's goals are. I will explain my plans as soon as I get done talking to Amsu." Charles quickly said.

Charles dialed Amsu's cell and waited for him to answer. "Old man do you still have a good relationship with Sophie?" Charles asked.

"In what way do you mean?" Amsu asked curious where Charles was going with this.

"If you ask her for information, would she try to get it for you?" Charles inquired.

"I believe so, but even if she wouldn't or couldn't I have many other resources. What do you need my son?" Amsu responded.

"I need all the information you can get me on a man named Uwais." Charles requested.

"W... Who is that? What does he have to do with threat to Emma?" Amsu asked, his trepidation showing.

"I am hoping you can find out more information on him. He is an assassin that was following Susan and me. Andrew managed to capture him alive and we are questioning him as we speak, but it will take time he is highly trained to resist interrogation. I am hoping that you can find out who he is working for." Charles stated with a smile. He realized he had hit a nerve with Amsu.

"I will do what I can but why don't you let me have a crack at him. I should be able to get through his mental defenses with ease." Amsu offered.

"For now, I like to keep our location a secret. I am sure they have a spy in my organization and do not want to take a chance on you being followed here. Amelia was the one who got his name and assignment from him already. Try to find out what you can and I will call you back in a couple hours and if we haven't made any progress with him then we will make arraignments to meet up and give you a crack at him." Charles suggested.

As they spoke, Charles wondered why Amsu was trying to take his territory. If he had wanted a territory, all he had to do was ask for one. Charles knew for a fact that Amsu could have had the Middle East including his beloved Egypt. He was beginning to wonder if Diamond's death had pushed her creator over the edge. He wondered why Amsu was going after him and his family, after all he had always thought of Amsu as a father figure and his betrayal hit Charles hard. He knew he would have to face him soon, but he would bide his time only striking when Amsu was at his weakest; in that moment the greatest chance of success presented itself

"OK my son, who knows maybe I will find out something form my contacts and we won't need to waste the time breaking through his mental defenses." Amsu replied carefully controlling the inflections of his voice.

While Charles was dealing with Amsu, Susan finished the task that Charles had assigned her. Susan then went to help Amelia with her task hoping that between the two of them they could get some clue as to Amsu plans. She was hoping that since she knew the members of Amsu's personal staff she would be able to help Amelia come up with something.

Once Charles was finished, he called everyone together so that the five of them could try to come up with a safe way to get their love ones out of danger. After discussing the problem for almost an hour, they came up with a working plan. Gloria would take the armored van and go meet their families. She would take them to Philadelphia International Airport to meet Charles' jet and have it taken them all to Scotland. Gloria had a piece of property there that until today no one but her knew about. The property had a large country estate located on it and was being cared for by an older couple that happened to be vampires.

Charles would call Amsu and ask him to meet them at a piece of property they had about an hour from Philly. He would claim that were unable to pierce Uwais' mental shield and they wanted him to try.

Amelia and Andrew would head to North Philly Airport, meet with Andrea and his team and then once they were sure that Gloria had gotten Emma, Catherine, and the rest out of town they would head towards the farm. If everything went perfect, they would be able to either capture or kill Amsu and end this mess before it got to out of hand.

Charles called Amsu's cell. "Hey old man, any luck?" Charles asked.

"Who you calling old man? I am sorry my son but either he is a relative nobody or you have the wrong name for him." Amsu retorted.

"Then as much as I hate to ask this, I am going to need you to get a bit more involved." Charles said.

"What do you need my son?" Amsu inquired.

"I am going to need you to help break through Uwais' mental shield. Both Susan and Amelia have failed to penetrate his defenses." Charles replied.

"I will be glad to assist you in any way I can. Where are we going to do this?" Amsu stated.

"I want to get him out of the city. I am thinking that farm Susan and I own about an hour north of here." Charles suggested.

"That sounds good. Do you want me to bring Emma and the rest with me?" Amsu asked.

"No, I agree with your earlier statement they are a lot safer there. I hate to admit this but I have a leak in my organization so I want this quiet so please don't tell anyone where you are going." Charles explained.

"I will get Layla to drive me if that is OK. I won't tell her our destination until we are on the road just to be extra sure of security," Amsu said.

"Thank you Amsu, I can't tell you how much I appreciate your support," Charles replied adding as much sincerity as he could.

"Anything for you, my son. When are you going to leave to head there?" Amsu inquired.

"We will be leaving within the hour and we will be taking a longer route to make sure we aren't followed. I would say it will be about three hours until we get there." Charles stated.

'OK, I will have Layla here within twenty minutes and head their directly to get things set-up" Amsu said.

"Great; with the addition of her we should have enough security in case things go sideways. Thanks, old man, I owe you one." Charles said before disconnecting the call.

Charles waited about thirty minutes then called Mitch. "Has Amsu left yet?" Charles asked and waited for him to confirm that Amsu had left before continuing, "Use the emergency tunnel that connects to the old sewage pipes. Gloria will meet you on the lot by alternate exit delta. Let me talk to Emma."

Mitch acknowledged Charles orders and asked him to hold while he got Emma. "Daddy, what is going on?" Emma asked clearly confused and concerned.

"Too much to go over on the phone; I need you to trust me and do exactly what Mitchel and the guards tell you to do. I will explain everything once we are together. I have a task for you. Go to the computer, bring up the security directives and type in "execute code 505", then press enter. It will prompt you to enter your personal pass word." Charles explained

"OK dad, I will do as you ask but I expect a full explanation when I see you." Emma responded. She had a sick feeling in her stomach. She then handed the phone back to Mitchel. While they were talking Emma went to the computer terminal and accessed the file that her father had asked her to use and typed in the execute order.

Charles finished with his call to Mitchel. Gloria was the first one to leave in a large van. Susan and Amelia had helped her stock the van with extra units of blood and snacks. Mainly for Catherine since she was pregnant. Gloria was to circle around for a bit and make sure she wasn't followed.

Amelia and Andrew were the next to leave; they also were in a large van. Their van was loaded with extra weapons for Andrea and his team. They would head directly to the airport and pick-up Andrea's team and then head to meet up with Charles to handle Amsu.

Charles and Susan would leave last and take the long way around to the farm. Charles tentatively planned to meet Andrew at a little farm store about fifteen miles from the farm. He had given Andrew a burn phone encase they needed to make any changes.

Emma was surprised and saddened when she saw. 45 seconds to core destruction. DO you wish to continue? Y/N. Emma pressed the "y" key then hesitated. She knew that it would be a long time until she would return to Philly, the city that she had called home for the last eighty years. She closed her eyes in an attempt to hold back the tears as she pushed the enter button.

Neil quietly walked up behind her and wrapped his strong arms around her. He could sense her distress even without their bond. "Ohtsévátanó (love) we will come back when this is over," Neil softly promised.

"Néméhotâtse éhame (I love you husband). Hohátséné' ónéé'tov tséhnéehóveto (My happiness is being with you)," Emma responded as she turned to face her mate.

"Néméhotâtse nâhtse'eme (I love you my wife)." Neil whispered as he kissed Emma lovingly.

Mitchel finished getting Charles instructions then hung up and he called in the additional guards that were needed. He then opened up the escape route and gathered the rest of the people for the move into the tunnel. He quietly walked over to Emma and Neil. ," I hate to break up this sweet moment but it is time to move."

Mitch then handed Emma and Neil each a holstered pistol. Emma had seen that Scott and Catherine were already in the passageway with Linda, Burt, and several others all of which were among her parent's most trusted people. Burt took the lead followed closely by Kathleen both of them were carrying an M-60 loaded with incendiary. Then it was Stan and Carper both carrying AK-47's, then it was the family group every one of them armed with side arms with exception of

Scott and Neil who had a Remington 12 gauge loaded with 00 buckshot.

Then behind the family group were Dawn and Sarah both carrying AK-47's and Sarah with an Army issue M24 sniper rifle on her back. Lastly was Mitch carrying an M-60 loaded with incendiary rounds. None of them had a light, but thankfully they could see just find without them and no one made a sound. Mitch knew it would take them about forty minutes to get to the meeting point. As they were walking, he couldn't help but wonder why they were running from Amsu; he had always been a trusted member of Charles inner circle. After walking for what felt like forever in the wonderful olfactory sensation of the city sewerage system, they arrived at the meeting point. Burt handed His M-60 to Stan and started to climb the ladder to the exit and fresh air.

"No! It is a trap, run!" Catherine screamed; her eyes glowing

No one questioned her they all turned to run when the manhole cover was opened and a square package with two small cylinders was dropped down the hole and they heard Amsu say, " Sorry Emma."

Gloria was setting in the parking lot where she was to meet Emma and the group about quarter of a mile away from where they would be coming out of the sewer system. She was to take them directly to the airport so the whole group was to be flown out of harm's way to a piece of property that Gloria had bought almost sixty years ago in Scotland. She felt a spike of gut-wrenching terror through her bond from Susan and from Amelia. Then she felt the ground shake and the sound of a muffled explosion.

Amelia felt the spike of fear from Catherine and knew she expected to die. She then felt the link between them shut down. "No!" She screamed as tears started to roll down her cheeks.

Andrew sensed her distress and knew that she was expecting Catherine to die. He could feel the dread and fear rolling off his mate and could hear her whimpering in pain. Seeing that they were trapped in traffic, he turned on to the first side street and parked the van. He pulled Amelia out of the truck with him as he let go of his human side and allowed his feral side to come forward. He grabbed Amelia in his arms and sped off towards the meeting point as fast as he could. He turned invisible after the first few steps to avoid drawing unwanted attention to himself.

Both Susan and Charles felt the spike of fear and sorrow from their daughter. Charles fought against his feral self to keep control. He quickly made a U-turn and raced towards the area that they were supposed to meet Gloria.

Susan also felt the spike of fear and then she felt her own fear. For the first time in centuries, she felt fear from Charles. He had always been able to keep his fear in check no matter what was happening. She knew in her heart they would be too late and tears started streaming down her face.

Both Susan and Charles felt Emma block off their link and it only deepened the pain they felt. Charles was barely holding on to his human side when his cell rang. "Black here," He said gruffly into the phone without looking to see who had called him.

"Hello son. I warned you that Emma would die if you tried to move them and now it has happened. Emma had to pay a terrible price for your incompetence." Amsu stated in a cold hard voice.

"Why? Why would you go after my daughter? If you wanted a territory, you could have had your choice. Any enforcer would of gladly gave you his territory and taken over another." Charles angrily stated as his feral side started to rush forward.

Susan watched as Charles battled with his feral side and she knew he had to keep his head clear if they were going to have a chance to avenge their daughter. Susan laid her hand on Charles shoulder and willed herself to remain calm in hopes it would help Charles to center himself. Charles glanced at Susan and gave her a sad smile letting her know he was back in control and grateful for her being there to help him.

"Charles my poor naïve boy, I don't want your territory. I want our race to go back to the strong race we once were. You and the other enforcers have let our race degrade to the point that humans, a race that is little more than bovines, managed to destroy my daughter. They turned her into a monster, and then killed her. Then, what do you do to avenge her? You assist those very same humans even going so far as to accept them into your inner circle," Amsu ranted his voice full of hatred.

"How the fuck does you killing my daughter help to further your cause? If you have a problem then you face me and not kill my child!" Charles demand now furious.

Amsu's maniacal laugh sent a chill down Charles back. "Charles my son you have become so weak that you were too afraid to even claim your mate, but now you are going to help me whether you like it or not. I have now made it to where you will have to be strong again if you want to avenge your daughter. And by coming after me you will help..." Amsu responded coldly.

"What do you mean I am going to help? I would never help you now. But you did get one thing right; I will kill you very slowly," Charles said interrupting Amsu.

"I know you will come after me, and no little territorial line is going to stop you. So you will be starting wars with everyone and you know as well as I do the council will never sanction my termination so you will have to act without their sanction which will start a war that will purge all of the weaker vampires," Amsu explained as if he was talking to child.

Charles knew for sure his sire had crossed over and was insane and dangerous. He also knew that he was correct about the council not sanctioning his termination, but he was wrong about it starting a war. He knew is there was going to be any justice for his family they would have to do it themselves and it would have to be done very carefully or Amsu would get his war.

"Know this, since you are too much of a coward to face me. I am coming for you old man enjoys what little time you have left," Charles quietly said mourning the loss if the man he had considered his father for over two Millennium.

"I will give you a starting point, head south young man. Do not worry; you and Susan will join your daughter soon," Amsu responded in a bone chilling cold voice

Catherine watched in slow motion as the device fell through the manhole and then exploded, she knew in an instant the flames would engulf her and she regretted that her baby would never get the chance to live. She watched in horror as the flames from the bomb engulfed Burt and Kathleen. She could not peel her eyes away as she watched the two of them slowly vaporize in slow motion. She wondered why they all did not run since the flames were moving so slowly. She felt Scott push her and Linda behind him in a futile attempt to shield them. The flames slowly reached out and touched Stan and then Carper engulfing them. They barely had chance to start to scream when they were gone.

Catherine looked at her mate for one last time as the flames came towards them sure, that it would be the last time she would see him in this world. She watched as the flames seemed to hit an invisible wall that was right behind Scott and instead of engulfing them the force of the explosion and the flames were directed up toward the roof of the sewer, they were in. the force of the explosion caused a cave in on the other side of the wall. Scott turned towards Catherine, the corner of his lips lifted to a small smile then his eyes rolled into the back of his head and he collapsed into her arms.

Emma heard Amsu's voice apologizing as she watched the bomb, he dropped fall carelessly through the opening. She watched in slow motion as its detonated spewing forth the flames of her destruction. She quickly closed of her link to her parents to spare them feeling her death and quickly turned wrapping her arms around her mate she wanted to feel his strong arms one last time. She felt his arms wrap around her and she closed her eyes and awaited her destruction. Minutes seemed as hours as she stood there. Finally, she was sure she should have already been dead and wonder why she wasn't. She carefully opened her eyes and surveyed the scene. She saw Scott collapsing into Catherine's arms in slow motion, and as soon as he touched her arms time seemed to speed up back to normal. She looked at Neil his eyes were open wide in shock he whispers, "He stopped the explosion."

Emma looked around to make sure that the others weren't injured; she saw Linda laying on the ground; her leg was bent at an odd angle. Emma rushed to Linda's side and immediately saw it was broken. "I tripped when he shoved me behind him. Damned clumsy of me huh?" Linda stated her voice hoarse with pain.

Mitch handed his M-60 to Dawn and quickly went to Linda's side. He was livid that Amsu had tried to kill his mate when he was supposed to be their ally. He quickly took hold of his mates' hand to lend her some support while Emma straightened out her leg.

"Dear, you know that neither Charles nor Susan will let this slight go. His day of reckoning will come soon and he will pay a hefty price," Linda softly stated.

Emma looked over at Catherine and saw that Scott was still unconscious. Both Neil and Sarah were helping her with him. Dawn who now had Mitch's M-60 was standing watch over them all. "Why did Amsu try to kill us? I thought he was our ally." Sarah asked.

"I do not know but when I get my hands on him, I am going to strip his skin off of his bones an inch at a time." Mitch replied still trying to recompose himself.

Emma went searching for something they could use to stabilize Linda's leg it did not seem to be a bad break but it did need to be stabilized for it to heal properly. She spotted what was left of the shotgun Scott had been carrying and quickly unloaded it and broke the rest of the stock off it. Mitch handed her his suit jacket and she quickly rendered it in to strips. She grabbed the other shotgun, removed the shells, and broke the stock off.

Mitch held his mate while Emma worked quickly to realign the bones of Linda's leg, then she used the shotguns to make a splint. Linda groaned in pain but kept from screaming out just in case Amsu or his friends were still around

Scott started to regain consciousness he was weak and claimed he had a massive headache but was otherwise uninjured. Neil was certain that a good feeding would cure what ailed him. When they tried to question him about how he did what he had done, Scott seemed to have no idea how he had done it but he said he was very glad he had.

Amelia and Andrew arrived near the last place that Amelia had sensed Catherine. They saw the smoke pouring out of the manhole cover. Andrew could sense that Amsu and another vampire were just at the edge of his perception to the north he could also sense Gloria to the south east of them; but what confused him was he sensed vampires about thirty feet and underground he could sense that they were alive he sensed eight of them.

"Try to sense Catherine love," Andrew telepathically suggested.

Amelia in all of the turmoil failed to realize that Catherine was still alive or she would have felt her death. "I can't sense her but I know she is alive." Amelia responded the same way. Amelia tried to mentally contact Catherine while Andrew used the phone to call Susan.

"Susan it is Andrew ... Amelia said that Catherine is alive. Do you know about the others...? You can tell she is alive, thank the maker.... We are at the manhole where they were supposed to come out of. Call Gloria and ask her to meet us here... I sensed him on the edge of my perception when we arrived moving out of the area. ... I am not sure how I knew it was him; I just did... OK I will see you two in few minutes. .. Gloria is pulling up now ... you just talked to Emma ... The passage is blocked. The next entrance is a mile up the road we will head there. Amsu just left the area he was heading north. If you and Charles are going to try to intercept him be careful please." Andrew said finishing the call.

Andrew and Amelia got into the van that Gloria was driving and told her where to go. While she was heading to the manhole, Amelia pulled all of the blood that was in the van. When Andrew saw what she was doing he asked." Why are you packing blood? We need to move quickly before the humans investigate?"

"Linda has a broken leg and Scott needs to feed as soon as we can get blood to him. He was the one the stopped the explosion. Catherine said that they lost four of their protection team." Amelia explained.

"When I get my hands on that cock-sucker he is going to wish he was never born," Andrew swore as he started to lose control. The temperature in the van started to rise rapidly.

"Enough already it is way too hot for all of this heat. Get a grip already." Amelia shouted while shaking him by the shoulders.

Gloria wondered why there was no response from the human authorities yet. She looked around getting an uneasy feeling because of the lack of response. "Andrew something isn't right. Where are the human authorities? I expected to be hearing sirens and see some form of response, if nothing else from their fire department," Gloria Stated concerned.

Andrew Looked around and realized she was right. The streets should have been filled with emergency service personnel. Andrew could not sense any other vampires in the area except for the group that was under ground and themselves. He wondered how long before they did finally come to investigate the large hole in the center of the street.

"Amelia try to get a message to Catherine and see if they can start heading this way. I am not sure how long we will have until the human authorities come and investigate the hole in the center of the street but I cannot imagine it will be much longer," Andrew requested.

Andrew looked around he tried to stretch his senses out further but he either didn't know how to or he was already at his maximum range. He thought for a moment and then said, "Gloria I think it would be better if you wait here. If the human response shows up call us then we will arrange for a meeting spot outside of their perimeter. Please be extra careful, I do not want to lose any more friends today."

"Andrew, I think it would be better if you were the one who stayed with the vehicle and let Amelia and me go. I know it goes against your instincts but please let me explain before you argue. With your abilities, it will be next to impossible for a vampire to sneak up on you. If there is a problem, you can use your connection with Amelia to warn us. I promise to keep Amelia safe." Gloria suggested knowing that Andrew wouldn't like the idea.

Andrew first reaction was to argue but he knew she was right and it was the safest way for everyone concerned. He quietly got out of the truck and helped Amelia out he then walked around to the driver's door and opened it to help Gloria out of the truck. "You two be extra careful and please do not make me regret this." He firmly stated.

Gloria couldn't believe he wasn't fighting this tooth and nail. She had fully expected him to tell her to go to hell. Gloria and Amelia went to the manhole and removed the cover before dropping down. Amelia took the lead since she could sense where the others were. The two of them moved quickly but cautiously. Amelia could sense that Catherine was getting closer and was unconsciously picking up speed to get to them

Catherine relayed Amelia's request that they try to start moving towards the exit. Mitch gently picked up his mate and was going to carry her when Neil suggested, "Mitch, why don't you allow me to help you with her? No sense taking a chance of injuring her anymore."

Mitch smiled and nodded his approval. Catherine and Emma were assisting Scott who was still weak from expending so much psychic energy to stop the explosion. Dawn would take the lead followed by Scott who was being assisted by the two women, then Neil and Mitch carrying Linda. Sarah would bring up the rear and would assist either group as needed.

Catherine was never so happy to see anyone as when she saw Amelia's smiling face. Amelia rushed to her and Scott and hugged them both while handing him a bottle of blood. She then handed Linda a bottle and paused long enough to allow them to finish their drinks. She then passed each of them a bottle and started to lead them out of the sewer system at Andrew's urging; apparently, the humans were finally responding to the large hole in the street and said it wouldn't be long until they decided to use this manhole to try to assess the damage from this side. The group had just finished loading themselves into the truck and were about to pull off when the water department truck pulled up and started to block the street off.

Charles and Susan headed to the Airport in hopes of intercepting Amsu and ending the trouble here. He pulled in to the customer pick–up area and Susan used her powers to convince the officer standing there, they were Federal agents and they were going into the airport on official business. The two of them rushed to the security lounge and Susan used her ability to convince airport security to quickly conduct a search to see if Amsu's plane had departed yet. The head of security had informed him that they had missed the plane by five minutes. They received a copy of the flight plan and found out he was scheduled to fly to Nevada with a layover in Denver for fuel.

Charles called to have the jet prepared. He knew it would take him a few hours before he could even get permission to enter Astin's territory; he was the head enforcer for the west coast, which included Vegas. He knew he could forget about trying to get permission for Denver; Elaina was loyal to Amsu.

"Susan, do you think the Amelia and Andrew would be willing to work for us?" Charles asked.

"Love I think you would be hard pressed to stop them from going after Amsu. My question is do you trust them? What are your long-term plans for them? I will not let you use them then kill them. I mean it love; I have never before made any demands of you before..." Susan replied cautiously.

"Love I swear to you I have no intentions of doing anything to them exempt trying to be their friend." Charles honestly interrupted.

"What do you have in mind for them?" Amelia inquired.

"Their anonymity will allow them to travel between territories unmolested. I want them to act as our investigators and to locate our target, then we will join them and the four of us will take care of Amsu. We will need to get them official identification and weapons permits. In addition, make sure that they have access to all of Diamond's assets. That lawyer you know do you think he would be able to handle getting that done. What is his name? "Charles asked.

"Mark will be able to handle all of it. You know you should put him on retainer like I do. As far as the rest, I will make arrangements through my contacts to make sure they have whatever they need. We need to keep them from becoming associated with you. I do not think we can afford to start that war he wants." Susan responded seriously. She then grinned and playfully said," It will be up to you to tell them that they cannot use their Hummer anymore."

"Why do I get all of the hard jobs?" Charles playfully whined.

Susan giggled and was about to respond when her phone rang, she quickly answered it," Emma god it is good to hear your voice... I know we will explain everything ... tell Gloria to go to the warehouse... Andrew is driving then tell him to go to where we spent last night.... We are heading their now see you within an hour ... I love you to call me if you have any problems."

Susan then called Mark and arranged for him to meet her, Charles, Amelia, and Andrew at her office in Philadelphia on Monday. She told him to bring his mate and her child; they would have to be here for a few weeks and they would pay any expenses including for a private tutor so that Johnny wouldn't fall behind in school.

Charles had taken a roundabout way back to the warehouse to make sure that they weren't being followed. The both of them were glad that the others were already there when they pulled in to the garage and locked the place down. The two of them knew that both theirs and Andrew's families were in danger and it was going to get more dangerous in the near future but for the next few days, they would all be together as one large, hopefully happy family.

When Emma saw her parents, she leaped into their waiting arms. Both Charles and Susan ran their hands over her checking for injuries while hugging her. They knew that she would take the news of Amsu crossing over hard but they would hash it out.

After everyone settled down and the building was locked down with all of the security systems activated Charles started to explain," Amsu has gone mad. He blames the vampire nation in general and me in specifically for the death of Diamond. He claims that the leaders of the nation have become weak and the only chance of us as a species to survive is to force a war that will eradicate all of the weak vampires. Emma the reason he targeted you was to get me to act; in his mind, I would have done anything to get my hands on him including starting his war by ignoring territory boundaries in order to chase him. He knows as well as I do that it will take time to get permission for me to chase him."

Charles paused to let the information settle in before he continued, "I have a plan and I know it is not going to be well liked by a few of you, but my decision has been made and most of you who are going to object have already sworn to follow my order. Those of you that didn't, I am sure I can get your sire to order you to follow my orders. Emma, Catherine, Armenia, Neil, and Scott you all are going to head to a secure location. Your guards will be Dawn, Sarah and Mitch from my organization and Gloria, Andrea, Greg and Samantha."

"Andrew and Amelia, we won't be telling you where they're going, it isn't that we do not trust you but there are vampires who like Amelia can read minds. Layla who is Amsu's most trusted assistant is able read minds like an open book. The assignment I have for the two of you may well bring you into contact with her but before you go, I will teach you how to strengthen your mental shield to offer you protection against her. "

Andrew looked at Amelia and she shrugged. "Umm, Charles where do you think you are sending us?" Andrew asked clearly bewildered.

"Susan why are you sending me away? You know I am your best tracker and my skills would only augment Amelia and Andrew's." Gloria asked through their bond a little hurt.

"I know they would but I am asking you for two reasons; first and fore most I trust you above all others to take care of my baby girl. Secondly, everyone involved knows you are my first and if you are with them, you will mark them. I'm asking you as my friend to please protect my child for me." Susan beseeched mentally

"Susan, you know very well that I'll gladly give my life for her." Gloria smiled as she replied telepathically

Susan gave Gloria quick hug and whispered, "I know you would but you better keep yourself safe also."

"Sorry I guess I did get a little ahead of myself. I would like to hire you and Amelia to hunt Amsu down and try to dismantle as much of his organization as you possibly can. If you find a part of it that is too large for the two of you to handle, then I will have a strike team ready to assist you. I need you two to promise me that once you find Amsu you call Susan and I in to assist you with his capture or termination."

"Andrew, I know you want his blood, as does everyone else in this room but this has to be done the right way or he will have his war. It is a war that none of us can afford. Humans have become excessively dangerous and if they get proof of our existence, they will haunt us. The governments will want to use us. The churches will haunt us out of fear that we are some kind of demonic creature," Charles explained trying not to leave anything important out.

"Charles, if we capture him what will happen to him?" Andrew asked.

"He will have to face the council of enforcers and if we prove he has gone feral, or insane however you like to think about it, he will be put down." Charles stated after thinking about his answer for a few moments.

Amelia started analyzing Amsu as if she was going to build a profile on him. She thought about what she knew of him and how he had acted. She also thought about how Diamond had acted.

"Charles, I do not think that Amsu has gone feral. From what you told me, feral vampires use mostly their instincts and do not plan for the future. Amsu has shown he still possesses a high degree of intelligence and he is planning. He is definitely going through some kind of psychological breakdown and I can develop a profile of him but I will need time and more information." Amelia explained her theory.

"I am sorry but the only thing I know of profiles is what I have seen on television. How will it help us in this case?" Charles asked his curiosity peaked.

Amelia considered best how to answer his question. She took a few minutes to decide how best to answer his question. "Charles it may help us in several ways. First, it will give us an understanding of his psychological state and his motivations. By using that information, it will help us to anticipate his next move. Secondly, if I can get enough information, I may even be able to use it to locate him and help to identify his potential allies. Lastly, I may be able to use the information to help others in the future," Amelia earnestly replied

Charles couldn't help but smile, He looked at Andrew and said, "I said it before and I will say it again, you have one hell of a woman there. Amelia I will make sure that all the files I have on Amsu and his associates are made available to the both of you first thing in the morning. Tonight, I want us all to relax and spend a pleasant evening with our families."

Everyone agreed with that idea and soon all of them were all working to make a wonderful meal consisting of lasagna, homemade garlic bread and a nice wine. The talk soon turned to planning for the future and deciding what they all would do after this mess was over. Charles admitted that he was thinking about possibly traveling to see the world again. He said that he and Susan had not done it since the end of the eighteenth century.

Amelia noted a bit of sadness when he talked about the last time him and Susan has traveled the world. Susan explained that they had lost a couple of dear friends during their travels and it rather put a damper on it. They all agreed to travel together. When Scott and Catherine acted a bit reluctant because of the new baby Charles quickly pointed out that, it could be seen as a learning experience for the child.

After they ate dinner, they decided to play a rather spirited game of monopoly that lasted well into the morning. Emma won when her father had the bad luck of hitting her park place followed by boardwalk on the next roll. They all knew that the near future would bring many challenges but for this one evening, they were a normal family enjoying a fun evening and even though they had yet to exchange blood, they all knew in their hearts that a new coven had been formed.

Following the game of Monopoly, each of the couples headed to bed leaving Gloria alone with her thoughts. A feeling of melancholy over took her as she poured herself another glass of wine started to wonder if she would ever be able to truly happy again. Since she had to put Lenard down, she has kept her heart tightly locked up. She knew they weren't mates but she loved him as much. The day that she had to kill him was the day she lost her heart and most of her soul. She quietly cried wishing she could move on.

"You can live again and even find love if you chose to." Amelia softly said startling Gloria.

"What do you mean? I was just thinking about my assignment" Gloria replied defensively as she wiped the tears from her face.

"Gloria even without my powers I can tell it is a lot more than that. Would you like to talk about him?" Amelia offered.

"I have no idea what you are talking about," Gloria quickly responded defensively.

"Gloria, I saw what happened in your mind and you have never gotten over what happened between you and Lenard. Please let me help you, I hate to see you suffering like this." Amelia beseeched.

Gloria's shoulders slumped and she looked at the floor as her tars started flow uninhibited. "He was a grandfather to me he taught me how to live and love life. How did I repay him? I killed him." Gloria said her voice broke and she cried harder.

Amelia held her friend and waited for her to be ready to continue with her story. She knew words would do little; what Gloria needed right now was her ears. After a while, Gloria recomposed herself and started again. "I was just sixteen when my parents were killed for helping with the Underground Railroad. My father's farm was close to the Ohio border so we would hide the escaped slaves until it was safe to send them to their freedom. Unfortunately, Colonel Robert Samuels caught a group of slaves and tortured them until they gave my family up. Samuels was hell bent on ending the Underground Railroad, He and his men raided the farm and killed my parents. But first, they abused my mother; they all took turns violating her then the dear colonel shot her in the stomach and left her laying there to die. They chained and collared me and dragged me to Virginia it was almost eighty miles. I was abused while being used as camp entertainment. I really didn't care how longed I lived as long as I lived long enough to kill each and every one of them." Gloria paused and took a sip of her wine.

After a couple moments, she continued, "After we crossed into Virginia the Colonel pronounced me guilty of aiding and abetting escaped slaves and I was to be hung at first light. That night most of the camp was in town celebrating when Susan showed up. My god she took out the four men that were guarding me so fast. I watched her as she drained the last of them and thought I was next but was too weak to resist. I hadn't had more than a couple of mouthfuls of water since I was captured. She carried me away from there and nursed me back to health after assuring me that I was safe. It took me two months to regain my strength. Susan had practically begged me to let the past go and keep a low profile but I was determined on getting my revenge.

I caught up to the first one from my list about three weeks later just west of Lynchburg. I gave him and three others to Susan. I took pleasure from watching the fear in their eyes as she was about to feed from them. The last one I feed to her was a young lad he was just sixteen when turned him over to Susan about a week before I was turned but I am getting ahead of myself here.

I had been tracking Samuels and caught him in a brothel in Shreveport. He was setting at a table with this fat whore on his lap when I walked in. He saw me and laughed as he went for his pistol. I can still see it; I pulled my Remington and fired once the bullet struck him in the left eye. I saw the look of shock in his remaining eye as he slowly raised his hand to his eye then slumped back into the chair. That is when all hell broke out the three men, he had been with started shooting at me I managed to dive for cover but not before I was hit twice, the first one was just a graze," Gloria said her voice low but steady. She paused for a moment as she relived the memory, 'The second one was in my right side as I was diving for cover, I fired and hit the one who had grazed me I hit him in the stomach and I remember he begged for his mother. I found out later he was just fifteen. A moment later, I killed the second one of them in the exchange of fire.

Now it was I and the man that killed my father left in the fight. I rotated the cylinder around to where two empty chambers. I squeezed the trigger and of course, when nothing fired, he thought I was out of ammo and stood. I fired again and this time he laughed at me. I fired for real this time and struck him in the chest the only problem was my gun was now empty. I watched as he raised his pistol and fired I remember feeling the round hit me in the right side of my chest it felt as if I was kicked by a mule the funny thing was I felt no pain. I watched as he cocked his pistol a second time and took aim. Just as he was ready to fire, his eyes glazed over and his expression went blank, he stood there frozen just for a second then fell to the ground. Everything went black after that my next memory is a hazy one of Susan giving me the choice of living or dying." Gloria pauses to refill her wine. She silently offers Amelia a glass, which she accepted.

"Love I may be a while Gloria really needs someone to talk to." Amelia telepathically said while waiting for Gloria to finish pouring their wine.

"Ok baby, I will be waiting for you when you are done." Andrew replied through their link sending her a mental kiss also.

Charles and Susan retired to their bedroom the day's events had taken a toll on them. Charles was lying there with his arm across his eyes and Susan spooned up against his side with her head on his chest. Susan had thought he had fallen asleep. When he quietly said, "Susan I know we agreed to mate on the first of January but I do not want to wait. Can we please mate tonight?"

"Charles my love I will mate with you whenever you want but what brought this on?" Susan asked slightly amused. She loved Charles since the first time she laid eyes on him but he was the one who always wanted to wait.

CHAPTER 10

****

A lot of things, first and foremost I love you more than I can express in words. The events of the day had some to do with it. I finally realized just how much of an ass I have been when I saw what Amelia and Andrew have together, watching them made me jealous. I realized just how much I want to have what the two of them have only I want it with you," Charles honestly explained.

Susan gave Charles a searing kiss and then nibbled her way across his chin slowly. When she got to his ear, she started sucking on his ear lobe. Her hands slid down his body to his rapidly hardening member. She wrapped her hand around his cock and slowly began to pump it up and down while she gently massaged his balls with her other hand. "Does this feel good baby?" She seductively asked.

Susan then dropped her fangs and started nibbling down his chest. She got to his nipples and sucked on the left one until it was hard then she took the nipple in her teeth and tugged on it sharply causing Charles to exhale rapidly as a shiver ran through his body. She repeated the process on the right nipple this time she nips his nipple with her fang. She continued down across his abdomen until she got to his belly button where she swirled her tongue around it slowly before continuing. Susan kissed her way across his pelvic bone then paused to look at his cock. She started to lick the head of it like an ice cream cone pausing every so often to blow across it causing Charles to shiver.

Charles was being drive nuts with desire and needed to get her to stop soon even though he wanted her to continue. Susan easily swallowed all of Charles and let her throat muscles massage the length of Charles' cock trying to milk his essence from him she could feel him getting close and felt Charles trying to pull her off him. Finally, she relented and let Charles pull her off his cock. He quickly laid her on her back and quickly repositioned himself at the entrance to her drenched pussy. He started to slide in slowly when Susan wrapped her legs around his backside and pulled him in in one quick motion. The pace the two of them set was bruising and they both were racing to their completion. Tries as he might Charles couldn't hold out and exploded inside her while biting down on her shoulder. The taste of Susan's blood was sweeter than the sweetest wine he had ever tasted. Susan felt Charles' bite and that shoved her over the edge. She started to scream her orgasm as she bit into Charles' shoulder. She quickly drank from Charles relishing each gulp of his blood as if it was ambrosia.

The two of them had the most intense orgasm of their long lives. They both were amazed as they felt their link snap into place. Hearing how amazing it was nothing like experiencing it firsthand. Susan grabbed a bottle of blood from the refrigerator beside the bed and poured each of them a goblet of blood. They toasted each other and quickly drank their goblets of blood followed by three more each. Susan pulled Charles into another searing kiss that he broke too soon, for Susan drawing a slight moan of frustration. "Before we got started again I just want to apologize to you for forcing you to wait all of these years. I love you my mate." Charles whispered to her.

Susan answer was another searing kiss that left no doubt in his mind he was forgiven and she was ready for the next round of lovemaking. Charles smiled as she began stroking his member back to life.

Gloria handed Amelia her drink then continued," After Susan turned me, she kept me close to her for the first few months insisting that I needed to learn how to control my hunger and learn the rules of my new life. As soon as I could, I resumed my hunt despite all of Susan's warnings. I quickly found my next victim In Richmond who I took great pleasure in slitting his throat. Over the next two and half years, I crisscrossed the south managing to track down another two from my list both of which I drained. Two weeks after the war ended, I was in Atlanta looking for Martin Samuels the colonel's oldest son he had been wounded and was back home when I found his father. I had truly become a monster without remorse. I found his homestead he was with his wife, who was pregnant, and I made him watch as I drained her. He begged for their lives especially the child's but I didn't care I wanted him to suffer" Gloria was in tears as she recalled the look on the poor girls face who only wrong was falling in love with the wrong man. She drained her glass of wine and had a faraway look in her eyes.

"How could I do that? I not only killed the woman but an unborn child and all I felt was satisfaction. I stayed with Martin for three days tormenting him while his dead wife lay on the floor in front of him. He begged me to kill him but I had no mercy, I repeatedly taunted him telling him this was just revenge and he had it coming after he violated my mother and murdering my parents. I left him alive tied up besides his wife's body so he could stare at his wife's dead face. I found out later he had managed to get free and hung himself. " Gloria paused a few minutes to recompose herself; "After I finished with Martin, I was a monster I only lived to avenge my parents. I did unspeakable things to get information on my next quarry. I thought nothing of using the families of people who I thought might have information I wanted. I once murdered a blacksmith's family while I made him watch. The man's only crime was he had hidden his uncle from me for a week."

"I had been wondering around for weeks, when I had heard that one of the men, I had been searching for had been hanging in a bar in Charleston. I was there in the process of questioning the barkeep when Lenard first saw me. He told me he could feel the emptiness in my soul and it was unbearable to him. He grabbed me and dragged me the bar after using his powers to erase the bar keeps memories of what had happened. He took me to his room and begged me to listen to him. He told me that I would be hunted as a rogue if I didn't stop my murdering spree. He warned me that Charles had ordered Susan to reign me in or put me down. Martin Samuels had left a note where he had admitted what his father, he and the rest of the unit had done to my mother and me. He said that I was the one who had murdered his wife. He had written that I had returned from the dead to avenge myself. He had written that I had drunk all of his wife's blood. He made me see that my actions were endangering everyone especially Susan, as me creator she could be held liable for my actions. "

"Lenard convinced me to talk to Susan and he went with me. Susan was less than thrilled with me at that point. She stated that she was considering just putting me down and warned me this was my last chance. I know he spent a long time talking to Susan to convince her to allow me to go to Sans Francisco with him. Susan had warned me that Lenard had taken responsibility for me and if I screwed up this time both Lenard and I would suffer the consequences."

"Two weeks later, we boarded a train and started our adventure. It took us months to make the trip by train and by stagecoach. Lenard was the most wonderful loving tolerant man I have ever known. He taught me that life was worth living. He had replaced the darkness in my soul. He not only showed me how to forgive those who had wronged me but more importantly how to forgive myself. He made sure I was educated and how to defend myself. Lenard was the one who helped me to hone my abilities. I was so fortunate that Susan was so understanding. "

"Lenard has kept in touch with Susan unbeknownst to me. He had been giving her updates on my progress. Lenard had been the one who had encouraged me to reach out to Susan who was now in Chicago. The two of us quickly renewed our friendship and became almost like sisters. Susan offered me a chance to become her personal assistant. Even in those days, Susan had her hands in many businesses including starting with providing blood to vampires. She opened her first blood bank and disguised it has a bordello. She had a special preferred area that was for vampires she would take some of her whores, take a bottle of blood from them, and sell it to her clients. The woman would have her memories altered that she had spent the evening with one of Susan's special clients and they were paid two to three times what they would make in a normal evening."

"I was happy for the first time since the night my parents were murdered. I loved life and enjoyed living it to the fullest. I took a sabbatical for five years so that Lenard and I could travel throughout the world. He would tell me about the history of each location. The things we experienced the first time we saw the world's fair or gone on a safari. Even once we got back, we were constantly going to places and doing things, I remember in nineteen- seventeen, I saw my first airplane. I know now days airplanes are common but in nineteen-seventeen, they were a novelty. I spent five dollars to take a ride in one it was the most thrilling ride of my life. Did I ever mention that I am a licensed pilot?" Gloria seemed to light up as she recalled her time with Lenard.

"No, you never did. I would love to take a ride with you one day." Amelia replied with a smile, "What kind of planes can you fly?"

"Ones with wings," Gloria replied with a chuckle. Amelia laughed as Gloria continued," I have my ATP certifications. Charles has a charter service he owns and makes sure I get enough hours to keep my licenses and I am rated to fly anything up to a Boeing Seven Sixty-Seven. Lenard was the one who convinced me to learn to fly in the twenties. When I hesitated, he goaded me into it by saying he figured it was too much for a girl like me. He used to tell me to try everything at least once. He went out, bought me a world war one surplus Jenny, he also hired David Leas; he had been a pilot in the war, to teach me how to fly. We had moved back to east coast by the time I had finished my flying lessons. I was working as a problem solver for Susan and occasionally Charles. When I wasn't on a job, I was with Lenard."

"The beginning of the thirties was a bit of blur. I remember spending a lot of time at Coney Island and going to the theatre. Of course, the late thirties were filled with talk of the war in Europe. Once the United States entered, the war I was busy; a group of vampires from the old country decided the world would be better off with Hitler in charge. Charles had tasked Susan with locating, monitoring, and preventing them from undermining the United States war effort. The vampires were using their powers of persuasion to help Germany either by finding out classified information like the date and the real locations we were going to land on D-Day. We managed to intercept the female vampire that had gotten it."

"Charles decided to openly, well at least as openly as we could; help the Allies so we also went hunting human spy networks we would either destroy them or feed them false information. We especially focused on finding the people who were watching for convoy movements along our coast. Charles personally prevented an assassination attempt against Roosevelt." Gloria paused to take a sip of her wine.

"After the war, we settled back into our quiet existence Susan started setting up her blood banks usually disguising them as some kind of drug or medical research company. By nineteen fifty-four she had at least one in every major city in the United States and plus over fifty location spread out through Europe. Then in Fifty --seven Lenard said, he had to go home for a while and that he had to go alone. He explained that he be gone for a few years and would contact me when he could. During the time he was gone I got a letter here and there. I knew something had changed he seemed cold and distracted in his letters and the last phone call I received from him I hardly recognized the man I knew.

After Lenard left, I started hunting rogues for Charles. I quickly found out that I had a talent for it. In October of Sixty-one, we started receiving reports of a rogue vampire in the French Quarter of New Orleans. Charles asked me to look in to it. By the time, I had gotten to New Orleans he had moved on so I started to track him. Twenty-three days later, I caught up to him in Charleston. He was in a bar two blocks from where the two of us had meant nearly a century beforehand. When I arrived, he was raping and drinking from this petite brunet. Everyone else was already dead he had frenzied in the bar. He ripped the throats out of the others in the bar."

"I was surprised when I saw it was Lenard but it was like he was expecting me. He stopped with the girl and quickly dressed. He turned to me then smiled and closed his eyes. I was in a fog as I swung the sword and removed his head. My god, even after all of this time I still see it every time I close my eyes. The blade arcing through the air then I felt the slight jolt as the blade contacts his neck; the sound it made was sickening. I watched as the blade cleanly passes through the rest of his neck. Then time seems to pause for just a second as I watch the light of life fades from the man that had taught me how to live and love again. I watched the body fall to the ground and as it did, I felt my heart die with him. I vowed to myself that I would never let anyone close enough to hurt me like that again." Gloria stopped unable to continue. She broke down and cried for her loss, not only Lenard but also her parents.

Amelia wrapped her arms around Gloria and held her as she cried her pain out. "Gloria, the man you knew as Lenard died and what you put down was just an empty shell. It may have looked like him and maybe somewhere deep inside was a shadow of the man he was but it was not him. I would like you to think about this; even the shadow of him didn't like what he had become. You said he smiled. Why do you think he did that?" Amelia gently asked.

Gloria looked into Amelia soft brown eyes, looking for the same contempt she felt for herself. She was surprised when al she seen was compassion. "I... I not sure," Gloria shakily replied.

"I think he was glad that you were going to end his pain. I also think he was glad it was you and not someone else. This way he died with someone who loved him by his side. That shadow of him knew he had to die and was glad that you were willing to release him and give him the peace he so desired somehow comforted him. I know it sounds crazy but think about it you knew him better than everyone else, do you think he would have wanted to live like that?" Amelia explained as she cradled Gloria in her arm trying to comfort her.

For the longest time all that could be heard was the soft sobbing from Gloria. "Do you really think that he understood why I had to do it?" Gloria softly asked sounding more like the nineteen-year-old girl then the hundred and fifty-year-old vampire.

"Yes, I do honestly believe that he not only understood, but was relieved that his suffering was over." Amelia assured her. Amelia hugged her friend as she asked, "Do you think the Lenard would want you to suffer? My guess is he would have wanted you to live and enjoy life to find love, most of all to find happiness."

"I am not even sure if I know how, even if I wanted to," Gloria quietly admitted.

"I think you want to be happy but you are feeling guilty. Let go of the guilt and live life to its fullest. I will help you as will Andrew, we will be here for you always," Amelia promised.

Gloria smiled and nodded slightly. "I already owe you and Andrew so much. The two of you saved my life and then invited me into your family. How can I ever repay you all?" Gloria asked solemnly

"Gloria you are family if it wasn't for you and Susan, Andrew and I would have been dead. You could never owe us anything." Amelia said hugging her friend.

"She is right Gloria, you are family, if you need anything just ask and if it is within our powers, we will do it." Andrew said as he entered the room. He walked over to Amelia and wrapped his arms around the two of them. After a moment, he released the two of them and gave Amelia a quick kiss.

"I am curious what happened to the girl that Lenard bit?" Amelia asked.

"I helped her through the change and she is a professor of law at Harvard and a close friend. She uses to work with Mark but wanted to take a break from the hassle of dealing with clients," Gloria explained.

"Let me ask you what would have normally happened to her?" Amelia asked already knowing the answer.

"She would have been prevented from being turned because without a mentor she would be a danger." Gloria responded automatically.

"So without you she would have been dead?" Amelia proposed.

Gloria started to answer then stopped she had never thought of it that way. Had she really saved Rose's life? She thought for a moment then a large smile spread across her face. "You been analyzing me, haven't you?" Gloria asked bemused.

"No, not really I was just trying to help you," Amelia explained.

After realizing, it was just after nine in the morning the three friends started making a large family breakfast for everyone. The three friends continued to talk. Gloria for her part felt a lot better than she had in years. Just her finally telling someone what had happened somehow made the load easier to bear. Unbeknownst to her at the time it was her first night of healing.

After the game had finished Catherine and Scott had retired to their room. Scott quickly helped Catherine to strip then lead her to the shower and washed her from head to toe while checking every inch of her body. He concerned not only for his mate but also for their unborn child even though both Susan and Gloria had said that Catherine and the child were fine and there had been no ill effects from the day's events. Scott wasn't happy about being excluded from the hunt for Amsu.

Catherine laid her head on Scott's chest quietly reflecting on the day's events. She could feel the anger building up in her mate and knew he would insist on being involved in the hunt for Amsu and in many ways agreed with him. While she didn't relish direct confrontation with Amsu, she wanted to help to bring him down. "Love we will talk with Andrew and Amelia in the morning. I want to help also," Catherine said telepathically.

"Do you think they will listen to us?" Scott asked the same way.

Catherine gave Scott a tender kiss." We will make them listen, my love," Catherine softly promised.

Catherine laid her head back onto Scott's chest and went to sleep. Scott laid there watching Catherine as she sleeps until he drifted off to sleep. The two of them we woke up a little after ten to the smell of coffee and food.

Emma and Neil took the dishes in to the kitchen area and quickly loaded them into the dishwasher before heading to their room. Neil quickly stripped Emma and started to suck on Emma's nipples causing her to moan. He slowly ran his hand down her taunt stomach heading to her nether region. He slowly worked his finger into her pussy. Emma's hips began working in time with Neil's fingers. When Neil started to rub her clit with his thumb, it pushed Emma over the edge.

Neil kept alternating sucking on one nipple then the other while working a second then third finger into her. He used his fingers to massage her spot sending her into her second orgasm for tonight. "Please take me," Emma begged.

Neil smiled as he positioned himself at the opening of her vagina and slowly feed himself in. He set a slow sensual pace taking full strokes each time. Emma used her fangs to nip at Neil's nipples she never broke the skin but bit hard enough so he could feel it. Neil was the first one to go over the edge firing ropes of red hot cum into her sodden pussy. Emma screamed through her orgasm.

Neil rolled the two of them on to their sides. The two of them in each other's arm while basking in the afterglow of their lovemaking. They fell asleep and slept like that not waking until little before ten am. The two of them quickly showered then headed out to find the food they smelled cooking.

Susan and Charles finished their last round of lovemaking at a little after four and fell asleep in each other's arms. Something woke Susan out of sleep around seven. She laid there watching Charles sleep as she thought about the first time, she saw him. It was twenty --six AD. she was the house slave of Pius Cassius Olcinius he was a Tribuni of the Praetorian Guard when she first saw Charles who went by Maahas in those days a wealthy Egyptian spice trader. She was assigned to serve him and her master refreshments. Charles visited her that night a fact she did not find out until much later as he had erased her memory of the visit. Three days later, he had purchased her. On the return trip to his home, he turned her and gave her, her freedom. Since that time, the two of them have been friends and lovers. Most of the time they were together or within a few days travel of one and another at most. Susan had been in love with Charles since the first time she had seen him and the highlight of her life up to last night was when she found out she was pregnant with Emma. According to everyone, it was just short of a miracle that she conceived without being mated. According to Agatha, it was only the second time she had delivered a baby to an unmated vampire and she had been delivering babies since seventy-three BC.

Charles was awake but laying there with his eyes closed well aware that Susan was watching him as he sleeps. He could feel the sense of foreboding that she felt. "What is a matter love? What has you worried?" Charles asked.

"I'm not sure I just feel that our end is near and I don't want to lose what we have especially now," Susan replied softly with a deep sense of sadness in her voice.

"Love if it is fated to happen there is nothing that we can do about it. Let enjoy the time we have left. Anyhow, you know that those premonitions rarely come true and if it does, I for one will still consider myself the luckiest man to ever have lived for having you at my side for all of those years," Charles stated then kissed her softly trying to convey all of his feelings through that one kiss. Susan gladly accepted the comfort that Charles was giving but she couldn't shake the feeling that they wouldn't survive this time. Charles stomach rumbled as the two of them smelled the food being prepared.

"I guess we better get up and feed you before you starve to death." Susan teased.

"Hey I burned a lot of energy last night. You were insatiable," Charles complained teasingly.

"Well mister it is your fault for making me wait so long and last night was just a very small down payment on what you owe me." Susan retorted while laughing.

Susan and Charles quickly showered and then dressed to go join the rest for breakfast. As soon as Susan walked into the room, Gloria ran over to congratulate her. She pulled Susan into a tight hug." About time, you two, I am so happy for you." Gloria practically yelled from excitement.

Emma was next to charge her parents she was so happy that tears were streaking down her face. She quickly wrapped her mother, father, and Gloria up in a hug. "I am so glad you two finally stopped fooling around and made it official. Congratulations and I love you both" Emma said.

Everyone else crowded around Susan and Charles to congratulate them and the breakfast quickly turned into a celebration. They opened a couple bottles of Perrier-Jouet to toast the couple. Linda volunteered to make a celebratory dinner with the help of Mitch whom she claimed was a world-class cook. After breakfast, everyone went into the sitting room to relax and to plan how they were going to deal with Amsu. "Amelia what kind of information would you need to make a profile of Amsu?" Charles asked.

"I could use whatever you have on him. I am not sure if his long life will make it easier or harder to profile him. Later on, I would like to interview you, Susan, Emma and anyone else who was close to Amsu." Amelia replied.

"After we finish our coffee, I will let you read over the information in the data base I keep on vampires. I have a good biography of him and most of his associates well at least the ones I know of and as much information as I have on them. I will also give you all of the information I have on the other enforcers and their top people. "Charles paused to take a drink of his coffee then continued," Susan will provide you with a list of places where can either purchase or acquire blood. She will also provide you with a list of safe houses and contacts in case you get into trouble or need a place to lay low for a few days. I will also need to know what other types of assets you will need at your disposal.

"From the sounds of it you have everything we need already in place. The only other things; we may need is tactical support and possible some help with intelligence." Andrew replied.

"It goes without saying we will be supporting you with as much intelligence as we can both Susan and I have large networks. There is one down side I have to insist that the hummer gets left behind." Charles stated.

"Where are the two of you thinking about starting your hunt?" Susan asked.

"We aren't sure yet I would like to get an idea of the man we are hunting then may be head to Nevada and try to pick up his trail. If you or Charles have any suggestions, we are all ears." Amelia replied while starting to prioritize what they needed to do over the next few days.

"I will try to use my contacts and find out where he is but I would suggest trying to weaken his organization by eliminating his key people. You two have to understand you are not going there to arrest them you will have to destroy them there is no other way. "Charles stated in a serious tone. He paused to let it sink in before he continued, "If you can't do this; please tell me now so we can get someone else. If you fail to kill them, they will turn on you and kill you. Use them to get the information you need then dispose of them. Once you start, trust no one,"

Andrew paused to consider Charles warning; he hadn't thought of this as an assassination mission but now it made sense to him. He knew that Charles was right and if they did not kill the vampires they were going to hunt, they would quickly be betrayed and destroyed. Andrew knew he had no problem with this but he wasn't sure if his mate would agree. He locked eyes with Amelia silent asking her what she wanted to do and was pleasantly surprised when she nodded.

"Charles, we understand and will be careful. We will have no problem doing what must be done to protect our family." Andrew stated firmly.

"I would like to offer Amelia and you the chance to form a coven with Susan and me, like you have with Gloria. I would also like to extend the offer to the rest of you here." Charles offered.

Everyone accepted and each took their turn joining the coven and allowing the link to form that would bind them all together throughout eternity. Susan took time to explain all of the benefits and even the few pit falls to forming an alliance through this way to those who had never had been a part of one before. The newly formed family set around enjoying a glass of wine with the exception of Catherine she had a goblet of blood since she was with child. Scott decided this was the time to broach the subject of them leaving.

Scott stood up and started." Charles, I know that you said that we are going to be going to some place for our safety but if it is all the same to you. Catherine and me would rather stay here and take our chances with you all." Scott said trying to remain respectful for the moment.

"I agree daddy I do not want to go hid I want to fight. Neil and I can take care of ourselves. Can you really say that anywhere you send us will be any safer than here with you and mother? Moreover, you are sending away a large portion of the people you know you can trust. Therefore, I am staying and you can forget about trying to pull rank on me. Emma sternly insisted.

"Neil would you please..." Charles started to argue.

"Sorry Charles not this time I happen to agree with her," Neil stated firmly cutting Charles off.

Charles looked to Susan for support but quickly realized that by the way she was smiling at him she would be no help. He slowly glanced around the room until he came to Andrew." What do you think?" Charles asked hoping to find support.

Andrew didn't answer right away he just slowly glanced around the room pausing at each person for a moment. He then locked eyes with his mate and smiled he knew her feelings on the subject, "Charles part of me does agree with you. However, when I ask myself this question I keep coming up with the same answer. Would they be safer if we sent them away? And my answer is no most likely not." Andrew replied in a calm even voice.

"How can you say that? We all know that he has spies in Susan and my organization. If doesn't already know they're alive he soon will be then he will make another attempt and this time he will make it such a way it doesn't fail." Charles angrily disputed.

"Charles, I do agree that he most likely already knows that they survived his attempt on their lives. Let me ask you, do you think you can keep them hidden from him if he wants to find them? Would you not agree that you are better prepared here to stop an attempt on their lives here?" Andrew asked.

"Charles, he is right it would be easier for us to guard our family here," Susan said agreeing with Andrew.

Charles threw his hands up in exasperation, "I hope the hell you two are right." Charles begrudgingly conceded.

The remainder of the morning was taken up with planning and preparation. The one thing that Emma, Catherine, and the others insisted on was that Amsu attempt on their lives wouldn't make them go into hiding. They would accept increased security but they were going to get back to as close as a normal life as they could. Emma insisted on reopening Sanguinem. When Charles objected Emma reminded him that he gave her the club to run as her own and if he wouldn't let her reopen that one, she would resign and open one of her own.

Once things finally settled down and all of the planning was finished. Charles gave Amelia and Andrew access to the files on Amsu and his associates to begin reviewing. Amelia used an old colleague's credentials to contact the Denver airport and was surprised to find out that the plane was still there. She also managed to find out that Amsu had purchased two tickets to LAX. She also managed to confirm that both Layla and he had boarded the plane. The flight left Denver at ten AM Mountain time this morning and about a two- and half-hour flight.

"We have a lead. Amsu just landed at LAX. He has Layla with him," Amelia happily announced.

"Why did he take a commercial flight is he has his own plane?" Andrew asked

"I am not sure; he may be trying to throw us off his trail. Hoping we will waste our time searching for him in the Denver but why L.A.?" Amelia wondered aloud

While Amelia was working on trying to profile Amsu, Andrew was trying to map out his entire network. When he heard Amelia announce that Amsu was on a commercial flight to LAX he had questioned why he had not used his own plane the Gulfstream had more than enough range. He was wondering the same thing that Amelia was why LA? "I'm not sure, but I think we should get to Los Angeles before we lose him," Andrew suggested.

"I am sorry but the two of you are not ready to go on the hunt yet. Layla by all accounts is an extremely powerful telepath. Amelia you may be able to defend yourself but Andrew you would be vulnerable," Charles stated from the door.

"Charles this may be our best chance to end this and if we lose him it may be a long time before we can pick up his trail," Andrew debated.

"If you and Amelia go out there before you are ready, we could lose you both and I do not want that," Charles responded.

Andrew agreed even though he was sure it was a mistake; over the next couple of days Amelia and Andrew worked long and hard to try to get an idea of what his next move would be. Amelia Profile was starting to take shape and it had given her some, what she hoped would be valuable insights into Amsu motives. She also had managed to flag him so if he decided to take another commercial flight she would know.

On Monday, much to both Amelia and Andrew's delight Denise and Mark arrived. Mark quickly set to his task of getting all diamond assets transferred to Amelia and Andrew. He also set them up with several sets of identities so they could switch as needed. Mark informed them that he would need about two to three weeks to get everything transferred over. He had also agreed to take a position on Charles staff.

Charles started Andrew and Amelia's training and they quickly found out he was a relentless taskmaster pushing them as much as seventy to eighty hours between rest periods. Not only had they learned to control their powers and shield their minds against intrusion but he also taught them how to wield a sword properly. He explained that a sword or an ax was much more dangerous to a vampire then a gun. Andrew took to the sword as if it was a part of him. Amelia quickly learned to use her mental abilities to make up for her lack of prowess with a sword.

Susan helped Amelia and Andrew with developing their mental skills and on controlling their primal side. Susan quickly realized that Amelia still had a lot of trouble controlling her jealousy and knew that this could be used against her. She started placing Andrew in circumstances where he closely interacted with women and made Amelia watch while Gloria, Catherine and herself restrained Amelia. Slowly Amelia learned to control her jealousy, which also helped her to control her baser self.

Scott, Neil, and Mitch were converting the family room into a proper command center. They set an area to sort and catalog any intelligence they received on Amsu or his cohorts. Mark was trying to map out all of

Amsu considerable assets. The longer he worked on it them more impressed he became with his accountant skills at hiding and protecting his client's resources. Mark had managed to piece enough together in order to show he was definitely receiving a large amount of money from Rodrigues and the Rios Cartel.

It had taken almost two months for Amelia and Andrew to learn enough to survive in their new world. The two for them had learned to control not only their powers but also more importantly their baser selves It quickly became apparent just how interdepended they were on each other. The two of them seemed to be able to strengthen one and another to the point that their individual weaknesses disappeared. Both Charles and Susan knew this was both a great asset but it could become a major liability. Both Charles and Susan knew that most likely, the surviving partner would die instantly and if by some off chance they didn't, he or she would definitely become a rogue.

During the time of Amelia and Andrew's training, Emma had reopened the club and it was busier than ever. She had hired Catherine to act as her personal assistant and to help her by managing the office for her. The two of them were quickly becoming like sisters. When Scott couldn't take her to her doctor visits, Emma would then they would go out to lunch and shopping. Emma was also helping Catherine with lose of her abilities.

Susan offered Scott a job as the managing Philadelphia's branch of Bio Medtronic. Scott seemed to take on his role like a fish to water the employees liked and respected him, as did the customers. He was willing to take a cut in his percentages for larger customers which invariable lead to him getting larger orders this made Susan extremely happy. He had also managed to hire a couple of human chemists that had developed a new preservative for blood and blood products while it would be years for the FDA to approve it the preservative was perfect for the true customers of the business. BRP-60 extended the shelf life of the blood products by three-fold and it allowed blood to be stored at room temperature. The only down side was slight after taste to the blood treated with the chemical.

Amelia and Andrew were finally ready to start their hunt for Amsu. The only trouble was it seemed after he landed at LAX a fact, confirmed by security cameras. He was seen getting into a taxicab and neither he nor the cab has been seen since. The owner of the cab had reported it stolen. He had parked it in front of his home after his shift the night before and it was gone when he went to leave for work the next day. Charles and Susan had used every contact they had to see if any of the other enforcers had had him assassinated. Every one of them had denied any knowledge of his disappearance.

After some, searching Charles had managed to track down why Amsu was in LA he was supposed to meet with Joseph Kingston he was the owner of a financial investment firm. It specialized in helping vampire to diversify their money and keep it hidden from the humans a task that was becoming increasingly more difficult with the advent of modern financial regulations especially in the United States. He claimed that Amsu had contacted about taking over managing his portfolio. He stated that Amsu had claimed he was having some legal issues and needed new blood to manage his assets. They were supposed to meet the night after he had arrived but Amsu never showed up.

Charles asked Mark and Andrew to look at the financial records of Layla and Amsu other top lieutenants. After an extensive search, they could find no movement of any capital out of any of Layla accounts. She was still receiving her salary and dividends form her investments. The only money that was being used was items that she had set up on automatic payments. It was as if she had dropped off the face of the earth. The rest of his top people all seem to be going on with business as usual but they are all in the Middle East and Northern Africa as far as they could tell.

The one major thing noted during Marks and Andrew's investigation was that Amsu was no longer receiving payments from the Rios Cartel. The payments to him were about one hundred and twenty-four million Pesos a month that were deposited into four vampire ran internet banks. The question is why the payments were suddenly stopped. Charles was sure that his creator was alive and as everyone knew, he would most definitely know if he wasn't.

Monday of the third week into their search for Amsu, Catherine had doctors and Scott had a meeting with a vampire that was also a scientist. He claimed he had a formula for a synthetic blood product that was almost perfected but he needed more capital to finish his research. Scott had requested that Susan and a couple of her top scientist be present at this meeting. Susan of course quickly agreed seeing the income potential as almost unlimited. Emma was happily going to go with Catherine. When Amelia heard she asked if Gloria and her could tag along then they all could go to lunch and then out shopping. Linda saw the other ladies getting ready to leave and excitedly asked if she could tag along. Mitch and Dawn went along to act as security. Andrew had insisted that Amelia carry her Glock. They went to the mid wife Agatha who reported that all was going perfect. They then headed down town to the shopping area. They all had a pleasant lunch then started their shopping there was a large crowd gathered around one of the entrances of the mall and a bunch of press there. They all decided it would be best to avoid the area and started to head back to where they were parked. They had just taken a step when they heard a young man shout, "Vampires!"

The man quickly withdrew a gun and started firing the first round struck Catherine in her right breast the second round grazed the side of her face. Amelia quickly knocked Catherine to the ground while she withdrew her weapon. She fired twice striking the man in the chest he shuddered with the impact of the bullets but didn't go down. Amelia was just about to change her aim to his head when a round from his weapon struck her in the right wrist causing her to drop her weapon. She was then hit in the shoulder.

Gloria heard the gunfire erupt and immediately tackled and bodily covered Emma. She watched the exchange of gunfire and saw Amelia lose her weapon when she was struck in the arm and Gloria wanted to retrieve the weapon but was afraid to expose Emma to the gunfire so she stayed put.

Dawn quickly moved Linda behind her and withdrew her weapon but unfortunately had no clear line of fire. She started to move to her right to clear her returning fire unfortunately all hell had broken lose when the gunfire had started and everyone was scrambling for cover. Mitch who had been at the back of the group had decided to race ahead to get the van opened for the ladies and as a result was out of position when the gun fire had erupted. He raced back just in time to see Amelia get wounded and quickly tackled the person who was firing at his charges. Just as he hit the guy, he heard the man shout, "Go back to hell!"

The man pulled a wire that was attached to two metal canisters strapped to his chest and instantly exploded into flames. Even before Mitch had a chance to scream, he was gone. Linda let lose a blood-curdling scream and her eyes went to black orbs as her body went rigid. She stopped moving and she had gone to join her mate.

Scott was in a meeting with Susan and the new scientist when he felt the pain and anger from his mate just before he felt Mitch and Linda die. He looked over to Susan and saw that she had felt them die also. Scott and Susan quickly excused themselves from the meeting and he called Catherine while Susan tried Emma.

Charles was talking with Andrew, Neil, and Mark when Andrews eyes went black for a moment then he quickly grabbed his cell and dialed Amelia's number he knew that something had happened and much to his dismay Mitch and Linda were no longer with them.

Neil had felt the loss also and his mates' distress and tried to call her. Charles was just getting ready to dial his cell when it rang.

Dawn heard Linda's scream and quickly turned but it was already too late she was gone and her body was already mummifying. She didn't survive the loss of her mate, which in a way Dawn was glad, it would have been a real disaster to have to deal with a rogue vampire while being filmed. It was already bad enough that they had been seen by so many witnesses and with all of the pandemonium, there was no way to contain it. She wondered how much the cameras had caught. She knew that they had been invisible to the cameras but the results of their actions weren't and neither was Linda's body. Dawn quickly gathered the others and started to herd them towards the van. She picked up Catherine, who was having a bit of trouble moving from her injuries, and carried her to the van. Thankfully none of the wounds were life threatening. Gloria went to retrieve Linda's body. "Leave it! We have to get out of here now." Dawn ordered.

Gloria grimaced but held her tongue and quickly followed the others. The Human authorities were quickly responding to the scene and they only had minutes to get away. They all got into the van and everyone cell phone started ringing.

Charles answered the phone and heard." Hello son I trust you are in good health. By the way have you seen the news, if not you should turn on channel six." Then the phone went dead.

Charles was shocked when he turned the television on.

Charles was shocked as he watched the replay of the gun battle between Amelia and the unknown gunman. He heard the person yell vampires and open fire then a fraction of a second later there was two muzzle flashes coming from an invisible weapon. Charles watched as the man shuddered from the impact of the rounds and then saw him returning fire. He watched as a Glock became visible as it hit the ground. The man was tackled by an invisible force and he screamed go to hell and then he set off the firebomb he had strapped to his chest that caused Mitch's flaming body to become visible. There was a scream a moment later and Linda's rapidly mummifying corpses appeared on the ground. The last image that Charles managed to see was the van the woman had used leaving the parking lot. While Charles was watching, the news reports Andrew and Neil managed to get in touch with their respective mates. Andrew was upset that both Amelia and Catherine were wounded but was glad to hear that their wounds were relatively minor. Amelia had reassured him that she was ok and they were heading back to Agatha's just make sure the baby was ok.

Charles received calls from the other enforcers wanting to know who was behind exposing them to the media like this. They wanted to know how he had allowed it to happen and what he was going to do to prevent any further damage. Half of the enforcer were threatening to have Charles replaced if he didn't get this situation rectified and soon. Only a few of the other enforcer would give him a chance to explain what had happened and only three of them believed that Amsu was behind it. Vladimir Demidov was the only one to offer his full support and if necessary, he would give Charles and his family a safe haven. He also pledged any assistance that Charles needed.

Susan talked to Emma and was relieved to hear that she was uninjured. She was not happy that Amelia and Catherine were wounded but was relieved that their wounds weren't life threatening and did agree that it was a good idea to have Catherine checked out by Agatha just to be sure the baby was uninjured. She told Emma that she was going to have Andrea, Greg, Samantha, and Sarah join them to act as additional security. She also stated that they weren't allowed to leave secure areas with less than a full security detail and they are to have a detailed itinerary logged before they leave. Emma knew full well it would be useless to argue with her mother and did agree that it was a good idea for the time being.

Scott started to go feral when Catherine told him she had been wounded it was only her reassurance that both her and the baby were fine that allowed him to stay in control of his baser side. He wanted to go meet Catherine at Agatha's but Catherine and Amelia both promised to call him if anything was wrong and to stop by Bio Medtronic so he could see her once they were done at the doctors, so finally he agreed to finish his meeting. Scott and Susan returned to the meeting and by the time that Catherine had arrive they had worked out a deal with the scientist his formula while not suitable for use yet was years ahead of the current research. His research also had produced several promising treatments for blood disorders. The deal was contingent on Susan's own scientist being able to reproduce the results that he claimed to have achieved.

Agatha quickly examined Catherine as soon as she arrived. She was pleased to reassure her that the baby was doing well. She said it was no need to remove the bullets from her chest they wouldn't cause Catherine any trouble. Agatha did remove the bullet from Amelia's wrist in order to allow her wrist heal properly with full range of motion and to prevent her from having discomfort. Once they were back on the road each of the mated woman called their other half to let them know what Agatha had said. Gloria called Susan then Charles.

Andrew calmed after finding Amelia was not injured seriously and started to wonder how Amsu had known where to find the woman. He used the computer to start making a list of suspects once he was done, he started to try to narrow it down. He knew he could cross off Neil and Scott off his list no vampire would risk their mate. He also crossed off Charles and Susan off the list if for no other reason he knew they would not risk Emma. Amelia, Gloria, and Catherine he trusted and eliminated them from the list. That left eleven people that had known that Emma and Catherine were going to the doctors and then to the mall.

It was no secret that Catherine and Emma would visit the mall after going to Catherine's appointment. Normally Dawn was their only security. Andrew was pondering a couple of things that didn't add up at first, first how Amsu found out that Emma and not Scott was taking Catherine to the doctors. Then assuming this was a planned operation how did Amsu arrange for the press to be there. How did he do it Scott had only realized a couple days ago that he had scheduled the meeting on the same day as Catherine's appointment.

He started his investigation by trying to identify the person who had attacked his family if he could find then maybe it would give him a clue to the traitor's identification. He used the news stations web site to try to get clear picture of the person. Andrew started by going through Charles' database that contained not only all of Charles and Susan's people but also all of the major players in the vampire world and their known associates. Andrew also ran a check through local and federal agencies. Emma and Gloria both were sure that the kid was not a vampire but he most certainly wasn't human. That meant he was a lycan.

While that search for the attacker's identity was going on, Andrew pulled up the files on his list of suspects and started going through them. He was about half way through the second file when he felt Amelia enter the room, he looked up with a smile seeing her standing there. He quickly rose and went over and cocooned her in his arms. The two of them stood there comforting each other not saying a word for several minutes. The two of them then shared a tender kiss before they separated.

"I will be back in a little bit I want to get a quick shower. Then I can help you with your search," Amelia said as she started to head to the bedroom they shared.

Andrew knew that Amelia had picked-up on his line of thinking from their bond and was thankful for it. He went back to the files he had been reading when Amelia came in. About twenty minutes later Amelia returned and quietly set down in the chair across from Andrew and started reading the next file. The two of them were soon lost in their work and the only communication was through their mental link.

Neil had been running interference for Charles since the attack had occurred. He was trying to reassure the local vampire population that they were already investigating the incident and trying to determine if it was an isolated event or some unknown group that somehow learned of the existence of vampires. When Emma walked into the office, Neil was in the middle of arguing with Erik Ferranti. "Erik, I don't give a dam how much money you have Charles is not available." Neil explained through clenched teeth. He had been telling this fool the same thing for the last twenty minutes. He thought because he was one of Charles main suppliers.

"I do not think you understand my good man I have to talk to him directly I know he would want to update me directly and not have one of his underlings do it." Erik said emphasizing each word.

"Erik I am not only Charles personal assistant but his son in-law so I am more than able to assist you." Neil stated firmly.

"I know who you are but you are not Charles so I demand that you put me through to him immediately. I have to know if it still safe for me to be your distributor after all I have many people who depend on me. " Erik ordered angrily.

"Who are you to demand a dam thing you are just some self-important asshole that thinks he is more important than he is. Now I would suggest that if you want any assistance today you tell me what your problem is so I can resolve it for you." Neil replied in a heated tone.

"You don't have the authority to handle it, now put me through to Charles and I may not mention how rude you have been to me." Erik smugly demanded.

Emma hearing the conversation and watched as Neil struggled for control. She watched as his eyes started to darken signaling that he was nearing the end of his tolerance. "Love, just tell him we are terminating his contract and if he has a problem let me have him," Emma mentally said with an evil grin on her face.

"Erik, I'm sorry to inform you that we no longer require your services please send us an itemized invoice for the work you have done for us since the last billing cycle and I will see it promptly settled." Neil replied in a cold hard voice. He knew that Charles had given Erik the contract so the he could save his business.

"Neil, do you think that Charles will allow you to cancel the contract? You really must be delusional." Erik challenged in a snug tone.

"Erik it is done and nothing you can say will change the fact that we are going to use a new supplier for Sanguinem. Good day sir." Neil ended the call with more than a bit of satisfaction. Erik was a pain in the ass on his best day and his self-important holier than thou attitude had always grated Neil's nerves. Neil looked at his mate and gave her a small smile. "Thank you, my love. He was demanding things he had no right to demand and insisted that he was too important to deal with me a mere underling. I didn't want you to have to get involved but I was never given authority to terminate a contract," Neil mentally explained.

Emma moved to her mate and wrapped her arms around his neck pulling him down for a kiss. Just as their lips meant the phone rang. Neil groaned when he saw Erik's number appear on the caller id. He was just about to answer it when Emma grabbed the phone. "He is busy Erik now fuck off." Emma growled into the phone.

"Emma please I need a moment of your time your mate is got this crazy notion that he can cancel the contract I have with your father," Erik nervously pleaded.

"That is because he can. If he said it is cancelled then the contract is cancelled. He has full authority to make decisions for the family businesses. Now is there anything else I can help you with Erik?" Emma sternly corrected Erik's earlier assessment.

"Emma please be reasonable it would be a major detriment to your father's business if you cancel the contract," Erik argued.

"You should feel lucky I am being reasonable because if I wasn't you would be looking for a new head for the way you spoke to my mate. If I were you, I would hang up now and start looking for a new area to operate in. Do I make myself clear?" Emma quietly warned. Neil knew that when she spoke in this quiet soft tone it didn't bold well for the person she was speaking to. He wondered if Erik was smart enough to realize he just went too far.

"Emma, I hope that you and your father can live with your decision. Tell your father I will have my legal department contact you all to work out the compensation I am due for you all reneging on the contract. I fully intend on making you honor this contract. This is not over Emma!" Erik angrily warned.

"Why Erik are you threatening me?" Emma asked in a sickie sweet voice.

"No; I am just warning you that there are consequences for your actions." Erik chastised Emma as if she was a child.

"Erik you seem to forget whom you are talking to. You will vacate my father's territories by sundown or you will not live to see tomorrow if I have to kill you myself. Am I in any way unclear?" Emma ordered not trying to hide her anger.

"Emma please don't do this my whole life is here. I have a business and my mate and her family are here." Erik pleaded realizing too late that he went too far. He knew if Emma forced him to relocate, his mate wouldn't be happy and worse yet her father would want his head. Thankfully, his father in-law couldn't take it without endangering Misha. Erik while he knew she was his mate had never really been bothered by the fact he was mated he took other woman into his bed and not just to feed. He knew if she were destroyed today, he wouldn't care one way or the other. Misha on the other hand wouldn't survive the loss of her mate and he had used it as a weapon against his in-laws more than once.

"The only reason I am allowing you to live long enough to leave is because of the great respect I have for your mate and her family normally I would have just had your head delivered to me. So I would advise you take advantage of my charitable mood and get the fuck out of town," Emma warned.

"Love you cannot kill him it would destroy Misha then we would lose a very old ally. You know Anatoly would start a war against us if we caused his daughter to die or go rogue by killing this piece of refuge." Neil mentally reminded her.

"Emma it would destroy Misha to have to be separated from her family," Erik pleaded a twinge of fear was leaching into his voice. He was getting worried he knew his father in-law would most likely cut him off and because of his mismanagement of the business he was broke. Misha did have a trust fund that paid her twenty thousand dollars a month and a sizable stock portfolio that was managed by her father. Erik knew that her monthly Stipend would never be able to support them.

"Neil you know how I feel about Misha but I am tired of this cocksucker using his being mated to her to get his way. I may not kill him but I will lock him in a room somewhere and only feed him enough blood to keep him alive." Emma replied to Neil using her mind while she coldly said," Erik you should of thought about that before you threatened my family. I would suggest you get a packing you have less than four hours to be out of here."

"Emma please don't hurt Misha this way; it will kill her if she has to leave Philly and her family," Erik pleaded.

"Good-bye Erik," Emma said before hanging up and cutting off any more of his whining. Emma then turned her attention to Neil," You are allowed to make any business decisions for the family never let pieces of shit like that tell you differently."

The two of them hugged as the phone started to ring again this time it was Nathan Rydal from the bank. He helped vampires to hide their holding within the banking system and was one of the few vampires that could call Charles directly. "What is up Nate?" Neil answered the phone knowing this wasn't a social call.

"I am just touching base with you to see if you need me to do anything. Should I be worried for my family?" Nathan asked.

"As far as we can tell it was an isolated incident. I believe for the time being Charles will be carrying on with business as usual. If anything changes, I will call you." Neil replied in a reassuring voice.

"I saw that Linda died so I am assuming it was Mitch that was the victim of the bomb. Was anyone else hurt seriously?" Nathan inquires his voice full of concern.

"Two others were hurt but their injuries were minor and have already healed. You are correct that Mitch was killed and Linda died from the shock of losing her mate." Neil responded sadly.

"Neil, I Am so sorry to hear about Mitch, please convey my condolences to your father for me," Nathan sadly said.

Neil promised he would and the two of them talked for a few minutes more before hanging up. Neil phone rang again as soon as he hung up this time it was the leader of one of the small covens; he glanced over and saw Emma was on another line. By the time, he had finished the call Emma was on her third call. The calls were along the same line. How much had the humans found out and how did they find it out? It was going to be a long day.

Andrew and Amelia had taken their time going over the suspect pool out of the eleven that Andrew had identified. They could find no proof that Agatha was involved not mention even if she had leaked the appointment time to Amsu she had no way of knowing about the mall trip. Amelia removed her form the potential suspect list. He also had looked at Andrea and two other people from Susan's security team who had known about the day's itinerary. Andrew was confident that they weren't the source of the leak.

Amelia started pulling the call logs for each of their suspect cell phones and tracking each number. Two of them had made a number of calls to phone numbers from the Middle East. Andrew realized that it was thin but it was something the two of them felt needed to be checked. He was unsure just how they should proceed since one of their suspects was Emma's office manager and the other was Mitch's second in command. He asked mark to discretely pull both of their financial records and look for anything suspicious. Amelia was looking into their personal and business e-mail accounts. She planned to ask Charles about getting access to both of their houses but knew she had to tread carefully so as not to alert them they were under suspicion. They had both considered using Amelia's mental abilities to probe their minds but decided it was best to hold off on that until they had more evidence.